With fond thoughts!
Rae

Unjustified

Unjustified

VALERIE KOSSEW DUNN

UNJUSTIFIED

iUniverse books may be ordered through booksellers or by contacting:

iUniverse
1663 Liberty Drive
Bloomington, IN 47403
www.iuniverse.com
1-800-Authors (1-800-288-4677)

ISBN: 978-1-4917-9504-0 (sc)
ISBN: 978-1-4917-9505-7 (e)

Library of Congress Control Number: 2016908000

Print information available on the last page.

iUniverse rev. date: 05/26/2016

1

PROFESSOR GODFREY MITCHELL WAS DEAD. NO QUESTION ABOUT IT.
His body was slumped behind his desk, a splatter of desiccated blood
and bits of brain and bone besmirching the upholstery of his chair.
His once handsome face was shattered and the back of his head was
missing. On the Oriental carpet, immediately below the lifeless
fingers of his right hand, lay a gun.

Heavy drapes covered the windows behind the desk and the
only illumination in the darkened room came from the glow of a
computer, its screen-saver endlessly running the name of a software
package. Well-stocked book-shelves lined one wall from floor to
ceiling. On the adjacent wall, amid Hogarth etchings in ornate gilt
frames, the mahogany paneling had been splintered by a bullet.

As Detectives Jackson Blaustein and Hugh Gardner, the Medical
Examiner and a pair of forensic technicians entered the professor's
study, they paused to take stock of the situation. Blaustein, the lead
detective, a transfer from Homicide in New York, led the group.
He was of medium height with a shock of dark hair graying at the
temples and thoughtful brown eyes. He had a reputation for dogged

persistence and the ability to separate the fundamentals of a case from the red herrings that too often got in the way of the truth. His partner, Hugh Gardner, was older taller and more than a little over-weight. His normally jovial expression had been replaced by a frown of concentration. All the men were still in their overcoats, their hands encased in surgical gloves and their shoes covered with plastic booties. Despite the fact that the temperature in the house was a mere fifty degrees, the smell of decay was overpowering

One of the lab technicians turned to Blaustein. "Any objection to opening a window, Detective?"

"Check to see if it's been tampered with first. And dust for prints. Then okay." Though he had been a homicide detective for more than twenty years, Blaustein had never grown accustomed to the stench of death. He welcomed the prospect of a little fresh air.

Going over to the computer Blaustein moved the mouse with the tip of a gloved finger. Instantly the screen saver vanished and in its place on an otherwise blank screen were two words, "I, Godfrey". Just the two words, there was nothing else.

"Impound the computer. See what's on it and check it for prints," Blaustein ordered before turning his attention to the Medical Examiner. "So what do you think, Doc?"

"Given that the house is so cold, it'll be difficult to give you an exact time of death. But it's safe to say that the victim's been dead quite a while, maybe three, four weeks," Aaron Priestley, the State's Chief Medical Examiner, was a man in his sixties with thinning gray hair, tired eyes, and the expression of one who was surprised by nothing because there was nothing to see that he had not seen before.

"The victim is indeed Godfrey Mitchell," Priestley said after opening the dead man's wallet and taking out his driver's license.

"Murder or suicide? What's your best bet, Doc?"

"Suicide could be a possibility. I'll give you a more definitive answer after I've done the test for powder residue on his hands and checked the bullet's entry angle," Priestley replied.

"You won't find a bullet when you do the post," Blaustein

2

gestured toward a hole amid the body fluids in the back of the chair. "Looks like it's embedded in the upholstery."

Before trying to recover the bullet or beginning the gruesome task of removing the body for post mortem, Blaustein and his crew began photographing the evidence in place. First they took shots of the body and the room in which the victim died. Then, after the body was removed, they photographed and checked the rest of the house and grounds and dusted for prints. They found no sign of forced entry. None of the doors or windows had been tampered with, and heavy snowfall in the preceding weeks had obscured any evidence there might have been of tire tracks or footprints. When they failed to find fingerprints in the professor's study or the front hall, it seemed obvious to Blaustein that a third party, in all probability, the killer, had cleaned up the area. These facts alone reinforced his decision to declare the area a crime scene.

An unused airline ticket to Atlanta in the professor's name lay on the hall stand. The departure date was December 27. If he had still been alive on December 27, then it had to have been the killer who stopped the professor from making his flight. Four weeks had elapsed since then, and that alone narrowed the probable time of death.

Other than the ticket, nothing seemed out of place. There was no pile of mail inside the front door and no stack of unread newspapers. Clearly someone, perhaps the victim, had canceled all deliveries in anticipation of his trip to Atlanta. But it was more than likely the killer who had turned down the thermostat in order to obscure the time of death. Considering all the possibilities, Blaustein was inclined to rule out suicide. His gut, and especially the absence of fingerprints in the professor's study, told him this was no suicide.

Except for a fine layer of dust, the remainder of the downstairs was obsessively neat. In the kitchen, the counters had been cleared, the dishwasher emptied and the dishes put away. Other than a single glass left in the sink, nothing was out of place. Hoping they might find useful prints on the glass, Blaustein told one of the technicians to bag it, then he turned his attention to the second floor. Like the rest of the house, the upstairs was inordinately tidy. Nothing was out of place in what were probably guest rooms. There were no personal items lying about, the bureau drawers were lined but empty and there were only empty hangers in the closets. Fresh, neatly folded towels hung in the spare bathroom but there were no toothbrushes or shaving paraphernalia in the medicine cabinet. The master bedroom told a different story. There the covers had been hastily thrown over rumpled sheets and pillows. A fully packed suitcase, containing a suit, slacks, shirts, underwear, ties and shaving gear, lay open atop a blanket chest. On the floor beside the blanket chest stood a briefcase. It contained a couple of copies of Mitchell's latest book, a legal-sized writing tablet, a card case holding several business cards, and notes for what looked like an acceptance speech. All indications were that Professor Mitchell had intended to make his flight to Atlanta. Clearly something or more probably someone had altered his plans. To Blaustein, the professor's death was looking more and more like murder.

"Check the sheets for hair samples just in case the victim had company," Blaustein directed.

In the master bathroom there were no towels, a fact that struck Blaustein as odd. He looked in the laundry hamper and finding it empty, went downstairs to the laundry room. There he found the missing towels in the dryer. Whatever evidence they may have held was gone, washed and dried away. But taking no chances, Blaustein collected the lint from the dryer filter and placed it in a plastic bag. He was not optimistic they would find anything helpful. Thus far, Mitchell's killer had been careful to hide his tracks.

2

IT HAD BEEN AN UNLIKELY LOCALE FOR A STAKEOUT. BUT THERE
were worse places to work undercover than the Whitney University
Library. Dina Barrett liked its dim recesses, the smell of old books
and the concentrated silence. Though almost thirty she was still
carded when she went to buy a six-pack. And being on campus
under cover, it helped that she looked like any other attractive
co-ed. With a lithe figure and dark rebellious curls, she blended
in. The students seemed to consider her presence among them
utterly unremarkable. It was in great part because of her youthful
appearance that she was tapped for her present assignment, her first
field job since the near-fatal incident in the casino parking lot.

Almost completely recovered from her gunshot wound, but not
yet back on normal duty, she had graduated from a desk job to
surveillance. Stakeouts were arguably more interesting than shuffling
paper. And she was able to put a positive spin on things. After all,
she had been extremely lucky. If the bullet had lodged a half-inch
to the right, she might have become a statistic. One more cop killed
in the line of duty and another name inscribed on the policeman's

memorial. In comparison, the after effects of pleurisy, lingering aches and pains, and recurring nightmares that gave her the sweats, seemed a small price to pay.

The reading room on the main floor of the university library was large and well lit. There was a circulation desk at one end and a reservation desk at the other. In the middle, separated by a wide, carpeted aisle, were rows of long, gleaming maple tables. Behind the tables and along the rear wall was a line of carrels. Seated in one of the carrels, Barrett had an unobstructed view of the reference desk and the librarians they suspected of passing dope to the students. A book and a notepad gave her the perfect cover. She could see what she needed to see and jot down her observations without being obvious about it because everyone else was also reading and taking notes. But even under the best of circumstances, and this was probably one of them, surveillance was a tedious job. By the end of her shift, she was more than ready to leave. And Edward Morrison was late. He should have relieved her ten minutes earlier. It was past time for the changing of the guard. For the third time in as many minutes, she checked the old-fashioned clock above the reservation desk. Its hands had barely moved from one Roman numeral to the next.

"Hi!" She said as a woman deposited her backpack, unzipped her parka and sat down in the adjacent carrel. The woman nodded a perfunctory greeting in return, and seeming disinclined to respond further, pulled a book from her backpack and opened it dismissively. She was without makeup of any kind, wore wire-rimmed glasses and was clad in a shapeless sweat-shirt and jeans that were worn at the knees. Everything about her announced her student status.

When Morrison finally arrived, Dina immediately stuffed her book and notepad into her backpack and reached for her coat. Meanwhile, shrugging off his parka without looking in her direction, Morrison threw his backpack onto a table in the center of the room and sat down with his back to her. They never acknowledged each other during the stake out. When they met to compare notes it was always in a safe house provided by the New Haven Police Department, their cooperating agency.

"Excuse me, are you Ms. Richmond?" The voice at her elbow made her jump.

"I'm Kelly Richmond," came a response from the new arrival in the adjacent carrel.

Dina glanced up as the speaker rose. A half-closed book was in one hand, the student's forefinger marking a page. Behind the metal-rimmed glasses her pale-lashed eyes looked puzzled, her eyebrows a question mark.

"This is for you, Ms. Richmond. You'll see it's marked 'urgent'. If you need to use an outside phone, please feel free to use the one in the main office," the head librarian handed the young woman a folded message slip and turned on her heel.

Putting her book face down on the desk, the student unfolded the message and read its contents. "What the hell?" Shock registered on her face.

"Everything okay?" Dina asked.

"Don't know. My advisor didn't show up for his lecture today and he isn't answering the phone. They think I might know how to reach him, but quite honestly, I haven't a clue. It could be he's not back from winter break yet," clearly distressed, Kelly Richmond bit her lower lip. "Even so, it's unlike Professor Mitchell to miss a class without notifying the History Department."

"It's possible he couldn't get to the phone for some reason. A fall, perhaps? Has someone been to check his house?"

"They haven't said," the student shook her head. "I'd go myself if I had wheels."

"Would you like a ride?" Dina's offer sprang less from altruism than from instinctive nosiness. Nosiness went with the territory when you were a detective.

"That's awfully kind," the student's relief evident, she grasped Dina's hand with both of her own. "Are you sure you want to do that? I don't even know your name."

"Diana Bassett," Dina gave the woman her undercover name without batting an eyelash.

"Kelly Richmond."

Gathering their books, the two women made their way to the glassed-in offices behind the reservation desk. While Barrett waited just outside the enclosure, Kelly went in to use the telephone. After a brief conversation, the student emerged and shook her head as if to affirm that there was still no news of the missing professor. Then they left the overheated library for the wintry sunshine of the quadrangle outside. Neither woman spoke as they hurried across campus to the student parking lot where Dina had left her SUV. They stowed their backpacks on the back seat and climbed in.

"Where exactly are we going?" Dina asked after turning the key in the ignition.

"Sorry, I should have told you. Professor Mitchell lives in Chisholm," Kelly Richmond looked tense, her face pale, the knuckles of her clenched hands showing white. "It's about ten miles from here. A bit of a hike, I'm afraid. Want to change your mind?"

"Not at all," Dina assured her as she pulled out of the parking lot and into the stream of traffic, though she hadn't bargained for quite such a lengthy drive.

"Do you know how to get there?"

Dina nodded. Chisholm was a pricey, small community much favored by senior Whitney faculty and business executives who considered the long commute to New York City a small price to pay for the privilege of living there.

Avoiding small talk, the two drove in silence as they left the Whitney campus, skirted the colleges of neighboring Yale, and turned north on Whitney Avenue. Once past the Peabody Museum and the residential area of New Haven proper, the traffic thinned. Soon even the suburbs were left behind as they headed north on a rural road that wound past shuttered farm stalls and fields that lay dormant under a blanket of snow.

Entering Chisholm, they circled the town green with its silent memorials to the local war dead, its white framed Congregational Church, its eclectic mix of eighteenth century colonials, rambling, whimsical Victorians, and tasteful, upscale boutiques and restaurants. Bricked, tree-lined side walks and old-fashioned lamp posts completed a picture that epitomized quaint New England. An image the town self-consciously cultivated.

"Turn left off Main onto Cedar Ridge," Dina's passenger told her. "The house is halfway up the block. I don't remember the number."

But there was no need for the number. Rounding the corner onto Cedar Ridge they were confronted by the flashing lights of police and emergency vehicles. Among them, Dina recognized the State's mobile forensics lab and several unmarked vehicles. She felt a jolt of envy. If not for being sidelined, she would have been part of the team. The State's Major Crime Squad was always brought in when serious crimes occurred in the smaller municipalities where understaffed and overworked police departments were not equipped to deal with major investigations. Chisholm, a town of only five thousand, fell into that category.

"Oh my God!" A gasp escaped Kelly's lips. "It looks as if something bad has happened."

A medical examiner's van was parked in front of the house as if to confirm the woman's fears. Worried that Kelly might rush the police barricade of yellow 'do not cross' tape, Dina pulled up next to the curb and put a restraining hand on the other woman's forearm. She did not want her companion to be around when body-bags were brought out.

"Even if you lived here, I doubt they would let you inside. At least not yet. Why don't you stay here? I'll see if I can find out what's going on."

Dina approached a local policeman guarding the perimeter of the property. "Excuse me Officer, my friend works for Professor Mitchell," she gestured toward the SUV. "She's naturally concerned about him. Can you tell us what's going on here?"

"Sorry Miss. There'll be a formal statement later."

To press the point, Dina could have pulled her badge. But she was reluctant to compromise her undercover assignment in front of Kelly. So she thanked the officer and returned to the car. "They're not saying anything yet and probably won't, pending an official statement," she said, sliding back into the driver's seat. "According to the officer, that could take hours. Why don't you let me take you back to Whitney?"

"I guess it doesn't make sense to hang around out here," the student conceded.

"Should I drop you at the library?" Dina asked as she started the car.

"No. I think I'd like to go home. Would you mind dropping me there?"

"Sure," Dina replied, hoping she was not in for another lengthy detour.

"It's on the way," her passenger said, as if reading Dina's mind. "I live just off campus. On Winslow Street."

Like its neighbors, the house on Winslow, where Kelly Richmond rented the top floor, had seen better days. The picket fence was green with mildew, the front porch sagged in the middle, the roof buckled, paint was peeling off the outside shingles and the street number was missing.

"Please come in for a cup of tea. You've been so kind," Kelly offered as they pulled up to the front door.

Preferring not to, Dina hesitated, an excuse on the tip of her tongue. Instead, she ended up accepting, less because she was being gracious, than because she wanted to learn more about the missing or more likely deceased Professor Mitchell. For her money, the scene on Cedar Street had all the hallmarks of a homicide investigation and her chance encounter with Kelly had given her an inside track.

Dina followed Kelly up to her third floor apartment. There was a bicycle with a broken back-light on the landing and a Connecticut Earth Day poster tacked to the door. The apartment itself was one large room: an attic bed-sitter with the bathroom and kitchenette partitioned off at one end. It had a dropped ceiling with stained tiles where the roof had leaked, old-fashioned iron radiators, and except where light filtered through the uncurtained gable window, was dark and unlovely. An armoire stood against one wall and along the other was a worn couch that presumably pulled out into a bed.

In addition, there were two threadbare upholstered chairs, an oak desk littered with papers and books, a gray metal filing cabinet and a goose-necked lamp. Kelly pulled the toggle switch on the lamp dispelling some of the gloom.

"Sorry. This place isn't exactly a palace. One's lucky to find an affordable, furnished apartment around here," Kelly apologized, picking up a stack of books from the sofa and adding them to the pile already on the desk. "Please sit down."

"You're lucky to have found a place within walking distance of campus," Dina said taking off her parka and hanging it on a wooden peg behind the door. Excusing herself, Kelly repaired to the kitchenette and turned on the burner under the kettle. "Do you take milk or sugar?" She called from behind the partition.

"Sugar please."

Preparing to wait while the water boiled, Dina went over to the desk and picked through the books so recently deposited there. Staring back at her from the dust-cover of one of them was an all too familiar name. It was her father's new biography of Thomas Carlyle. Turning to the dedication page, her eyes misted and her breath caught. He had inscribed his life's work simply, 'In memory of my son, Jeremy, Jr.'. Much as she resented her father, she nodded her approval.

"Have you had a chance to read Barrett's biography of Thomas Carlyle?" Kelly asked as she came into the room carrying matching porcelain mugs with 'Save the Whale' logos on them.

"No," Dina did not elaborate.

"The author, Jeremy Haywood Barrett, Sr. is a professor at the University of Connecticut. A well-known scholar and a nice gentleman."

"You know him personally then?"

"Not really. I once heard him deliver a paper at the Pickwick Club. Are you familiar with the Pickwick Club?"

"No, afraid not."

"Its members are Victorian scholars from all the Connecticut colleges. They meet quarterly to present their latest research.

Sometimes they invite graduate students to report on their work. I was hoping for an invitation, but Godfrey hadn't gotten around to it yet," she shrugged. "Anyway, that's where I heard J.H. Barrett give a paper on Carlyle. His biography's been very well reviewed. In fact, it's been on my 'must read' list for some time." Kelly handed Dina one of the mugs, placed the other on the desk and began rummaging through a pile of journals. When she found the one she wanted, she flipped through the pages, found the page she was looking for and passed the journal to Dina.

"Here's the latest review," she said.

"Impressive," Dina replied noncommittally, after reading the review. She had always suspected that researching Carlyle was her father's excuse to spend every summer in England and away from his family.

"You don't sound overly impressed," Kelly cocked her head quizzically.

"Not my field," Dina didn't provide any additional enlightenment. Being nonspecific went with the territory when you were under cover.

"No, or I'd have seen you in the Arts Department if you were."

Dina chose not to respond. Instead, taking her mug with her, she took a seat on the sofa. "Do you think he's all right? Professor Mitchell?" Kelly sat down on the armchair and tucked her feet under her.

"I have no idea. Are you very close to him?" Dina parried, making sure to use the present tense though her gut was telling her the woman's professor was more than likely a victim of foul play. She took a sip of tea which was some kind of herbal and far too sweet. This, combined with her reluctance to impart assurances she could not give, made Dina regret her impulse to accept the other woman's invitation.

"Not really," Kelly shook her head. "I've only been Professor Mitchell's teaching assistant since September. That's when I started Graduate School."

"Does he have family?" It was not an idle question. The family of the victim was always the first place one looked for suspects in a homicide.

"An ex-wife and a son living in the South somewhere. North Carolina I believe." Kelly replied.

"So he lives alone in that big house?"

Kelly nodded, distractedly pulling at a loose strand of hair.

"Who sent you the note?"

"Note?"

"The one they handed you in the library. The one asking if you knew how to get hold of the professor," Dina reminded her.

"Oh. . . that note. It was a message from Sidney Lawrence, the History Department Chairperson."

"And he told you something had happened to Professor Mitchell?"

"Not exactly. When Godfrey didn't show up for his class, and the Department could not get hold of him, Professor Lawrence got in touch with me because I'm Professor Mitchell's Teaching Assistant," Kelly explained. "But I'm as mystified as he was. In the few months I've been the Professor's T.A., I've never known him to skip a class."

"So you have a hunch something's wrong?" Dina asked the question casually. She didn't want it to sound as if she was interrogating the woman.

Kelly nodded. "Teaching is a passion with him. If you'd ever been to one of his lectures, you'd understand. Even if history's not your subject, you should try and go some time. His lectures are exceptional. Sometimes students who haven't even registered for his classes show up. Most of the faculty are more interested in doing research than lecturing to a bunch of undergraduates, but Godfrey actually gets a kick out of it. He enjoys lecturing almost as much as he does writing," she stopped to take a breath. "He's very well known. I'm surprised you have never heard of him. I thought that everyone in Connecticut had heard of Godfrey Mitchell. He's a best-selling author"

"Maybe I have heard the name," Dina admitted.

"Actually, around campus, he's more famous for his lectures than he is for his books. He's a bit of a ham. And no one enjoys his

lectures more than he does." The smile that had briefly replaced
Kelly's worried expression faded. "Barring a dire emergency, there's
no way he'd miss a lecture. Especially, without letting someone
know. Especially the first lecture of the semester with a new group
of freshman to wow."

"Who would take over for him if he couldn't give his lecture?
Would you as his T.A?"

"Oh no, his assistants only teach the tutorials, never the lectures,"
the very thought seemed to strike Kelly as outlandish.

"When is the last time you saw Professor Mitchell?" To be polite,
Dina took another tentative sip of her tea.

"Around Christmas. Just before he left for the annual meeting of
the AHA -- the American Historical Association."

"About a month ago?"

Kelly nodded numbly, "Just as we went on break."

With an effort Dina finished her tea and carried the cup to the
kitchen area. "If you think you'll be all right, I ought to be leaving."

After rinsing the cup in the sink and setting it to dry on the
draining board, Dina dug a small notepad and pen from her coat
pocket. Maintaining her undercover role, she scribbled down the
name 'Diana Bassett' and her cell phone number, tore off the sheet
and handed it to Kelly. "In case you'd like to get in touch."

"You've been very kind, Diana," though still looking pale, Kelly
seemed calmer as she walked Dina to the door.

Her curiosity getting the better of her, Dina drove back to
Chisholm after leaving Kelly's apartment. The medical examiner's
van was no longer there, but police cars and the State's mobile crime
lab were still parked in front of the Mitchell place. Pulling up at the
curb, she parked her vehicle and walked over to the police barricade.

"Is Detective Blaustein still here?" She showed her badge to the
local cop on duty.

"In the house," the policeman gestured with his thumb.

"Would you tell him that Detective Barrett is here?" Much as she was tempted to, Dina was reluctant to enter the crime scene uninvited.

She waited outside the police barricade, impatiently stamping her feet against the cold and wishing she'd worn her warm boots as she looked at the grounds. Mitchell's property was not particularly large, about an acre and a half, with a stand of well-established evergreens bordering his neighbors on either side. It had not snowed in some time and the street was clear, but the driveway lay under a pristine blanket of snow. Crusted-over snow covered the front lawn and capped the boxwoods that lined the icy walkway. At the head of the walkway stood the house, a large brick neo-colonial. It had chimneys at the gable ends, twelve-over twelve windows, a double front door decorated with twin Christmas wreaths and a closed two-car garage. The combination of Christmas wreaths in late January and the closed-up garage gave the place a desolate look.

Grinning broadly, Blaustein burst out of the door and made his way toward her, "Partner!" He exclaimed taking Dina's hand warmly in two of his own. "How the Hell did you know I was here?"

"Sheer coincidence," she smiled at him.

"Well, your timing is excellent. I've just finished up here. Want to go for a cup of coffee?"

"Fine. I noticed a Starbucks near the Chisholm green. That okay?"

"Dandy. I'll follow you there."

Jackson Blaustein had been Dina's partner for almost a year before she was sidelined by the casino shooting. Blaustein had transferred to the Connecticut State Police when Dina was still fairly new on the force. Though a bit of an odd couple - Blaustein, a savvy, city-bred, middle-aged Jew, and Dina, a native New Englander, attractive, smart and barely thirty - they were temperamentally compatible and professionally well matched. He had experience, she had great instincts, and both were outsiders. Because of this and their mutual respect, they made an effective team. Or had done, till Dina was shot. But the bond between them was stronger than ever now. When she went down, it was Blaustein who disabled her attacker. And it was Blaustein who stanched the bleeding till the EMTs arrived. She owed him her life.

"So how's the undercover game?" Blaustein asked after they had paid for their cappuccinos and taken them to a table by the window. "You're working with Edward Morrison now, right?"

"I am. He was with the New Haven P. D. before he joined the State's Major Crime Squad, so he not only knows the area but has a good working relationship with the New Haven detectives working the case with us."

"A good man?"

"Yes." She did not mention that Morrison's tendency to be late was driving her nuts. "Edward and I split the day shift. A team from NHPD takes over at night."

"Any suspects?"

"We're almost sure it's one of the reserve desk librarians. The reserve desk is right in the middle of the reading room which makes the stakeout dead simple. In fact, it'a the easiest surveillance I've ever been on. Not to mention the fact that it's a real bonus to be working indoors where it's warm and not outside in the freezing cold. As covert operations go, it's a breeze. Boring but not bad"

"Are you close to an arrest?"

"Not really. We have yet to catch the suspect actually handing out the goodies and even when we do, we don't want to simply get a dealer for possession with intent to sell. We'd prefer to go after the supplier."

"What made you think your dealer was a librarian?"

"We caught a break when a female student at Whitney over-dosed. Fortunately the victim, Polly Obermeier, survived. You remember the case?"

"I do."

"Well, a glycine bag with traces of coke was found in the back of her library book. The book was stamped 'on reserve', but when we checked the reserve list, we found that none of the faculty had placed it there. That narrowed the list of possible suspects to one of the reserve desk librarians. We're working on the theory that the dealer has a bogus reserve list. What we don't know is how the students find out about it."

"Student grapevines are wonderful things."

Dina nodded her agreement. "So we're keeping an eye on the reserve desk until we know which librarian is dealing. We intend to catch him or her in the act."

"How do you figure they make the transfer?"

"We're pretty sure the buy occurs when the buyer and the dealer exchange books. The student's book has cash in it. The librarian's contains a small bag of coke."

"A tidy arrangement."

"It is. And hopefully it leads to a big bust. Like I said, it won't end with the arrest of the dealer. We want the supplier. Arresting one dealer won't stop the drug trafficking. We're after bigger fish."

"Is the University cooperating?"

"Reluctantly. They would like to fire the dealer as soon as we make a positive I. D. In fact, they'd prefer to handle the entire matter in-house. It's been tough trying to make the Dean see the big picture," Dina tore open a packet of sugar and stirred it into her coffee. "How about you? How's your new partner working out?"

"Fortunately I didn't have to break in anyone new. Huey Gardner has stepped in as my sidekick. We get along fine. He's solid and methodical, even if he doesn't have half your instincts," he stirred his cappuccino and took a sip. "Speaking of which, Chisholm is way out of your bailiwick. You still haven't told me how you knew I was here. ESP?"

"Just a freaky coincidence. I was in the Whitney library when Mitchell's teaching assistant was told that he was AWOL. Apparently it isn't like him to miss a lecture, so she got worried. Being nosy, I offered to drive her to his house. But when we got there and I saw emergency vehicles all over the place, I thought it best to take her back to New Haven," Dina said, scooping some foam off the top of her cappuccino and licking the teaspoon.

"And after that your natural inquisitiveness continued to get the better of you, so you came back to Chisholm?"

Dina nodded, "He's dead, isn't he?"

"As a doornail. Been so for some time."

"That's what I figured. It's obvious the driveway hasn't been plowed since the last snowfall. And that was more than a week ago."

"My guess is he's been dead longer than that. The heat had been turned way down in the house. It was barely warm enough to keep the pipes from freezing. Even so, the body was pretty far gone. We won't know for sure when he died until after the autopsy. But it was probably sometime around Christmas. We found an unused airline ticket to Atlanta. He was booked to leave Bradley at 3:45 p.m. on December 27 and return on the evening of January 3."

"His T.A. mentioned that he was supposed to go to an American Historical Association meeting. Maybe that was in Atlanta."

"We'll check on it."

"How did death occur?"

"Shot in the head. Close range. Blew the back of his skull out." Blaustein appreciatively munched an éclair, apparently unaffected by the grisly discovery on Cedar Ridge.

"Self-inflicted?"

"Don't know yet. There were a couple of words on his computer, perhaps the beginning of a suicide note. There was no sign of a struggle. He was shot at close range and there are scorch marks on the face. So of course we bagged his hands just in case he ate his gun. Priestley will test for residue. But my gut tells me we're looking at a homicide."

"What about a weapon?"

"A .38 found beside the body. But even if it was registered to the victim, it still doesn't eliminate the possibility that someone else popped him."

"Any sign of forced entry?"

"Place was locked up tight as a drum. And of course right now the snow makes it impossible to check for external evidence. After the snow melts we'll have a go at the grounds, but I'm not optimistic we'll find anything."

"Strange that he hasn't been missed in almost four weeks. I guess everyone must have been on winter break."

"What's his graduate student's name? The one you drove over here. I'll need to interview her."

"Kelly Richmond."

Blaustein wrote down the name.

"She rents a third floor walk-up on Winslow Street in New Haven. The number was unreadable or I'd give it to you."

"I'll get it."

"She doesn't know yet that Mitchell's dead and seems pretty shaken up. What do you want to do about notification?"

"First, of course, we have to inform the next of kin," Blaustein finished the éclair and wiped his lips with his napkin.

"He has a son and an ex-wife. I don't know if there are other relatives."

"I'm surprised there's something you don't know yet," he teased. "Too bad you're not on the case."

"You mean like a mole?" Dina's eyes danced at the prospect.

"I was joking."

"I wasn't," Dina challenged him.

"You're still working the drug investigation," he pointed out.

"I could easily work part time on the Mitchell case," she said reasonably. "Mitchell worked at Whitney. I am on campus all the time. I could poke around."

"You're barely ready to take on one case, let alone two," Blaustein reminded her, crumpling his napkin into a ball.

"I blend in well and I already have an in with Mitchell's graduate student. I see her in the library a lot," Dina pleaded her case.

"I don't know...."

When Blaustein hesitated, Dina knew she had won him over but she decided not to press the point just yet. She switched gears. "Who notified you about the body?"

"The local police. They had a call this morning from Mitchell's boss, Sidney Lawrence, the History Department chairman. Possible missing person. When they investigated, they found the body and called us."

"Given that Mitchell missed class just this morning, wasn't it a little premature to be filing a missing persons? I'd interview this Lawrence character if I were you."

"Anything else I should be doing?" Blaustein grinned.

"Not for the moment," Dina countered, ignoring the jab. "Except to give my best to Greta. How is she?" Dina was very fond of Jackson's invalid wife.

"Still teaching English Lit. And enjoying every minute of it," Blaustein beamed proudly. Being tied to a wheelchair, did not keep his wife from teaching part-time at the University of Connecticut's West Hartford campus.

"I guess I'd better be getting back to the New Haven safe house to compare notes with Edward," Dina rose. "I don't want to be late."

"You seem to have adjusted to the New Haven environment. Found some place convenient to stay?" Blaustein asked helping Dina on with her coat.

"You'll never guess where," Dina smiled impishly at him.

"You're right. I'll never guess," Blaustein let Dina precede him through the door.

"I've rented a couple of rooms in Freddie Hathaway's house. She's away a lot, so most of the time I have the place to myself. And I don't mind it even when she's there. She's such a neat old lady."

"Freddie eh? Small world. How did that come about?" Winifred Applegate Hathaway had been a witness in their first case together.

"When she read I'd been shot, Freddie sent me a potted plant with a solicitous note. I wrote to thank her and since then we've kept in touch. When the condo I was renting was sold, she insisted I stay with her, at least till I find something more permanent. She wouldn't take no for an answer. And to be honest her offer couldn't have come at a better time. Being undercover in New Haven makes it extremely convenient. I have a self-contained suite on the second floor and I can come and go as I please without disturbing her. Though sharing a kitchen can be a bit hairy at times."

"Tell her 'hi' for me," Blaustein said, seeing Dina to her car.

"Please keep me in the loop," she pleaded unlocking the door of her vehicle.

"Dina, forget about it.

"Please."

"If this does turn out to be a homicide, you'll be out there on your own, it could be dangerous."

3

NO MATTER HOW MANY TIMES HE HAD DONE IT BEFORE, BLAUSTEIN never found it easy to observe an autopsy. So it was a relief when the medical examiner finally peeled off his surgical gloves and discarded them in the medical waste bin. As usual, Dr. Priestley, had been methodical and thorough, explaining each step as he went along in clear nontechnical terms, making it easy for the layman to understand. If he was unsure, he said so. He never hedged. And he had no reason to hedge now.

"Nothing complicated here. There was a single shot to the right temporal area and death was instantaneous. I'll provide the details in my report. But to put it succinctly, the bullet entered the side of the head somewhat obliquely, shattered the skull and penetrated the brain. It caused massive trauma before exiting at the base of the skull. I'm sorry, but it isn't possible to state definitively whether the shot was self-inflicted. Just that, judging by the angle, it could have been," Priestley said as he covered the body with a sheet. "The powder burns on the right side of the head indicate that the shot was fired at very close range. There was also powder residue on the victim's right hand. But I'm not totally convinced it was he who fired the gun. The powder on Mitchell's hand was not pronounced, and not everywhere one would expect to find it. But it may be possible he fired the gun. As you no doubt know, normally when one fires a gun, there's powder along the index finger and thumb, the area most exposed when shooting a handgun. In this case there's some residue on the thumb, but hardly any on the index finger. We know the gun was fired twice. So we can't rule out the possibility that it was Mitchell who fired the shot that was found in the paneling. He may have done it voluntarily or the killer held his hand, pre- or postmortem, and fired the shot to make the death look like a suicide ." Priestley washed his hands at the stainless steel sink and dried them on a paper towel. "I expect the crime lab found the victim's finger prints on the gun?"

"They did, and only the victim's prints. For my money, the most likely scenario is that the gun was wiped clean after the fatal shot was fired and then placed it in the victim's hand."

"Have you checked yet to see if the bullet that killed Mitchell matches the second bullet found at the scene?" The pathologist asked.

"There's no question about it. Both bullets were fired from the same .38. Huey Gardner is checking the registration." Blaustein confirmed. "So we're faced with a couple of possibilities here. Either the slug we found in the wall was fired in self-defense before Mitchell was killed -- which would account for the powder on the vic's hand. Or, it bolsters the theory that whoever killed Mitchell tried to make it look like suicide by putting the gun in the Professor's hand and firing the second shot. That would account for both the prints and the powder residue. What's your best guess, Doc? Do you think we're looking at a homicide here?"

"It's impossible to say for certain, so I don't want to guess."

"Fair enough." Blaustein's eyes involuntarily strayed to the white mound on the examining table. "What's your estimate for the time of death?"

"At least three weeks, possibly four. Hard to say for sure. The temperature in the house was barely fifty. Warm enough to keep the pipes from freezing and just cold enough to keep the body from deteriorating too rapidly."

"Four weeks would jibe with the date on the airline ticket," Blaustein confirmed with a nod. "Was there any physical evidence that the victim tried to fight off his attacker?"

"Negative. No foreign skin under the finger-nails. And no cuts or abrasions. But there is another factor to be considered."

"What?"

"The victim had sexual intercourse just prior to his death."

"That doesn't surprise me. We found two sets of pubic hair in the bed in the master bedroom. We're also running fingerprints on a glass we found in the kitchen. If the hair and the prints came from the same person, we could have our killer. But my gut tells me it's unlikely. A killer who was careful not to leave prints at the scene would not have left such incriminating evidence elsewhere in the house. Mitchell probably had two different visitors in the hours before his death. The first one slept with him. The second one killed him. That's if we can rule out suicide." Blaustein watched as Priestley pulled a pack of cigarettes from his lab coat, and wished that he hadn't given up smoking. A smoke would have tasted great right about now.

"You can't totally rule that out." The medical examiner lit his cigarette, put his disposable lighter back in his pocket and inhaled.

"Then we have to find a reason he would want to kill himself. Any sign he was suffering from a fatal or debilitating disease?"

"The man was sound as a bell. More like a thirty-five year old than a man of over fifty. Organs all sound. No sign of disease. No excess fatty deposits. Muscular-skeletal system in excellent shape. No hint of arthritis. No drugs or medications in his system. If death was self- inflicted, then it certainly wasn't for health reasons. In fact I'd guess he devoted a lot of time to keeping fit. Not exactly the typical profile of a suicide."

"Well there could have been financial reasons, I suppose. We can't rule those out until we've completed a check into his credit record," Blaustein got off the stool and took a step toward the door. "When can we expect the official report?"

"Probably the day after tomorrow. That okay? We're short-staffed at the moment."

"Not a problem. Thanks, Doc."

Outside the air was cold with a hint of snow. As he unlocked the door of his unmarked car, Blaustein took a deep breath, relieved to escape the smell of death and antiseptics. Before getting in, he pulled out his cell phone and dialed the command center.

"Blaustein. Put me through to Detective Gardner please," he said waiting for Huey to come on the line. "It's me, Huey. Anything on the gun yet?"

"Yup. The .38 was in fact registered to Godfrey Mitchell. And the lab confirmed that his were the only prints found on the weapon. What's Doc Priestley's verdict?"

"Doc found some powder residue on the vic's right hand but doesn't think it proves conclusively that Mitchell fired the shot that killed him. For my money, the slug we dug out of the wall could have come from a gun in a dead man's hand. It's probable the shot was fired so that the victim's hand would be covered with powder residue and his prints would be on on the weapon."

"In an attempt to make Mitchell's death look like a suicide," Gardner nodded before continuing. "Whoever killed him was also careful not to leave his own prints on the gun or in the study or foyer. Both places were wiped clean."

"Anything else of interest in the rest of the house?"

"Yes, actually. The techs found two sets of prints in addition to the victim's. Judging by size, both were made by females. One set matched the prints on the drinking glass. We're still checking to see if they are on file."

"What about the second set?"

"Found all over the place. Even on the knick knacks. Could belong to the cleaning lady."

"That would account for the fact that except for the master

bedroom, the house was immaculate. The cleaning lady probably came and went before whoever left pubic hair in the bed arrived. Either way, don't you think it's strange that neither woman raised an alarm when Mitchell didn't come back on schedule?"

"Makes one wonder, doesn't it?"

"Listen Huey, before you hang up, can you connect me with Lennie Hoffimeyer in the computer lab?"

"Can do."

"Lennie, it's Jackson Blaustein." Blaustein said when he got through. "I need a credit check done on Godfrey Mitchell, 234 Cedar Ridge, Chisholm."

"He's that Whitney professor right? I caught the squeal on the scanner."

"Yes. We need to rule out suicide. The man was in perfect health. And it seems unlikely the victim had money problems. He lived in an expensive house with a Beamer parked in his garage. But you never know. He could have owed big time on both. So we need to check his finances. Also I'd like a bank statement to see if he made any large withdrawals lately."

"Right, he could have been into drugs or had a gambling habit."

"Drugs aren't likely. The M.E. has given him a clean bill of health. But blackmail's always a possibility. Which of course would leave homicide on the table. Either way we'll need a financial profile. I'll make the request official tomorrow but do you mind doing what you can in the meantime? I know it's almost quitting time." Blaustein apologized.

"Not a problem." As far as anyone knew, Lennie didn't have much of a social life. The computer lab was his universe. He never needed an excuse to beaver away in front of a computer screen.

Before going home that evening, Blaustein stopped off at the command center that had been set up in the Chisholm Town Hall. Lieutenant Gordon, who headed the Major Crime Squad had commandeered a conference room on the second floor and in short order equipped it with phone lines, a fax machine, a copier and a shredder. The phones and fax machine were set up on a large oval conference table in the middle of the room. Wires and extension cords crisscrossed the floor. Except for Huey Gardner, the room was deserted. Gardner, an old timer biding his time till retirement, was happy to be Blaustein's new partner and Dina Barrett's replacement. With his pleasant face, and gentle demeanor, he seemed more like a Papa Bear than a Popeye Doyle. In any good cop-bad cop routine he was inevitably the good cop. Anything else would have been totally out of character. He was a genuinely nice man but no longer running on all four cylinders. So Blaustein was frankly surprised to find him still in the command room after everyone else had already gone home. He had a telephone cradled against one ear and was taking notes. When he hung up he turned to Blaustein. "I've located Mitchell's cleaning lady. If it's okay with you, I told her we'd stop by there tomorrow morning. We'll also need to get her prints if only to determine whether they match either of the sets we found in the house"

"Fine with me."

"I also called the *New York Times*. The paper Mitchell took. Seems he canceled delivery just after Christmas himself. Said he would call to restart. Same story at the local post office. He went in there on Christmas eve and filled out an authorization to hold his mail. He didn't give a date for resumption of delivery and indicated he would pick up the mail himself. I guess we'll need a warrant to go get the mail?"

"That's taken care of." Blaustein patted his breast pocket. "Why don't we stop off at the post office first thing tomorrow morning? After we've gone through the mail, we can pay the cleaning lady a visit. Then there are a few people at Whitney University we need to talk to."

Gardner looked at his watch as he levered himself out of his chair. "Time for my preprandial. Care to join me at the local pub?"

"Thanks Huey. But I want to finish up the lead sheet and drop the report on Gordon's desk before I leave," Blaustein tossed a clipboard onto the table and sat down. "I don't want to give him a reason to chew me out first thing in the morning."

"See you in the morning then," Gardner shrugged on his coat and drew a pair of gloves from one of the pockets.

"Before you go, what do you think about adding Dina to the team? She's still involved with the Whitney case, but they're fairly close to wrapping it up from what I gather. It would be useful to have an extra pair of eyes while she's still on campus."

"It's fine with me," Huey said as he pulled on his gloves. "But doesn't Lieutenant Gordon have to okay it first?"

"Of course. I'll make sure it's kosher with him before we say anything to her."

After Gardner had gone and Blaustein had finished his paper work, he turned off the lights, locked the door and went to retrieve his personal car from the lot. There was a layer of soft snow on the windows and before getting into the car, he wiped it off with a gloved hand. He ran the engine for half a minute and then, putting the car in gear, drove off through quiet streets under a darkening sky. The snow-plows had not yet gotten around to clearing the local roads and it took longer than usual to reach the highway. Blaustein did not mind. Being New York City born and bred, he reveled in the Connecticut countryside, especially at this time of the year. Fields bordered by winding, stone walls lay dormant under a cover of snow, and smoke curled from the chimneys of clapboarded farm houses in a real-life Currier and Ives world.

It was a different story heading north on Interstate 91. There was nothing picturesque about it. Though the snow had been cleared from the road, a long line of red taillights stretched ahead for miles. Cursing as he slowed to a crawl, Blaustein tuned into the police band radio for an update. A jack-knifed tractor-trailer had blocked two lanes of the highway just north of Meriden and long delays were anticipated. With a sigh he used his cell phone to tell Greta he would be late for dinner.

"That's all right, Darling. I'll keep dinner warm for you," she said, as usual accepting his tardiness without complaint.

Her easygoing acquiescence made him wish that sometimes she would complain just a little. He might have felt less guilty if she bitched a bit. But with major inconveniences to contend with in her life, Greta's philosophy was never to let the minor ones get her down. Since the attack in Central Park that left her a paraplegic, she had developed a far better perspective on life than most people. Maybe she had always been that way, but Blaustein had not really known her before the attack. It had been pure serendipity that his beat happened to take him to the Park on the night she was mugged. A stroke of good fortune that saved her life and ended up enriching his.

The snow was letting up by the time Blaustein reached the outskirts of his West Hartford neighborhood. The streets had been plowed but the municipal snowplows had left a solid ridge of snow blocking the entrance to his driveway. Switching to first gear, wheels spinning, he willed the car over the snow bank and came to a sliding stop in front of the garage. Faced by the unpleasant prospect of shoveling the driveway after dinner, he trudged morosely up the pathway to the front steps.

But his cantankerousness ebbed the moment he opened the door. The house glowed with warmth and the aroma of good cooking. And, as always, a smiling Greta was there to meet him in the entrance hall. Despite the encumbrance of the wheelchair, she looked beautiful to him. Her fair hair, now prematurely white, framed a delicately defined face with wide-set gray eyes that danced with pleasure at seeing him. He kissed her gently on the lips and hung his damp coat on a rack in the hall.

"Have I ever told you how much I enjoy coming home to you?" He asked.

"A few times. But I never get tired of hearing it," she laughed. "Do you mind eating right away?"

"Try and stop me. I'm starved."

Greta swung the wheelchair around and led the way to the dining room with its cheerful William Morris wallpaper and matching drapes. The table was set for two and on the sideboard, beside the silver Sabbath candlesticks and the Queen Anne tea service, was a warming tray with a covered serving dish on it. Greta wheeled herself to the table and waited while Blaustein carved and served the pot roast and vegetables.

"I saw Dina Barrett today. She said to say 'hello'," Blaustein said, pouring them each a glass of Cabernet.

"I hope she's back to full strength."

"Seems to be. She's on assignment in New Haven," Blaustein took a sip of wine. "This is good wine. What is it?"

"Gran Corona. My sister brought it the last time they ate here," Greta replied, breaking off a piece of roll and nibbling it. "How did you happen to be in New Haven?"

"I wasn't. I was on a case in Chisholm when Dina appeared out of the blue."

"I heard on the evening news that a Whitney professor was murdered there. Is that the case you're on?"

"The news report said 'murdered'? That hasn't been established yet. Trust the media to jump to conclusions," Blaustein growled between mouthfuls of pot roast.

"Now that you mention it, I don't remember whether they actually said he'd been murdered. I may be oversimplifying. But that was the implication. They said his body was found under suspicious circumstances and that he appears to have been shot. That certainly sounds like murder to me."

"Mitchell was shot at close range, so there's an outside chance it may have been suicide. There was no evidence of forced entry, no self-defense wounds and no signs of a struggle. But if it was suicide, the reasons for it aren't obvious. The man was in excellent health and apparently at the top of his profession. So unless we find that he had some other reason to end his life, I strongly suspect someone else did it for him. On the other hand, we're not about to dismiss the fact that he may have started to write a suicide note."

"Did it read like a suicide note?"

"Hard to tell. There were just two words, 'I, Godfrey'."

"I suppose that could be the beginning of a suicide note," she suggested. "Or a last will and testament that he didn't get to finish."

"Or it could have nothing to do with his death. You see our dilemma? We can't dismiss the possibility of suicide but we also have to assume that this could be a homicide."

"An intruder or someone he knew?"

"So far, we have nothing to go on. But it's early days, maybe something will turn up."

"Like Mister Micawber, the eternal optimist!" She smiled.

"It sure sounds that way, doesn't it?" Blaustein rose, plate in hand. "More pot roast? I'm getting seconds."

"No thanks," Greta shook her head. "So how did Dina happen to be in Chisholm. Has she been assigned to your case?"

"Actually no. She was in the Whitney library, working another case when Mitchell's teaching assistant was notified that he was missing. Dina happened to be in the adjacent carrel. That's how she got involved. She showed up as I was leaving the scene and I gave her a summary of the situation over a cup of coffee. You could just see the wheels turning. She's obviously dying to get involved in this one."

"Any harm in that?" Greta speared her last piece of potato and dipped it in gravy.

"It would actually be quite helpful to have an extra pair of eyes and ears on campus. But though Dina claims she's fine, she's still on a reduced schedule. We'll need to get Gordon's approval before adding her to the team."

"What about Huey Gardner? Would he still be your partner?"

"Oh yes. Dina's role, if she has one, would be secondary. I discussed it with Huey this evening and he's agreeable. But then he always is." Blaustein returned to his seat with a fresh helping of meat and potatoes. "So it'll be up to Gordon. And I hope he approves. If she isn't officially anointed, Dina's likely to snoop around on her own. And that could really muddy the chain of evidence."

"She wouldn't do that, surely." Greta put her knife and fork down and wiped her lips on her napkin. "Snoop, as you put it, on her own?"

"I don't know. She had a gleam in her eye that I didn't quite trust," Blaustein conceded. "Besides, it might be dangerous if it really is murder. Someone who's killed once won't hesitate to do it again. If she's working solo, she won't have any back up," Blaustein said pouring himself another glass of wine. "I'd rather have Dina where we can protect her. If only from herself."

"She's not irresponsible," Greta protested.

"No, but we don't know who she might be up against."

Greta changed the subject. "We should ask her over for dinner some time soon. Does she still have the same phone number?"

"No, actually she's got temporary digs in New Haven. Seems her landlord sold the condo she was renting and she had to leave. Her current landlady is Freddie Hathaway, a victim in a burglary Dina and I investigated when we first started working together. Talk about coincidence!"

"And you always say there's no such thing as coincidence." Greta teased.

"Well, there isn't, not where crime is concerned."

4

THE SAFE HOUSE DINA WAS HEADED FOR WAS IN THE FAIR HAVEN
section of New Haven, about as far away from the Whitney campus
as one could get and still be in New Haven. It was the last house on
a cul-de-sac and ideal for the purpose. Sparsely furnished but with
state-of-art computers and high speed hookups, the small Cape was
surrounded by an overgrown hedge of Hemlocks and so isolated
that people could come and go without being noticed. For the
moment, the only ones using the safe house besides Dina Barrett
was Edward Morrison. Except for their contacts in the New Haven
Police Department, no one else knew they were there.

Dina was making coffee in the small rudimentary kitchen when
Edward Morrison arrived. He was on time for a change and Dina
rewarded him with a smile as he unzipped his ski jacket; sat down
at the breakfast bar, and helped himself from a box of doughnuts.

"None too warm in here," he said.

"Coffee will help," she handed him a steaming mug.

Edward was in his thirties and married with an infant on the way,
but he looked a lot younger than he was with an incongruous baby

face atop the body of a linebacker. His hands were gloveless and on his feet he wore salt–stained Timberlands. Under his ski jacket he had on corduroy pants, baggy at the knees and a plaid flannel shirt. His fair, straight hair was combed back from his face and worn long in the back. Like Dina he was able to pass as a student and like Dina he encouraged the impression by dressing the part.

"I caught a break today," Edward said, his hands wrapped around the coffee mug.

"It's about time we caught a break," Dina took her coffee over to the breakfast bar and sat down. "Tell me."

"After you left the library, a student came in. He looked at the reserve desk for a second or two and then took a seat at the end of my table. He seemed real nervous. Kept fidgeting. Instead of opening the book he had in front of him, he kept looking up at the reserve desk. I figured him for a user in need of a fix, and guessed that he might be stalling till the right librarian showed up at the desk."

"Which librarian was there when he first got there?" Dina selected a doughnut from the box and took a bite.

"Myra Sullivan. And the fact that he didn't react till after she left seems to put her in the clear." Edward took a sip of coffee before continuing. "Anyway, the longer this guy waited, the more nervous he got. Kept staring at the reserve desk. Kept drumming his fingers on the table. Ignored his book. Just watching him was starting to make me nervous. In fact, I was just as jumpy as the kid by the time Sullivan took her break and Herman Archer came to relieve her. The second Archer showed up behind the reserve desk, the kid picked up his book and went over to him."

"Herman Archer, the one the students call Archie? He seems like such a nice guy."

"He's obviously not that nice."

"Did you actually see an exchange take place?"

"Wait. It gets better and better," Edward grinned. "The student handed over his library card and the book. Archer scanned the library card, took the book and then checked inside the back cover. I was guessing he found the correct amount of cash there, because he then went to the reserve shelves and retrieved a second book."

"Archie could have been checking to make sure the book was handed in on time," Dina sounded skeptical.

"Exactly. That's why I had to find out for sure," Edward grinned. "And why, when the student left the library, I followed him out and tailed him to his dorm room."

"He didn't make you, I hope?" To Dina it seemed incongruous that a man as large as Edward Morrison could tail someone and not be noticed.

"Of course not."

"Of course not," Dina echoed. "Sorry for the interruption. Go on."

"I gave the student a couple of minutes inside his dorm room. Then I knocked on the door and went in without waiting for an invitation. He had drug paraphernalia spread out on the desk in front of him. So I acted real cool. I knew I couldn't nail him without a search warrant, so I asked him where I could find some coke. Obviously, he couldn't deny that he knew where to get it. In fact, he was so anxious to take a hit and get me out of his hair that he spilled the beans. "If you want any coke," he told me, 'return a book, any book, to Herman Archer at the reserve desk put fifty bucks in the back of it. You'll get your coke."

"Any book?"

"Right. When Archie sees it's not on the reserve list, he checks the back of the book for cash. He then hands the student a new book, which has a bag of coke taped to the back inside cover."

"The books aren't on the reserve list?" Dina was puzzled.

"No. And I don't think there is a bogus reserve list. The student doesn't ask for a particular book. He just takes whatever the librarian gives him."

"So if there isn't a bogus reserve list, how did Polly Obermeier's book get to be stamped 'on reserve'?"

"Archie stamped it during the transaction, I guess."

"He stamps the books he hands out 'reserve list' to make sure he gets them back?"

"I guess so."

"Great work Ed!" Dina beamed at him. "A real break in the case."

"So where do we go from here?"

"Next we find out who Archer's supplier is. Keep an eye on him round-the-clock to see what he does in his off hours. And who he contacts."

"We'll need to brief the NHPD and see what they want to do about expanding surveillance."

"We also need to run a background check on our Mr. Archer."

"I'll stop by the NHPD on my way home, if you'll take care of the background check."

"Fine, I'll get started as soon as I've written up today's report."

After writing and faxing the report to Head Quarters, Dina left the safe house and went home. She let herself in, made a bee-line for the kitchen, put on the kettle, helped herself to a slice of leftover pizza from her shelf in the refrigerator, and popped it in the microwave. She felt achy and exhausted. Not yet fully recovered from the bullet that almost took her life, she still tired easily. She was also ravenous. Except for the stale doughnut at the safe house, she hadn't eaten since breakfast.

"Is that what you call dinner?" Freddie, dressed in a navy blue Polartek robe and fur-lined slippers, had appeared in the kitchen doorway. Her short gray hair, damp from the shower, was brushed back behind her ears, and her remarkably unlined face had been scrubbed so clean it glowed. A pair of reading glasses dangled from a chain around her neck. "I roasted a chicken this evening. Why don't you have some of it?"

"That's nice of you, Freddie. But I thought we agreed to keep our larders separate."

"What's a little chicken between friends?" Freddie asked

rhetorically, knowing that the subject was closed as far as Dina was concerned. She took a mug and a tin of cocoa from the cabinet above the counter. "Mind if I piggyback on your hot water?"

"Of course not." Dina said, transferring her warmed-over pizza from the microwave to the kitchen table.

"I've decided it's time for a little sunshine and a lot of golf," Freddie informed her as she poured measured spoonfuls of cocoa into a mug. "It's not warm enough yet in the Carolinas, so I'll be going to Florida. I take off first thing on Saturday morning, which means you'll have the house to yourself for a few days."

"Florida sounds wonderful right now. I envy you," Dina turned off the burner under the kettle and poured steaming water into the two mugs. After handing Freddie hers, they sat down on opposite sides of the kitchen table.

"It'll be a comfort knowing you'll be here to keep an eye on things." Freddie said, stirring a heaped spoon of sugar into her cocoa. "If you mind being here alone, invite a friend to stay with you. They can use the front guest room."

"Thanks. But I won't mind being alone."

"Well if you change your mind, feel free. This big old Victorian can be a bit intimidating, even for me. And I grew up here. Zelda will come in to clean as usual. Just tell her of anything extra that needs doing."

Dina nodded. "I saw Jackson Blaustein today. He said to say 'hello.'"

"How is he?"

"Busy on a new case out in Chisholm. The Mitchell case. You might have heard about it on the evening news," Dina said between bites of pizza.

"I did. And I was shocked. Shocked and saddened," Freddie's normally cheerful face composed itself into lines of solemnity. "I knew him, you know. Not well. But still, it made me sad to hear that he'd been killed. Such a horrible end for a fine man and a good writer."

"How did you know him?"

VALERIE KOSSEW DUNN

"I met him years ago when he was new on the faculty, a young assistant professor working toward a tenure track position. Reggie and I saw him occasionally at faculty parties, Godfrey and Alison, his wife... ex-wife now I guess, were a handsome couple. Reggie was a Dean of Faculty at Whitney back when it was a sister school to Yale. In the days before it went co-ed. We were always entertaining in those days. It's not something I do much anymore, thank goodness. I always found college soirees a bit of a bore. The men always talked shop, and the women, there weren't too many females on the faculty back then, always talked about their children. As I didn't have any, I found it tedious in the extreme. I went because of Reggie. After he died, I stopped giving and going to faculty parties altogether. A rite of passage, I suppose," she took a long sip and set her mug down. "But as usual I digress. To cut to the chase: I haven't seen Godfrey Mitchell in years but I've followed his career with considerable interest. Apart from being one of the more distinguished professors in the History Department, he's twice topped the *New York Times* best sellers' list. His books read like fiction. Pretty rare for an academic."

Dina knew most of that since meeting his graduate student. She was more interested in the personal stuff, "What was he like as a person?"

"He had all the right credentials. Born with a silver spoon you might say. He attended Choate as a boy. Then Penn. He got his doctorate at Harvard before joining the Whitney faculty as an assistant professor. Personally, I thought him a bit of an apple polisher. A little too smooth if you know what I mean. But one can't blame youngsters jockeying for a tenure spot. They all have to grease the skids a bit," she paused, remembering. "He became a reluctant hero some twenty years ago."

"Why reluctant?"

"It had something to do with him testifying against a colleague in court. I'm not sure I remember all the details. Something about a stolen manuscript. A rare manuscript. The prosecutor considered Godfrey a hostile witness. He had to be subpoenaed because he didn't want to give evidence against a friend. Even so, it was Godfrey's testimony that sent his colleague to jail. Such a scandal." She sighed.

"Do you remember the man's name? The accused?"

"Sorry, I don't," Freddie shook her head, adding. "I wonder what happened to that poor misguided young man?"

Dina wondered too. And whether Mitchell's erstwhile colleague may have come back to seek a dreadful vengeance. But if so, why so many years later? And why such a violent retribution? At most theft, especially for a first-time offender, would have meant just a few months in jail. And if Mitchell had been a reluctant witness, why retaliate at all? As a motive for murder, that long ago incident was at best a long shot. But she decided to follow up on it anyway.

After Freddie had retired to her room and Dina had cleaned up in the kitchen, she called Jackson at home.

"I hope you're not eating."

"Just finished. What's up?"

"I was talking to Freddie about the Mitchell case. She knew him years ago, when he was an assistant professor at Whitney. Apparently he was a reluctant witness in a case that sent a colleague to jail. It all happened a long time ago. And she doesn't remember the man's name. But it ought to be checked out, don't you think?"

"What was the crime?"

"The theft of a manuscript," she paused. "I know it doesn't sound like much of a crime. And I don't know what kind of sentence the man served. As a first-timer, it probably wasn't a long one."

"I agree. It doesn't sound much like a motive for murder especially if it happened long ago, but you're right, we should follow up on it. Thanks for telling me," Jackson responded. "Do you happen to know when exactly the theft occurred?"

"Twenty or so years ago. Freddie wasn't very precise."

"And Mitchell was a reluctant witness?" Blaustein sounded doubtful. "I don't know. Twenty years does seem a long time to bear a grudge. But thanks for letting me know."

"I'll let you know if anything else comes up."

Blaustein hesitated before speaking again, "Look Dina, this is premature, but Huey and I were discussing the possibility of adding you to the team on a part-time basis. We both think you'll be an asset but I have to run it by Gordon first, so don't get your hopes up."

"They already are!" Dina's spirits rose at the prospect.

"Well don't count on it. You know what a tight-ass our Loo is."

The next morning, as soon as he had taken off his coat, Blaustein marched into Lieutenant Gordon's office. The latter was at his desk going through the previous day's reports.

"What is it?" he said gruffly without looking up.

"And a good morning to you too," Blaustein responded light heartedly.

"Cut the crap. You look as if you want something. What is it?'

"Gardner and I think it would be a real plus if Detective Barrett could be added to the Mitchell team on a part-time basis," he hurried on before Gordon could object. "It won't distract from her present assignment. But as she's already under cover on campus….."

Gordon started shaking his head.

"Having her on campus has already paid off. Not only does she have an in with Mitchell's graduate student, but she's given us a lead."

"What kind of lead?"

"It turns out that some years ago, Mitchell provided testimony that sent a colleague to jail. It could be a motive for murder."

"Tell me about it."

Blaustein explained the circumstances as far as he knew them, "I know it's a stretch. The man probably served very little time and it happened a long time ago, but it's worth looking into."

"No one would wait that long for a pay-back." Gordon sounded unconvinced.

"Perhaps it's a dead-end," Blaustein conceded. "but we should still look into it."

"I don't have the manpower to go chasing dead-ends."

"It's something Barrett could do for us if she were part of the team."

When Gordon hesitated, Blaustein knew he had him at least partially convinced.,"Look, Blaustein, the case Barrett's working on needs to be watertight. They're a long way from an arrest. She can assist on the Mitchell case only if she is willing to put in the extra time, okay. I'll call and tell her to follow up on the lead she's given you. After that we'll see."

And that was as far as Gordon was prepared to go. For the time being it was far enough for Dina. After she completed her stint in the library, she walked over to the *New Haven Register* building and went in. Her badge gave her access to the paper's research library and a helpful librarian helped her locate microfilm editions going back twenty-five years. The story first broke in February 1991 with the headline: "Assistant Professor Arrested". According to the report, Harvey Thomas, an assistant professor in the History Department at Whitney was found in possession of a manuscript taken from the Grosvenor Rare Book Library. The manuscript, an anti-slavery protestation written by the great British abolitionist William Wilberforce to Thomas Jefferson, was conservatively valued at six figures. Also found in Thomas' possession, and even more incriminating, was a typewritten, though unsigned letter from Thomas to a wealthy Manhattan collector. It offered the document for sale at a price to be negotiated. The discovery of the Wilberforce letter in Thomas's office and the fact that he had been working on the Wilberforce-Jefferson correspondence in the Grosvenor on the day the loss was discovered, convinced the authorities they had an open and shut case. He was charged and bound over for trial. The article made no mention of Godfrey Mitchell.

The story was no longer front page news by the time the trial took place. Nevertheless, it was reported in some detail in a later edition of the *Register*. Here for the first time Godfrey Mitchell's name was mentioned as a witness for the prosecution but, as a colleague and friend of the accused man, a hostile witness. He testified that while waiting in Thomas's office to discuss a seminar they were teaching jointly, he noticed the Wilberforce letter on Thomas' desk. A scholar himself, Mitchell recognized it for what it was and knew that it did not belong there. Unwilling to confront his friend and reluctant to report him, he hesitated before turning the matter over to the Department Chairman, Adrian Needham. It was he who summoned the police.

According to Miles Acton, the reporter who covered the story, Mitchell looked uncomfortable testifying for the prosecution and was even a character witness for the defense. But nothing he or other character witnesses could say undermined the incriminating evidence against Thomas. The jury did not buy the argument that Thomas had been doing research in the Grosvenor Rare Book Library on the day the manuscript disappeared to explain away his fingerprints on the Wilberforce letter. Nor could the defense explain how a typewriter found in Thomas' home came to be used to type the memo to the Manhattan collector. And then there was also a possible motive. Thomas was known to be hard up. On a Whitney assistant professor's salary, money had been tight. His young wife had quit her part-time job because she was having a difficult pregnancy. The couple owed back rent and Thomas still had to pay off his student loans. The prosecutor's case seemed solid.

To back up the argument that Thomas had been using the Jefferson papers to do legitimate research, his attorney produced Grosvenor Library logs and the testimony of a finger print expert to show that Thomas's prints were on several other documents in the Grosvenor. He argued that the letter and the memo to the dealer had been planted in order to frame Thomas and proved that there were no prints, either his client's or anyone else's, on the memo to the collector. But he was unable to prove how or by whom the letters had been planted, and he offered no explanation for the inescapable fact that the letter to the collector had been written on Thomas' home typewriter. Though he told the jury that the man in the dock was not a criminal but a victim, his argument did not sway them. After deliberating for only two hours, they voted to convict.

In a later issue, *The Register* reported that after being found guilty and sentenced to a year in jail, Whitney had terminated Thomas's contract. There were no follow-up stories and no mention of Thomas in any other context. Presumably after serving his time he had picked up the pieces of his shattered life and moved on. It was a sad, sordid story, and Dina was inclined to dismiss it as nothing more than a sideline to the current case. Even though Mitchell reported the stolen letter and testified to that effect, he had done so with obvious reluctance. And it all happened so very long ago. Still, Dina was disinclined to close the book on the whole affair until she had spoken to the reporter, Miles Acton, assuming he was still around.

Dina's opportunity to find out more about Godfrey Mitchell came from an unexpected source the very same evening. She had just picked up her mail from the table in the front hall and was rifling through the usual bills and solicitations when Freddy called out from the front parlor.

"Dina there's someone here I'd like you to meet."

Dina had noticed a vintage Jaguar parked in the driveway, and as Freddie only entertained in the front parlor on rare occasions, she guessed that her guest was someone special. Putting her mail back on the table and smoothing her obstinate hair, she crossed to the archway that lead into the parlor.

Though a large room and high-ceilinged, she always found the parlor oppressive. Even the fire burning in the fireplace failed to bring cheer. The room had dark mahogany paneling and heavy velvet drapes. One of Freddie's forebears, a dyspeptic-looking gentleman with whiskers and sideburns glowered from above the marble fireplace. Straight-backed Victorian chairs with needlepoint seats, overstuffed wing chairs with ball and claw feet, and a monstrous cranberry velvet sofa with an ornate mahogany frame fought for space with an assortment of pie-crust tables. The latter and the mantle over the fireplace were cluttered with bric-a brac: a brass clock with an erratic chime, elaborate lamps with fringed shades and delicate porcelain figurines. Also, crammed into every conceivable space there were vases and lacquered boxes brought from China long ago by an old Applegate sea captain.

As Dina entered the parlor, an elderly gentleman rose from the wing chair in which he had been sitting.

"Dina, I'd like you to meet Adrian Needham, Professor Emeritus and formerly Chairman of Whitney's History Department," Freddie grinned at her, rather like Alice's Cheshire cat. Clearly she had invited the elderly professor to tea so that Dina could pump him. And Dina, suspecting that her landlady rather enjoyed the idea of playing detective, had a hard time keeping a straight face.

"Pleased to meet you, Professor," Dina shook his hand politely and purposely avoided looking at Freddie.

"Please join us for tea," Freddie waved Dina to a chair.

"Thank you," Dina sat down, crossing her legs demurely at the ankles.

"When I invited Adrian, I told him my ulterior reason was to talk about the Harvey Thomas incident. I explained that you were a detective working on the Godfrey Mitchell case," she handed Dina a delicate cup and saucer decorated with little pink roses. "So don't be shy about asking questions. Adrian won't mind."

"I won't mind at all, my dear. But it's all so long ago. I can't guarantee I'll remember the details," the old man inclined his head apologetically. He was a small man, perhaps five foot five. With a round body, a plump, cherubic face, glasses that he wore halfway down his nose and a healthy head of white hair. Except that he was clean shaven, he could have been the jolly old elf himself.

"Jackson Blaustein, is the State detective in charge of the case. I might suggest that he talk to you as well. Is that all right?" Dina said, helping herself to two lumps of sugar with a pair of silver tongs.

"As long as nothing I say can be taken down and used as evidence against me?" the old man chuckled at his little joke.

"I promise that he'll read you your rights first," Dina joked back, thinking no one looked less like a criminal than the rotund little man.

"Well the way I remember it," he began, "Godfrey Mitchell

came to me that day looking upset. I was dashing off somewhere. Don't remember now where that would have been. But because the chap looked so harried, I told him to sit down and tell me what was wrong. What he told me came as a shock. He'd come across a letter from William Wilberforce to Thomas Jefferson on Thomas' desk. It was a rare manuscript normally housed in the Grosvenor and it had no business being on Thomas' desk. Not knowing what to do, and preferring not to confront Thomas directly, he had brought the matter to me. Put the monkey on my back as it were.

"Well, I remember feeling as if I had been hit in the solar plexus. Thomas, you see, was one of the History Department's bright young stars and in line for a tenured position at Whitney. I had taken a chance on hiring him in the first place because he didn't come from the usual background. He did not get his undergraduate degree from any of the great universities. In fact, he was a poor boy from the South End of Boston with a doctorate from U. Mass. But he was a Woodrow Wilson Fellow and according to his references, quite brilliant. So despite objections from some of the senior faculty, I hired him as an assistant professor. At first, before the mess over the Wilberforce letter, he made me look good. Completely justified my faith in him. So much promise!" he sighed and shook his head. "You see, he was beginning to make quite a name for himself. He had published several seminal articles. Brilliant, insightful articles. And he was working on a history of the anti-slavery movement in England – which to my knowledge he never published, much is the shame. To find out that he'd stolen a valuable manuscript from the Grosvenor and planned to sell it, came as a devastating blow. Simply devastating," he sighed again. "Admittedly we paid our assistant professors very poorly back then. Barely a living wage. And he did have a child on the way. So one can understand his desperation. But understanding it does not mean condoning it. Even if the chap was hard up, there was no excuse for what he did.

"So," he continued, after pausing to take a sip of his tea, before summoning the police, I called the Grosvenor. I had them check the Wilberforce papers, just in case Mitchell was wrong. They kept me on hold while they looked. And when they came back with an answer, it was one I didn't want to hear. There was a letter missing all right. The very one Godfrey Mitchell had seen on Harvey Thomas's desk. I had no choice then but to call the police."

"Did Mitchell go with you when you confronted Thomas?"

"No. I didn't think it appropriate to involve him further."

"What did Thomas have to say when you accused him of taking the letter?"

"He was very flustered. Claimed he had no idea how the letter came to be on his desk and couldn't imagine how it got there. But the letter was there all right. Out in the open. He couldn't deny it. If he had only borrowed it to do research, all would have been forgiven, but the police also found a letter to a collector, a man by the name of Sutton, in which Harvey offered to sell the Wilberforce letter and vouched for its authenticity. He never offered an explanation, either then or later. And when the prosecutor proved that the Sutton letter had been typed on an old typewriter Thomas had at home, it was the final nail in his coffin. No one else could have typed that note."

"His wife perhaps?" Dina suggested.

"Only if she was in it with him," Needham shook his head, "and any way, she could not have taken the Wilberforce letter. Her husband was the one with access to the Grosvenor."

"Strange he left his office door open with the letter just sitting on his desk," Dina said, playing devil's advocate.

Instead of taking the bait, the old scholar took her comment at face value, "Not only brazen but careless," he said. "Thomas had closed the door but hadn't locked it, you see. I guess he didn't think anyone would come in uninvited. We tend to respect other people's closed doors as a rule, don't we?"

"But the closed door didn't stop Mitchell," Dina reminded him.

"Godfrey knew he was expected, and when Thomas didn't answer his knock, he simply walked in and dumped the books he was carrying on the desk. That's when he noticed the Wilberforce letter."

"What was Godfrey Mitchell like as a young man?"

"Handsome," Freddie interposed with a twinkle.

"He was all Ivy," Needham said, ignoring the interruption. "A likable, pleasant young man. Came from a wealthy family and had a fairly good academic background. But though an adequate scholar, he wasn't brilliant like Thomas and probably would have been passed over for tenure if not for Thomas's dismissal."

"Do you know what happened to Thomas after he was released from prison?"

"Can't say that I do," Needham admitted regretfully. "I'm afraid I was so disappointed in the man that I didn't much care. He may have ended up teaching somewhere, but if so he didn't have the nerve to ask for references. So if he continued his academic career, my guess is it was at some place that didn't check credentials too carefully. Either that or he dropped out of academia completely. I never saw his name on any subsequent publications. An unfortunate waste. He had so much potential. A brilliant, analytic mind. And he knew how to write. An enviable talent, that not all historians share, alas."

"Did he have many friends?" Dina broke into the old man's reverie.

"Except perhaps for Godfrey Mitchell, I don't think so. At least not on the faculty. He was a bit of a loner."

"Given the fact that Godfrey Mitchell turned him in, would Thomas be likely to have taken revenge?"

"Now? You mean all these years later? I doubt it. Besides, why would he? Godfrey had to be virtually dragged into court to testify against him," Needham sat silently contemplating the fire. "In any case, I think it most unlikely. Harvey would never have considered violence of any sort, no matter how provoked. Not in his character. He was a declared pacifist. Never in the least confrontational. And except to proclaim his innocence just prior to sentencing, he didn't even take the stand in his own defense. Besides, he didn't like guns. And whoever killed Godfrey, apparently used a gun, didn't they? No, Harvey didn't kill him. You can be sure of that. He may have been a broken man, a saddened man. But I don't see him as a vengeful one."

"Is there anyone else who may have had a grudge against Professor Mitchell?" Dina asked, mentally scratching Harvey Thomas off her list of suspects.

"Probably a few husbands," added Freddie, hitherto a silent spectator during the exchange. "He was quite the lady's man. Even before his divorce."

"But was it just salacious gossip, or was it fact?" Needham looked uncomfortable.

"Most likely just faculty wife gossip," Freddie admitted with a shrug. "But you know what they say. Where there's smoke…. Speaking of which." She rose and added a log to the fire.

"Time to feed the dog. I really ought to get home. Thank you for tea, Freddie." Putting down his cup and saucer, Needham hoisted himself out of the chair, "It's been very nice meeting you, Dina. I hope you catch whoever did this to Godfrey."

"Hope so too. I'll pass on what you've told me to Detective Blaustein. He may want to pick your brain himself. So don't be surprised if he calls you."

Dina and Freddie walked the old gentleman to the door and helped him on with his overcoat. Outside the snow was falling in large, gentle flakes coating the bare branches of the maple trees and sugarcoating the hedgerows.

"Will you be all right driving in this?" Freddie asked anxiously from the doorway.

"Been driving in snow for more years than I care to remember," Needham replied as he turned to wave. He got into his car and started it up. With his windshield wipers going and his headlights on, he backed down the driveway. But before turning onto the street, he rolled down his window and called out, "You might want to speak to a colleague of Godfrey's, Augusta Scott. She knew him as well as anyone. I'll tell her you'll be in touch." Then rolling up the window, he was gone.

5

FIRST THING NEXT MORNING BLAUSTEIN AND GARDNER, ARMED WITH their subpoena, retrieved Mitchell's mail from the post office. Along with a pile of junk mail, there were solicitations from charitable causes, two letters from fans, neither of them threatening, and several bills. One, a telephone bill, confirmed what they had already learned from the victim's telephone records. On the days immediately preceding December 27, several long distance calls had been made from the Mitchell house: the first to a ski lodge in Vermont, a second to an Atlanta hotel, presumably to confirm his reservation there, and a half dozen or so to out-of-state acquaintances. When contacted, none of the latter, admitted to being anywhere near Connecticut at the time of Mitchell's death. Claims that would have to be verified. The call to the ski lodge was still a bit of a mystery as the lodge did not keep a record of incoming calls.

After leaving the post office, the two detectives headed south to the home of Ada Jennings, Mitchell's cleaning lady. She lived in a working class neighborhood of New Haven where the lots were tiny and the houses all needed a coat of paint. They parked on the street in front of the house and picked their way along the icy, shovel-wide path that led to the front door. The front window curtain moved aside as they approached and before they could ring the bell, the door opened.

"You're from the police?" The middle-aged woman who greeted them was red-faced, big bosomed and wide hipped. Her salt and pepper hair was cut sensibly short. She was wearing an oversized blue sweat-shirt, jeans that were threadbare at the knees, and sneakers that were worn at the toes.

"Yes, Ms. Jennings, thank you for agreeing to meet with us. Detectives Blaustein and Gardner." They showed her their badges.

"Yes, yes. Come on in. Don't want to heat up the outside," her response was brusque without being rude.

After their coats had been deposited on a coat-rack in the hall, they were shown into a small, overheated parlor.

"If you don't mind, we'd like to ask you a few questions about Professor Mitchell."

"So you said when you called. Do sit down," she clucked.

"You've been Godfrey Mitchell's cleaning lady for how long, Ms. Jennings?" Blaustein asked, as he and Gardner took a seat on the couch.

"Don't remember exactly but a lot of years. Since before his divorce," the cleaning lady pulled up a chair so that she was facing them.

"How often do you clean his house?"

"Twice a week, Tuesdays and Thursdays."

"When was the last time you went there?"

"Two days after Christmas."

"Not since then?"

"No, Sir. I was due to start again this week."

"How come you haven't been to clean the Mitchell place in so long?"

"I was away taking care of my sister in Ohio the week after Christmas. She had back surgery and needed a hand. And seeing as the Professor was planning to be away anyways, it worked out just fine for the both of us."

"When did you get back from Ohio, Ms. Jennings?"

"Day before yesterday. On the Greyhound."

"So the professor planned to be away all this time?"

"Don't know if he did. But he knew I wouldn't be back for a few weeks and it was okay with him."

"Did you keep your bus ticket receipt by any chance?"

She nodded.

"Mind showing it to us?"

She gave him a questioning look from beneath her eyebrows and got up, "I didn't kill him if that's what you think."

"Not at all, but why don't we look at your ticket any way?" Blaustein answered patiently. "That way you'll be officially in the clear."

After the ticket had been produced and verified she sat down again with a grunt. Crossed one beefy leg over the other and waited for the next question with an air of martyrdom.

"Tell us Ms. Jennings, about the last time you saw the professor. Was he still in the house when you left?"

"Yes he was."

"And that was when?"

"The time I left, you mean'?"

Blaustein nodded.

"It was around one thirty," which would have made it more than two hours before Mitchell was due to fly to Atlanta.

"Ms. Jennings, do you know if Professor Mitchell was expecting any visitors later that day?"

"Not that I know of."

"Did he have any regular visitors?"

"Used to be that Heather Leopold, his teaching assistant, came by quite a bit, but she graduated last summer and I haven't seen her since." Blaustein nodded at Gardner who made a note. "The new one doesn't come by at all. Professor Mitchell told me she doesn't have a car."

"What about girl friends? Did Professor Mitchell have any girl friends that you know about?"

"Well," she licked her lips with a lizard-like flick of the tongue. "It isn't my place to pry into my employer's private business, but I reckon, he did have a lady friend come visit now and then."

"Did you meet her?"

"No, I never did."

"Then how do you know he had a lady friend?" Blaustein prodded.

"The trash. Tissues with lipstick marks," she reddened. "And condom wrappers in the master bath room."

"Did Professor Mitchell ever give you reason to believe he was afraid of anyone?"

"Mr. Mitchell afraid?" she snorted. "Not likely."

"Ms. Jennings, do you customarily change the linens?'

"Change, launder and put them away. I do it once a week."

"And did you change the linens on Professor Mitchell's bed the last time you were there?"

"Yes, Sir."

Blaustein and Gardner exchanged glances. Ada Jennings' clean linens in the master bedroom were no longer clean when Godfrey Mitchell went to meet his killer downstairs. This tidbit of information nailed down the time of death much more precisely.

"As far as you know, was Professor Mitchell alone when you went to clean the house that day?"

"No, Master Brian was there too. He was just leaving when I drove up just before ten. He'd left his usual mess in the guest room. The way kids do. So Mr. Mitchell, bless his heart, paid me a little extra to clean the place up. That was on top of a nice Christmas bonus. Real good to me he always was," she sighed.

"Brian is Professor Mitchell's son?"

Blaustein had previously verified the fact.

She nodded, "I guess you could say that."

"Why do you put it that way? Didn't they get along?" Blaustein's interest was piqued.

"I don't think they were real close, no," she said with a disapproving sniff.

"You say Brain was just leaving when you arrived?"

"Yes, Sir. With his skis on top of his car."

Which might account for the phone call to the ski lodge in Vermont. "And you're sure you saw him drive off?"

She nodded. Obviously a woman of few words.

"And you did not see Brian or anyone else in the house after that?"

Again she confirmed the question with a nod.

Additional questions provided few revelations other than to confirm the impression that Ada Jennings thought the world of her late employer. But at least they had narrowed down the possible time of death and had learned that Mitchell's son Brian was one of the last people to see the professor alive.

"Mrs. Jennings, our temporary command center is located in the basement of the Chisholm town hall. Please come down there as soon as possible so that we can take your fingerprints."

"What for?" Instantly on guard, her eyes narrowed.

"It's just routine," Gardner hastened to reassure her. "We need to identify your fingerprints, in order to determine who else may have left fingerprints in the house."

"Oh," with a nod of comprehension, she relaxed visibly.

Leaving the cleaning lady with their business cards, and relieved to escape the stuffy little house, Blaustein and Gardner drove back to New Haven. They parked in front of the Whitney History Department and went in. After a brief wait, the two detectives were ushered into the office of the Chairman, a large room filled floor-to-ceiling with books, primitive masks and maps of Southern Africa, which subcontinent was Sidney Lawrence's specialty. He rose to greet them from behind his desk. He was a tall, gaunt man with tanned almost leathery skin, prominent cheekbones and a mop of unruly sandy hair. He wore a Tweed jacket with elbow patches, a dark green turtle neck, a wedding ring and a sports watch. Blaustein figured him to be in his late forties.

VALERIE KOSSEW DUNN

"Please gentlemen, be seated," Lawrence waved at a pair of
leather chairs and resumed his seat behind the desk. "You're here
about Godfrey Mitchell. A sad, very sad business."

"Yes, we hope you can provide us with some background on
Professor Mitchell," Blaustein confirmed. "We'd like to find out who
his friends were and which colleagues he was close to. We need to
talk to everyone who knew him."

"Well, except for the obligatory faculty parties, Godfrey didn't
socialize much with his colleagues," the chairman hesitated as if
reluctant to point a finger at anyone. "If he was friendly with anyone,
it would have been our other Victorian specialist, Augusta Scott."
Gardner wrote down the name.

"Did he get along with his students?"

"The undergraduates seemed to like him. He was a very popular
lecturer."

"What about his graduate students?"

"I can't answer that with any accuracy, and if you absolutely have
to question them, go ahead. Though I'd much rather you didn't,"
Lawrence answered shortly.

Gardner made a note on his lead sheet to follow up on Godfrey
Mitchell's relationships with his graduate students.

"How about his colleagues, did he get along with them?"
Blaustein returned to his original line of questioning.

"Godfrey was generally well respected by his colleagues,"
Lawrence answered after the briefest of pauses, "but he had his
detractors."

"Oh really?" Blaustein pricked up his ears. "Anyone with enough
of an axe to grind to want to kill him?"

"I doubt that," Lawrence honored Blaustein with a humorless
smile. "Academia can be a pretty cutthroat business, but for the
most part it's 'cutthroat' in the figurative sense. It's true that ours is a
game of publish or perish, but as far as I know, the use of the phrase
is purely metaphorical."

"Anyone with a particular bone to pick? You'd be surprised how
little it takes sometimes to set someone off," Blaustein prodded.

54

"Well, there's always a certain amount of envy when someone is very successful. And Godfrey was, you know. Most of us are lucky to get one or two books published. And generally when we do, our work is read by only a handful of fellow historians. For most of us, decades of hard work is usually left to gather dust in academic libraries. Godfrey Mitchell was different. A rare exception in our world. His books are immensely popular with the general reading public."

"Why do you think that is?" Gardner was genuinely interested.

"He tapped into a mother lode when he started publishing his series, *Lives of The Victorians*. There's a taste in this country for the salacious, and the lives of the nineteenth century British aristocracy provided that in abundance. Each new book in Godfrey's series has made the *New York Times* best seller's list. And his popularity as an author carried over here on campus. Because of his celebrity, his courses and seminars have always been over-enrolled."

"And the other faculty members resented his popularity?" Gardner looked doubtful.

"It's not quite as straight forward as that. You have to understand that we academics tend to decry what we call 'popular history.' However irrational and snobbish it may sound, it's an inescapable fact. We ought to cheer when the general public is turned on to history. Instead we tend to scoff at popular historians for pandering to the great unwashed."

"In other words if the public likes it, it can't be academically sound?" Gardner queried.

"Something like that," Lawrence nodded. "But it's hog wash you know. There's no reason why history can't be both well-researched and fun."

Fun? Blaustein grimaced. He had hated history when he was a kid in school. "Did his colleagues consider Mitchell's stuff academically unsound?"

"Well, Victorian England isn't my field, but that's the opinion of his fellow Victorians." Lawrence shrugged apologetically. "In my opinion, they tend to quibble the details. My impression was that on the whole Godfrey's research seemed pretty thorough," he paused, as if debating whether or not what he had to say next could be misinterpreted. "There is something else. Rumor has it that a lot of his research was done by graduate students. Ordinarily that is taken care of with some sort of acknowledgment, but Godfrey never gave his students credit for their contributions. The only one to challenge him left the University under a cloud."

"Did Mitchell and that student have a confrontation?"

"The student accused him of plagiarism but never actually proved it."

"And left with his tail between his legs?"

"You could say that. He transferred to another university. But the whole thing was a tempest in a teacup and hardly to my way of thinking, a motive for murder."

"The student's name, the one who challenged Mitchell?"

"Curt Daniels."

Gardener wrote it down. "Present whereabouts?"

"Don't really know."

"What about Mitchell's other graduate students, past and present? Could you give us a list?" It wasn't much to go on, but at this point Blaustein felt he was just grabbing at straws anyway.

"I'll have my secretary prepare it for you," Lawrence picked up the telephone and made the request.

"Professor Mitchell was scheduled to fly to Atlanta just after Christmas," Gardner interposed. "Would you have any way of knowing the reason for his trip?"

"Yes, I would. The annual American Historical Association meeting was being held in Atlanta. I attended myself. But I didn't see Godfrey there."

"When did you fly out?" It was Blaustein asking the question this time.

"On December 28th."

The day after Mitchell was scheduled to fly out and presumably the day after Mitchell was killed. Could that be significant? Blaustein and Gardner exchanged glances and Gardner made a note.

"Were you surprised that you didn't see Professor Mitchell at the conference?" Blaustein did not miss a beat.

Lawrence shook his head. "Not really. In fact, it wouldn't have registered that I hadn't seen him. You see, we're in different fields and usually attend different sessions. Besides, roughly a thousand people came to this year's conference. It was a mob scene," the fingertips of his right hand began drumming a barely audible staccato on his desk blotter, perhaps an indication that the facade of patient cooperation was cracking.

Nevertheless, Blaustein decided to push the envelope a bit further. Something about the chairman's careful responses bothered him. "One more question. Were you on friendly terms with the deceased?"

"Not exactly," Lawrence responded stiffly, his fingers had stopped drumming. "I might as well be up front with you about that, because you're likely to hear it elsewhere." But he chose not to elaborate.

"Mind explaining?"

"Yes I would," Lawrence bristled.

Blaustein decided not to push it for the time being. Instead he fumbled in his breast pocket and produced a warrant, "Now, if you'll steer us in the right direction, we'd like to take a look at Professor Mitchell's office.

"Of course. Not a problem," Lawrence rose. "I'll show you where it is."

Blaustein and Gardner accompanied the chairman down the corridor to a closed door at the end of the hall.

"I took the precaution of ensuring the door was locked as soon as I heard what had happened to Godfrey."

"And had the door been locked prior to that?"

"It had. And I'm confident it has been since Godfrey was last here. Our cleaning crews don't enter or clean locked offices. We historians are all a little paranoid. Have been ever since the nineteenth century when John Stuart Mill's maid used the only copy of Carlyle's *French Revolution* for kindling."

"We expect to be joined here shortly by our crime lab technicians.

The room will be officially off-limits until further notice," Blaustein informed him, as he waited for Lawrence to unlock the door with his master key.

"I'll notify staff and students," Lawrence flung open the door and stepped aside to let the two detectives enter.

As befitted a senior member of the faculty, Mitchell's office was fairly spacious. Where there weren't bookshelves, the walls were covered with framed caricatures from *Punch*. In the middle of the room stood a large cherry desk with a leather chair behind it and two side-chairs in front of it. There was an old-fashioned oak filing cabinet against one wall, and beside it a table with computer paraphernalia and a swivel chair. A leaded window looked out onto the street below. The window was securely latched.

"We'll be taking the computer, the files and any other papers or documents we consider relevant to the case," Blaustein informed the chairman, who hovered at the door. "We'll give you a receipt."

"You ought to know that anything Godfrey has written is automatically covered by copyright. Even his lecture notes."

"Don't worry we don't plan to publish any of it," Blaustein grinned, amused by the other man's instinctive reaction, and making a mental note to share the comment with Greta when he got home. She'd relate.

"Has anyone, to your knowledge, ever infringed Mitchell's copyright?" Gardner asked.

"Not to my knowledge," Lawrence rejoined.

"What about the other way around?" Blaustein nodded appreciatively at his partner for bringing up the subject.

"Again, not to my knowledge. And I would have heard if any suits had been filed."

"Well, thank you for your help. We'll probably be back with more questions later," Blaustein said, donning a pair of surgical gloves.

When the chairman had closed the door behind him, Blaustein turned to his partner. "Why don't you take the file cabinet, I'll go through the desk?"

"I don't expect we'll find anything here. Do you?" Gardner put on a pair of gloves, opened the file cabinet and started flipping through the files. "Looks like nothing but academic material. Copious articles and notes."

"Maybe we'll get lucky and come across some personal stuff mixed in," Blaustein had opened the drawers of the desk and was pawing through the contents: student grades in one drawer, lecture notes in neat folders in another, and in a third, letters from admirers who had read Godfrey Mitchell's books. Fan mail. On the surface the letters seemed laudatory but they would need to be carefully examined.

Blaustein sighed, "Obviously someone had reason to kill this guy, but so far we've got bubkes."

And bubkes was what they had after the lab technicians had dusted for fingerprints, packed up the computer, wheeled out boxes of files and sealed off the room. The confiscated material would be meticulously sorted and inspected back at head quarters: even the student grades. Blaustein did not want to ignore the possibility that a student, possibly upset about poor grades, had gotten back at Mitchell. Someone had hated the guy enough to kill him. But who?

"I didn't get the impression Professor Lawrence was too fond of his late colleague did you?" Gardner asked as they walked to where their unmarked car was double-parked.

"Apparently he wasn't alone."

"No, Mitchell was a big man on campus but not a popular one. At least not with peers who looked down their noses at his commercial success. And certainly not with his graduate students. Hell, if I did someone's research and got no credit for it, I'd resent him too."

"But enough to murder him? I think it's more likely that his killer had a personal motive rather than a professional one. Perhaps Professor Augusta Scott will shed some light on the subject. I got the impression that she and Mitchell may have been more than mere colleagues."

"We should also get a hold of his graduate students. Especially Heather Leopold. Ada Jennings said she came to the Mitchell house fairly often. There could have been some hanky-panky going on."

"And his current graduate student, Kelly Richmond, the one Dina Barrett met in the library."

"Perhaps Dina's in a better position to sound out Richmond than we are, now that she's officially part of the team. It would be a subtler approach." They had reached their car and Gardner waited on the passenger side for Blaustein to unlock it.

"Good thought, Huey," Blaustein got into the car and pulled out his cell phone. "Let's see if she'd like to join us for lunch."

An hour later, Detectives Barrett, Blaustein and Gardner were at a restaurant on Wooster Square sharing a large pizza with everything on it.

"I have to get back to the library, so I must eat and run," Dina apologized, helping herself to a slice. "Meanwhile," she began, " I've been looking into that stolen manuscript ."

"Nailed it down as the motive already?" Blaustein teased.

Ignoring the jibe, Dina continued, "No, in fact I've probably eliminated it as a motive. Harvey Thomas, the man who was accused of the theft, ended up losing his job and spending a year in the slammer. But that was more than twenty years ago, and though Godfrey Mitchell was the whistle blower, he was a hostile prosecution witness. He even testified as a character witness for the defense."

"Whistle blowers can end up paying a steep price, but if it all happened twenty years ago, that's a pretty long time to nurse a grudge," Gardner said with a mouth full of pizza.

"It doesn't make a lot of sense does it? But I checked back issues of the local newspaper anyway," Dina dug into her purse and handed Blaustein the articles she had copied from the *New Haven Register.*

Blaustein unfolded the articles and after scanning each of them, passed them along to Huey Gardener, "I'm inclined to agree that even if Harvey Thomas blamed Mitchell for turning him in, it's unlikely he'd have waited this long to get back at him. It's far too long after the fact. Besides, Mitchell had little choice in the matter. He was morally and intellectually obligated to report the theft."

"My thinking exactly," Dina nibbled on a pizza crust. "Besides, violence was apparently out of character for Thomas. Adrian Needham, the former chairman of the Department, remembers him as a pacifist who hated guns. Not exactly the profile of someone likely to commit murder with a firearm. People don't change that much."

Gardner nodded in agreement, took a third piece of pizza and offered Dina another.

"No more for me, thanks," Dina shook her head. "Apparently Thomas was having financial difficulties. Trying to make it on an assistant professor's salary with a pregnant wife to support. That wasn't easy back in the nineties. Pay for junior faculty at Whitney was only a cut above the poverty level. But the irony is that Thomas had it made. He was quite brilliant and in line for a tenure spot. His need for money must have been dire for him to have risked it all."

"Any idea what happened to him?" Blaustein asked, helping himself to more pizza.

"No, I asked Needham that question, but he didn't seem to know. Thomas served his time and the rest is murky. He obviously didn't have the gall to ask Whitney for references, so Needham has no idea where he ended up teaching. Or even whether he published anything subsequently."

"We'll check into Thomas's present whereabouts if only to eliminate him as a suspect. Unless he's changed his identity and faked a new social security number, it shouldn't be difficult locating a convicted felon. I'll put someone on it. But it looks like just another case of spinning our wheels," Blaustein sighed. "Our occupational hazard. But what else is new?"

"I'm still trying to locate the reporter who broke the story. He might be able to shed some additional light on the subject," Dina nodded her thanks to the waiter as he refreshed her water glass.

"Don't spend too much time on it. It looks like a dead end. Just keep your ears open and let us know if you hear anything useful while you're still under cover on campus."

"Oh, I plan to," came the animated response from Dina.

Blaustein laughed at her enthusiasm, "Just don't ask too many obvious questions. We don't want you taking any chances and we don't want you to blow your cover and jeopardize the drug-bust you're working on. Gordon will have both our heads if you do. So, just blend in the way you've been doing and keep tuned into the campus grapevine."

"That shouldn't be difficult."

"Great. You'll find out a lot more that way than we can with a jackboots approach."

"No one would ever accuse you two of having a jackboots approach," Dina laughed. "But I agree in principle. I know how people clam up when they're talking to the cops."

"Whatever you can find out about Mitchell's graduate assistants past and present would be helpful too. Lawrence mentioned that they resented him because they did a lot of his research and were never given credit for their contributions. So we'll have to interview them, but your acquaintance with Kelly Richmond is a plus there. Find out what you can from her."

"Will do. But remember, if you interview Kelly in her walk-up, don't let her serve you tea. It's undrinkable!"

6

DINA EXPECTED TO FIND OUT MORE FROM KELLY RICHMOND THE VERY
next afternoon when, along with Whitney University students,
faculty and local dignitaries, she filed into Sussex Hall for the Godfrey
Mitchell memorial service. Taking her place in the balcony, she
watched as the crowd took their seats below. The History Department
faculty and graduate students filed in as a group, taking their places
in a reserved section up front. Among them, was Kelly Richmond.
She was dressed, as suited such a somber occasion, in a long black
skirt with a matching jacket, a white turtleneck and black ankle-
length boots. Her fair hair had been pulled back into a French braid
threaded with black ribbon. Without make-up of any kind, her face
looked strained and pale.

Against a backdrop of massive organ pipes, three dignitaries attired
in academic robes had taken their place on the platform. They had
been announced in the official program as the President of Whitney,
the University chaplain and the History Department chairman, Sidney
Lawrence. There were no family members or personal friends on the
stage and Dina was frankly puzzled by the omission.

A hush fell over the crowd as the service began. It started with the chaplain's benediction, overly long and delivered in appropriately sonorous tones. The benediction was followed by eulogies from the President and Chairman Lawrence. Given the occasion, the two men were necessarily laudatory about their fallen colleague, a nationally acclaimed lecturer and best selling author. His latest book, a life of George IV had already been translated into French, Spanish and German and was being made into a PBS documentary. His earlier works were all now available in paperback. Virtually a matinee idol among the undergraduates who clamored to enroll in his courses, his death was seen as a major blow to the History Department, the Whitney community and the cultural climate of the nation at large. To underscore the latter point, telegrams from the President of the United States and the Governor of Connecticut were read to rounds of polite applause. But Dina noted that the accolades were all for Godfrey Mitchell the academic, the teacher and the successful author. Virtually nothing was said about the man himself. Again, she wondered at the omission.

After a harmonious rendition of "Nearer My God Unto Thee," sung a cappella by a choir from the Music School, the service ended with a final prayer. Dina followed the crowd outside and positioned herself on the steps. From this vantage point she hoped she would see Kelly Richmond when she emerged from the recesses of Sussex Hall. Her intention was to 'bump into' Mitchell's former T.A. as if by chance. Be solicitous. Take her for coffee, or tea which Kelly seemed to prefer, and pump her for information about the man who had been her mentor. But instead of encountering her intended target, Dina came face to face with someone really unexpected: her own father.

"Dina!" He said, sounding surprised. "I hadn't thought to see you here."

"Nor I you, Dad," Dina responded, trying to sound pleased. But the timing could not have been worse. She did not want Kelly Richmond to see her talking to the author of a book she claimed never to have read. Her cover would have been blown for sure.

"Well Godfrey Mitchell is an acquaintance of mine, so I came to pay my respects. We've been colleagues for years. A great tragedy," her father paused and looked at her quizzically. "You aren't here. . . er. . . professionally are you?"

"You mean on the case? Not actually, I'm here working on a completely different case," Dina said, nervously scanning the crowd and trying not to look obvious about it.

"A case here? At Whitney?" Her father persisted, as someone pushed passed them, jostling his program from his hand.

"I happen to know Mitchell's graduate assistant," Dina replied, retrieving the errant program and handing it back to her father. "I was with her when she heard what happened to him. Attending the memorial service seemed the right thing to do under the circumstances."

"Look, let me take you for a cup of coffee. Your mother wouldn't forgive me if I were to let you go without finding out how you're getting on."

"There's a coffee shop not far from here if you don't mind a short walk," she suggested, relieved to be getting away from campus and at the same time resigned to the fact that she would have to manufacture another chance meeting with Kelly Richmond.

Shouldering the backpack that had been lying at her feet, she accompanied her father down the steps. She could not remember him ever taking her, just her, anywhere before. He had never been a nurturing parent. But as they walked toward the commercial district, her long-held ambivalence toward him began to erode. She noticed for the first time how old her father looked. Though still an impressive looking man, tall and lean, with a full head of snow-white hair, his rangy frame was stooped against the wind and the harsh winter light emphasized the lines etched into his otherwise handsome face. Smitten with a guilt she had no reason to feel, Dina was touched by this evidence of his vulnerability. Dina and her father had never been close, in fact the contrary was true. For the sin of having been born a girl, she had always lingered on the fringes of his world, waiting patiently for a sign of his interest which never came. Even as a little child she had sensed his indifference. Though he was the one person she had always wanted to please, he never seemed to give a damn. No matter how hard she tried to earn his approval, her efforts always fell short. Her mother, beautiful, aloof, and wrapped up entirely in her own all-consuming world of committees and charities, did not provide an alternative haven. And but for the unconditional love of her younger brother Jeremy, there would have been no reciprocal warmth in her young life. That was why the accident that took Jeremy's life had so devastated her. Jeremy had been the glue that bound an otherwise dysfunctional family together. With his death, the fissures in the family facade deepened. Instead of the three remaining Barretts drawing closer together, the distances between them had widened. With Jeremy Junior gone, her mother had buried herself more than ever in her social activities. She became a cipher: a presence in Dina's life but not a factor. And her father had retreated behind an impervious barricade of books and papers, a wall of indifference that he breached only once, during her senior year in college, when he voiced strong opposition to her becoming a policewoman.

"I am very disappointed in you Dina," he had said, as if her career choice were a personal affront to him. "I didn't send you to the University so that you could be a cop." He said 'cop' as if it were a dirty word.

"You never had any expectations of me, so why would you be disappointed!" she had flashed back heatedly. It was the first time she had given voice to a resentment engendered by countless perceived slights over the years.

Though the hurts diminished with time, and her parents had shown genuine concern when she was shot, the rift never completely healed. She continued to perform such basic filial obligations as remembering her parents' birthdays and making dutiful visits on all the holidays, but she lived her own life now. Her parents were no longer a major part of it, a fact that caused her a twinge of regret as she looked at her father grown suddenly older and more shrunken. Without over- analyzing her emotions, she linked a cautious arm through his and was unreasonably gratified when he looked down at her and smiled.

They found a booth in a small, overheated sandwich shop ahead of the lunchtime crowd. Apart from a few late breakfast stragglers lingering over their newspapers, the place was empty. A bus-boy cleared a table for them and a tired-looking waitress with a pink pinafore took their order. Dina ordered an espresso, her father a cup of tea and a pineapple Danish.

"Sure you don't want something to eat?" he asked.

"No thanks. Not hungry," she replied.

"You're too thin," he said with sniff.

"You doing okay, Dad?" She asked, changing the subject.

"Yes. Right as rain,"

"How about Mom?"

"She's fine. Busy as usual."

There was an awkward pause as they waited for the waitress to set their order down. Dina added two packets of sugar to her espresso and stirred. Her father jiggled his teabag up and down a few times and then added a squeeze of lemon.

"According to the eulogies, Godfrey Mitchell appears to have been a giant in his field. Was he really?" Dina asked.

"For the most part what you heard was just the usual laudatory claptrap one gets at funerals. But there's no denying his popular success as an historian. He left the rest of us in the dust when it came to the sheer volume of his book sales. Except for the occasional positive review from our peers, most of us are destined to labor in the half-light of obscurity. We read each other's books because nobody else does. In fact, we'd all starve if we had to rely on royalties. Godfrey Mitchell on the other hand raked it in. To put it crudely, He was a huge success. A publishing phenomenon. Getting onto the *New York Times* best sellers' list tends to guarantee that. But his peers were not among his admirers."

"Did that include you?"

"Yes, to be blunt. I thought his work superficial. But because the public liked his stuff, enrollments in British history courses have jumped in the past few years. I know mine have."

It had taken her father years to complete and publish his book on Carlyle, and few would read it. If he was a little envious, it was understandable. Dina wondered if others were envious too. But envious enough to kill the professor?

"Do I hear a 'but' when it comes to your praise?" Dina prodded.

"Yes, there is a but.. .," he emphasized the word before taking a bite of his Danish. "Sure you don't want one? This is very good."

"Sure," Dina repeated, concealing her impatience

"But," he continued his thought, "Godfrey was what we derogatively call 'a popular historian'. In academic circles there's a stigma attached to being a 'popular historian'. It goes along with the assumption that the multitude can't appreciate history *veritas*. But to give the man his due, his research was usually pretty sound. And he helped to cultivate a taste for history as opposed to historical fiction. The nay-sayers should acknowledge that in the broadest sense, Godfrey was a great teacher. Most of us teach a handful of reluctant under-graduates. He managed to teach the masses. He got them to read history. No small feat."

"Is it true he used his students' research and never gave them credit?" Dina took a sip of her espresso, found it still too hot and replaced the cup in its saucer.

"I had not heard that. But it's highly possible. He was so prolific that it would be reasonable to assume he had help with his research. But if so, he should have acknowledged his debt to whoever helped him," her father took a last bite of his Danish. "To be fair though, the fellow had a facility with words and that may account in large part for the sheer volume of his work. He was a man who probably never suffered from writer's block."

"He probably made quite a bit of money if his books were so popular," Dina said half to herself, wondering if Mitchell had an heir. An heir with a motive.

"Probably did. Most of us are lucky if a handful of royalties dribble in. He probably received sizable advances."

"How well did you know him?"

"He and I were both members of the Pickwick Club, a Connecticut association of British historians. We meet quarterly, sometimes at U. Conn, and sometimes at Whitney, Yale, Wesleyan or Trinity. Members take turns to report on their research. We mail our papers to each other ahead of time which gives members time to cogitate. And get out the knives, so to speak. Turnout is generally sporadic. But whenever Godfrey was the speaker, we always had a full house. I'm not sure whether that was because of his reputation or because people wanted to nitpick his research."

"What was Godfrey Mitchell like as a person? Was he generally well liked? I didn't get an impression one way or the other from the eulogies today. Neither the President nor Lawrence said anything about him as a person. The omission made me wonder if perhaps he was *dis*liked."

"Well, he wasn't what you would call affable. To be quite frank, I thought him a supercilious bastard. But I don't know if the feeling I had was general. From what I've heard, the ladies liked him," her father gave Dina a rare, confiding smile. "He was what one would call a fine figure of a man. Handsome. Very polished. And wealthy."

"Wealthy because of his publications?" Dina's espresso was almost cool enough to drink and she sipped it tentatively.

"In part, perhaps, but I gather he inherited money. A lot of money. His family was in railways back in the days before the railways needed government subsidies to survive."

"Was his family at the funeral? I was surprised the ceremony didn't include a eulogy from a member of the family. The whole service seemed very impersonal."

"Godfrey was divorced. He had a son, I think," her father paused before continuing, and Dina knew he was thinking about Jeremy, Jr. because a shadow crossed his face. "The son and Godfrey's ex-wife may have been at the funeral, but I've never met them, so I don't know if they showed up. I don't really know whether he was close to other members of the family. Or even if he had any other relatives. I knew him on a professional rather than a personal level."

How like her father, Dina thought, to know people only on a professional level. Never to break down the barriers. Had Godfrey Mitchell been like that? She had the impression that the man had few close male friends. But what about women? Her father's remark about the ladies echoed Freddie Hathaway's comment and it would certainly bear investigating.

After dutifully escorting her father to his car, Dina set off on foot for the library. It was her turn to relieve Edward Morrison, and this time it was he who would be kept waiting. Trying to out-pace a stiff wind that had turned icy, her chest began to hurt and her breathing became labored. Cursing the wound that still plagued her on occasion, she slowed to an amble as she passed Sussex Hall. It was silent now, its massive doors shut, its steps deserted, a handful of discarded memorial programs the only reminder of the man who had been honored there barely an hour earlier. Lugging a backpack that seemed heavier with each yard, she crossed the campus and headed up the library stairs. With the pain in her chest now impossible to ignore, she took the steps one at a time and went inside.

She walked past Edward who was sitting at one of the long tables facing the reserve desk, he gave an imperceptible shake of the head to signal that there was nothing new to report then got his gear together and left. Meanwhile, Dina dumped a couple of books and some writing materials onto a nearby table, shrugged off her coat and sat down. She selected a book at random and paged through it. Pretending to be engrossed, she kept a close eye on the librarian on duty behind the reference desk. His name was Herman Archer. In school he had been known as 'Archie', which was what the students at Whitney also called him. Barrett's research into his background had been about as revealing as his high school yearbook, according to which he had not belonged to any clubs, competed on any teams or distinguished himself in any other way. He had graduated with a degree in library science from a state school in Iowa and his employment history had been erratic until he was hired by

Whitney. Perhaps Social Security would be able to fill in some other blanks.

"Hello, Diana," the speaker, Kelly Richmond, was wearing an unbuttoned coat over the black skirt and jacket she had worn to the memorial service.

"How have you been holding up, Kelly?" Dina asked, looking up.

"Okay, I suppose, if waiting for the other shoe to drop can be called okay," the graduate student shrugged off her coat and sat down in the adjacent carrel. "I'm seriously worried about losing my T.A. And I'm still waiting to be assigned a new dissertation advisor. It's like being in a rowboat without a paddle."

"That's really rough."

"Tell me about it," Kelly smiled ruefully.

"Learning about Professor Mitchell's death must have come as a shock."

"It was devastating. Godfrey was not only my professor. He was my mentor. That was what first hit me, the personal loss. It wasn't till later that I realized there would be other consequences for me," she smiled shamefacedly. "I really need the stipend I was getting as his T.A."

"Doesn't Whitney have an obligation to keep you on as a T. A.? Don't you have some sort of contract?"

Kelly leaned back in her chair and sighed, "Oh, they'll probably feel obligated to carry me for the rest of the semester, but teaching assistantships don't come with tenure unfortunately."

"You were Godfrey Mitchell's only graduate assistant?"

"Yes. But not his only graduate student. He was advisor to three other graduate students and there were several others in his graduate seminars. We all feel the loss. He was our guru."

"I'm surprised by such loyalty, I heard that he used his students to research his books and never gave them credit," Dina broached the subject tentatively not knowing how the question would be received.

"Where did you hear that?" The retort was unexpectedly sharp.

"Just a rumor that's floating around," Dina countered casually.

"Well I guess there's some truth to it," Kelly's shoulders sagged as she made the admission. "It was one of the things I didn't like about him. He made a practice of assigning specific research topics for his seminars. Perfectly legitimate of course, except I suspect his assignments were less for instructional purposes than because he needed the material for his books. And you're right. He never credited anyone."

"And he got away with it?"

"What could a bunch of students do? Sue him? Research papers aren't exactly copyrighted. Besides, we were dependent on him for our grades. No one wanted to challenge him. He could hold up graduation if we crossed him."

"Too bad no one ever spoke up. What he did sounds to me like exploitation."

"I'm afraid that Godfrey's graduate students are used to being his helots. The only student who ever dared to stand up to him lived to regret it. A man named Curt Daniels. He not only challenged Godfrey. He did it publicly."

"Publicly?"

Kelly nodded. "He went so far as to write a letter to the student newspaper accusing Professor Mitchell of plagiarism. Because it was such a serious charge, there was an official on-campus hearing. Godfrey argued that research assignments were merely exercises and that he assigned topics based on work he himself had previously researched. Which may or may not have been true, but it was impossible for Daniels to disprove it. Especially as not a single student backed him up. No one was willing to put their own degrees on the line. So Daniels was hung out to dry. He was essentially finished here. By the time the dust cleared he was gone. As I understand it, he transferred to some other university the following semester."

"Did he get his degree there?" Dina asked, making a mental note to follow up on Curt Daniels. He seemed like a man with a legitimate chip on his shoulder.

"I don't really know. I doubt anyone here openly associated with Curt Daniels after the story broke. As I understand it, he became something of a pariah: the epitome of what not to do if you want

UNJUSTIFIED

to get ahead. His failed crusade was used as a warning to all new graduate students, including me," Kelly opened a book, signaling an end to the conversation.

Taking her cue, Dina turned back to her own book, "Let's have lunch some day soon," she said, vowing to make it sooner rather than later.

7

WHILE DINA WAS CHATTING WITH KELLY RICHMOND, BLAUSTEIN AND
Gardner were knocking on the door to a suite in the Savoy Hotel in
downtown New Haven. It was answered by a jacketless young man
in dark suit pants, a white shirt open at the neck and a tie hanging
loosely from beneath his collar. He would have been handsome, like
his father, for he was tall, with classic features, tousled blond hair and
cobalt blue eyes, but a surly expression and a spoiled mouth ruined
the impression.

Blaustein introduced himself and his partner, "I know this is a
difficult time for you," he acknowledged, "but I wonder if we could
have a word with you and your mother."

"Well it is a difficult time right now . . .," Brian Mitchell objected.

"It's all right Brian. Tell them to come in," came a female voice
from within.

Stepping aside grudgingly, the young man admitted the two
detectives. On a couch by the window sat Alison Mitchell, Godfrey's
ex-wife. She was wearing the slim-fitting, black wool dress she had
worn to the memorial service, a double string of pearls at the neck,

a gold Rolex on one wrist and three or four gold bracelets on the other. Her skin had a uniform all-over tan. Her dark hair, worn stylishly short, was streaked with silver. She sat with her stockinged feet tucked beneath her, her high-heeled pumps on the floor beside the couch. She did not get up to greet her visitors.

"Please sit down, gentlemen," she waved them to a pair of armchairs facing her while her son took his place behind the couch, a protective hand resting on each of his mother's shoulders.

"We're sorry to intrude at such a trying time," Blaustein apologized.

"It's as good a time as any," she shrugged. "We'll be here for the funeral tomorrow and our plans are indefinite after that. So you may as well speak to us now."

"A determination has not yet been made whether or not your husband's death was self-inflicted. It has not officially been ruled a homicide."

"Suicide? Godfrey?" she laughed mirthlessly. "No way."

"Why do you say that, Ma'am?" Blaustein queried.

"You'll forgive me if I'm cynical, Detective," she brushed her hair back with one hand, making her bracelets rattle "but my ex-husband was too much in love with himself and his success to end it all," she hesitated. "Unless he was suffering from some fatal disease I didn't know about."

"Not according to the autopsy report. Your former husband was in perfect health, Mrs. Mitchell. So we can rule out poor health as a motive for suicide."

"What else could there be? He certainly wasn't broke," she gave a bitter laugh. "Unless one of his ex-girlfriends was blackmailing him."

"We've checked his bank account and his only substantial payments have been to you and to your son's trust fund. There have been no significant cash withdrawals of any kind, which makes blackmail seem rather unlikely. Any reason you're suggesting it?"

"No, none at all. Frankly, it's more likely he ran afoul of some husband who decided to shoot the bastard. Godfrey was a libertine," she patted her son's hand, "Sorry, darling."

Brian Mitchell shrugged off his mother's apology, "Dad's fooling around was no secret."

"You think it's possible a jealous husband may have shot your husband?"

"Given his overactive libido, I think it's highly possible," she absently coiled a strand of pearls around her fore finger.

"Can you give us any names?"

"Detective, I left my husband ten years ago and live about as far away from him as I can get. I don't know anything about his latest dalliances, and as long as the alimony checks keep coming in, I don't much care."

"What about previously, when you were still married to him, was marital infidelity the reason you sued for divorce?" Blaustein phrased the question as delicately as he could.

"Yes," the question did not seem to upset her in the least. "To put it bluntly, I found him in our bed with a nymphet from the university. One of his undergraduates. She wasn't the first, but she was the final straw. Funny, I don't even remember her name now. I suppose that's Freudian."

"Jillian Davis," Brian reminded her. "She was supposed to be babysitting me."

"Right," his mother pursed her lips. "Brian was eleven at the time and thought he was too old for a baby sitter. Too bad his father didn't realize he was the one too old for a baby sitter."

"Do you know anyone who might be able to provide information about Professor Mitchell's alleged liaisons?"

"No I don't. And there was nothing alleged about Godfrey's philandering, Detective. Godfrey loved women almost as much as he loved himself. Even so, I doubt he took any of his little flings seriously. He was a user of women. Of people in general. Knowing him, I doubt he would have made any commitments, especially commitments he had no intention of keeping. He was too careful a man. And he had no trouble attracting female admirers. For some reason women, especially younger women, and there are a lot of them on a campus, found dear Godfrey irresistible. But I seriously doubt he inspired the kind of passion that would make a woman want to shoot him." Her words were laced with ill-concealed venom.

"Which brings us back to a jealous husband or boy friend."

"That's possible, I suppose," she admitted. "Darling, pass me a cigarette from my purse will you?"

Brian left his place from behind the couch, rummaged through a black Prada purse that lay on the coffee table and passed his mother a pack of cigarettes and a gold lighter.

She paused to light up and exhale a lungful of smoke before continuing. "But it's mere conjecture, Detective. I don't know if he was seeing anyone because I haven't seen Godfrey in years and I haven't kept up with Whitney gossip. When I left here, I made a clean break. So you'll have to get your information about Godfrey and his love-life from someone else. I don't know anything about it and I don't much care. I also don't know if anyone had it in for him for any other reasons. Except me that is," her laugh was bitter. "But if you're looking for a suspect, don't look at me. I may have hated the bastard but my alibi is ironclad. I've been staying at the Prince of Orange in Sint Maarten for the past six weeks."

"Mind if we check your passport? You have the right to refuse."

"Sure," she shrugged. "It's in my purse. Mind getting it Brian?"

Brian grudgingly retrieved his mother's purse a second time and handed it to her. She dug out the passport and passed it to Blaustein who checked the passport photo and flipped to the visas in the back. The lady had traveled regularly to Sint Maarten over the past several winters, generally arriving there in early December and leaving at the end of March. Except for her abrupt return to the States to attend her late husband's funeral, her most recent trip followed the same pattern. It looked as if she had been in Sint Maarten since the first of December, but Blaustein made a mental note to double-check with the airlines, the hotel, and the immigration authorities.

"Of course vengeance isn't the only motive for murder," Blaustein conceded, handing back the passport. "In murder-mysteries they say *cherchez la femme*. But in reality it's more often *cherchez* the almighty dollar. Perhaps we should be looking for someone who would benefit from your ex-husband's death. Do you know who the chief beneficiary of his will is?"

"I am," Brian answered without hesitation. "But I didn't kill dear old Dad if that's what you think."

"When is the last time you saw your father, Brian?" Blaustein asked.

"Mom was away, so I spent Christmas with Dad," he took a seat next to his mother on the couch and she took his hand.

"So you were in Connecticut just before he was due to leave for his conference?" Blaustein exchanged a glance with Gardner. That confirmed what Mitchell's cleaning lady had already told them.

"Yes. He was flying out on the 27th and I took off for Vermont the same morning."

"Did your father seem unusually preoccupied or upset?"

"My father was always preoccupied. He was a workaholic."

"Do you recall any unusual comments he made, or any out-of-the-ordinary events that occurred?"

"No, I don't. Especially to the comments part. Dad and I barely spoke to each other. But then we seldom do." This last was uttered derisively. "I arrived on Christmas eve and the most intimate thing we did was to go shopping for my Christmas present. He bought me this sport's watch." Brian pushed back his shirt sleeve to reveal a multifunctional timepiece with a complex series of protruding knobs. "We spent the next two days under the same roof and we ate some of our meals together. But we didn't exactly communicate."

"What about visitors? Did your father have any visitors or keep any appointments while you were with him?"

"Except for a group of carolers on Christmas Eve, I can't recall anyone coming to the house. But I crashed early most of the time, so I can't say for sure."

"Did your father retire at the same time you did?"

"No, he generally went to his study after dinner and worked at his computer. I sometimes went to visit one of my childhood friends."

"And the day after Christmas?"

"Ditto."

"Same friend?"

"Yes."

"Do you mind telling us your friend's name?" Gardner asked, preparing to write the information down on the lead sheet attached to his clipboard.

"No, I guess not," Brian answered, looking uncomfortable. "Tony Marx. But I don't see the relevance..."

"Can you tell me why it was you came home for just three days, and spent so little time with your father?" Blaustein cut off Brian's question, leaving it hanging in the air.

"First of all, I wasn't home, not in any really sense. I don't consider where my father lives to be home." He and his mother exchanged confirming glances, and she patted his hand again. "Secondly, I've never spent much time with my father, even as a kid. Dad was always too busy." Brian couldn't quite keep the whine out of his voice.

"Where did you go when you left your father's house?" Blaustein asked.

"I drove to Stowe, Vermont."

"What kind of vehicle do you drive."

"A Beamer."

"It's registered to you?"

"Yes it is."

"Did you drive up to Vermont alone?"

The young man nodded.

The fact that Brian Mitchell had been unaccompanied left open the possibility that he might have come back to the house after the cleaning lady left. But there would be no way to prove it. The neighborhood had already been canvassed and they had drawn nothing but blanks. Neither Brian nor his Beamer had been seen again after his initial departure. So Blaustein tried another angle. "When you arrived at your father's house on Christmas eve, did you drive up from North Carolina?"

"No from New York actually. That's where I go to school, Columbia."

"And in Vermont, where did you stay?"

"Look Detective, I don't see the point of any of your questions, and I certainly do not like what you are insinuating. I will not allow my son to answer any further questions, at least not unless our attorney is present. Uncoiling from the couch like a snake preparing to strike, Allison Mitchell slipped her feet into her shoes and stood up. "Your business here is done, gentlemen, so I'll ask you to leave," her obsidian eyes flashed venomously.

"Mrs. Mitchell, we are conducting an investigation into the murder of your ex-husband. Your son may have been one of the last people to see his father alive," Blaustein explained patiently, if not altogether honestly. "Any information he can give us may help solve this homicide."

"That's not the way it sounded to me," her words were icy but her eyes blazed.

"Mother, I have nothing to hide. I don't mind telling them where I stayed. Or whom I was with. Or anything else for that matter," he placed a restraining hand on her elbow and turned to look first at Blaustein and then at Gardner. "I had reservations for a week at the Alpen Ski Lodge. But the conditions were lousy. It sleeted and the slopes were icy. So after a couple of days, I drove back to New York. I spent New Year's Eve in Time's Square with a few friends and the rest of humanity watching the ball drop." Under the circumstances, Brian Mitchell looked remarkably unruffled. In fact, for a young man, he struck Blaustein as unusually self-possessed. Was it a reflection of innocence or merely an indication of exceptional self-control?

"Have you quite finished now?" Alison Mitchell asked imperiously. "Brian has been extremely forthcoming."

"Just a couple more questions, if you don't mind," Blaustein caught and held her gaze. With his big brown puppy eyes he could be very disarming. Apparently mollified, she shrugged her acquiescence.

"Did your father generally take safety precautions? Did he keep the doors and windows locked, for instance?"

"The outside doors, front and back, are the self-locking kind.

I've locked myself out often enough so I've learned to always take a house-key when I leave. Dad unlatched the doors only when he was expecting guests. But for the most part the Old Man kept the doors locked. It didn't help him much, did it?"

"Do you know whether he was expecting guests that morning?"

"Probably just Ada Jennings, his cleaning lady, and she has her own key."

"Do you remember if any of the downstairs windows were open?"

"Dad kept them closed in the winter but the latches didn't work too well. He talked about getting them replaced but it was never a priority. It's always been a safe neighborhood. At least it was till now."

"Who besides you, your father and Ms. Jennings had a key to the house?"

"No one that I know of."

"Did you see Ms. Jennings at all while you were staying with your father?"

"She cooked dinner for us on Christmas Eve and came in to clean on the morning I left. She arrived as I was loading my car. My father was alive at the time. She'll vouch for that," Brian said, with more than a touch of bravado.

"Don't tell me you're planning to question Ada," Alison Mitchell did not try to hide her scorn. "You can't be considering her a suspect. However misguided her loyalties, Detective, Ada adored Godfrey. She's worked for the family for years. Since Godfrey and I were first married in fact."

"At this stage of an investigation Ma'am, we question everyone who knew or had contact with the victim." By depersonalizing the questioning and steering it away from Brian, Blaustein took the opportunity to diffuse the tension in the air. He did not let on that they had already spoken to Ada Jennings, nor that she had confirmed seeing Brian leave. "Like you, Ms. Jennings may be able to give us some valuable information. But just because we question her doesn't make her a suspect. And the same applies to both of you," Blaustein explained patiently. "Which is why we may need to talk to both of you again. So please let us know when you plan to leave the hotel and where we can find you when you do."

The two detectives rose and Blaustein handed each of the Mitchells his card. "Now we'll be on our way," Blaustein said as he and Gardner made their way to the door. "We regret the inconvenience, especially at a time like this." His apology was offered pro forma. For his money, and depending on the details of Mitchell's will and the size of his estate, each of the surviving Mitchells might have had a very good reason to kill the man. Certainly neither of them seemed too cut up about the eminent professor's demise.

"So what do you think?" Gardner asked as they took the elevator down to the hotel lobby.

"I think, Huey, it's possible, even though the cleaning lady saw the kid leave, he could have hung around until the coast was clear, slipped in, and killed his old man."

"It takes about five hours to drive up to Stowe. So if he left his father's house around ten and didn't stop for lunch, then he should have arrived at the Alpen Lodge no later than three. Anything much after that and he'll have some explaining to do."

Blaustein nodded. "There was obviously little love lost between him and his father, and the kid probably stands to inherit a bundle. So let's check the time of his arrival at the Lodge. Get a copy of Mitchell's will. And look into Brian's trust fund."

"Can it wait until after lunch? I'm famished."

"You're always famished," Blaustein laughed. "Which is why having you as a partner is having a negative effect on my waistline. At least with Dina I felt guilty when I scarfed down food. With you I don't have any inhibitions even if it means doing penance in the gym later." He patted his middle with one hand. "So Huey, now that I've done my *mea culpa* for the day, where do you want to eat?"

They settled on a New York-style deli where Blaustein ordered corned beef on rye and Gardner a Reuben. While they waited for their meals to arrive, they ate half-sour pickles and drank bottomless cups of coffee.

"It takes something away from the pure pleasure of drinking

coffee when you can't smoke a cigarette," Gardner complained as he usually did about the no-smoking rule in restaurants.

"Sorry to disagree, Partner. Nonsmokers really can't stand it, that's why, even when I used to smoke, I never did it indoors."

"That so? Your wife complained?"

"Bless her, Greta never complains. About anything. But I knew how much my smoking bothered her, so whenever I felt the urge to smoke, I went onto the back porch to light up."

"Greta still teaching English Lit. at the University?"

"Yes she is," Blaustein answered as he helped himself to another pickle.

"She gets around okay then?" Huey hesitated before asking the question.

But Blaustein was not embarrassed by it. "She has a new, specially equipped van with hand controls and manages pretty well on her own. But she still needs someone at either end to help her load and retrieve her wheelchair. I help her in the morning; her sister Helen comes over to help out after class, and a University volunteer fills in at their end. It works out okay and Greta's grateful for all the help, but I know it still hurts like hell to be so dependent." Blaustein looked up as the waitress placed an overstuffed sandwich in front of each of them. He immediately discarded the decorative toothpick and took an appreciative bite.

"What did you make of the Mitchells?" Gardner asked, with a mouthful of Swiss and pastrami.

"Overly defensive. It makes me wonder what they have to hide," Blaustein replied.

"Not much love lost between them and the deceased from what I could see," Gardner finished the first half of his sandwich and prepared to start on the second, "and if the kid stands to inherit, he definitely had motive. I doubt he had the guts though. He struck me as a spoilt-rotten young man without much backbone. The wife on the other hand...."

"Yeah, a tough cookie. You'd think after ten years her anger would have cooled some." But Blaustein knew from experience that when the emotions were involved, especially with a woman as complex as Alison Mitchell, appeared to be, anything was possible. "We can rule out the possibility that Mitchell killed himself. The man had no reason to. But with no sign of forced entry and no evidence of a struggle, the perp must have been someone who knew him well. Someone who didn't need to break in. Someone Mitchell admitted to the house. Or someone who had a key. Possibly whoever was under the covers with Mitchell that day. As far as we know, Ada Jennings, Brian Mitchell and the victim's lover were the last people to see the man alive. Except for his killer. If it wasn't any of them."

"Too bad it took so long for the body to be discovered. It makes proving the exact time of death damn difficult," Gardner, having polished off the last of his sandwich, folded his napkin and signaled the waitress for the check.

"We have at most a two-hour window between the time Ada Jennings left and the time Mitchell was due at Bradley Airport. We'll have to order a second canvass of the neighborhood. Maybe mentioning the kid's BMW will jog a few memories. But as far as we can tell, Mitchell's absence went completely unnoticed. He had several lights on timers, so people naturally assumed he was home."

"You'd have thought the fact that the driveway hadn't been plowed would have tipped someone off."

"I guess people just aren't nosey about their neighbors these days," Blaustein pulled out his wallet and reached for the check. "What's the damage here?"

After leaving the deli they drove to the office of Mitchell's attorney with a warrant to obtain a copy of his will. The attorney was busy with a client when they arrived so they cooled their heels in an anteroom. Gardner was content with the crossword in an abandoned *New York Times*. Blaustein checked his watch every two minutes and looked put out until, after what seemed an interminable delay, they finally left with their copy of Mitchell's will.

They read the will over cups of Dunkin Donuts coffee in the front seat of their unmarked car. The will bore out Brian Mitchell's claim that he was his father's chief beneficiary, and did little to diminish the young man's motive. Brian's father had died a wealthy man by any standards. Besides his success as an author, Godfrey Mitchell had been the only son and heir of a very wealthy father. Now the bulk of his estate reverted to his son's trust fund. But there was a catch. Brian would not have control of the trust fund until he was twenty-five: four years hence. Till then, he would continue to receive a generous allowance in addition to his college expenses.

If greed was the motive for Godfrey Mitchell's death, then Alison Mitchell had a stronger reason to kill her former spouse. Mitchell's will made provision not only for the continuation of alimony, but also for the payment to his ex-wife of 50 percent of posthumous royalties from his publications and films. Still, even if she knew about the royalties, according to her passport the woman was in Sint Maarten when her ex-husband was murdered. She appeared to have an iron-clad alibi.

Apart from some small legacies, the rest of the late professor's estate was left to fatten the Whitney endowment. Craving recognition even after death, Mitchell had endowed a history chair in his own name. It was a gesture that must have satisfied both his enormous ego and his sense of delicious irony. How he must have chuckled at the prospect of his colleagues, the very colleagues who had criticized him in life, scrambling for the honor to sit in a chair with his name on it.

"Everybody wins except for the dear deceased," Blaustein said, clearing off the fogged up windshield with a gloved hand. "So who else had a reason to kill him?"

Gardner pulled a pack of Kents from his pocket, "Mind if I smoke?"

"Actually I would. It'll make me want one. But go ahead," steeling himself to resist the temptation, Blaustein focused on the matter at hand. "Please remind me to get a subpoena for the financial records of the mother and son."

"Why do I have the feeling we're back to square one?" Gardner said as he cracked the window and lit up his cigarette.

"Because we are," Blaustein said, crumpling his paper coffee cup. After tossing it into the plastic trash-bag that hung below the dash, he put the car in gear and they drove off. "We don't even have a circumstantial case here. We have nothing but supposition."

8

PHILIP POTTER WAS A COMPUTER ENGINEER WITH A DEGREE FROM
M. I. T. Tall and lean with a pleasant face, a ready sense of humor
and an infectious laugh, he was easy to like and Dina liked him a lot.
They had known each other only as classmates in high school. When
they met again years later, they were both getting over shattered
relationships and each began to fill a void in the other's life. After
Dina was shot, Philip had sent flowers and chocolates and was a
source of comfort. But after that, they had seen each other only
intermittently, and Dina knew it was her fault. Though she barely
admitted it to herself, her move to New Haven had been an attempt
to put some distance between them. Ever since the night when he
confessed to something more than friendship, she had been sending
him mixed signals. She was fond of him, more than just fond. But
fond was a lot less than he was looking for. She knew it would be
kindest to make a clean break. It was the only thing that would be
fair to him. But would he see it that way and could she bring herself
to do it? Which is why she felt something akin to panic when Philip
called that morning.

"Hey," she said when she recognized his voice.

"Hey, yourself, stranger," he sounded absurdly pleased.

"Not out of choice," she said, not quite truthfully.

"I understand. Look, I'll be in New Haven for a meeting today, would you have time for a cup of coffee this afternoon?"

"I'll make the time," she answered, trying to sound more upbeat than she felt.

"If you don't mind, I'd like to combine duty with pleasure. I'd like to have your help picking out a birthday present for my Mom. I haven't a clue about that sort of thing."

"Don't mind at all."

"Would it suit you if we met at Andy's Book Café? I'm planning to buy a book for Mom and their coffee is always great."

"Perfect," she agreed, thinking their interchange had been a bit awkward and wondering if their meeting would be the same..

He was in the biography section when she arrived, a copy of David McCullough's *John Adams* open in his hands. "My mother's a history buff, I think she may like this," he said when she came up to him. "Have you read it?'

"As a matter of fact, I have and I thought it was wonderful. It was a get-well present from my parents. They gave it to me after I was shot . It turned out to be the perfect gift. Being laid up, I had loads of time to read." She was talking too fast, trying to cover her nervousness, but he did not seem to notice as he examined the back cover.

"If your Mom likes the book and when it gets warmer, you may want to take your mother to Quincy."

"What's in Quincy?"

"Three Adams homes all perfectly preserved, including the furnishings Abigail brought back from Paris. I went there with my father and Jeremy when my brother and I were in high school."

"You've talked me into it. Let me pay for the book and then I'll grab us some coffee. Do you want anything with it? Danish, a sandwich?"

"Coffee will be fine, thanks. My landlady's invited me to dinner tonight and I won't eat a thing if I load up on Danish."

At an unoccupied table they exchanged pleasantries, like a couple of strangers on a blind date. Both of them felt awkward. She because she knew she had to do the honorable thing and cut him loose. He for very different reasons. And when they had exhausted small talk, it was Philip who broke the silence. He put down his coffee mug and cleared his throat. "My company is sending me to Atlanta."

"Will you be gone long?"

"It's not a trip. It's a permanent reassignment. Actually a promotion. I'll be heading up a new research department."

"Congratulations." Her throat felt constricted. "When do you leave?"

"At the end of the month."

"That soon?" Instead of feeling relieved, it was as if the wind had been taken out of her sails.

"I'd feel a lot happier about it if you were coming with me," he reached out and stroked the back of her hand. "We could make a good life there together."

Dina hesitated for just a second before replying. "Thank you Philip. A big part of me wants to say yes," Dina looked at Philip over the rim of her coffee mug, her eyes misting, her cheeks flushed, "but I have a job here."

"They need first class detectives in Atlanta too," he coaxed, his tawny eyes unfaltering as they met her blue-gray ones.

"Philip. . . ." She hesitated.

"Uh oh, I think I know what's coming."

Dina put down her coffee mug and took both his hands in hers. "This is very difficult for me because I'm torn. Really torn. I don't want to lose you and I know I'm going to regret what I'm about to say as long as I live. But I just can't make the kind of commitment you're looking for. I'm not ready to take that extra step and I don't know if I ever will be. I also know that I can't expect our relationship to stay as it is forever. It would be selfish of me and totally unfair to you. You have to get on with your life."

"I'll take that as a 'no'," he said, trying to make light of it.

"Perhaps this Atlanta job has come at a good time," Dina rationalized. "You can make a new start."

"I don't have much choice. Do I?"

"I hope we can always be close, Philip. It would mean a lot to me."

"It would mean a lot to me too," he said wistfully, taking her hand in both of his and kissing it.

Later that day, in her little sitting-room, Dina turned on the computer. She felt tired and down, but she needed to research a couple of people before dinner. One was Curt Daniels, the former graduate student who had accused Godfrey Mitchell of plagiarism. The other was Miles Acton, the *New Haven Register* reporter who had covered the Harvey Thomas trial. Locating Daniels was literally a click away. He had addresses in both Hadley and Amherst, Massachusetts. Locating Acton, however, proved impossible no matter which search engine she tried. Vowing to check with the *Register* in the morning, Dina printed out the information on Daniels and logged off. Then, feeling as if she'd been used as someone's punching bag, she straightened up and got to her feet. Getting back to normal was taking too darn long.

Off her little sitting room was a bedroom and en suite an old fashioned white-tiled bathroom with vintage fixtures and white lace curtains. The bedroom, its decor unchanged since the thirties, had a double bed with an art-deco headboard, an intricately veneered armoire, a dresser with a beveled mirror, a chaise almost buried in petite point cushions, and on the wall behind the chaise, a single portrait in a gilt frame. The subject of the portrait was a young woman in a deep red velvet gown that set off her creamy skin. At her throat was a diamond necklace and in her raven hair a matching comb. But it was the woman's dark eyes, eyes that fascinated Dina. No matter where she was in the room, they held her gaze. The woman, Freddie's Great Aunt Mildred Turner, had been considered a beauty when the portrait was painted in the late nineteenth century. Courted by the most eligible young men of her day, she had married well and life for the young couple had been a grand social whirl. But years after the portrait was painted, during the Depression and after the suicide of her banker husband, she had lost everything. With nowhere else to turn, she had come to live in New Haven with her brother and sister-in-law, Freddie's grandparents. And there she remained, outlasting her sibling and his wife by several years. She was still living in the house when Freddie's father inherited it and moved in with his family.

According to Freddie, Mildred Turner had been a wraithlike, unobtrusive presence. She spent her days alone in what was now Dina's second floor suite, reclining on the chaise with her remembrances and her embroidery, the very petite point cushions that still adorned every sofa and love-seat in the house. She took her meals on a tray in her room and never came downstairs. To a young, imaginative Freddie, whose duty it was to bring up her great aunt's dinner tray, the frail old lady seemed like a sorrowful apparition, a creature not quite of this world, a faded replica of the vibrant portrait in the gilt frame. And her presence still permeated the room. Dina couldn't enter it without remembering that it was here Mildred Turner had spent her last days and where she died, taking her sad memories with her.

To dispel the gloom, Dina switched on the light and closed the drapes, shutting out the encroaching darkness. All she wanted to do was collapse on the bed. But having promised to eat dinner with Freddie on the eve of the latter's departure for Florida, Dina pulled herself together, ran a brush through her hair, buttoned the collar of her shirt, smoothed her skirt, and made her way downstairs. The table had been set, not in the breakfast room where they customarily dined, but in the formal dining room. The candles in the silver candelabra had been lit, the table was laid with a fine linen cloth, neatly folded napkins, crystal wine goblets, gleaming silverware and a fine Bone China dinner service. Freddie had really gone all out.

"Isn't this grand!" Dina exclaimed, regretting that she had not contributed a bottle of wine to the proceedings, or at least changed for dinner. Freddie, who usually walked around the house in sweaters and jeans was wearing a long black dress with Mildred's diamond pendant around her neck and diamond studs in her ears.

"I thought it would be fun to dine formally for a change," Freddie said with a laugh.

"It looks like you've gone to a lot of trouble. Can I belatedly offer to help with something?"

"Zelda was my sous chef before she left this evening. It's all done. But you can help me bring out the dishes."

Twinkling at Dina, Freddie presided over a meal of poached salmon with a lemon sauce, avocado tossed with walnuts on a bed of fresh spinach, crisp French bread and a fine California Sauvignon Blanc. The dinner concluded with a creme brulee and coffee served in demi tasse cups.

"I didn't realize you were such a gourmet cook," Dina said, dabbing her lips and setting her linen napkin aside.

"One of my long lost arts. As a Whitney wife, I entertained quite a bit in the old days. I don't do it much now and I don't miss it. But I had the urge to put on the dog tonight. It's always fun to fuss when one doesn't have to."

Dina stood up to take the empty plates, "You're to let me clean up. I won't take no for an answer."

"Gratefully accepted. I'll just pour myself another cup of coffee and keep you company in the kitchen."

While Dina rinsed dishes and loaded the dishwasher, she realized how much she'd miss Freddie. The small dynamo kept up an endless stream of chatter and without her effervescent presence, the house was going to seem very large and very empty.

"Now don't forget," Freddie was saying, "Zelda will be in twice a week to clean as usual. If there's a problem, call me. I've left my Florida phone number by the downstairs telephone. And please make yourself right at home. Use the whole house. Entertain if you'd like to."

"Thanks but I don't think. . .," Dina loaded the last of the dishes in the dishwasher and wiped her hands on a paper towel.

"No, I mean it," as always Freddie was incapable of taking no for an answer. "I'm terribly relieved that you'll be house-sitting for me. Ever since the robbery, I've been reluctant to go away and leave the place empty. Which reminds me, I set several lights on timers. They'll automatically turn off at eleven each night. So don't worry if you go away for a day or two, the house will look inhabited. And please, don't forget to turn the heat down before you go to bed. You know where the thermostat is. This old monster of a place eats heating oil."

"I'll remember," Dina poured herself another cup of coffee and sat down at the kitchen table opposite Freddie. "Jackson Blaustein and Huey Gardner interviewed Godfrey Mitchell's ex-wife after the memorial service. He had the impression there wasn't much love lost there. Did you know Alison Mitchell at all?"

"Not well. She wasn't an easy person to get to know. She kept to herself for the most part, especially after the rumors started."

"What rumors?"

"Well, to put it bluntly, it was common knowledge that Godfrey was fooling around. A lot of men begin to feel their oats when they hit middle age, but I suspect in Godfrey's case it may have started long before that. He was very good looking and knew it. Knew it and flaunted it. To add to his allure he'd published his first best seller by the time he was forty, and had become a celebrity. So women fluttered around him like moths. I don't think he tried too hard to fend them off."

"And his wife was understandably jealous?" Dina said as she stirred sugar into her cup.

"If she was, she didn't show it. At least not in public. Alison wasn't what you'd call the demonstrative type. She played the dutiful wife right up to the end when, rumor had it, she caught him in their bed with a student. That was about ten years ago. She divorced him shortly afterwards."

"Has there been any talk about Mitchell's love life since his divorce?"

"I don't really keep up with campus gossip these days," Freddie responded primly, but her eyes held a mischievous twinkle and Dina knew she was holding something back.

"Come on, out with it," Dina coaxed.

"Well if I thought it was just idle talk, my lips would be sealed. But in the interest of providing my house detective with fodder...." Freddie teased. "I'll tell you what I know. Apparently, Godfrey and Deirdre Lawrence were a hot item this past summer. It happened while her husband was away doing research in Africa."

"Sidney Lawrence? The History Department chairman?" Dina felt a rush of surprise.

"The very one."

"But his eulogy at the memorial service was so laudatory?"

"Well that's not surprising. Sidney is nothing if not a gentleman and a scholar. Even if he knew about his wife and Godfrey, his duty was to act as spokesman for the Department. And from what I know about him, it may have given him a perverse sense of satisfaction to honor the man who had dishonored him."

"Or to cover up a murder?" Dina suggested tentatively, not knowing how Freddie would react to the suggestion but figuring it was worth the gamble.

"No, not Sidney!" Freddie looked horrified.

"You'd be surprised what sets some people off."

"I suppose you cops have to be suspicious of everyone," Freddie wagged an accusatory finger at Dina. "But in this case you're wrong, dead wrong. Besides, Sidney may not have known about Deirdre and Godfrey. The injured spouse is usually the last to know."

"But what if he did find out about it? Wouldn't the sense of betrayal be enough to send him over the edge. Maybe he lost it when he confronted Mitchell. Maybe he blew Mitchell away without really intending to."

"Blew him away?" Freddie winced at Dina's choice of phrase.

"Sorry," Dina apologized, getting up to rinse her coffee cup and put it in the dish washer.

"I know that you're only doing your job," Freddie pursed her lips, "but, if you don't mind me being frank, it worries me. You've already been shot once. Shouldn't you be considering another line of work?"

"You sound just like my parents now! But don't worry. I'll try not to poke into anything dangerous," Dina said, not knowing if it was a promise she could keep. "I'll just snoop around a little. Whatever I find out, I'll pass on to Jackson. In fact, I'll call him tonight and let him know about the Deidre-Godfrey rumor."

Somewhat mollified, Freddie got to her feet, "Now I really must say good night. I have an early plane to catch and I haven't quite finished packing. Not that it matters what I pack, so long as I don't forget my golf clubs."

"How are you getting to the airport? I can give you a ride."

"Thank you dear, but I'm fine. I won't be away that long, so I plan to leave my car at the airport. It's convenient to have it waiting for me there when I get back," and with those words, Freddie retired upstairs.

True to her word, Dina called Jackson that evening. She passed on the gossip about Mitchell and Sidney Lawrence's wife. She gave him the Hadley and Amherst addresses for Curt Daniels, Mitchell's former graduate student. And she told him that she planned to locate the *Register* reporter, Miles Acton in the morning.

Before setting up in the library the next day, Dina drove to the *New Haven Register,* went straight to the personnel office and displayed her detective's badge. "I'm trying to locate Miles Acton, one of your reporters," she asked the woman behind the front desk.

The woman peered at her from over the tops of her half-glasses, "Miles Acton? The name isn't familiar. Are you sure he works here?"

"He did about twenty years ago. Would you mind checking?"

The woman obligingly turned on her computer and scrolled through a list of names. "Sorry. He's not showing up in our active file."

"Do you have an inactive file?" Dina wasn't giving up easily.

The woman turned back to her computer and tried again. This

time she hit pay-dirt. "Here it is. Miles Acton. He's still in the area. Lives in Hamden. I'll print the address for you."

Armed with the address, Dina wasted no time. She hopped in her SUV and drove north on Whitney Avenue to Hamden. Acton's house was located on a quiet, wooded cul-de-sac. After parking her car, she walked up a brick pathway and knocked on the door. When he heard why she had come, the burly, balding man who answered was only too willing to talk to her.

"Come in. Come in and sit down," he said, waving her into a sunny front parlor and shooing a cat off the sofa.

Now in his late seventies, Miles Acton had a pleasant basset hound of a face, with heavy jowls and brown, soft eyes. He wore an unbuttoned cardigan over a plaid flannel shirt, baggy, brown corduroy pants and leather slippers that flopped as he walked. Like him, Acton's parlor had a comfortable lived-in look: the sofa sagged, the carpet was threadbare in places, and the finish on the coffee table was nicked, scratched and water-stained.

"I haven't thought about the Thomas case in years. What's your interest in it?" Clearly Acton was more used to asking questions than answering them.

"We're looking into Godfrey Mitchell's background and Thomas's name came up."

"Of course," Acton seemed like a straight shooter.

"You covered the Thomas case for the *Register*." It was a statement rather than a question.

"Yup, I was a court reporter before I was put out to pasture. Since then I've been freelancing," he twinkled at her. "Just couldn't go quietly. Now I only write when the mood strikes me. And I have to admit it's a relief not having the pressure of deadlines anymore."

"Did you report on court cases exclusively?"

"Yeah, for the most part my regular beat involved murder, embezzlement, arson and fraud. You name the crime. I covered the trial. The Thomas case was a little different though."

"How so?"

"Small potatoes for one thing. It would not have made the front page if Whitney University hadn't been involved. For another, the matter should never have been brought to trial in the first place. In my opinion, Whitney should have handled the whole thing internally. Charging that young man with grand theft seemed like overkill. Even though the letter's value was estimated to be six figures, it was just a guesstimate. No one ever put an exact price on the damn thing," clearly Acton's sympathies were with the defendant in this case.

"So you didn't agree with the guilty verdict?"

"I felt sorry for the defendant but if I had been on the jury, I would probably have voted to convict anyway. The evidence against Thomas was pretty convincing and the court-appointed lawyer defending him did nothing to refute it."

"What was his lawyer's argument?"

"That the case was circumstantial. That his client was the victim of a frame. But he had no evidence to back up his argument. All he had in his client's defense were a bunch of people who knew Thomas and called him a stand-up guy, a great scholar, hard working, etc. Character witnesses. Even the chief witness against him said he didn't want to believe Thomas was capable of stealing from the Grosvenor."

"Godfrey Mitchell?"

"Yes. He was the one who discovered the stolen letter in Thomas's office. He was the prosecution's star witness. But right from the start it seemed obvious that he did not relish the role."

"A hostile witness?"

"In spades. The information had to be dragged out of him."

"Did you happen to notice Thomas's attitude toward Mitchell? His reaction during Mitchell's testimony?"

"Thomas didn't react visibly to anything Mitchell or any of the other witnesses said. He just sat there impassively. He looked like a man who'd had the stuffing knocked out of him. You had to feel sorry for the guy. His whole future was blown. No matter what the verdict, there would always be the suspicion that he couldn't be trusted."

"I read your report on the sentencing but couldn't find a follow-up story. Do you know what happened to Thomas after he was released from prison?"

"Sorry I can't help you there. I guess he served his time and moved on," he gave Dina a quizzical look. "You don't think he was involved in Godfrey Mitchell's murder?"

"Just covering all the bases. Do you?"

"Not I. Thomas didn't seem the type. He was a gentle reed of a man. A reed who had been broken. Besides, Mitchell was obviously uncomfortable testifying against someone he considered a friend. There seemed to be no malice in his testimony."

"Scratch one suspect," Dina said, getting to her feet. "Thank you. You've helped a great deal."

"Not at all, it was my pleasure," he said as he saw her to the door.

9

"AUGUSTA SCOTT PREFERS NOT TO BE INTERVIEWED IN HER OFFICE,"
Blaustein told Huey Gardner on their drive down to the shoreline.
"She didn't say why."

"Let's hope it's because she has something significant to tell us
and doesn't want to do it within earshot of her colleagues."

"Let's hope.

It was a bright sunny day, redolent with the promise of a January
thaw. The piles of dirty brown slush that bordered the streets were
noticeably shrinking. Icicles hanging from the eaves had begun to
drip, dimpling the crusty snow on the ground beneath. Hungry sea
gulls were making noisy discourse on the beaches bordering the
Sound. But spring was still a long way off and the temporary break
in the weather wasn't fooling anybody. Groundhog day was still a
couple of weeks away, and the little rodent never predicted anything
better than another six weeks of winter.

Augusta Scott lived in a two-story gray clapboard with a wide
wraparound porch, wind chimes and white rockers. It overlooked
a rocky beach. On the landward side, tips of grass showed through

the melting snow that covered the lawn. Slushy puddles had pooled on the driveway and on the fieldstone path that encircled the house. Across the gray expanse of the Sound, the faint outline of Long Island hugged the horizon. After parking their car in front of the closed-up doors of a two-car garage, the two detectives made their way to the front door and rang the doorbell.

"Must be pleasant here in the summer," Gardner observed. "Not much of a beach though."

"Big enough when you don't have to share it with the likes of you and me." Blaustein grunted.

The sound of footsteps announced Augusta Scott before she opened the door. She was a statuesque woman in her early forties, handsome in the Wagnerian manner, with straight fair hair worn with bangs and a page boy, well-chiseled features and a no nonsense manner. She was wearing a plaid skirt and a twin set with the Peter Pan collar of a white blouse showing at the neck.

"Detective Blaustein?" She said, extending a hand in greeting.

"And Detective Gardner," Blaustein introduced his partner.

"Please come in," she stood aside and waved them into the hall. "Would you like to hang up your coats?"

After depositing their coats in the vestibule closet, she ushered the two detectives into the living room. It was furnished eclectically: a Danish modern sofa and chairs, modern paintings on the walls and several antiques, a grandfather clock, a roll-top desk, ball and claw end tables, and a couple of straight-backed Victorian chairs. French windows opened onto a porch with a view of the Sound. A Royal Doulton tea service had been placed on the coffee table. When they were all seated, and preliminary to any discussion, she observed the niceties by serving tea and offering them whisper-thin ginger cookies.

"All right," she smoothed her skirt with one hand, "tell me what it is you'd like to know."

"Whatever you can tell us about Godfrey Mitchell. Especially what you know about his friends and whether he had any enemies," Blaustein said as he helped himself to sugar and stirred before continuing. "Don't discount anything. No detail is too small or too unimportant."

"Does this mean it wasn't suicide?"

"It would be premature to jump to any conclusions," Blaustein answered, though he preferred to ask the questions rather than answer them. "That's why we're here, to get some background on the late professor. We understand that you might be the person who can provide that information. We were told that you knew Godfrey Mitchell well."

"You'll probably hear this elsewhere, so I might as well tell you that I knew him intimately at one time," the calm gray eyes met his without wavering, and to Blaustein it seemed that the woman had ice in her veins.

"When was that?"

"I'd known Godfrey and Alison for years, but not well. We had met at faculty parties, played the occasional game of bridge, that sort of thing. But I didn't really get to know him until well after his divorce. About six years ago, I had an extra ticket to the Long Wharf Theater and invited him to join me. You could say I shamelessly made the first move," she laughed, but without humor. "Our relationship went pretty quickly from that innocuous beginning to something purely physical. But I realized early on that Godfrey was incapable of making a commitment, and worse, that he wasn't bound by any loyalties. To be frank, dating me didn't stop him from fooling around. It was as if the man couldn't help himself. I began to feel a lot of sympathy for Alison."

"Was she still living in the area?"

"No, she moved out-of-state immediately after the divorce was finalized. I didn't see her again until the memorial service." She set down her cup and saucer and handed the plate of cookies around. "Anyway, when I found out that I was not the only love of Godfrey's life, we had a candid discussion about his. . . er. . . promiscuity. I hadn't invested any capital in the relationship so it was a very adult conversation and without rancor. We both came to the conclusion that we preferred the status quo ante. So we went back to being simply colleagues and stopped seeing each other except for an occasional luncheon. I didn't need the distraction of a faithless lover and he apparently didn't want to change the habits of a lifetime. We both recognized that an amicable break was best for both of us."

"Thank you for being so frank," Blaustein acknowledged, though he couldn't shake the impression that the recital had been too pat, and he wondered whether it might mask deeper, still unresolved feelings. Augusta Scott was such a cool customer that it was hard to tell. "You described Mitchell as being promiscuous. Do you know anything about the other women in his life?"

"I didn't keep track, Detective. Godfrey didn't confide the details of that aspect of his life to me, so I can't quote chapter and verse. But knowing his proclivities, I'd say that he managed to have a few trysts, probably with the younger, more attractive faculty wives. His charms were hard to resist. But after a divorce that was triggered by a relationship with an undergraduate, I suspect he pretty much stayed away from students. Nowadays, with the fear of sexual harassment suits, even Godfrey probably curbed his libido. But as I said, I don't really know. My own relationship with him moved to a purely platonic plane. Both being British historians, we had quite a bit in common. When we met, we talked about our work. His books. Our mutual preoccupation with current research. He was not forthcoming about his love life, and I certainly wasn't interested in discussing it."

She hadn't mentioned Deirdre Lawrence and Blaustein wondered if she knew about the rumor that she and Mitchell were an item. So he asked, somewhat innocuously, "Do you happen to know how well Mitchell knew Deirdre Lawrence?"

"I heard some gossip over the summer. But that's probably all it was, gossip," offering to refill their cups, she effectively shut off that particular line of questioning and didn't apologize for not mentioning the rumors during her earlier narration. It made Blaustein wonder what else she had failed to mention.

"What about Mitchell's professional relationships?" Blaustein asked, accepting the refill as he changed the subject. "Did he have any academic rivals? Anyone who was openly antagonistic toward him?

Or anyone who may have lodged complaints against him, formal or otherwise?"

"You have to understand, Detective, that when it came to publishing, Godfrey had a lot of rivals. A lot of rivals but not many equals. He was prolific and his books were immensely popular. On both sides of the Atlantic," she sipped her coffee thoughtfully. "There's no denying that some of his fellow academics resented his success. They quibbled about his scholarship and nickel and dimed his interpretations. And that hurt him. He wanted to be accepted by his peers. It was one of the things he often talked about when we lunched together."

"Did he think anyone in particular was out to get him?"

"It was more like everyone in particular. There was a fairly pervasive 'Get Godfrey' attitude in the Department. It came out in faculty meetings when, like I said, his colleagues quibbled about his research. But no, he never mentioned anyone in particular."

"No anti-Mitchell ring leaders?"

"Not that I'm aware of."

Blaustein sensed that a wall had come down between them. Augusta Scott was either unable or unwilling to name names. Was she blameless herself? Or was she protecting one of her colleagues? He glanced over at Gardner who had been taking diligent notes on the lead sheet. "Any other questions, Detective Gardner?"

Just a couple," Gardner looked up from his clipboard. "Before we talk to Professor Mitchell's graduate assistant, Kelly Richmond, I'd like your take on the young woman, Professor Scott."

"I've never met her, and know very little about her except that she had an outstanding undergraduate record at Rutgers University. She began her graduate studies at Whitney this academic year, replacing Godfrey's previous T.A. who graduated last May. From what I'd gathered, Godfrey thought Kelly was an okay student and a dependable teaching assistant. He described her to me as very conscientious and reliable, but he fell far short of calling her brilliant. I had the feeling that she lacked the little extra something that we always hope to find in our students, but so rarely do," she sighed.

"And the student she replaced?"

"Heather Leopold. She was a career graduate student who took forever to write her dissertation. I don't know exactly what her problem was. She finally defended last spring and moved on. I don't know where she is now."

"Any reason she may have resented Mitchell?"

"As far as I know she and Godfrey had an amicable relationship. Initially her main job for him was to grade papers, and because Godfrey's classes were enormously over-subscribed, she had her hands full. Later, as his literary endeavors took up more and more of his time, she also took over some of his undergraduate seminars. Heather was quite likable. She had a robust personality and a sense of humor which I suspect will stand her in good stead when she gets her own faculty position somewhere. The undergraduates here seemed to like her. At least I never heard any complaints."

"Do you know where she's teaching now?"

"No, I don't. Nor whether she is. Though I hate to admit it, postgraduate degrees in history don't guarantee college positions, even for Whitney Ph.Ds. If you'd like to get in touch with her, try the placement office."

"What about Jillian Davis? She was an undergraduate here about ten years ago. Know anything about her?" Gardner persisted.

Augusta Scott frowned slightly and tapped her manicured fingertip on the arm of the sofa. "You're asking about Jillian Davis because you've probably heard that she was the ultimate cause of Godfrey's divorce. Where did you hear about her?"

"Why don't you just tell us what you know about the relationship between Jillian Davis and Godfrey Mitchell," Blaustein ignored her question, unwilling to yield the inquisitor's role to Augusta Scott.

"He admitted to me once that Alison found them in bed together," she shrugged, ceding the high ground once again. "I don't know whether that was the first time, but it was the last as far as Alison was concerned. Jillian baby-sat for Brian Mitchell who was about ten or eleven at the time. Shortly after the incident, she left school. I don't know what's happened to her since." She put down her cup and glanced at her wrist watch. "If there's nothing else, I really must get back to campus."

"Just a couple more questions. Where were you, Professor Scott, in the days immediately after Christmas?" Blaustein resumed the interrogation.

"Most of the time I was right here in Connecticut."

"You didn't attend the conference in Atlanta?"

"My sister was in Europe and I was taking care of my niece Kendra."

"Your niece is how old?"

"Eleven going on thirty. Just after Christmas we went to New York. We took in a show at Radio City Music Hall and skated at Rockefeller Plaza."

"Would you mind telling us where you stayed in New York?"

"At the Algonquin," she stood up abruptly. "And if you have any additional questions for me, I think I'll insist on having an attorney present. This is beginning to sound like the third degree, Detective. And I must tell you that I resent it."

"Of course you have every right to an attorney," Blaustein placated her as the two detectives got to their feet and followed Augusta Scott to the front hall to retrieve their coats. "But these questions are just routine. We're asking them of everyone who was associated with the victim."

Acknowledging the explanation, she inclined her head regally. "I do hope you find whoever committed this horrible crime, Detective."

"Thank you for your help, Professor Scott," Blaustein said, taking a business card from his wallet and handing it to her. "Please get in touch if you think of anything else."

"Full disclosure was not her intent! What do you make of her?" Blaustein asked, as he turned the key in the ignition.

"Well she certainly jumped on you when you began asking about her whereabouts. Maybe she does have something to hide."

"Well, she didn't try to hide her previous relationship with

Mitchell but on the other hand, she didn't volunteer the rumor about him and Lawrence's wife," Blaustein looked over his shoulder as he backed out of the driveway and swung into the road. "Maybe, as a member of the faculty, she just prefers not to discuss her colleagues."

"Let's hope Mitchell's students are more forthcoming. Someone out there must know something. After all, somebody hated the guy enough to kill him."

"Well the first student on our list is Kelly Richmond and she may not be able to tell us much. She's only been Mitchell's student for a few months," Blaustein checked the clock on the dashboard. "With luck she'll still be at home."

Leaving Long Island Sound behind them, they made their way back to the highway where brake lights ahead signaled a traffic problem ahead. Blaustein fumed silently as the car inched forward one excruciating yard at a time until they eventually passed the stalled vehicle that had caused the problem. After crossing the Quinnipiac Bridge, they circled north onto Interstate 91 and headed for the Winslow Street exit where they parked in front of the multi-family house where Kelly Richmond lived. The house was as woebegone as Dina had described it, with peeling paint, missing shingles and a sagging front porch. The door to the entry hall was unlocked, so they went upstairs to the third floor. On the unswept landing outside Richmond's door, Blaustein noticed a road bike with muddy tires and a broken reflector. Hoping this meant the graduate student was home, he knocked, and did not have to wait long to find out.

"Who is it?" came a female voice from behind the door.

"Detectives Blaustein and Gardner, Major Crime Squad."

A safety chain slid into place and a second later, the door opened a crack. Blaustein held up his badge. "May we speak with you Ms. Richmond?"

"Of course."

The chain slid back. The door opened. And Blaustein had his first glimpse of the student Dina had told him about. Her fair hair was pulled back into a French braid and her gray eyes looked back at him from behind metal-rimmed glasses. She wore no makeup and dressed in jeans, an oversized fisherman's knit sweater and Timberland boots, she looked like any one of a hundred students.

The apartment into which she ushered them was a bedsitter, furnished with what looked like the leavings of a secondhand store. The sofa bed that took up a third of the space had not yet been made. She scooped up the bedclothes, dumped them on a nearby end table and in a single, practiced motion folded the bed back.

"Excuse the mess," she apologized, replacing the seat cushions. "Please sit down." She indicated a couple of shabby upholstered chairs and plonked herself down on the sofa, one leg tucked beneath her. The gray eyes behind the glasses looked from one to the other and then came to rest on the hands folded in her lap.

"Ms. Richmond, I understand you've been Professor Mitchell's teaching assistant since the start of this academic year?" Blaustein began the questioning.

She inclined her head, "Yes."

"Had you known the professor before you came to Whitney?"

"Only by reputation. I considered myself fortunate to get the assignment."

"And why was that?" Blaustein thought he already knew the answer, but he wanted to hear it from her.

"Godfrey Mitchell is. . . was. . . quite famous. I thought I was lucky to be his teaching assistant."

"And how was it that you, a first year graduate student, was given such a plum assignment?"

"Partly because of my undergraduate record, I suppose," she fiddled with a loose tendril of hair. "And partly because the job wasn't so plum after all."

Surprised by this response, Blaustein pressed the point. "Please explain."

"He worked his teaching assistants hard," she shrugged, "harder than most."

"Do T.As. have set duties?"

"Well, the more senior graduate students teach undergraduate seminars but the rest of us mostly grade papers and exams."

"Did Professor Mitchell require anything more of you than grading papers and exams?" Blaustein persisted, despite her obvious reluctance to speak ill of her late mentor.

The student hesitated. "Well, in addition to taking graduate courses and researching our dissertations, Professor Mitchell expected us to do assigned research. It got to be a bit much at times. The T. A. who preceded me took eight years to finish her dissertation and I understand that part of the reason was the unrelated research she was required to do."

"Unrelated how?"

"Well," she looked down at her hands, "the research she was required to do wasn't for her dissertation at all, but for a book Godfrey was working on himself."

"Did you know about his reputation when you accepted the position?"

"No, being new on campus, I didn't know that Mitchell was something of a slave driver," she looked frankly at Blaustein this time, her gray eyes steady. "At the time I felt pretty lucky. I thought that with Godfrey Mitchell's reputation and contacts, it would be easier down the road to get a job. Of course that's not going to happen now that he's been shot."

"Will you get reassigned to another professor?" Gardner asked, looking up from the notes he was taking.

"I'm still waiting to find out about that. They haven't decided what to do with me yet," she said with a matter-of-fact shrug and seemingly without self-pity.

"Are you relying on your stipend to stay in school?" Blaustein couldn't help feeling sorry for the earnest young woman. "Can they just take away your stipend? Don't you have a contract of some sort?"

"Well my fellowship pays my tuition. But being a graduate assistant helped pay the other bills."

"Tell me about your relationship with Professor Mitchell. How did you get along with him?" Blaustein abruptly switched gears.

"Fine. I always handed in his class grades on time. And he was happy with the research I did for him. At least I guess he was, he never sent me back to go over the same ground."

"That's the research you did for your dissertation or your research for him personally?"

"Mostly the latter. But his emphasis was on the early nineteenth century, which is my period, so I was really killing two birds with one stone. My predecessor, Heather Leopold wasn't so lucky, which is why she took eight years to get out of here. Her dissertation was on William Morris who came much later in the century. So there was no connection between her own research and his. As far as I know, she didn't make any waves. But some years ago, one of his T.As. did, and ended up paying for it. He ended up doing the lion's share of the research Mitchell used in one of his books, and got no credit for it. So he publicly accused the professor of plagiarism. Exploitation might have been a more appropriate charge."

"Know the student's name?" Blaustein asked, though he already knew it.

"Curt Daniels. He ended up leaving Whitney." She stood up abruptly. "I'm having tea. Want some?"

"No thank you," they both said in unison, remembering Dina's warning about the woman's tea.

"Well, do you mind if I do?" she asked rhetorically, making her way to the partitioned off area at the back of the room

When they heard water running as the kettle filled, and the clink of a teaspoon on china, Blaustein walked over to the kitchenette and peered in. On the other side of the partition was a space no wider than four feet, half of which seemed to be taken over by a noisy, nineteen- fifties–style refrigerator with rounded contours. The rest of the cramped quarters consisted of a working area that ran along one wall. It had a cracked Formica countertop which incorporated a two-burner plate and a sink overflowing with dirty dishes. Above and beneath the counter were cabinets, once white, now badly in need of a coat of paint. The wallpaper was splattered with grease stains and peeling at the edges. The floor was covered by discolored linoleum tiles. Blaustein remained in the doorway, one hand resting on the partition, "Tell me," he said, pausing so as to force her to look at him, "did you have a social relationship with Godfrey Mitchell?"

"You mean did I sleep with him?" There were those unwavering gray eyes meeting his again.

"Yes, to be blunt," Blaustein held her gaze.

"Then no, absolutely not." The kettle whistled and she took it off the burner.

"He never put any moves on you?" Blaustein sounded unbelieving.

"I wouldn't exactly say that. Godfrey was. . . well... suggestive. And when I first started working for him it embarrassed me. But he seemed to realize that he was making me uncomfortable and knew enough not to push the envelope. So after some initial awkwardness we learned to get along on a purely professional footing." She poured the hot water into a mug and added a tea bag.

"You weren't intimidated by such provocative behavior?" Blaustein sounded incredulous. "It sounds a lot like sexual harassment to me."

"Godfrey never let it get that far. His advances, if you could call them that, were much more subtle. He was too clever to be caught harassing one of his students."

"And you didn't resent him for this kind of behavior?"

"Not at all. It was just Mitchell being Mitchell. He would have flirted with a bag lady." She jiggled the teabag and turned, her back to the counter. "Shall we go where we can sit down?"

When they were once again seated, Blaustein picked up where he had left off. "Tell me what you know about your predecessor and her relationship with Mitchell?" Blaustein knew he was on shaky ground here. Everything Richmond told him would be hearsay. Still, it might serve to flesh out his picture of the victim.

"Heather Leopold? Well, we didn't overlap so there isn't much I can tell you. She graduated in May and I arrived on campus in September. I never actually met her."

"What about the grapevine?"

"She may have had a crush on him. Which would explain why she didn't mind hanging around for so long. She could also afford to take eight years to write her dissertation. I understand her Daddy is well off. But the Prof may not have made any sexual advances. I understand that Heather wasn't exactly Godfrey's type. According to campus gossip, he only went for lookers. And from what I've been told Heather wasn't a pin-up girl. So, I doubt they had a sexual relationship."

"Know what she's doing now?"

"Not a clue."

"Ms. Richmond, where were you on the days immediately after Christmas?"

"I was here for the entire Christmas break." She gave him an amused look. "Does that make me a suspect?"

"If you were, we would be reading you your rights," Blaustein reassured her.

10

IF THERE WERE A STEREOTYPICAL MALE LIBRARIAN, THEN HERMAN Archer seemed to fit the mold. He was meticulous to a fault, perfectly nondescript and the epitome of a fussbudget. Short and a trifle over-weight, he wore his prematurely thinning hair cut short on the sides, an out-at-the-elbows jacket and thick-lensed glasses. He was in his mid-thirties but looked middle aged. A creature of habit, today as usual, he took his lunch-break at a desk in the glassed-in office behind the registration desk. Dina watched him unwrap a sandwich and take the cap off his thermos. She was used to the routine, visible as it always was through the glass-walled enclosure that separated the office from the registration desk. But today something happened to alter Archie's normal routine. He took a call at his desk, his hand cupped over the mouthpiece as if what he had to say was for the caller's ears alone. Of course Dina could not hear Archie's end of the conversation, but she was able to read the tension in his body language as he put down the receiver. She watched as he carefully rewrapped his sandwich and put the cap back on his thermos. Then he grabbed his coat and left the library.

Though Dina had been prepared to wait out Archie's lunch break till Edward arrived to relieve her, she immediately shrugged into her coat, shoved her writing materials into her book-bag and hoisting it over her shoulder, left the library. Archie was halfway across the quadrangle by the time she emerged outside bareheaded. Pausing for just a minute to pull a wool cap and a pair of dark glasses from her coat pocket and put them on, she followed, keeping a safe distance behind the librarian as he left the campus.

Walking briskly and purposefully, Archie made his way to a bus stop on the corner of Broadway and Dixwell. Dina, shielded behind an F150 truck that was parked on the opposite side of the street, watched as he joined two men already waiting at the bus stop. As he neither communicated nor even made eye contact with the other two men, it seemed unlikely that either was his supplier. It looked as if Archie was just waiting for the bus.

Dina knew that tailing someone taking a bus was easier with two people: preferably one on the bus and the other following by car. But there wasn't time to call Edward, so Dina's only option was to follow Archie onto the bus. To avoid being recognized, she waited till the bus lumbered around the corner. Then dashing across the street, she ran up to the bus as the last of the riders was boarding, pulled a handful of change from her wallet and fed the fare box.

Archie was seated on the left, five rows from the front. Face averted, she made her way past him and took a seat on the same side of the bus, three rows further back. As soon as the bus was underway, she pulled a cell phone from her backpack and dialed Edward. No answer. That probably meant he had turned the ringer off while in the library. All she could do was leave a message.

"Edward," she whispered, cupping her mouth behind her hand, "I followed Archie onto a Dixwell Avenue bus. I don't know where he's headed yet. I'll call you back when I know more."

The bus made its leisurely way north, every now and then stopping to pick up and discharge passengers. Gradually the stops became less frequent and the number of passengers dwindled. Archie stayed put until the bus reached a down-at-heels strip mall with a mostly empty parking lot. By this time, Dina and Archie were the only passengers aboard.

If she got off now, she risked being made. So she watched as Archie disembarked and after the bus had gone a hundred yards, she made her way down the aisle to the driver and tapped him on the shoulder.

"I'm so sorry," she smiled sweetly. "I've missed my stop. Would you mind letting me off here?"

As no man in his right mind was ever able to resist Dina's smile, the driver pulled over to the curb and Dina was off and running. When she reached the plaza, she slowed to a walk, partly to catch her breath but also as a precaution. She needed to see but not be seen. An ice cream kiosk, closed for the winter, seemed the ideal shelter. From behind it she could survey the parking lot without being noticed. The plaza consisted of a half dozen stores, three of them empty and boarded up, a small convenience store, a barber shop and, at the far end, a laundromat. There was no one going into any of the stores and no one was coming out. At first she thought she had lost Archie. But just as the whole escapade was beginning to look like a wild goose chase, a black Lincoln Continental drove into the lot and parked at the farthest end of it. Seconds later Archie appeared from the doorway of the laundromat. He made his way across the lot and got into the passenger-side of the Lincoln. A few minutes passed. Then Archie got out carrying what looked like a shoe box. He left the parking lot without looking back, walked to the curb, looked both ways, and crossed to the bus stop on the opposite side of the street.

This time Dina could not follow the librarian and without a car, she couldn't follow the Lincoln either. So looking on helplessly, she watched the vehicle back out of its parking space, drive to the exit and then head south on Dixwell Avenue leaving Archie to wait for his bus. She had not been able to make out the face of the driver, but she did manage to take down the license plate number. Hoping against hope that the car didn't have stolen plates, she phoned headquarters and asked them to run the license. Then she called a cab.

"Dina? Can it really be you?"

The voice behind her was very familiar. Halfway across the New

Haven Green and on her way back to the campus, Dina spun around and came face to face with her old beau, Clive Atkinson.

"You're the last person I expected to see here, Clive," despite herself, her pulses raced.

"I'm here to give a series of lectures at the Law School."

He looked great, as always. Tall, fair haired, patrician, and impeccably dressed. He could have posed for an advertisement in G.Q.

"At the Law School?" She was impressed in spite of herself. "What's your topic?"

"Environmental law."

"How to enforce environmental law? Or how to help companies circumvent it?" She knew she sounded bitchy.

"Still the liberal. Still tilting at windmills. Not everything is black and white, you know." He admonished. "I like to think I help companies litigate unfair legislation."

"Just as I thought," she flung back at him, her chin tilted, her eyes flashing. "Aiding and abetting industrial polluters after the EPA has nailed them."

"I assume you're not here to study the economics of capitalism," he mocked.

"No, it isn't exactly my field."

"And have you finally seen the light, or are you still a cop?" He managed not to sound too censorious.

"I've always seen the light," after all the arguments they'd had about her decision to enter the police force, she opted not to elaborate.

"How are your parents?" It seemed safest to change the subject.

"The same, only older."

"It happens." He smiled his old charming smile and her resistance faltered.

"And what about you?"

"The same, only older," he caught her hand and noticed the absence of rings. "Not married, I see."

"Marriage isn't all it's cracked up to be from what I hear," she snatched her hand back. "Or do you have a different take on it?"

"Actually I'm glad we agree on something. I tried it for a while, you know. Soon, perhaps too soon, after you and I broke up. It didn't last."

"Doubtless she had better social pretensions than I did," Dina shot back.

"Well she wasn't planning to become a cop, that's for sure," he laughed. "She's what you'd describe as a New York City socialite. A culture maven but an emotional and intellectual void. She didn't have any of your spark and I found that I missed it." His unexpected wistfulness caught Dina by surprise and she averted her eyes.

"You must have made it professionally to be an invited speaker at Whitney." It was her turn to change the subject. "Congratulations."

"If you'll let me take you to dinner tonight, Dee, I'll tell you all about it."

"Is that a good idea?" Her curiosity was getting the better of her but her reluctance to stir up the embers of their past and a lingering loyalty to Philip made her hesitate.

"I won't rehash any old arguments, what would be the point?" He mistook the reason for her reluctance.

"Thank you, then I accept," she said grudgingly.

"The Faculty Club suit you? As a guest of the Law School I have privileges there?"

"Of course you do," she teased, knowing his penchant for snobbish pretension and wondering why she had ever been impressed by it. "I'll meet you there. Is eight o'clock all right? I'm driving up to see my parents this afternoon but should be back in plenty of time. If there's a chance I'll be late I'll leave a message for you."

Racing up the Interstate a short time later and with time to think, Dina wondered whether accepting Clive's invitation had been altogether wise. It was like building a bridge to a void. A bridge that went nowhere but to the past. A hurtful past that began one summer on the Cape where they first met. She was barely twenty then and had just completed her sophomore year in college. He was handsome, sophisticated, and already close to graduating from Harvard Law School. Initially surprised and flattered by his attentions, she had been shy, almost tongue-tied. But with persistence he wore down her reticence along with her resistance. As the summer ripened into fall, their romance ripened with it. They dated for almost two years and their plan was to get married at the end of her senior year. Then, after her brother's fatal accident, came her announcement that she planned to enter the Police Academy. A huge shouting match ensued and everything changed between them. It was as if blinders had been removed. She realized for the first time how very much like her father he was. And that being so very much like her father, it would be a mistake to spend her life married to him. Upon sober reflection it was like being drenched by the ice-cold water of reality.

Clive, she suspected, had not changed an iota since then. If first impressions were any gauge then he was as much in love with his rarified bloodlines and his social and intellectual superiority as ever. And just as stubborn. A trait they shared. Obstinacy was not a characteristic that eroded with time. No, there was no future in seeing Clive again. All the signposts warned against it. She toyed with the idea of calling to cancel their dinner date. But she didn't. Instead of pulling out her cell phone, she put Cliive out of her mind, turned up the volume on the radio and watched the miles melt away.

Since meeting her father at the Mitchell memorial service and remembering how much he had aged, Dina had felt the stirrings of filial guilt. Life was just too short to harbor grudges. Deciding it was time to mend fences, she had called her parents and invited herself for lunch. "I'll bring the dessert, and please don't go to a lot of trouble, Mother," she had said.

That was why, after dropping off a report at headquarters in Meriden, she had taken Route 66 to Middlefield and Lyman Orchards. Encountering bumper-to-bumper traffic on the two-lane road and anxious not to be late, she took a short cut past Powder Ridge. To the west were the hills that separated Middlefield from Meriden and all around were rows and rows of gnarled, leafless fruit trees, their bountiful harvest dormant until the summer. Empty too were the

Quonset huts that housed migrant workers. And absent were the parents and little children who came in season to 'pick their own'. But the country store was alive with shoppers when Dina arrived there. She parked and went inside. Bypassing the fruit and vegetable aisles, she followed the heady aroma that led her to the bake section. There, without hesitation, she selected a still warm-from-the-oven apple pie, paid at the checkout counter and left.

The drive to Storrs was a trip she had made countless times, usually with a sense of dread. But her chance meeting with her father had enabled her to turn a corner in their relationship. Today she felt upbeat despite the fact that the weather did not mirror her good mood. It had turned gloomy, overcast and raw. By the time she drove up to the eighteenth century colonial that was her parents' home, sleet was lashing at the twelve-over-twelve windows of the old house and making them rattle. Bowing her head against the wind she grabbed the apple pie and scurried from the car. Her mother greeted her at the door.

"Hello, Dina," she gave her daughter a peck on the cheek. "Hang up your coat and then join your father in the keeping room while I finish up in the kitchen."

Unlike Dina's father, her mother seemed ageless. And though her fair hair was threaded with gray, the years and the tragedy of losing a son had barely changed her. Elegant even in an apron, she still seemed like the distant, beautiful mother who had always kept Dina at arms' length. But Dina was not prepared to let the chill of their past relationship get in the way of her determination to thaw the wall of ice that had always separated them. She had thought about her mother a lot lately and was prepared to concede that her remoteness was due to reserve rather than indifference. Some people just weren't given to demonstrations of affection. Her very proper mother was one of them.

"Can I help you with anything, Mother?"

"There's nothing much left to do. I'll join you shortly," her mother said, relieving Dina of the apple pie as Dina took off her coat and hung it in the hall closet.

"At least let me put my contribution to the meal in the kitchen," Dina offered.

"No need. I'll do it."

"Thank you, Mother," Dina sighed as she closed the closet door.

In the keeping room beside its huge stone fireplace, her father was so engrossed in the book he was reading that the fire had been reduced to embers. He closed his book when Dina entered and started to get out of his chair.

"Don't get up," she bent and kissed him on the cheek.

"I have to. I've neglected the fire."

"No, stay where you are. I'll take care of it."

She selected a handful of kindling and a couple of good sized logs from the customary stack of wood beside the fireplace, placed them carefully on top of the grate and then raked the glowing embers until sparks flew up the chimney. When she was satisfied that the logs had caught, she sat down in the armchair opposite her father.

"I have an appointment to meet with Augusta Scott. Do you know her?" She asked after the usual small talk had petered out.

"Yes, as a matter of fact, she's a member of the Pickwick Club. I told you about the Pickwick Club didn't I?"

Dina nodded. "What do you think of her, Dad?"

"Well, between you and me, I think Augusta's actually a better historian than Godfrey Mitchell ever was. Her research is sounder," he answered, placing a bookmark in his tome and putting it on the table beside him.

"What's she like a person?" Dina was not particularly interested in Scott's academic credentials.

"Until last summer she was just a nodding acquaintance, then she sat next to me on a plane from England and I got to know her a little better. We'd both been attending a conference in Oxford and had shared a cab to Heathrow. Naturally we talked shop the whole way back to Bradley. A charming woman with a wry sense of humor. Having her as a travel companion made the trip go much faster and far more pleasantly than usual. Is your meeting with her connected to the Mitchell case?" He took off his reading glasses and polished them with his pocket handkerchief.

"It is."

"I thought you weren't involved in that investigation." He may have aged, but her father still did not miss a trick.

"That was true when we last met, and I'm still primarily on another case, but I now have a limited involvement with the Mitchell case," she continued without elaborating. " Actually my interview with Augusta Scott came about indirectly. I met a former chairman of the History Department socially and he suggested that I talk to Professor Scott. Adrian Needham. Do you know him?"

"Know of him. He was in a different field. We historians are a narrow bunch. Don't have much to do with each other if we don't have a common specialty. But how is it you met Needham?"

"He and my landlady, Freddie, are old friends. I'm pretty sure she invited him over so that I could pump him about Mitchell. And he was quite helpful. Among other things he suggested I speak to Augusta Scott. He said she knew Godfrey Mitchell as well as anyone in the Department. I immediately passed the information on to Jackson Blaustein, who's heading up the investigation. Turns out that he'd already interviewed her, so I was somewhat mystified when she called me to set up an appointment."

"Maybe as a courtesy to Adrian Needham. He may have told her to get in touch with you, and she felt obliged to follow through."

"That may be it."

"Perhaps you ought to know that once upon a time it was rumored that Augusta and Godfrey were an item. I haven't heard anything about that for some time though," he got up, stirred the fire with a large wrought-iron poker that hung beside the hearth and changed the subject. "Isn't it rather dangerous poking about in a murder investigation? You've taken a bullet once already."

"That's because I let my guard down. I'll be sure not to do that again."

"I sincerely hope so. Your mother and I find it very unsettling having a daughter on the front lines as it were. We have already lost one child. It would be insupportable to lose two." The gray-blue eyes that were just like Dina's held her gaze. "You'll never know how distressed we were the night your partner arrived with the news that you'd been shot."

Surprised by this rare expression of concern, Dina said nothing as her father resumed his chair by the fireside and went on speaking. "I know we've had our differences in the past. But I think it's time to put all that behind us. I realize that nothing I say will change your mind. It's too late for that. And your mother and I have come to terms with your line of work. But," his eyes were still holding hers, "that doesn't mean that we'll ever get used to the idea that you are constantly putting yourself in harm's way."

"Amen to that," came her mother's voice from the doorway. "Lunch is on the table."

They ate lunch in the kitchen, as they had always done when Dina and Jeremy were children. The kitchen had always been Dina's favorite room in the house. Like the keeping room, it had a fireplace with a stone hearth, wide walnut floorboards and wainscoting. There were four windsor chairs, one on each side of the table. One of them empty now. No one commented. But each knew what the others were thinking.

"Roast chicken and potatoes with lots of gravy. Just the way you like it, Dina."

"You've gone to an awful lot of trouble, Mother. Sandwiches would have been just fine."

"Nonsense," her mother said as she handed each of them a serving. "Help yourselves to salad."

"Your mother and I are thinking of getting a dog."

"Actually it's your father who wants a dog, not I."

"Teddy Two?" Dina said with a smile.

"No, not a Beagle this time. Something a bit bigger. More athletic. I was thinking about a Lab. Or better yet, a dog from the animal shelter." Her father said, pouring gravy over his roast potatoes.

"The shelters have a hard time placing large, older dogs. You'll be doing a good thing," Dina said with obvious approval.

But her mother said nothing. Clearly this was a controversial topic. And after a brief lull in the conversation, Mrs. Barrett abruptly changed the subject. She was making it abundantly clear that getting a dog was not up for discussion. "Your father's *Carlyle* has been very well reviewed,"

"I know. I read the review in *Victorian Studies*. I should have said something earlier. Congratulations."

"Since when do you read *Victorian Studies*?"

"I don't as a rule," she laughed but didn't offer any further explanation.

"Remind me to give you a copy of my book before you leave," her father said, looking pleased.

"You father's been invited to England for a series of summer seminars."

"Dad, that's wonderful. Will you be going with him, Mother?"

"I'm thinking about it."

And so the conversation went. They stuck to the safe subjects and skirted the difficult ones. Just like always. After lunch, Dina washed the dishes and her mother dried them.

"I'll put the dishes away. I know where everything goes, her mother said. Though Dina had lived in the house most of her life and knew quite well where everything went, she still felt as if she did not quite belong there.

On the drive back to New Haven from her parent's house, and with time to think, Dina watched the miles melt away and allowed her thoughts to return to the crime that had taken Godfrey Mitchell's life. If Mitchell and Scott had once been 'an item', as her father put it, then what if he had rejected her? Could the motive behind Mitchell's murder be that primitive? Was it possible that Scott found out about the woman who had been in his bed on the day of his murder? Was it a case of jealousy-fueled revenge?

Dina wondered what it was like to feel such intense passion. It was so unlike her gentle fondness for Philip or, for that matter, the ashes of her relationship with Clive. Deep down she dreaded the possibility that the ashes might be waiting to burst into flame again. She did not want to go down that road a second time. And as the distance to New Haven lessened with each mile, she was more convinced than ever that seeing him again was a mistake. The two of them could never be simply friends. And anything else was unthinkable. Pulling out her cell phone, she dialed the Faculty Club. But Clive was not there. She did not leave a message. Was that because she was still unsure? Irresolutely she drove home and once there, again tried calling the Faculty Club. Again without result. So still harboring misgivings, she showered and changed for dinner.

The Faculty Club, she figured, would be strictly for the twin-set and pearls crowd. So in defiance, she chose a racy pair of moss green velvet pants with a matching jacket. Of course the fact that it was her most flattering outfit, that the color complemented the creaminess of her complexion and set off the highlights in her shoulder-length brown hair had nothing to do with the fact that she wanted to impress Clive. Nor, she told herself, was impressing Clive the reason she applied her make up with more care than usual, brushing her cheeks with a trace of rouge, touching her lips lightly with gloss and highlighting the blue-gray eyes that looked back at her from the mirror. But if impressing Clive had been her intention, then judging by the appreciative look on his face when he met her in the Faculty Club foyer, she had succeeded.

"I had cold feet about seeing you this evening and tried to call you," she said, after they had been seated and handed their menus.

"There's nothing sinister about dining with an old friend," he replied, not looking up from the menu. "So I'm glad your misplaced scruples, or whatever they were, didn't deprive me of the pleasure of escorting the best looking woman in the place."

"Even if she's a cop?" Dina regretted the comment the minute she uttered it.

But Clive was unfazed. "What you do for a living is your business, not mine."

Silenced by this unexpected concession, Dina decided that maybe it wouldn't be such a bad evening after all. And it wasn't. They shared a spinach salad served with poached pears and glazed walnuts. Then followed it with a rack of lamb for Clive and for Dina, a filet mignon served rare with mushrooms and a Bearnaise sauce. Between them they polished off a bottle of Cabernet and during it all, they chatted amicably. He told her about his legal practice and his failed marriage. She told him about Philip and confided her ambivalence. They stayed away from politics, always a source of tension between them, and away from the contentious subject of her occupation. But she knew he'd broach the latter topic again sooner or later. So it wasn't a surprise when the issue came up while they were relaxing over dessert and coffee.

"Is New Haven your beat these days?" He asked.

"Not permanently. I'm on temporary assignment here. Light duty until I'm a hundred percent." She stopped herself, realizing she did not want to go there.

"And why aren't you a hundred percent?" He paused, his coffee cup halfway to his lips.

"A bad guy took a shot at me," she tried to sound nonchalant.

"And missed, I hope!"

"Not quite. But luckily he didn't take out any vital organs," she tried to make light of it. "This is my first real assignment since coming back. Before this they had me shuffling papers."

"Considerate of them. But wouldn't an entirely different line of work have been more appropriate?" He was skirting close to danger and knew it when he saw the flash in her eyes.

Though gearing up to fire back, Dina was distracted by the arrival of a party of five at the adjacent table. She instantly recognized two of the men. One was the History Department Chairman, Sidney Lawrence, who had delivered Godfrey Mitchell's eulogy the previous day. The other she remembered from an article in the *New Haven Register* that week. He was Henry Stowe Wright, a Pulitzer Prize winning historian and a visiting Fellow. The third man was not familiar to her, neither were the two women. One was a mousy fifty-something who, judging by her possessive manner, was married to the third man. The fifth member of the party was a handsome woman in her forties, statuesque, with straight fair hair worn shoulder length. Her features were well-chiseled. Her manner somewhat aloof. She was dressed in a classic high-necked navy dress adorned with the inevitable pearls.

After being seated and having placed their orders for cocktails, the two women excused themselves and walked off in the direction of the restrooms. Curious to learn the latest campus gossip, Dina waited a minute before excusing herself and following suit. She let herself into the ladies' room quietly and began combing her hair at the vanity. The other two women were talking to each from behind closed stall doors.

"Why do you think Deirdre Lawrence didn't come tonight?" Came the first voice. "Do you think the rumors are true?"

"What rumors?" Was the noncommittal reply.

"You know, about Deirdre having had an affair with Godfrey Mitchell. Don't tell me you haven't heard?" The speaker continued without so much as taking a breath. "According to the rumor mill, the affair began when Sidney went to Africa this past summer."

This was the second time that someone had mentioned a Godfrey Mitchell/Deidre Lawrence affair. Did it have something to do with his murder? Or was it just a side issue? A red herring? Dina thought to herself.

"I've heard it," the reply was curt, inviting no further discussion.

"Well, do you think it's true, Augusta?" the other woman persisted.

"I really don't know, nor frankly care," came the response. "It's their business."

Augusta? Augusta Scott? How many Augustas could there be at Whitney. And did Augusta Scott really not care that Mitchell had been having an affair?

"I wouldn't be surprised if it was Sidney who killed Godfrey," the other woman continued, "and frankly, I wouldn't blame him if he did."

There was the sound of flushing water and a moment later one of the stall doors opened and one of the women came out. The tall elegant one. She hesitated a moment when she noticed Dina, then proceeded to the adjacent sink to wash her hands. Dina turned away from the mirror. If this was indeed Augusta Scott, she did not want to be recognized later. But instead of leaving, she went into the vacated stall.

"I wonder whether Deirdre suspects Sidney?" Came the insistent voice from behind the adjacent stall. "Imagine living with someone you think is a murderer!"

The other woman did not answer, "I'll see you at the table," she said and let herself out.

After the second woman left, Dina followed. And although nothing she had overheard confirmed the rumor linking Deirdre Lawrence and Godfrey Mitchell, it left open the possibility that Augusta Scott may have known about it. And did that mean anything? Scott seemed very close mouthed and Dina wondered how much she would be able to learn when they met. Absolutely nothing if Augusta Scott recognized her from the Faculty Club ladies' room.

Clive had settled the check by the time she came out, and was waiting with her coat. He helped her into it, his hands resting momentarily on her shoulders. She could feel the warmth of them through the fabric, uncomfortably intimate, almost a caress. And she wasn't sure how to discourage the intimacy without seeming rude. She and Clive were so much at odds on so many fronts that it made it convenient to deny an attraction on simply logical grounds. She should have denied it and would have denied it, if asked. Even to herself. Especially out of loyalty to Philip.

Outside, in contrast to her inner unease, a calm, frosty stillness had settled over the city. The paths that crisscrossed the New Haven Green were deserted. The historic churches, silent sentinels guarding the Green, stood dark and empty. The silence that hung in the air was palpable. And Clive's proximity was unnerving. Before he could say anything she was afraid to hear, she took a step away from him.

"Thank you for a lovely evening," her words sounded abrupt even to her ears.

"Where did you park?" He countered with icy politeness.

"Just down the street, not far," she put her hands in her pockets.

"I'll walk you."

"I'll be okay, thank you," she protested, knowing it would do no good.

"Don't give me that tough cop talk. I'm walking you to your car," he replied in a tone that brooked no argument. He did not take her arm. A fact for which she was at once grateful and chastened.

She had hurt his feelings by the curt farewell and she instantly regretted her brusqueness. Glancing at his profile, she noted the familiar obstinacy in the set of his jaw and fought the impulse to loop her arm through his. Instead they walked on in silence, their footsteps echoing forlornly behind them. When they reached her car, she turned to face him, her keys already in her hand. She did not want him to kiss her, but was oddly disappointed when he didn't.

"Good to see you again," he said formally, handing her into her car. "I'll be in touch before I leave Connecticut."

He waited dutifully at the curb till she had driven off, and she watched him in the rear- view mirror till his figure merged with the shadows and he was lost from sight.

11

THE BLACK LINCOLN DINA HAD SEEN LEAVING THE PARKING LOT ON
Dixwell Avenue belonged to Carmen Mendoza, a big-time drug
dealer. The authorities had been after him for years but, despite
several arrests, he always managed to walk. Smart lawyers and lack
of evidence were sufficient to spring him. With a chance to finally
nail the man, Lieutenant Gordon had summoned Edward Morrison
and Dina Barrett to Major Crime Squad headquarters in Meriden.
The three of them were seated in his office.

"Morrison, we need to be able to prove conclusively that Herman
Archer sold cocaine to a Whitney student. Can we?" Lieutenant
Gordon asked.

"I can testify to what I saw," Edward replied confidently, " And
I'm pretty certain we can get the student to spill his guts."

"What about physical evidence?"

"Archer walked away from Mendoza's car with a shoe box. And
he wasn't carrying shoes," Barrett added. "If we find the box and it
contains a controlled substance, or traces of a controlled substance,
we'll have Archer cold. I think he'll talk."

"That's my thinking too," Gordon nodded in agreement. "I've talked it over with the NHPD and we agree it's time to move in on Archer. I've already asked the court to swear out a search warrant for his apartment. We've got enough for probable cause,"

"If Archer's at home when the search is conducted, he might be able to tip off Mendoza," Edward frowned. "I think it should be carried out while he's on duty at the library. He doesn't have to be there if we have a warrant to raid the place. One of us can be in the library to keep an eye on him."

"Does he live alone?" Gordon asked.

"He does," Dina confirmed. "In a one-bedroom apartment."

"Not too many places one can stash coke in a one-bedroom apartment," Edward grinned.

"Okay, we'll conduct the search while Archer's at work in the library. Morrison, I want you to work with New Haven on this. Barrett, I want you to keep an eye on Archer in the library. If he makes any kind of a move call it in immediately. Do we know his hours?"

"We do. He works from nine to five and takes a one-hour lunch break from noon to one," Barrett answered, disappointed that she was stuck with the surveillance.

"All right. Thanks for coming in," Gordon signaled their dismissal. "And Detective Barrett, this is your top priority. I don't want you distracted by the Mitchell case."

As Dina had drawn the short straw, it was she who went to the Whitney library the next morning to keep an eye on Herman Archer while Edward and the NHPD searched the librarian's house. When she got to the library, Kelly Richmond was in her usual spot, her fair head bent over a book.

"How've you been?" Dina asked, shrugging off her backpack and taking off her coat.

"Fine," Kelly responded barely looking up from her book.

"Does that mean you've been assigned a new advisor?" Dina wasn't about to be put off by the other woman's monosyllabic answer.

"Yes. In fact I have a meeting scheduled with Professor Scott. She's offered to take me on."

"That's great news. I hope she treats her graduate students with more consideration than Godfrey Mitchell did."

"I understand she does," Kelly smiled. "At least she doesn't expect them to do her research for her. And she's a great resource."

"Sounds like an ideal arrangement. I hope it works out for you."

"So do I," Kelly pointedly picked up her book.

Dina got the hint but didn't take it. She wanted to keep the student talking. See what if anything she could find out. "It just so happens that I saw Augusta Scott yesterday. Or should I say, I eavesdropped on a conversation she was having. It was a juicy bit of gossip about Godfrey Mitchell and one of the faculty wives."

"Augusta doesn't strike me as a gossip," Kelly's voice was dismissive, flat and incurious.

"Well she didn't say much actually. It was the other woman who did the talking, and it was quite obvious her comments made Professor Scott uncomfortable. I had the impression that Augusta Scott doesn't like to encourage rumors."

"Who was the woman with Augusta?"

"I don't know. But according to her, Deirdre Lawrence was having an affair with Godfrey Mitchell.

"Really? That's a new one on me," the graduate student's interest had finally been piqued. No one is completely immune from discussing the latest scandal.

"Supposedly the affair began when Sidney Lawrence went to Africa last summer. The woman's theory was that when Lawrence found out about his wife's affair with Mitchell, he flipped and shot the man."

"Sounds like a pretty wild theory. Sidney Lawrence doesn't seem to be someone who'd lose his head and shoot someone," Kelly replied thoughtfully, as if mulling over the possibility and rejecting it. An overhead light reflected in the student's glasses making it difficult to read her expression.

"I thought it sounded pretty far-fetched myself. Especially given the glowing eulogy Lawrence gave at the Mitchell memorial service. It would be bizarre, to say the least, if he turned out to be the killer. A regular soap opera."

"You were at the memorial service? That was decent of you seeing you didn't really know Godfrey."

"I almost felt that I did. Thanks to you."

"We didn't exactly meet under pleasant circumstances, did we?" The comment was made without rancor as the graduate student picked up her book and smoothed the pages with the flat of both hands.

This time the gesture was unmistakable and Dina decided it was time to back off before her probing seemed obvious. "We should have coffee some time. Or tea. Can I have your phone number?"

"Of course, that would be nice," Kelly said politely, but without enthusiasm. Her thoughts had already returned to her book but she obligingly wrote her phone number on a note pad, tore off the page and handed it to Dina.

Meanwhile, Blaustein and Gardner had just been admitted to a home in Woodbridge, a western suburb of New Haven. It was a pleasant rather than imposing house on a treed lot in a well-to-do neighborhood. According to town records, the house was jointly owned by Sidney Lawrence and his wife Deirdre. Blaustein knew with some certainty by now hat the rumors concerning a relationship between Deirdre Lawrence and Godfrey Mitchell were true. The fingerprints on the glass found in the murdered man's kitchen belonged to the professor's wife. During a campus sit-in when she was a student, she had been arrested and her fingerprints were still on file.

"Thank you for agreeing to see us," Blaustein said as Deidre Lawrence showed them into the living room.

As expected, given Godfrey Mitchell's proclivities, Mrs. Lawrence was an attractive woman. But having met the stylish Alison Mitchell and the statuesque Augusta Scott, Blaustein had pictured someone cast in the same mold. Surprisingly, Deidre Lawrence turned out to be quite different. She was tiny, with a neat little figure, a youthful, pretty face and flyaway auburn hair that matched her eyes. She was dressed in a brown sweater with a cowl collar, a brown and gray plaid skirt and low-heeled loafers.

"Please sit down," she said with what Blaustein detected as a discernible Southern accent: elongated vowels and lazy consonants.

"May I get you some coffee?" She was clearly nervous.

"Coffee would be nice," Blaustein acquiesced, taking a seat on the sofa beside Gardner.

He didn't really want coffee, but sensed that playing hostess would put the woman at ease. Absenting herself, she went to the kitchen where, to the sounds of tinkling china and a gurgling percolator, she busied herself preparing the brew. When she returned, carrying a tray, her face seemed unnaturally pale and she was obviously trying hard to appear calm. But her hands gave her away. They trembled as she decanted the coffee. And the elegant china cups rattled in their matching saucers as she passed them to the two policemen.

"Mrs. Lawrence, we're here in connection with the Godfrey Mitchell case," Blaustein began, "But you probably already guessed that."

She nodded numbly.

"Could you describe your relationship with Professor Mitchell," Blaustein added sugar to his coffee and stirred.

"You probably already know or you wouldn't be here."

"That may well be, but we'd rather hear about it from you," Blaustein said as politely as possible. "We really don't wish to embarrass you, but we need your answers to a few questions."

"I admit I had a relationship with Godfrey," her voice was barely audible, and looking down at her hands, she twisted her wedding and engagement rings as if to underscore her sense of shame.

"When did you first start seeing him?" The poor woman was

so close to tears that Blaustein felt almost guilty having to pose the question. They already had proof of the liaison because of Deidre Lawrence's fingerprints on the glass found in Mitchell's house but he wanted to gauge her reaction to the question.

"This past summer," she said shamefacedly. "While Sidney was away in Africa."

"Does your husband know about the relationship?"

Deidre nodded her affirmation.

"When did he find out?"

"In September, after he got back."

"What was your husband's reaction when he found out?" Blaustein willed her to look at him. "Was he very angry?"

"More hurt than angry," she said defensively, looking at him directly for the first time.

"And did you end the relationship after he found out about it?" Blaustein sipped his coffee, observing that Deirdre had barely touched hers.

"I said I would... but I didn't. I wish I had." She shook her head, looking down at her hands, again twisting her rings. "It's not that I loved Godfrey. And I knew he didn't love me. I also knew that sooner or later our relationship would run its course and he'd tire of me. But it was like an addiction. I just couldn't quit cold turkey. I rationalized that it didn't really matter much to Sidney anyway," she admitted, her voice catching. "Our marriage has always been a pretty one-sided affair. I was the one who made it work. With Sidney work always comes first. He loves his work with much more passion than he loves me. He treats me like a pair of old sneakers. I make his life comfortable. It's convenient to have me around. But that kind of relationship wasn't enough for me any more. I was bored and tired of playing second fiddle to the research project of the moment. That's when Godfrey happened to come along," she said looking up at Blaustein, her amber eyes shiny with unshed tears. "I know that's a poor excuse."

Blaustein, thinking she didn't look anything like a pair of old sneakers, bored in on her with his next question. "Did your husband know you were still seeing Professor Mitchell?"

"I don't know," she looked miserable.

"If he knew, would he have confronted Professor Mitchell?"

"If you think Sidney had anything to do with Godfrey's death, you're wrong!" She sat ramrod straight, her chin tilted upward, her mouth set in a determined line. "Perhaps I shouldn't be talking to you."

"Mrs. Lawrence, right now we're less interested in your husband than we are in you. We believe you to be, at the very least, a material witness."

"I?" Her face grew even paler than before, her eyes widening with apprehension.

"We have evidence that proves you were in the house just prior to Professor Mitchell's death."

"How could you possibly know if I was there? Or when?" Her voice trailed off helplessly.

"Ma'am, we found your fingerprints. And we can also prove you were in Mitchell's house with DNA tests."

"DNA?"

"Genetic fingerprinting."

"Detective, I know what DNA is."

"Then you also probably know that we can test evidence recovered from the victim's bedroom to prove that you were in his bed just prior to his death." He did not mention that he would need a court order to get a DNA sample if she did not cooperate. He was hoping for voluntary cooperation so that neither a DNA test nor a court order would be necessary.

"Just prior?" She echoed, her voice barely audible.

"Yes, immediately prior to his death," he held her gaze, his meaning clear, his words ominous and his voice stern. But she looked so distraught, he regretted having to play the heavy.

"Alright, I was in his house," she admitted after a pause, squaring her shoulders and looking frankly from one detective to the other. "But I didn't kill him, if that's what you think."

"We're not saying that you killed him," Gardener soothed. "We just think you can help us find out who did."

"I'd like to help. I really would. But I haven't a clue who killed him and I honestly don't know anything that would shed any light. Truly, he was alive when I left his house."

"For the record, when was the last time you saw the professor?" Blaustein continued.

"On December 27th. He was leaving for Atlanta that day and I went to say good bye." Tears came to her eyes and she wiped them away with a forefinger.

Blaustein gave her a moment to recover before asking his next question. "Did you see anyone besides the professor while you were there?"

"As I drew up to the house, I saw his cleaning lady come out the front door. I waited till she had driven off before I went in." She had the grace to blush.

"Was the house locked when you arrived?"

"No, the door was unlatched. I rang the bell and went in."

"About what time of day was that?"

"A little after one," her hand shook as she put down her coffee cup, rattling it in its saucer.

"And you left when?"

"I don't know exactly, around two I think."

Just enough time for a quickie, Blaustein thought remembering the rumpled bed in the master bedroom. But he didn't pursue the matter. He didn't need to. If needed in court the pubic hair recovered from between the sheets would provide the proof that she had been there. But they still had no proof that it was she who pulled the trigger. And they had nothing else on her, certainly no obvious motive. No evidence of a lover's quarrel. Not a shred of evidence that she had been in his study. Besides, there was a guilelessness about her that made him want to believe she was innocent even though Blaustein knew that both distress and guilelessness could be faked. The book on Deirdre Lawrence would have to be kept open even if gut instinct told him the pages would be blank. With this in mind, he observed her closely as Gardner continued the questioning.

"Did you see anyone else besides Godfrey Mitchell while you were there?"

She shook her head, making her curls bounce, "No one."

"How about when you left? Did you notice any cars parked out front?"

She shook her head again.

"How about delivery vans or pedestrians?"

Again she shook her head, "Not that I noticed."

"What about phone calls? Did Professor Mitchell make or receive any while you were there?"

"I don't really remember, but I don't think so."

Gardner looked at Blaustein. "Do you have any additional questions you'd like to ask, Detective Blaustein?"

"Just a couple. Mrs. Lawrence, did Professor Mitchell say anything at all to you about having enemies or about threats to his safety?"

"That day?"

"That day or at any other time."

She took a moment to answer. "He was fond of saying that his colleagues in the Department were 'hyenas' just itching to tear into his carcass. But I don't think he considered them a physical threat," she paused. "You don't think one of them could have ... ?"

Instead of answering her, Blaustein followed up with a second question. "What about his ex-wife Alison? Do you know what their relationship was like?"

"They hated each other," she smiled a small, knowing smile.

"Is that what he told you?"

"Only indirectly. But I could tell from the little things he said."

Blaustein watched her as she spoke, trying to decide whether she was as innocent as she looked. He did not want to eliminate the possibility that Mitchell may have decided to dump the enchanting little Mrs. Lawrence and that she shot him in the heat of the moment. But this murder did not have the hallmarks of a crime of passion. Everything about the crime scene pointed to cold premeditation. Whoever killed Godfrey Mitchell had left the study sanitized.

Mitchell's were the only fingerprints on the gun. The powder stains on the victim's right hand and his fingerprints on the gun could have been staged to imply a suicide. And though the message left on the computer could have been the final words of a penitent, anyone could have written them. But none of this seemed consistent with an individual who had carelessly left fingerprints on the glass found in the kitchen sink. He decided to switch tracks.

"Are you personally acquainted with Alison Mitchell?"

"I met her for the first time at the memorial service. The Mitchells divorced the year before Sidney and I came to Whitney."

"So you don't know for a fact that Alison and her husband hated each other," Blaustein was nothing if not persistent.

"Just from his reaction to her phone calls," her lip curled. "She always said something to annoy the hell out of him."

"You were in the room when she called?"

"A few times."

"And the phone calls were about what?"

"Money. Always about money. Her alimony check was late, or didn't meet her expenses, something like that." She shrugged expressively and as if to underscore the point added, "I wouldn't mind having some of her expenses!"

"Like what?"

"Like escaping to Sint Maarten for months on end each winter. Like a beach house on the Outer Banks every summer. Like driving a Mercedes. I could go on."

"The lady has a tough life," Blaustein acknowledged with a raised eyebrow. "Do you know whether she has any other sources of income?"

"You mean other than alimony? No, I don't really know," she shrugged.

Blaustein nodded at Gardner and the latter took up the questioning, "What was Mitchell's reaction to his ex-wife when she called to complain about money?"

"Polite. He was always under control."

"I suppose he would be in front of you," Blaustein interjected.

"Do you think he might have reacted differently if you weren't there?"

"He might have. But I don't think he would have. He resented being pressured but I don't think money mattered a great deal to Godfrey."

No, it wouldn't have, Blaustein thought. From all accounts, Mitchell was more concerned about his reputation, his image, and his libido. A few more questions convinced him they had learned all they could from Deirdre Lawrence. But for now he still could not rule out either Deidre or her husband as suspects. He signaled his partner and the pair rose. "Thank you for your time and for the coffee," Gardner said as they left.

12

"I JUST CHECKED THE MAJOR AIRLINES THAT SERVE SINT MAARTEN. They have no record of Alison Mitchell on any flight either entering or leaving the States during the time in question. But that doesn't exclude the possibility that she did. There are puddle jumpers that will fly you just about anywhere in the Caribbean, and there's no way to check them all," Blaustein told Gardener while they were on their lunch break, eating Chinese takeout at their desks.

"So, Alison Mitchell could have come back to the States. Done her ex. Returned to Sint Maarten and it would not have shown on her passport?" Gardner said between mouthfuls of Lo Mein.

"Somehow I have trouble believing Mrs. Mitchell killed her ex. For starters, I don't think she had sufficient motive. She couldn't have been sure that she would benefit from his will."

"Even if she suspected that she might inherit a bundle, do you see her sneaking to and from the Caribbean and risking being caught doing so? Uh uh." Gardner scooped the last of the Lo Mein from the carton.

"On the other hand, we *are* talking about quite a lot of money.

His books are still on the best seller's list and he had a movie in the works. If she'd known she was in line to get a share of his royalties it would have been a pretty powerful motive," Blaustein tore open a fortune cookie, discarding the fortune without reading it, and popping the cookie in his mouth.

"Perhaps she was still sore that he cheated on her?"

"Not after all this time. Passions fade. Greed is something else."

"So let's check out her alibi."

"Do you think Gordon will okay a trip to Sint Maarten? It's bound to be nice this time of year," Blaustein grinned.

"Dream on."

Of course Joe Gordon nixed the idea of traveling to Sint Maarten. So instead of experiencing first hand the undulating hills, sparkling white sands, gently waving palm trees and rolling surf, Blaustein had to content himself with a long-distance telephone call and flipping through travel brochures. While waiting for his call to go through, he read about the island's premier hotel, The Prince of Orange which offered luxurious accommodations, a private beach, fine dining and excellent service. It was where Alison Mitchell was renting an ocean front suite: further proof that Alison Mitchell liked indulging in the finer things.

Fortunately, the hotel manager spoke excellent English, "Yes, Mrs. Mitchell has a suite here," he confirmed. "She is in the States at the moment, but we are expecting her back. Would you care to leave a message?"

"Actually, I'd like to ask you a few questions, if I may. My name is Jackson Blaustein, I am a detective with the Connecticut Major Crime Squad. If you've checked your fax machine recently, you should have received a communication from the Police Department in Philipsburg. It will have authenticated my identity. I am investigating the death of Mrs. Mitchell's ex-husband, and I have a few questions."

He waited for the manager to retrieve the fax.

"I'm convinced you are who you say you are, but that doesn't alter the fact that I really would prefer not to discuss our hotel guests," the manager protested primly.

"I won't ask you to," Blaustein assured him. "I would merely like you to tell me whether or not Mrs. Mitchell was registered at your hotel this past December."

"She's booked in here for the entire winter season, but I'll check the December guest list if you like." There was a resigned sigh and a rustle of pages.

Blaustein could tell this wasn't going to be easy, "Just tell me whether she was away at all toward the end of December?"

"She did not check out at any time in December." The iciness at the end of the line was as frosty as the bleak winter landscape outside Blaustein's window.

"Maybe she didn't check out, but she may have taken off for a few days without actually checking out. If so, your cleaning crew may have noticed that her linens didn't need changing for a few days," Blaustein wasn't going to let him off the hook too easily.

"They might," the manager conceded.

"Would you check with the housekeeper please and then call me back collect?" Blaustein provided the number. "I'll wait at my desk for your call."

If Blaustein were a betting man, he would not have laid odds against a return call. But there was one, about half an hour later.

"The housekeeper believes that except for right now, when Mrs. Mitchell left to attend her ex-husband's funeral, her suite has been in daily use since she checked in at the start of the season," the manager said, sounding smug.

"Believes? But she isn't sure?" Blaustein wasn't giving up yet.

"Detective," the manager replied, adding a much-put-upon sigh, "our busiest time is over the Christmas holidays. We hire extra help, most of whom we have since let go. If on any particular day or days in December there was no need to change the linens in Mrs. Mitchell's suite, then no one on our present staff remembers it."

So that was that. No point in beating a dead horse.

After he hung up, Blaustein flipped through the financial report on Alison Mitchell. It made for interesting reading. According to the terms of the divorce settlement, Alison received generous alimony and child support payments. She had acquired outright ownership of the couple's unencumbered beach houses in North Carolina and Florida (pieces of property Godfrey had inherited from his father), and half the couple's joint savings and investments which at the time of the divorce were relatively modest because Godfrey had not yet exploded onto the *New York Times* best seller's list. The money the professor inherited from his father had been placed in trust for Brian. Godfrey was left with the house in Chisholm and what remained of his Whitney salary. Apparently he had paid dearly for his roll in the hay with Jillian Davis. In fact, if he hadn't struck literary gold he might have had a lean time of it.

Alison on the other hand looked like a winner. Besides monthly alimony checks, she had an additional, if somewhat irregular, source of income from freelance articles she published in one of the more up-scale fashion magazines. She had the proceeds from the Florida beach house which she sold for a handsome profit shortly after the divorce. And when her father died a couple of years later, she inherited a sizable amount in tax-free bonds. Cumulatively, all this should have kept the wolf from the door quite nicely, thank you. But apparently it hadn't. Alison Mitchell's cash reserves were negligible. The bonds inherited from her father had been cashed in over the years and most of the money from the Florida property was gone. Relying almost entirely on her monthly check from Godfrey, she barely had sufficient income to cover her considerable expenses. So where had all the money gone? And could this relative penury be a reason to kill her ex-husband?

Digging into Alison's bank records next, Blaustein picked up on the fact that the Professor's ex-wife frequently made sizable cash withdrawals from her checking account, odd amounts at odd times. Did this mean an expensive drug habit? He thought back to when he and Gardner interviewed her but could not remember noticing any of the usual symptoms he associated with addiction. True he had not been looking for them. So perhaps it was time to pay the lady a return visit. Acting on this conclusion he dialed the Savoy Hotel half-expecting her to have flown the coop but to his relief the receptionist at the hotel assured him otherwise.

"Yes Mrs. Mitchell is registered here," he said. "Would you like me to put you through to her room'?"

When Alison Mitchell answered at the other end, Blaustein muttered something about a wrong number and hung up. The best way to catch her, he figured, was unawares. Without any real plan in mind, he grabbed his overcoat and left for downtown New Haven. There, as usual, parking was at a premium. He found a metered spot near the hotel put a police sign on the dash and went inside.

"I'll be with you in a minute, Sir." The uniformed clerk at the front desk told him, briefly covering the mouthpiece of the telephone. "Garage? Will you have the valet bring Mrs. Mitchell's car to the front please." The clerk put down the receiver and turned to address Blaustein.

But Blaustein had already left. If Mrs. Mitchell was going somewhere, he wanted to find out where that was. He returned to his car and pulled up to the curb in the front of the hotel. From there he had a good view of the garage exit. After a couple of minutes, a white Lexus was driven down the ramp of the garage and into the circle in front of the hotel. The driver's side door opened and a parking valet got out. He waited at attention until the glass doors of the hotel opened and a mink-wrapped Alison Mitchell came out. Handing her the keys with a slight bow, the valet ushered her smartly into the car. She gave him a tip. He closed the car door. And she drove off.

Blaustein followed at a distance as the white Lexus made for the northbound lanes of Interstate 95. She was driving fast. He hoped not so fast that she would attract the attention of a State Trooper. Keeping a couple of cars behind her, he followed as she crossed the Quinnipiac River Bridge and passed the shoreline towns of Branford, Guilford, Madison and Clinton. At Old Saybrook, she crossed the Connecticut River, slowed briefly for a right lane closure and then kept on going. By now Blaustein was beginning to have an inkling as to where she was headed. The inkling turned into certainty when the

Lexus turned north on Route 2A, the road that led to the Mohegan Sun Casino. Could it be that the lady had a gambling problem?

Blaustein did not gamble. One gambler in the family was enough. His Uncle Maurice, with a thing for the Atlantic City tables and also a weakness for the ponies, always expected to have a winner with the next hand or on the next race. He seldom if ever did. Uncle Mo had made and lost a fortune. He was a salutary example. But Blaustein could understand the lure: the inability to resist just one more chance with a one-armed bandit that seldom paid out, or one last bet on a sure-fire winner that never won. Was that Alison Mitchell's problem? Could it be that she had gambled away a fortune? Could gambling debts be a motive for murder? He watched from a distance as she drove up to the Casino of the Sky and left her car with a valet. Hoping that he would not lose her, Blaustein parked as close to the entrance as he could, and prepared to follow.

But he paused as he crossed the parking lot, slowed by a flood of memories. All bad ones. This was the precise spot where Dina had been shot. Caught in a tangled web of recollection, he could almost hear the sound of a gun being fired and see his partner as she slumped to the ground. They had been on surveillance that night and were just coming off duty. Dina, ahead of him by a few yards, was unlocking their unmarked car when the shot rang out. Instinctively unholstering his gun, keeping low and dodging behind parked cars, he had raced to her side.

"I'm okay," she gasped.

But he could see she was not. Dragging her out of the line of fire, he propped her up against the front wheel of the nearest car, fumbled for his cell phone and called in an emergency crew.

"Officer down! Officer down!" He uttered words no cop ever wanted to say. He gave their location. Left the line open. And crouching over his recumbent partner, stood guard.

After an ominous silence, he heard a noise over to his left. Scooting forward gun in hand, he poked his head around the front of the car. It was enough to cause a flurry of gunfire from what sounded like a semiautomatic. But it was also just sufficient to give away the position of the stalker: the man they had been trying to nail for weeks. Jackson aimed in the direction of the gunfire and fired a single shot into the semi-darkness. His shot missed, ricocheted off someone's hapless car and provoked another volley aimed in his direction. He still had bullets left in his chamber and there was also Dina's gun. But he was clearly out-gunned. Meanwhile next to him, Dina was silent, a blood stain soaking through her jacket. Where was the ambulance? Where was the back up? Why were they taking so damn long? He had lost a partner once and was determined not to let it happen again. He'd turn in his badge first. So with gun cocked, he inched forward again.

"Peek-a-boo." Came a taunting voice from behind him.

Spinning around he saw the barrel of a gun leveled at him and he fired instinctively, not missing this time. A lucky shot? Yes. But it was the taunt that had saved him. Saved him and saved his partner. It had given him the fraction of a second he needed to turn and fire before his opponent could get off a shot. If the man had resisted the impulse to gloat, he could have shot him in the back and killed them both.

Shaking off the memory that still haunted him on nights he could not sleep, Blaustein crossed the parking lot in pursuit of Alison Mitchell. Welcomed by a blast of warm air and the pervasive ringing of slot machines, he entered the casino. Alison Mitchell's mink coat was just disappearing past the martini bar. He followed in her wake, past the upscale stores and past a bank of ATMs. Clearly, she had a goal in mind. And her destination turned out to be a high stakes gaming table. Minimum bet $500.00. After checking her mink, and being escorted to an empty seat at a black jack table, she placed an order with a cocktail waitress clad in a sexy adaptation of Native American apparel, and got down to serious business. Baustein stayed just long enough to know that Mrs. Alison Mitchell was not a novice at the game. She studied her cards and when she bets, she bets big.

On his way out of the casino Blaustein was recognized by an off-duty State Trooper.

"The Major Crime Squad here for some reason I don't know about?" The trooper asked.

"Just checking on a potential suspect who seems to have a gambling habit. The woman at the $500.00 table over there," Blaustein nodded in Alison Mitchell's direction.

"Want me to keep an eye on her?"

"It's probably not necessary, but if you happen to still be around and something unusual strikes you, give me a call." They exchanged phone numbers, shook hands and Blaustein left.

While Blaustein was checking on Alison Mitchell, Gardner was checking out her son's alibi. Predictably, Lieutenant Gordon had been far more accommodating when it came to sending one of his detectives on a four-hour drive to nearby Vermont than he had been to the suggestion that they fly to Sint Maarten. In this case Gardner drew the short straw. He got the Vermont assignment. Bemoaning his bad luck, Huey stopped to pick up a newspaper, donuts and a thermos of coffee, then made for the highway. He had set off early enough to dodge Hartford's morning rush hour but did not manage to avoid rush hour gridlock when he hit Springfield some thirty minutes to the north. After that, the traffic thinned and it was a straight run. Perhaps too much of a straight run, he was stopped for speeding by a trooper just before reaching the Massachusetts–Vermont border.

"I should throw the book at you," the trooper said when Gardner flashed his badge. But brotherhood prevailed and he sent Gardner on his way with only a caution.

By the time he reached the Alpen Lodge where Brian Mitchell claimed to have stayed after leaving his father's house, Gardner's thermos of coffee was empty, his donuts were long gone, and lunch had become his first priority. He made for the Lodge restaurant, the decor of which was predictable given the name of the place: pine floors, exposed post and beam construction, solid wooden tables, Swiss-style chairs with daisies painted on them and leaded casement windows that overlooked the ski slopes. A welcoming fire glowed in the large stone fireplace. And the waitresses were all dressed to look like Heidi.

Gardner had his choice of tables. Except for him the place was empty. He selected a spot by a window and took off his coat and muffler.

"It's such a heavenly day. Everyone is out on the slopes," the waitress explained. "We'll probably get a rush later on."

Ignoring his waistline and his conscience, Gardner ordered meat loaf with mashed potatoes and gravy. He said 'yes' to coffee and worked *The Hartford Courant* crossword while waiting for his order. When his meal arrived, he did ample justice to his meat and potatoes and had to resist the temptation to mop up the gravy with a slice of bread. After he had settled his check, Gardner strolled over to the registration desk. By this time the foyer was swarming with skiers in bright parkas, sun-kissed faces and plenty of noisy *bon homie*.

"I wonder if you can help me?" He asked over the din.

"Certainly, Sir," the clerk smiled pleasantly.

"I'd like to verify that a Brian Mitchell checked in here on December 27?" Gardner produced his badge.

The clerk's smile disappeared but he obligingly checked his computer. "Yes, Mr. Mitchell checked in on December 27 and checked out again on the 30th."

"Do you happen to know at what time he checked in?"

"At two p.m. Sir."

"Would you mind printing that out for me?"

By checking in at two p.m., Brian Mitchell could automatically be eliminated from the list of suspects. It was a four-hour drive from Connecticut to the Alpen Lodge. Gardner had just timed it himself. Ada Jennings had seen Brian leave his father's house at ten and Deirdre Lawrence had left around one. So there was no way Brian could have slipped back into the house, killed his father and arrived at the ski lodge by two. Whoever was guilty of killing Godfrey Mitchell, it could not have been his son and heir.

While still in Vermont, Gardner had planned to question Jillian Davis, the student who had been Brian's baby-sitter and the proximate reason for his parents' divorce. She now lived and taught school in Vermont and it had been relatively easy locating her. By prearrangement, Huey Gardner and Jillian Davis were to meet at a coffee shop after school got out.

Mitchell's former student and a male companion were already seated when a slightly windblown Gardner arrived. He went straight to their table and they rose in unison when he approached.

"Detective Gardner, Connecticut Major Crime Squad," he said, extending his hand in greeting.

"Jillian Davis," she confirmed. She was fair-haired, very pretty, wore a diamond engagement ring on her left hand and dimpled when she smiled. "This is my fiancé Adrian Hughes. I brought him along for moral support, I hope you don't mind. He knows all about me and the Mitchells."

"Not at all," Gardner replied as they shook hands and sat down. He cleared his throat. "As I told you when I called, I'm working on the Godfrey Mitchell case."

"Yes," came the monosyllabic reply. But Gardner noticed that her face clouded over when she said it.

After they had ordered coffee and declined anything to go with it, Jillian Davis told the Connecticut detective about the time Alison Mitchell found her in bed with her husband.

"I never saw Professor Mitchell after that dreadful day. And at the end of the semester, I transferred out of Whitney. I just couldn't bear to stay there after what had happened. At first I was in denial. I blamed it all on Professor Mitchell. For coming onto me in the first place. For cheating on his wife. For taking me upstairs to his bedroom when I was supposed to be babysitting Brian. For making me feel dirty and ashamed. And for the humiliation of being discovered in his bed. Then, when I heard that Professor Mitchell and his wife were getting a divorce, I started blaming myself. I went on a major guilt trip. I could have said 'no'. I should have said 'no'. But I hadn't said 'no'. To be honest, I was so flattered by his attentions and so swept off my feet that I didn't say 'no'. That made me just as guilty as he was." She took a sip of her coffee before continuing.

"I never told my parents why I wanted to transfer. I was far too embarrassed. Instead I made up a cock-and-bull story about preferring the countryside to the city. I finished my degree at Dartmouth and went on to get a Master's in Education from the University of Massachusetts. So, after a few years, I was able to put the whole nasty incident behind me. Till now. Godfrey Mitchell's murder has brought it all back." She shivered involuntarily. "Except for Adrian and now you, I've never told a living soul about the sorry affair." She reached across the table and patted her fiancé's hand.

"So you haven't seen any of the Mitchells since that incident?" Gardner asked, signaling the waitress for another cup of coffee.

"Actually we saw Brian quite recently. Remember Adrian?"

He nodded his acquiescence.

"Do you happen to remember when and where it was that you saw Brian?"

"It was up at the Alpen Lodge, not far from here. Do you know it?"

"I do." Of course, Gardner knew exactly where it was.

"I'm not sure precisely when it was that we saw him. We spend a lot of our weekends up there. Do you remember, Darling?"

"We went there the day after Christmas and stayed till New Year's eve. Remember how awful the weather was?"

"Yes, it was miserable," she confirmed with a frown.

It also confirmed that, even had she been a suspect in the death of Godfrey Mitchell, just after Christmas Jillian Davis was nowhere near the Mitchell house.

"Did Brian say anything to you on that occasion?"

"We never spoke. Once I realized he was there, I made a point of avoiding him. It wasn't difficult. He stayed only a couple of days. Probably because the weather was so bad. It kept all the skiers indoors. Brian and his friends spent most of the time playing pool. So it was easy to keep out of his way. We simply avoided the pool room."

"Why did you think it was necessary to avoid Brian?"

"Adrian's been trying to persuade me to file a suit against Mitchell."

148

"I think that predators like Mitchell should not be allowed to get away with it," her fiancé volunteered.

"Adrian does legal work for a child advocacy group in Vermont," Jillian explained, "and when I told him about my experience, his second reaction, after his concern for me, was to consider filing a sexual harassment suit that would stop Mitchell from exploiting other young women."

"Have you gone ahead with the suit?" Gardner asked.

"Actually, no," Adrian shook his head. "Jillian was dead set against it."

"Maybe it was selfish of me but I didn't want to relive the worst experience of my life. I didn't have the courage to go through it again. And now that Mitchell is dead, obviously it's a moot point."

After crossing the Vermont-Massachusetts border on his way back to Connecticut, Gardner detoured into Amherst. He left the highway behind him and descended into the Pioneer Valley. Proceeding past flat alluvial farmland that lay fallow beneath a layer of melting snow, closed-for-the-season farm stalls and cheaper-than-Connecticut gas stations, he came to the outskirts of Amherst and the sprawling campus of the University of Massachusetts. There he planned to interrogate Daniels, the graduate student who had charged Mitchell with plagiarism. Abandoning his car in the visitors' parking lot, he stopped to ask a passing student for directions to the History Department and then headed toward it across the windswept campus.

Daniels' office door was open when he arrived, and he rapped on the jamb.

"Come in," Daniels called, looking up from behind his desk.

"Detective Gardner. I phoned." He said by way of introduction.

"Yes, please come in," Daniels rose and solemnly presented Gardner with a large freckled hand. He was a man of perhaps thirty, tall and angular, with bony wrists that jutted out of his sleeves, straight red hair that was thinning on top, and a prominent nose topped by horn-rimmed glasses.

"You wanted to talk to me about Godfrey Mitchell. But if you're looking for a testimonial you won't get it," Daniels said bluntly when they were both seated.

"No testimonials necessary. Just anything you can tell us that helps to find his killer."

"You mean whoever it was who finally did the world a favor?" Daniels permitted himself a sardonic grin.

"You were a graduate assistant of his at Whitney?" Gardner chose to ignore the remark.

"More like his drudge," Daniels conceded, the bitterness in his voice evident. "While I was his graduate assistant, I spent most of my time doing research for him but never got any credit for it. No academic credit and no acknowledgment when his book was finally published. It made me pretty mad. Mad enough to try and expose him with a letter to the student newspaper, but not mad enough to kill him ten years later, if that's what you think." Daniels drummed the fingers of his large freckled hand on the desk and his eyes challenged Gardner from behind his thick-lensed glasses.

"You're not being accused of anything. And we are aware of your charge of plagiarism."

"Yes, that's what I accused him of: plagiarism." One reddish eyebrow raised itself above the rim of his spectacles.

"It was a gutsy move."

"Gutsy maybe. Foolish, most definitely. I was the one who left Whitney with my tail between my legs. Mitchell went on to make a fortune off the book. That's justice for you," he sighed. "But I didn't try to mete out retroactive vengeance myself. Not now and not then. Though I admit, I may have been tempted when it all happened."

"Sounds like you still resent him. Do you?"

"Look, if I'm being accused of something, come right out and say it," Daniels challenged, his face reddening and his body tensing.

"No one's accusing you. It's routine to question everyone who knew the victim."

"What exactly is it you're looking for?" Daniels still sounded wary, scarcely mollified, but obviously itching to unload on Mitchell.

"There are a whole lot of people who thought the bastard had it coming."

"People he exploited?"

"The exploitation, was professional as well as sexual. It came with the territory as you'll find if you check with Godfrey Mitchell's students and former students." Some of the wariness had evaporated.

"Can you tell me what you know about his relations with his female students? I gather he had something of a reputation where women were concerned."

"You've got that right. Godfrey Mitchell had female students begging for him to get into their pants," he reddened slightly. "I don't mean to be offensive, but you get my meaning."

"No need to apologize. When one's looking for a motive one ends up digging up a lot of dirt. Besides, what you said confirms what we've already heard about him. But particulars would help, if you can recall anything."

"Well, Mitchell was either very careful, very lucky, or both. So I can't name you any names." He paused, as if searching his memory. "Except one, that is. I was personally involved in an incident during my last year at Whitney."

"That would be about ten years ago?" Gardener figured he knew what was coming.

"Yes. I went to his house one day to drop off some research. I had just arrived when his wife drove up. So instead of ringing the doorbell, I waited on the front steps for her and we went inside together. When Mitchell wasn't downstairs, she went upstairs to get him and I waited in the hall. Next thing I knew, I heard the Mitchells screaming at each other. I can tell you that it made me pretty uncomfortable. I didn't want to be there with a family fight going on, but because he was expecting me, I waited. I didn't know what else to do. Then, while all the ruckus was going on upstairs, I saw one of Godfrey's undergraduates come running down the stairs. Her shirt was unbuttoned and she was carrying her shoes."

"Did you recognize her?"

"I did. Her name was Jillian Davis. She was a junior in Godfreys survey class and I tutored her in one of his seminars. Nice looking kid, blonde, pert, a cheerleader type. She rushed right by me as if I wasn't there, burst out of the front door and then just stood there in her bare feet. I could tell she was wondering how she would get back to Whitney. Mitchell must have driven her to his house because his was the only car in the driveway when I got there and his place was about ten miles from campus. Anyway, the Professor and his Mrs. were still going at it upstairs, so I decided not to stick around. I dropped my research info on the coffee table and drove Jillian back to campus."

"Did she discuss the incident with you?"

"No, but she didn't have to. It was all pretty obvious what had happened. And, anyway, she was too shaken up to talk. She just sat there and cried the whole way back to New Haven."

"Do you know what happened to her after that?"

"She left Whitney. I don't know if she managed to finish the semester."

"Did either of the Mitchells ever say anything to you about the incident?"

"Alison did. She called me the next day to say she was getting a divorce and asked me if I would be willing to testify, if necessary."

"What did you say?"

"Even though I sympathized with her, I said 'no'. I was getting to the breaking point with Godfrey myself, and I didn't think getting mixed up in his messy divorce would help any. As it was, Godfrey didn't like the fact that I'd been there and had witnessed the whole sordid mess. The next time I saw him, he was short with me. And a bit later, when I asked for an acknowledgment in his upcoming publication, he acted as if I were using the incident to blackmail him. He not only turned me down flat, he threatened to destroy me. That's when I decided to destroy him first. I accused him of plagiarism in an open letter to the Whitney Student News." He shrugged. "You probably know the rest."

Gardner nodded. "Probably, but give me the details any way."

"Nothing much left to tell. He turned the tables on me. I couldn't get anyone to back me up. His other grad students, people I thought were my friends, were all more interested in covering their asses. No one agreed to testify for me. In the hearing that was held on campus, Mitchell made me look like a disgruntled student with an axe to grind. He emerged from the hearing without a mark on him. And I was dead meat as far as Whitney was concerned. So I transferred my credits to U. Mass. and finished up my doctorate here. A U.Mass. Ph.D. doesn't have as much cachet as a Whitney degree, but I liked the atmosphere here. They have a great faculty and there's less academic cannibalism. Besides, I lucked into an Assistant Professorship after I graduated and this is a great place to stick around. Coming here was like getting to the promised land. Godfrey Mitchell actually did me a favor. So you see, Detective, I didn't have a reason to kill the old bastard. Though I'd be a hypocrite if I were to say I was sorry someone did. End of story as far as I'm concerned." He leaned back in his chair, his eyes still alert, watching the detective's reaction from behind his horn-rimmed glasses.

"One last question," Gardner hesitated for a fraction of a second before asking it, knowing what Daniels' reaction would be. "Where were you in the days immediately following Christmas?"

Daniels did not move but his body tensed, his hands fisted and his knuckles whitened. "I was here. Alone. And no, I do not have a corroborating witness. But not having an airtight alibi doesn't make me guilty of anything, does it? I didn't kill Mitchell, Detective. And I don't know who did."

"You've filled in the picture for me nicely, thank you," Gardner got up and prepared to leave. "Please call me if you think of anything else." He took a card from his wallet and handed it to Daniels. "Don't get up. I'll see myself out."

13

"COME IN I'VE BEEN EXPECTING YOU," THE WOMAN WHO OPENED THE
door after Blaustein and Gardner had flashed their identification was
heavy-boned, solid rather than fat, ruddy complexioned and red
haired. Below pale eyebrows, white lashes fringed her pale green
eyes. She was dressed in a beige fisherman's knit sweater, practical
brown corduroy pants and brown leather Birkenstocks.

"Then you know why we're here, I take it?" Blaustein said when
they were seated in the living room.

"Godfrey Mitchell," Heather Leopold acknowledged with a
shrug. "It doesn't take a rocket scientist to figure out that sooner or
later you'd want to question his former graduate students. Especially
me. I was his factotum for eight years. And everyone knew I resented
him. I made no secret of it. But I didn't resent him enough to kill
him, honest," she raised both hands in mock surrender. "If I'd wanted
to do him in, I would have done it years ago."

"I understand you graduated this past May and that you're on
the faculty at City College in New York," Blaustein didn't bother

mentioning that he had earned a degree from City College taking night classes. This was not a social call.

She nodded. "It's only a one year appointment. So when I'm not preparing lectures and grading papers, I'm writing countless cover letters for my resume."

"It's quite a commute from here," Blaustein said in a conversational tone designed to put her at ease.

"Not too bad. I take the train into the City and it gives me time to gather myself," she explained. "When you're preparing lectures for four different courses, you definitely need time to gather yourself."

"Four different courses? Quite a load."

"Not unusual for a rookie assistant professor. That's the irony of the game I'm in. To get tenure, they expect you to publish, but they don't give you enough time to do it. Hopefully this too shall pass. But I can promise you that one day, when I eventually get tenure, I won't treat my T.As. as my vassals." Her lips curled as she said this.

"Unlike Godfrey Mitchell?"

"Yes, God willing. Not at all like Godfrey Mitchell." From beneath the pale lashes the green eyes did not waver.

"You didn't like him much, did you?"

"No, I didn't. Is that a terrible thing to say now that he's dead?" Still the eyes did not flinch.

"It's an honest answer and we appreciate that. But you ought to know that you're entitled to say nothing at all."

"I understand that. I've nothing to hide."

"Then tell us, Ms. Leopold, what in particular was it about Professor Mitchell that you didn't like?"

"If you'd asked what it was I liked about him, it would be a shorter list," she giggled but there was no mirth in it. "Let me see. What was it about Godfrey Mitchell that I didn't like?" She began counting off the fingers of her left hand beginning with the thumb. "Well, besides being arrogant and opinionated and a shameless philanderer, he used people. He used women to service his libido and he used his graduate assistants to supply his academic research. You've probably heard my depressing story already, so there's no point in lying to you, Mitchell exploited me shamelessly. As his T.A., I did his research for eight years in addition to grading his exams and term papers and tutoring his undergraduates. Grading papers or tutoring undergraduates is a given when you're a T.A. I had no complaints about that. It was spending the bulk of my time doing his research instead of my own that had me really frosted," she sighed. "That's mostly why it took me eight years to finish my dissertation."

"Did you get any publications out of your research for him? Your name on any papers? Any acknowledgments?" Blaustein asked, already knowing the answer.

"Surely you jest," she snorted.

"Did you complain to any of the other faculty?"

"Only to fellow graduate students."

"Why didn't you complain to the Department Chairman? Or the Dean?"

"That would have been an academic death sentence," she aimed her fore-finger at her temple and pulled an imaginary trigger. "Whoops. I didn't mean. . . ." She flushed, realizing the implication of the gesture.

"I understand that was the fate of one of your predecessors when he challenged Professor Mitchell. It must have had an inhibiting effect on you."

"You bet it did. After that incident, all his graduate students towed the line. That's why I continued to do grunt work even though I never got so much as a 'thank you'. You see," she explained, "a 'thank you' would have been an acknowledgment that he owed me something."

"Tell me, Ms. Leopold, did you ever go to Professor Mitchell's house?"

"All the time. Mostly to drop off whatever I had researched for him. Sometimes to ferry other materials. I was Godfrey Mitchell's very own, private Fed Ex service: at his beck and call whenever he needed something from his office or from the library." Again her body language reflected her resentment.

"You had a car?"

"Yes, unfortunately. I understand his new T.A. doesn't have wheels. So he wasn't able to use her as a gofer. What an inconvenience for dear old Godfrey! And how lucky for her."

"Do you have a key to the Mitchell house?"

"Present tense?" She frowned, her light-colored brows meeting at the bridge of her nose. "I didn't have a key then and I don't now. Look, Godfrey was a bastard and I resented him. Deeply. But not nearly enough to kill him. Especially now that I have my degree and he is out of my hair. Why on earth would I want to kill him now?"

"I understand that Godfrey Mitchell was something of a lady's man," Blaustein ignored her rhetorical question and changed the subject. "Was there ever anything more to your relationship with him than that of professor and student?"

"He never made a pass at me, if that's what you mean. Which, given his reputation, should have been a devastating blow to my fragile ego. But frankly it would have been much more embarrassing if he had. Fortunately, Detective, I wasn't his type. Not nearly pretty enough." She laughed good-naturedly.

"Tell us, Ms. Leopold, where did you spend the Christmas break?"

"I went up to Poughkeepsie to be with my folks."

"And you were there for how long?"

"I went up on Christmas eve and stayed through New Year's Day," she paused, the color in her cheeks heightening. "Look, Detective, if I'm under suspicion, you should come right out and say so. Then I'd get a lawyer to do my talking for me."

"These are routine questions, Ms. Leopold. We've asked them of everyone who has ever had anything to do with Godfrey Mitchell," Blaustein countered

"Okay," she sounded mollified. "I know you're only doing your job. And even though I'm not about to cry crocodile tears for Godfrey Mitchell, I hope you find the person responsible for his death. I truly do."

Just before leaving Heather Leopold's house, Blaustein's pager went off. He glanced at it, frowned and put it back in his pocket.

"Thank you for your frankness, Ms. Leopold," he said handing her his card "If anything relevant comes to mind, do give me a call."

"She didn't hide the fact that she bears a grudge," Gardner said when they were back in their state car. "But I doubt she would have shown such open hostility if she were Mitchell's killer. She would have been much more guarded than than she was."

"Agreed. Unless her relationship with Mitchell was a lot more complicated than she let on."

They had driven for several miles in companionable silence before Blaustein remembered that there was a message on his pager.

"That was Augusta Scott's home number," he said, digging the pager out of his pocket and handing it to his partner.

"I'll call her back," Gardner replied, using his cell phone to dial.

At the other end, the phone rang and rang but no one answered.

"Odd that she wouldn't be there if she called just a few minutes ago," Gardner said, disconnecting.

"Maybe she's on the way to her office. Try her cell."

Gardner checked his notes, found the number and dialed. But again Scott did not respond. All he got was a recorded message.

"I'll try the History Department," he said, dialing a third time. "May I speak with Professor Scott?" He asked when a secretary answered.

"She hasn't come in yet."

"Are you expecting her?"

"Not sure. All I know is that she called a few minutes ago to cancel an appointment."

"Somehow I doubt Augusta Scott would call you unless there was a good reason for it," Gardener turned to look at Blaustein after disconnecting the call.

"Let's drive by her house and check it out. Meanwhile, keep calling her."

Gardner tried the professor's number again a couple of times before giving up with a shrug. "I don't have a good feeling about this."

Blaustein turned on his flashers and siren. "Why don't you call

Dina Barrett? She's closer than we are. Ask her if it's possible to meet us at Scott's house."

As they drove east in the high speed lane of I95 North, Blaustein's thoughts were speeding ahead of him. In their interview with Augusta Scott she had struck him as collected, circumspect and, except for admitting to a relationship with Mitchell, which they probably would have found out about eventually, she was not particularly forthright or cooperative. If she was calling, it could be the break in the case they were looking for.

Meanwhile, before beginning her tour of duty in the library, Dina had gone to the History Department for her interview with Augusta Scott. But Scott was not in her office when Dina arrived and the office was locked. She waited in the hallway for a few minutes but when there was still no sign of the professor, she went to the Department office to leave a note.

"The only appointment I have down for Professor Scott is with one of her students. And the professor called to cancel that," the Department secretary informed her.

Frustrated and a little annoyed, Dina was turning to leave when her cell phone rang. It was Huey Gardner asking her to meet them at Augusta Scott's house in East Haven.

"Let me call Edward Morrison and ask him to cover for me in the library," Dina said without a moment's hesitation. Then, when Edward agreed to the substitution, she set off, delighted to have a temporary respite from the boredom of surveillance duty.

Traffic was light and she beat Blaustein and Gardner to the Scott house. There were no cars parked outside the professor's two-story gray clapboard when Dina drove up, and the doors to the two-car garage were both closed. Hoping the bird had not already flown the coop, she parked her vehicle, marched onto the wraparound porch, rang the door bell and waited. When there was no response, she tried again. This time she tried using the knocker but as she did, the door opened a crack. With a gentle push of her gloved hand, she opened it further.

"Hello, Professor Scott," she called.

The only answer was an intermittent banging sound. Entering the otherwise silent vestibule, Dina stopped short. On the rug at her feet lay an open briefcase. She knelt down and without touching the case or its contents, examined it. Except for a set of car keys and a couple of pens it was empty.

"Ms. Scott! Professor Scott! It's Detective Barrett," she called, her voice echoing off the walls in the ominously quiet house.

Now the cop in Dina took charge. Keeping on her coat and gloves, she removed her boots, took her gun from her shoulder bag and started looking around. In the living room the drapes were closed, barely filtering in the winter sunlight. That struck her as odd. It was midmorning. Perhaps the professor had not yet come downstairs? What if she was in the shower and simply had not heard her? Feeling intrusive and a little foolish, Dina retraced her steps to the foyer and called out again from the foot of the stairs. But again there was no response. She listened for sounds of a shower or a radio, and heard nothing but the sporadic banging she had heard before. After a cursory survey of the downstairs, she made her way upstairs, cautiously, one tread at a time, her gun in hand and keeping her back to the wall. By now her instincts were telling her that something was very wrong.

When she reached the upper landing, she found herself facing several doors, none of them closed. Still with her back to the wall, she entered the first room on her left. It appeared to be a study, with book-filled shelves, a desk, two chairs, and a computer table. Otherwise, the room was empty and the computer monitor blank. Next to the study was a bedroom. It had the look of a guest room, overly neat with a double bed, a chintz coverlet, matching curtains, and seascapes on the walls. She opened the closet. Just a row of empty hangers. On the other side of the hall was a bathroom, its door ajar and to all appearances it too was empty. Steeling herself, she entered and grasped the shower curtain. The rings rattled as she pulled the curtain aside. Nothing. Her relief was palpable. She hadn't seen *Psycho* three times for nothing.

Finally there was the master bedroom. Her heart in her throat, anticipating the worst she hesitated before entering. Like the other rooms it was neat but empty. A purse bad been emptied onto the bed. Still feeling intrusive, Dina checked out its contents. The wallet contained about thirty dollars, some silver and a few credit cards. Apart from two pens, a lipstick and a comb, the rest of the purse, like the briefcase downstairs, was devoid of paper of any kind: no address book, no notes, not even a shopping list. Turning to leave, Dina was stopped in her tracks by another loud bang. She spun around, gun at the ready, her heart in her throat. But she was immediately relieved to see that the culprit was merely an errant shutter that had not been properly latched.

Opening the window, she leaned out, reached for the shutter mounting on the outside wall, and attached the shutter. Below she could see waves breaking onto a deserted beach and out to sea a lone tanker silhouetted against the bleak winter sky. Turning, she closed the window and returned downstairs. She methodically checked the living room again. Except for a copy of *Newsweek* that lay open on the coffee table, nothing seemed out of place. Neatness and order prevailed everywhere.

Next she surveyed the dining room. It too was empty. The powder room likewise. In the kitchen the percolator light was on and a half-carafe of coffee was warming. Beside it on the counter stood an empty cup and saucer and an untouched Danish on a matching plate. At least a sign of human habitation, but there was still nothing to explain the absence of the professor. There were two doors that led off the kitchen. She opened them both. One opened onto a stairway that went to the basement and the other led to the garage. She tried the basement first. It had been finished with a tile floor and faux wooden paneling. Not too bad for a basement. At the foot of the staircase were shelves of bottled preserves and a substantial wine rack. The far end had been converted into a workroom. Tools hung on a pegboard above a worktable. Pots of paint were stacked beneath it on wooden pallets. Very orderly. The other side of the basement was being used as a laundry. Dina checked the washer and dryer. Both were empty. There was a door that presumably led to the exterior. It was locked and latched from the inside. She went back upstairs to the kitchen and tried the second door. This one lead to the garage. Half the garage was used for the storage of garden furniture, rakes, shovels, empty flowerpots, bags of mulch and a lawn mower. In the other half stood Scott's car. Removing a glove, Dina touched the hood with the back of her hand. It was ice cold.

With an ever growing sense of foreboding, she returned to the main part of the house and retraced her steps to the living room. It was unlikely that Augusta Scott had simply walked out leaving her house unlocked. But there was no point in jumping to conclusions. There could be a simple explanation. Scott could be out jogging, or taking a stroll on the beach. Turning to the window, Dina pulled aside the drapes. A seagull on the porch railing stared at her through the window and then flew off squawking. A weak winter sun struggled to break through the clouds. Beyond lay the Sound, its gray waves breaking onto the deserted beach.

With every muscle taut and her ribcage aching, she forced herself to relax and was about to put the gun back in her purse when she tensed. Someone was out on the porch. Someone was sitting in one of the wooden rockers. Someone who seemed ominously still. She pulled open the unlocked French windows admitting a gust of frigid air and hesitating just long enough to check the chambers of her gun, she stepped outside. But she saw at once that she had no need for a weapon. Augusta Scott sat motionless in the rocker. Only her hair stirred in the sea breeze. She had been duct-taped hand and foot. Her mouth was taped shut. Her head lolled against the seat cushion, her bulging eyes stared unseeing at the gray expanse of sea and sky. She no longer heard the melodic dirge of the wind chimes, or the gentle rush of the waves as they tumbled onto the beach in a ceaseless, mocking reminder of the transience of the human condition.

Looking closer Dina saw that there was a deep reddish purple welt around the professor's neck. It had bled slightly, soiling the collar of her white shirt with relatively fresh blood, bright red and not yet congealed. A bloodied rope lay draped over the porch railing, where a wooden stairway led down to the beach.

Recovering from her initial shock, Dina stepped back into the house. There was a phone on the end table beside the couch. Her hand trembling, she dialed 911. The East Haven Police Department would have jurisdiction over this one. But before she could tell the dispatcher why she was calling, she stopped. Footsteps were approaching the front door. Placing the receiver on the counter but leaving the line open, she crouched behind the couch. Barely breathing, she waited. Whoever was at the door would have noticed her car outside. They would know she was here. Too late now to do anything about that. The doorbell rang. Twice. The door was still ajar and no deterrent to whoever wanted to come inside. When she heard it open she cursed herself for not locking it. From the front hall came the sound of a whispered conversation and of someone stamping his or her boots on the mat.

"Professor Scott!" Blaustein's voice.

Relief coursing through her like a spring freshet, Dina put her gun back in its holster and stood up. Framed in the doorway, like a pair of guardian angels, stood Jackson Blaustein and Huey Gardener. She could have kissed them both.

"Hello Dina. Thanks for heading over here. . . ." Blaustein hesitated. One look at Dina's chalk-white face told him that something was wrong.

"She's out on the porch, Jackson."

14

THOUGH DINA NEVER COMPLETED HER 911 CALL FROM AUGUSTA
Scott's house, the East Haven emergency switchboard operator had
been able to pinpoint the location of the call. In response, an East
Haven patrol car had shown up moments after the discovery of
Scott's body. And despite the fact that the Scott murder had taken
place in East Haven, and could have come under local jurisdiction,
the East Haven Police Department agreed to a joint investigation
with the State's Major Crime Squad. In the first place, there was
an apparent link between the Mitchell and Scott homicides. Also,
Barrett, Blaustein and Gardner of the Major Crime Squad had been
the first law enforcement officers on the scene. So the local and state
police departments joined forces and for the sake of efficiency, the
Chisholm command center was transferred to a conference room
in the East Haven Police Department. Blaustein and Gardner were
assigned to head up the joint investigation assisted by East Haven
Detectives, Charlie Latima and Josh Seymour.

Josh Seymour was an old-timer who had not been promoted
in years and did not expect to be. In contrast, Latima was young,

ambitious and bucking for promotion. He saw the Scott murder as exactly the sort of high profile case that could boost his career and he made no secret of the fact that he resented the intrusion of the State cops. Blaustein did not need to be hit over the head to recognize the signs. He knew all about out-of-joint noses. He had met a lot of cops like Latima. So, summing up the situation immediately, he made a point of including Latima and his partner in all the official briefings and he involved them in every aspect of the investigation. He did not have time to worry about backbiting. But he made sure when parceling out team assignments, that Latima was kept out from under his own feet.

For the sake of efficiency, Latima's crew was assigned to question the beachfront residents and to comb the beach for clues. Their first find was a broom found at the high water mark about a half-mile from the Scott house. It was quite new and still bore the tag of a local hardware store. As new brooms aren't customarily discarded on wintery beaches, the cops figured that it may well have been used to eliminate all trace of the perpetrator's footprints. The broom itself yielded no answers however, not even a useful fingerprint. But it did turn out to be Augusta Scott's broom. At the local hardware store, the owner remembered selling it to her.

"A nice lady. Real pleasant. Such a shame," The storekeeper said, shaking his head. "She was a real do-it-yourselfer. She came in here for one thing or another damn near every Saturday morning."

The questioning of Scott's neighbors likewise turned up little. With one exception, most of them had been away at work when Scott was killed. The exception was a retired school teacher who had walked her dog along the beach that morning.

"Augusta was sweeping her porch," She told the detectives. "Being almost midmorning on a weekday, it seemed a bit unusual. I asked her if she was playing hooky. She said 'no', that she was waiting for a call and planned to go into work later. She seemed a bit tense, now that I think about it, and obviously didn't want to talk, but she was too polite to give me the brush off. You can always tell when people don't feel like being sociable. So I just waved and kept walking. I don't remember what the exact time was. Retirees," she informed them with a twinkle, "aren't on the clock."

While Latima and Seymour were taking statements from Augusta Scott's neighbors, Blaustein and Gardner found themselves once again in the Whitney Graduate School. Word of Scott's murder had not yet reached the School but rumors were flying following the removal of her computer and the sealing of her office. The buzz was that Scott had killed Mitchell. And the fact that she had not come to work that morning added fuel to a rumor that she was already in custody. So it was curious stares and a cold, expectant silence that met the two detectives as they made their way down the hall to Sidney Lawrence's office.

Without a clear motive in the Mitchell case, the History Department Chairman was still a likely suspect. But though it was logical to think he may have murdered Godfrey Mitchell in a jealous rage, the murder of Augusta Scott did not quite fit. What could possibly be his motive for killing Augusta Scott?

"Professor Lawrence?" Blaustein knocked on the jamb of the chairman's open door and entered without waiting for an invitation.

"Detectives Blaustein and Gardner yet again," Lawrence sighed. He did not get up from behind his desk, or invite them to sit down. "It would have been a courtesy to inform me before sealing Professor Scott's office and removing her computer. So, I can't say I'm delighted to see you."

Blaustein nodded at Gardner and they both sat down uninvited. "I regret to inform you, Sir, that Professor Augusta Scott, was found dead this morning."

Lawrence's shoulders tensed and Blaustein noted that beneath the suntan, his gaunt face had paled. Except for a muscle working in his jaw, his expression, however, like those of the African masks on the wall behind him, was wooden.

"Murdered?" It was almost as much a statement as a question, his voice steady.

Blaustein made note of the fact that the Department Chairman was assuming foul play even though no mention of it had been made. Of course, given the confiscation of Scott's computer, such an assumption was understandable.

"We would like to ask you, Professor," Blaustein said, with a show of polite deference. "Where you were between ten and eleven thirty this morning? But let me advise you before you respond, that you may refuse to answer and that you have the right to an attorney if you do."

"Am I being charged with something?" The question was posed coolly. The mask still in place.

"Not at this time."

"Then I'll be happy to answer your questions. I have nothing to hide and have no need for an attorney." He seemed totally unruffled, almost arrogant.

"Then, as you don't object, please tell us where you were between ten and eleven thirty this morning?" Blaustein repeated.

"I was checking out journal articles in the library all morning," his impassive face still revealed nothing, but his hands betrayed him. They were gripping the armrests of his chair, and the knuckles showed white beneath the tanned skin. He was a man struggling for control.

"Anyone who can verify that?" Blaustein persisted.

"I was in the stacks," Lawrence responded, letting go of the arm-rests and leaning back in his chair as if forcing himself to relax. "I don't know if anyone either saw me or recognized me. If I were trying to establish an alibi, I certainly would have made sure they did, he added sarcastically.

"Well, if you can think of anyone who may have seen you, let us know. Meanwhile, we have another question we'd like answered. You remember telling us that you left for Atlanta on December 28th?"

Lawrence nodded.

"Could you tell us where you were and what you were doing the day before your departure?"

"I spent the day splitting logs in my backyard. A friend helped me. We started in the morning after breakfast and kept at it, with a couple of breaks till it was dark. About five o'clock. Then we went inside for a drink. He was with me the whole time. You can check with him." He steepled his fingers, tapping them together.

"His name?" Blaustein noted that Lawrence still wore his wedding ring, so all was not lost for the lovely Deirdre.

"Dan Desmond, a neighbor of mine."

"What about later that night?"

"My wife and I had dinner at a colleague's house. There were six of us there. Ask them." Not missing a beat, Lawrence spelled the names so that Gardner could take them down.

"And after you left there?"

"My wife and I went home. She was with me the whole time. And drove me to the airport the next morning like the dutiful little woman she is." This time there was no mistaking the sarcasm. "You told us before, that you were not exactly on friendly terms with the late Professor Mitchell. But you didn't tell us why. Would you please elaborate?"

"Really Detective, you know the answer to that question or you wouldn't have asked it. And surely you wouldn't have wasted your time interviewing my wife."

"Suppose you tell us in your own words," Blaustein challenged.

"Would you be on friendly terms with someone who was humping your woman?" Lawrence leaned forward resting his elbows on the desk, his hands clasped, and daring Blaustein to respond.

Blaustein didn't. Instead he changed the subject. "Do you know of any reason someone would want to kill Augusta Scott?"

Lawrence sat back, evidently relieved that the questioning had taken another tack. "No I don't. She was very well liked and highly respected. The news is going to devastate the Department. Especially coming so soon after Godfrey's death."

"Did you know that Professor Scott had a relationship with Mitchell?"

"That was some years ago. They remained on friendly terms."

"Her telephone records indicate that she made a call to your office this morning. Mind telling us what that was about?"

"She left a message," Lawrence rustled through a pile of telephone slips but did not find what he was looking for. "Something about wanting to meet with me as soon as possible. And for the Department secretary to cancel a meeting she had scheduled with a graduate student. Apparently she was unable to reach the student at home."

"She didn't indicate why she wanted to meet with you?"

"No."

"Did she give a reason for canceling her meeting with the student?"

"No," Lawrence shook his head.

"Who was the student?"

"Kelly Richmond. Before his death, Godfrey Mitchell was Kelly's faculty advisor. She's been without one since Godfrey was killed. Augusta had agreed to take her on."

Lawrence's recitation tallied with Scott's telephone records. Just before calling the History Department, she had placed a call to Kelly Richmond's apartment. Maybe Scott said something to the student that might shed some light.

"I guess, Professor Scott's death makes Ms. Richmond a two-time loser," Gardner was in his 'good cop' mode.

"Yes. If I were superstitious, I certainly wouldn't volunteer to take her on. She seems to be jinxed, poor kid," Lawrence brushed back his sandy forelock and sighed. "But, to be brutally honest, right now I have more pressing concerns than replacing Kelly Richmond's advisor. To be pragmatic, I have to think about the rest of the Department. Besides the effect all this will have on morale, we've now lost two of our professors. Both our Victorians. They can't be replaced midyear. That's out of the question. Somehow the rest of our faculty will have to pick up the slack. And they already consider themselves overloaded."

"Who took Professor Scott's call this morning if you weren't here?" Lawrence's personnel problems were not Blaustein's concern. His interest was in finding out why two of Lawrence's faculty members had been killed and whether their deaths were connected.

"Actually my secretary took the call," Lawrence reshuffled the sheaf of papers on his desk and this time came up with a slip of paper from a standard yellow message pad. He handed it to Blaustein. It gave the time of Scott's call -- which had been placed two minutes after the call to Richmond's apartment and tallied with the telephone records -- as well as the notation that she had called to arrange a meeting with Lawrence and to cancel her meeting with Kelly Richmond."

"Were you in the building at the time?"

"No, I hadn't gotten in yet."

"Do you normally come in after ten, Professor Lawrence?"

"Not usually." Lawrence didn't offer a further explanation and his expression didn't change.

"What was unusual about this morning then?" Blaustein asked as casually as he could. He didn't want to put the man's guard up.

"Nothing. I went for a run first thing, the way I usually do and then, as I told you, I went to the library."

Blaustein decided to leave it there for the time being. "Do you know if your secretary was able to notify the student about the postponement?" He asked, changing the subject and noting the look of evident relief on Lawrence's face.

"You'll have to ask her, Detective," Lawrence snapped, his irritation this time ill-concealed.

"Right. We'll speak to her when we're through here. In the meantime, I'd like you to look at a list of calls Professor Scott made from her office in the twenty-four hours prior to her death. Tell me if anything strikes you as significant in any way. In any way at all," Blaustein took the telephone log from his jacket pocket, unfolded it and passed it to Lawrence.

Looking it over, Lawrence shook his head, "A call to a garage downtown. That's because she had her car serviced yesterday. And a couple of calls to universities out of state. Those don't strike me as out of the ordinary. Augusta was chairing a colloquium in the spring and she was probably sounding out potential speakers." He handed the log back to Blaustein. "Looks run of the mill to me, Detective."

Blaustein folded the log and put it back in his inside breast pocket. Augusta Scott had called some of the same universities from her home as well. If she was arranging a colloquium in the spring, then Lawrence's explanation seemed reasonable. Even so they would need to check out her calls.

"When is the last time you saw Professor Scott?" He asked, deliberately changing the subject again.

"Late yesterday afternoon as she was leaving, I passed her in the hall."

"How did she appear to you?"

"Augusta always seemed calm and collected. That's how she appeared to me yesterday."

"What if anything did she say to you?"

Lawrence frowned, as if trying to recollect, "Actually, now that I think about it, something quite odd. She said that things weren't always what they seemed. She didn't explain what she meant, and I didn't ask. Perhaps I should have."

"Tell us, Professor Lawrence, did you see anyone when you were out jogging?"

"Running," Lawrence corrected him. Serious runners didn't jog.

"See anyone you recognized?" Blaustein repeated with more patience than he felt..

"You seem to be insisting that I produce some sort of alibi." Lawrence's comment was made with an attempt at wry humor, but Blaustein could tell the man was close to losing his temper. The muscles of his jaw had tightened, and once again his knuckles showed white beneath the skin as he gripped the armrests of his chair. It might have been productive to push him further, but Blaustein decided he had pushed him far enough. If Lawrence was guilty, chances were he had been sufficiently provoked. Perhaps enough to cause a reaction, if so, it wouldn't be a bad idea to set up surveillance on him. He'd arrange it without Lieutenant Gordon's okay. Tell him about it once it was a fait accompli. If he waited for Gordon's approval it might never happen. Gordon wasn't one to stick his neck out. And with a member of the faculty involved, the Loo would be reluctant as Hell to upset the Whitney establishment.

Blaustein turned to his partner, "Detective Gardner, is there anything else you'd like to ask?" Huey started to shake his head and then changed his mind, "Yes, and you have the right to refuse, Professor Lawrence. Would you mind showing me the palms of your hands?" Unless he had worn substantial gloves, there would be conspicuous rope-burns across the palms of Scott's killer.

Hesitating for just a moment before complying, Lawrence turned his hands over so that they lay open on the desk exposing the palms. Except for a fine layer of perspiration, his hands were unmarked. Disappointed and feeling as much in the dark as ever, they thanked Lawrence and rose to leave. They had come seeking answers and were leaving with more questions than before. More questions, more suppositions and still no hard evidence.

As usual when Dina reached the part of New Haven where the Whitney campus merged with city blocks, parking was at a premium. The Whitney lots were all full and so were the parking spaces along the side streets. After circling the block a couple of times, she saw a woman in a mini-van pulling out and grabbed the parking space. She fed all the quarters she had into the meter, and then set off across campus.

When she got to the library, she settled down in her usual spot, switched her cell phone to vibrate and put it in her jeans pocket. No sooner had she done so than she felt the phone's tremor. She immediately got up from the desk, walked over to the corridor that led to the rest rooms and seeing the caller was Blaustein, answered it at once.

"We've tried reaching Kelly Richmond at home and struck out," he said. "Any idea where she might be?"

"She's in the Whitney library. From where I'm standing I can see her."

"Okay. Don't want you to blow your cover. Just tell me where in the library I can find her."

"She's in one of the desks on the main floor. You'll see her when you come in. The desks will be along the far wall to the left."

"Let's hope she's still there when we get there."

"I'll make sure she sticks around till you do."

"That would be helpful. Thanks."

"Where are you now?"

"Just wrapping up in the History Department and none too soon. We've been interviewing some very stressed-out staff."

"If Richmond leaves before you get here, I'll call you at once. Either way, I'd like to catch up with you afterwards. We can grab a cup of coffee at Freddie's place later if you'd like."

Dina hung up, slipped the phone back into her pocket and walked over to where Kelly was hunched over a book taking notes. It was cold in the library, a lot colder than usual and the graduate student was still wearing her coat and gloves, a scarf wrapped around her neck. Her nose was red, her eyes, behind their steel-rimmed glasses, watery. Yet there were beads of perspiration on her forehead.

"I think I'm coming down with something. You had better keep your distance," she warned with a shiver.

Dina took a step back. The last thing she needed after battling pleurisy was a chest cold. "Sorry you're under the weather but I'm afraid you'll feel even worse when you hear what I'm about to tell you," Dina apologized.

"What is it?" Dina had Kelly's full attention now.

"It's Professor Scott. I'm sorry to be blunt, but she's dead." There was no delicate way to break the news.

Kelly's jaw dropped, "Oh no! It can't be!" Shivering visibly, she hugged herself, a hand under each armpit, her shoulders hunched.

"Unfortunately it's all too true. They think she was killed some time this morning. I'm sorry to be the bearer of bad tidings."

"Killed? In an accident?"

"I don't know the details but it's all over campus by now. I'm surprised you haven't heard." It probably was not all over campus just yet but Dina did not want to give the impression that she had an inside track.

"Damn, I always liked her. And especially now. I was feeling really down before she offered to replace Godfrey as my advisor," Kelly responded forlornly.

Dina shrugged. There was nothing she could say.

"You probably think I'm being selfish, thinking of myself when I should be thinking about her," the graduate student said, half to herself.

"It's an understandable reaction. Don't be too hard on yourself."

"I'd better get over to the History Department," Kelly closed her book with a snap and began putting her things into her backpack. "I'd like to find out what's going on."

"So what will you do now?" Dina needed to stall Kelly till Blaustein and Gardner arrived.

"I guess what I've been doing since Godfrey Mitchell died, prepping for my exams and doing my dissertation research." She stood, zipped up her coat and flinging one end of her woolen scarf over her neck, she hefted her backpack over one shoulder. But before taking a step toward the exit, she stopped in her tracks. Blocking her path were Blaustein and Gardner.

"Hello Ms. Richmond, Detectives Blaustein and Gardener. We've met before," Blaustein said by way of introduction.

"Yes?" Kelly replied uncertainly, her brow creasing in a puzzled frown.

"If you don't mind stepping outside, we would like you to answer a few questions," Blaustein said without preamble.

Although badly wanting to stick around for the questioning, Dina excused herself, dumped her backpack on an adjacent desk and went back to her surveillance of Herman Archer.

15

"I HOPE YOU DIDN'T CATCH HELL WHEN LIEUTENANT GORDON FOUND out you were the one who found the body," Blaustein, Gardner and Dina were comfortably seated at Freddie's kitchen table later that afternoon.

"There was no way to avoid it. Nevertheless, it paled in comparison with what happened earlier today," Dina admitted. She was still trying to shake off the memory of the gruesome discovery on the porch.

"I'm sorry now that we sent you on ahead of us."

"Actually I might have been the first one on the scene anyway. A friend of Freddie's set up an interview with Scott. And when she didn't show up at her office, I thought about driving out to see her. With a referral from a personal acquaintance, she may have been more forthcoming with me than she was when you guys interviewed her."

"Unfortunately we'll never know. Apart from the rather candid admission that she and Godfrey Mitchell had a brief affair some time ago, she gave us bubkes," Blaustein said, getting up and helping himself to another cup of coffee. "Any takers?"

Dina and Huey both shook their heads.

"Which friend of Freddie's?" Blaustein and Gardener asked simultaneously.

"Adrian Needham, the former Chairman of the History Department. I thought I mentioned that Freddie introduced us."

"Oh yes, you did. Wasn't he the one who told you about the theft of that rare manuscript from the library?"

"He was," she took a sip of her by now tepid coffee. "I don't suppose you've had time to follow up on the present whereabouts of Harvey Thomas?"

"A dead end," Gardner informed her. "We checked with Internal Revenue as well as the Social Services Administration only to find that Harvey Thomas, kicked off a few years ago."

"Did he ever go back to teaching?" Dina asked, more out of a latent sympathy for the man than anything else.

"He did. Some place where they weren't too fussy about his background. He wound up at a small two-year college in Jersey."

"Quite a comedown from Whitney," Dina shook her head at the waste.

"He had it coming," the comment from Gardner, was unexpectedly harsh.

"Learn anything new from Kelly Richmond?" Dina asked.

"No," they answered simultaneously.

"She didn't speak to Scott then?"

"She said that Scott left a message postponing their meeting but she didn't speak to her directly," Blaustein responded.

"Richmond doesn't remember Scott saying anything other than that she was postponing their meeting. And unfortunately she erased the message. We'll pick up the tape some time tomorrow, just in case the lab can do something with it."

"Any other new developments?"

"Not really. We spoke to Lawrence but got nowhere. With luck we can get something from Scott's office computer which we now have in custody. Whoever killed her, erased her home computer. We're hoping that Lennie Hoffman will be able to restore it. And her office computer does not look very promising. So far we haven't seen anything but official correspondence, lesson plans and several chapters of a book Scott was writing. No useful leads."

"What about phone records?"

"We checked both her home and office phone records. Neither looks promising. Today she made only three calls from her home phone. The last one was to my pager. The earlier two we assume were to postpone her meeting with Richmond. One to the History Department and the other to Richmond's home. What we don't know is why she postponed the meeting."

"Maybe one of the calls she made yesterday will tell us something," Barrett suggested.

"Unfortunately it doesn't look as if the calls she made yesterday will tell us much at all. They were all from her office phone. One was to her garage. The rest were all work-related," Blaustein pulled the telephone log from his pocket and passed it to Dina. "Make anything of this?"

Dina took the log, scanned it, shook her head and handed it back.

"All the calls Augusta Scott made from her office phone in the last twenty-four hours were to other universities. Lawrence thought that in all probability she might have been contacting potential speakers to a colloquium she was organizing," Blaustein ran a finger down the names listed on the log. "According to this list, it looks like he was right. On our way here Huey called a couple of the numbers on the list and the people he spoke to confirmed that Scott had called about the colloquium. He's checked off the two he managed to contact and we'd like you to check out the others. Sorry to dump this on you. It's not likely to be a productive use of your time."

"No problem," Dina took the list, folded it and put it in her backpack. "How come you guys were headed to Augusta Scott's house today?" Dina asked after a pause.

"She left a message on my pager. When Huey couldn't raise her on the phone, we decided to go to her house, but knew it would be a while before we could get there. That's when we called you. At the time, we thought she might have some new information for us, but from what we know now, her call may have been a cry for help."

"Even if she didn't know who killed Godfrey Mitchell when she called you, she did in the end," Dina shuddered, "because whoever killed Mitchell also killed her."

"A better than even bet. But if the murders were committed by the same individual, then we can at least cross one suspect off our list," Gardner volunteered. "Heather Leopold. She was with us when Scott called."

"If the same perp committed both crimes, he certainly used very different MOs." Blaustein added, "the two murders couldn't be more different."

"Even though the murder weapons were different, the MOs were actually fairly similar," Gardner offered thoughtfully.

"True, in both cases the weapon belonged to the victim, almost as if the killer was forced to ad lib," Barrett chipped in.

"And there was another point of similarity," Gardner reminded them. "In both instances the victim knew the killer. There was no evidence of a break-in in either home. The killer was undoubtedly admitted voluntarily."

"Which should narrow the list of suspects but so far hasn't given us a thing," Blaustein ran his fingers through his hair in frustration.

"In the Mitchell case, the killer staged a suicide. But given the fact that Scott was strangled and duct-taped, staging a suicide wasn't an option."

"We do know that the killer is computer savvy. We know he did a pretty thorough job of purging Scott's computer. At least that's what the computer people tell me," Blaustein finished his coffee and put down his cup. "Everything on Scott's computer was erased. Even the software. Let's hope that Lennie Hoffman can put that Humpty Dumpty back together again."

"What about the tire tracks at Scott's house?" Dina suggested, touching all the bases.

"The killer must have parked elsewhere and walked," Blaustein replied. "But not along the beach. There was no beach sand in the house. Not even microscopic amounts. Best guess is that Scott let him in through the front door. But we know that he didn't leave that way. After killing her, he chose the scenic route. Down the porch steps and along the beach."

"Why, I wonder?" Dina asked.

"Perhaps he heard you arriving and didn't have a choice," Blaustein suggested. "But even so, he kept his cool. Made sure that he didn't leave his footprints in the sand. He swiped a broom from the vic's porch and used it to obliterate his trail. The brush marks led from the porch to the water's edge. And once he reached the water, the perp probably made his getaway through the surf. There are no prints anywhere. A local cop spotted the broom further down the beach, near the high-water mark. It's been identified as belonging to Scott."

"Surf's pretty cold this time of year."

"Maybe he was wearing boots."

"If he was walking in the surf it's possible someone may have noticed him. One doesn't see too many people walking in the surf this time of year. Or, for that matter, at any time of the year fully clothed, which I assume he was," Dina added.

"That's what we're hoping. The local cops are still canvassing the neighborhood but they'll be lucky to find a useful eye witness. Most people are at work on weekdays."

"Did the Medical Examiner confirm that strangulation was the cause of death?" Dina asked.

"Yes, the proximate cause being a crushed trachea. She did not put up a fight. There are no defensive wounds. And so unfortunately no foreign skin particles beneath her fingernails. We'll have to wait for the official autopsy report to get the precise details."

They sat in silence for a few minutes. Blaustein was leaning forward on his elbows, his empty coffee mug on the table in front of him. Gardner was slumped in his chair, his legs stretched out under the table, his hands folded over his middle-aged belly. Neither of them looked as if they cared to move. Both were bone-weary. But they had taken about as long a break as they dared to. They didn't have the luxury of goofing off. Not with two unsolved murders and no leads. Looking at each other, they nodded and simultaneously stood up.

"Thanks for the coffee Dina," Blaustein grabbed his coat from the back of his chair. "Again, I apologize for sending you in there without backup. I hate to think what might have happened if you'd walked in on the killer."

"How could you possibly know that I was going into a situation that might need backup?" Dina shook her head dismissively.

Blaustein waved her off. "Maybe not, Dina, but think about it. Augusta Scott wasn't dead long when you found her. If you had arrived a few minutes earlier, you'd have come face to face with her killer. He'd have heard you ring the doorbell. And he would have been waiting for you. Face it, no way would it have been a fair contest. He would have had the drop on you even under normal circumstances, and you're still a long way from being back to your usual strength. So for a change I have to agree with Lieutenant Gordon. Go do the Whitney job and forget the Mitchell case." Blaustein hoped his cautionary message would sink in, but he could tell from the obstinate look on Dina's face that she wasn't buying it. She had her teeth into this one and she wasn't about to let go. Instead of answering, she gave each of her guests a hug and saw them to the front door.

Though Blaustein's words resonated with her, Dina had no intention of sitting on the sidelines. She would not admit, even to herself, that her earlier brush with death had scared her. She had recurring nightmares, but only a jumbled memory of what had actually happened. Like fragments of a half-remembered dream: the feeling of impotence as she lay wounded in the casino parking lot, the vague memory of Blaustein kneeling beside her his gun in hand, the searing pain, the sirens, the flashing lights, the wail of the ambulance and the omnipresent fear of dying as she went in and out of consciousness. These recollections still found their way into her nightmares and left her damp with sweat, her pulses pounding, every muscle tense, and fully awake. They called it post traumatic stress disorder: the same recurring nightmares, night after night and in the early morning hours before daybreak. Nightmares that did not always fade in the cold light of day. But in the brutal light of reality,

180

her near-death experience had taught her a valuable lesson, one the young seldom heeded: she was not invulnerable. Life was not to be taken for granted. And the incident had left her shaken. Less trusting. But like a rider who has been thrown, she knew she had to get back in the saddle. Which is why, though forewarned, she dismissed Blaustein's warning with barely a second thought.

16

DINA WAS IN THE KITCHEN AND ABOUT TO HEAT A T. V. DINNER IN the microwave when the doorbell rang. She walked through the darkened, empty house to the front door, turned on the porch light. Leaving the latch in place, she opened the door a crack. Clive Atkinson stood on the doorstep, a bottle of Chianti in one hand, a pizza box balanced on the palm of the other, and a semi-apologetic grin on his face.

"I hope you don't mind me dropping in unannounced. I did try calling first."

Taken aback and not knowing whether to be angry or pleased, she settled for ambivalence. As an old friend she guessed it was okay to show up uninvited and okay not to stand on ceremony, but if he still harbored romantic feelings for her, then he was presuming too much. She definitely did not want whatever it was they had once shared. In fact, she couldn't fathom what, if anything, she felt for Clive. So she remained rooted in the doorway, wordless.

"Are you going to let me in while the pizza's still hot or do you want to eat it cold?"

She drew back the latch and stepping aside, admitted him.

"Nice digs," he said, looking around at the high-ceilinged foyer with its age-darkened mahogany paneling.

From the foyer she led him through the even more impressive formal dining room with its shimmering Waterford chandelier, its massive Sheraton dining table and chairs, its sideboard laden with ornate silver, its antique Persian rugs and heavy velvet drapes.

"If you don't mind, we won't eat in here. It's far too gloomy."

"It's a magnificent room," Clive said. "But I agree, somehow pizza in a box does not seem appropriate."

"My landlady grew up in this house," Dina explained, falling naturally into the role of docent. "It was built by her great-grandfather early in the last century, around 1900. I have a suite on the second floor but pretty much the run of the place."

"Not a bad place to have the run of," Clive commented, as they passed through a set of swinging doors into what was once a butler's pantry outfitted with glass-fronted china cabinets and mahogany counters. The pantry in turn opened into a large country kitchen with an oak table in the center. Dina put the pizza box down on the table.

"We'll eat in here. It's by far the most cheerful room in the house," she found a corkscrew in one of the drawers and handed it to him. "After you've taken your coat off, you can get to work opening the vino. I'm glad you remembered how much I like Chianti."

"I remember quite a lot about you," their eyes met for a brief second before she looked away. Trying to ignore the implications of his comment, Dina turned her attention to what was in the pizza box. "You got eggplant and Portobello mushrooms! I thought you preferred pepperoni?"

"I do. But I remembered that you don't," he said, taking off his coat and scarf and placing them on the back of a chair.

"That was very noble of you," she was unexpectedly touched. "You could have ordered half-and-half."

He shrugged dismissively and went to work with the corkscrew while Dina set out plates, flatware and wine goblets.

"Please sit down," she said, after he poured the wine. "And help yourself while it's still hot."

"There's nothing quite like New Haven pizza," he said, helping himself to a slice.

"A whole lot better than the T.V. dinner I had planned for tonight," she tried to sound casual and cover the awkwardness she felt. But she was talking too fast and knew the awkwardness showed.

Clive on the other hand seemed perfectly at ease, as if sharing a pizza with her in Freddie Hathaway's kitchen was the most normal thing in the world. But then people like Clive usually felt at home anywhere. Like other members of the upper crust, he was accustomed to taking command whatever his surroundings. Nothing phased him. Everything came easily. It was a trait Dina envied and knew she could never emulate. It was one of the reasons she had never really felt at home in the rarefied atmosphere of Clive's world.

"I'm leaving Connecticut tomorrow," Clive said, placing a second slice of pizza on his plate. "I didn't want to leave without saying good-bye."

"Where are you off to?" She felt an unexpected stab of disappointment at the news.

"I have a case pending in North Carolina."

"Defending an environmental polluter no doubt?" The second the words were uttered, she regretted them.

But be chose to ignore the remark. "When the North Carolina case is settled, I'll be going back to New York," he reached a hand across the table and took hers. "I'll call you when I get there if you'd like?" His voice was unexpectedly wistful.

Dina merely nodded, not knowing whether she liked the idea or not. But she did not immediately reclaim her hand, and her reluctance to do so sent a message. Perhaps the wrong message. She knew instinctively that it would be a mistake to encourage him. That resuming their aborted relationship would never work. So why was she unwilling to let go? Banishing the thought, she took a bite of pizza. But she had lost whatever appetite she had had. Suddenly it tasted like the cardboard in which it had been packed and she had a hard time getting it down. So pouring herself another glass of wine, she changed to a safer subject, "Will you be pleading the case in Raleigh?"

"Yes. Probably in a month or two, unless both parties decide to settle. I'm going down tomorrow to take depositions."

"Does your job take you on the road a lot?" She asked, nibbling on a crust, dawdling with her food, the way she used to as a child when she wanted to postpone doing homework.

"Depends. Most of our clients are New York firms. If their companies are located out-of-state, then we go to wherever it takes us."

"That means spending a lot of time in hotel rooms. I'd hate that."

"Yes, it gets old after a while. Not to mention unhealthy. Restaurant food is insidious. I'm glad hotels at least have workout facilities, otherwise it would creep up on you." He patted his stomach.

The conversation drifted on in this vein. Circumspect and tentative, it steered a safe course by avoiding all the topics that were off limits -- which was everything that was on top of both their minds. Avoidance made for civil discussion, but every now then Dina caught the old spark in his eyes when he looked at her. And it made her uncomfortable. She was convinced that there was too much scorched earth between them for anything to ever grow again. With lingering misgivings, she strengthened her resolve to burn the remaining bridges.

When they had drunk the last of the Chianti and eaten more than enough pizza, they returned the remainder to the refrigerator and Dina rinsed the dishes and the wine glasses and loaded them into the dishwasher. Clive, standing behind her, put a hand on her shoulder and spun her around to face him. She felt the warmth of his proximity and the invisible bond that still drew her. For a moment, on the brink of succumbing, she hesitated. But only for a moment. It was far too late to go back. Steeling herself, she leaned forward and gave him an unmistakably platonic kiss on the cheek.

"Thank you for the pizza and the Chianti and for still being a friend," she said, knowing the words sounded cold and final.

"It was good to see you again too," repulsed, his reply was icily polite. He retrieved his coat and shrugged into it.

"When you're in town again, I'll buy the pizza," she said, knowing full well that she probably would never see him again. Clive had never taken rebuffs very well.

They walked to the front door in silence where she kissed him on the cheek again, a sisterly kiss which he did not return. Instead he merely said good bye, and turned to go, leaving her with a momentary twinge of remorse.

Blaustein did not expect to make it home for dinner that night. So like Dina and Clive, he, Huey Gardner and the two East Haven cops, Latima and Seymour, were likewise eating pizza. It was Blaustein's treat. The pizza offering and the atmosphere of camaraderie at the East Haven command center were going a long way toward soothing Latima's ruffled feathers. The young cop seemed almost eager now to cooperate, if only to prove how capable he was.

"You guys have done a terrific job canvassing the neighborhood," Blaustein was saying between mouthfuls of pizza and swigs of Pepsi. "By confirming alibis for the time of the murder you've pretty much eliminated any of the neighbors as suspects. That hugely narrows the field."

"It really helps too that you managed to unearth Linda Kirk," Gardner added. "The fact that she saw Augusta Scott alive around ten gives us a good fix on the time of death."

"Less than a two-hour window," agreed Latima. "When Linda Kirk set out on her walk along the beach, it was 10:00 a.m. and Scott was still alive. The 911 call from Detective Barrett came in at noon."

"I'd guess it was even less than a two-hour window. By the time Detective Barrett arrived Scott was already dead and the perp had taken off down the beach," Gardner continued. "The way I see it, Scott's killer arrived sometime after ten. And with no forced entry and no traces of beach sand anywhere, he obviously came through the front door. That means Scott admitted someone she knew. The fact that there are no signs of a struggle also seem to confirm that. Then, once inside the house, the perp either persuaded or muscled her onto the porch. Tied her to the chair. Taped her mouth, hands and feet and strangled her. But before leaving the premises, he took the time to go through her purse and her briefcase and purge her computer. Possibly in that order," Gardner popped the top of a can of Pepsi and took a swallow. "He probably took off down the beach when he heard Dina's car in the driveway."

"Good," his partner added, "I like that scenario. But I think we can narrow the time frame even more. Remember, it was around eleven that my pager went off. So we know that Scott was still alive then and that her call to us may have been a cry for help. Minutes later, when we called back, she didn't answer," Blaustein shook his head, "Perhaps, if she had called 911 instead of us, your local guys would have got to her house faster and she might still be alive. A witness rather than a victim."

"And the killer could have been in custody. Or at the very least we'd have had a decent description of him," Gardener added, helping himself to another slice of pizza and passing the box to the two East Haven cops.

"Thanks." Seymour accepted a slice.

"Not right now thanks," Latima shook his head.

"Anything else Mrs. Kirk had to say?" Blaustein prompted.

"Not much. Her impression was that Scott was preoccupied and did not want to be sociable. Usually Scott made a fuss of the dog. She didn't that morning."

"This was on Kirk's outbound walk," Seymour chipped in. "On the way back, she remembers seeing Scott sitting in one of the rockers. But she didn't answer when Kirk called out to her. Kirk thought she was asleep. But she was probably dead by then."

"She didn't notice the duct tape on the victim's mouth?" Blaustein was incredulous.

"No she didn't. The old lady doesn't see too well, I guess."

"Does she remember what time that was?"

"Unfortunately she wasn't specific. She'd stopped to chat with a friend who lives at the other end of the beach and lost track of time."

"Did she see anyone else walking along the beach?"

"Negative," Latima eyed the pizza but didn't take any.

"Did she happen to notice whether the living room drapes were open or closed?"

"We didn't think to ask."

"Well it's a minor point," Blaustein conceded. "One would expect the drapes to be open at that time of day. But they were closed by the time Detective Barrett arrived. The perp probably closed them while he searched the place."

"We can definitely rule out that this was a B and E gone wrong. No valuables seem to be missing and whatever the killer took seems to have come from Scott's briefcase." Gardner added.

"Except for the broom," Seymour reminded him.

"Right. That was good work finding the broom," Blaustein acknowledged. "It confirms that the perp made his getaway down the beach and that he was probably parked several blocks away. It's just too bad that the broom didn't give us any prints. I expect he wore gloves. As did Detective Barrett. The professor's were the only prints in the house."

After debating with himself, Gardner took another slice of pizza, "I seem to be the only one eating."

"Tell me, Huey," Blaustein asked, obliging his partner by taking another slice of pizza, "do you think Lawrence was on the up and up when he claimed not to know why Scott called asking to see him?"

"It's hard to tell with him. He's as stony-faced as those African masks of his. We'll probably never know what Scott had in mind when she called him, " Gardner acknowledged regretfully.

"Does Lawrence have an alibi for the Mitchell case?" Latima asked.

"He flew to Atlanta on the 28th, the day after Mitchell was booked to fly out. But we assume that Mitchell was killed on the 27th because in all likelihood he would have made his flight that day if he were still alive. But on the day he was murdered, Lawrence claims he was splitting logs with a neighbor, a Mr. Desmond. We haven't confirmed that yet, unfortunately Desmond is out of town.

Which is why Lawrence remains a person of interest in the Mitchell homicide."

"What about his alibi for the Scott murder?"

"Lawrence claims he went running earlier and saw no one who can corroborate. Then he went to the library but didn't remember seeing anyone there either. Not even a librarian. It seems like a pretty flimsy alibi if you ask me. We still need to examine Lawrence's jogging shoes to see if there's any beach sand on them. But we'll need a warrant to do that."

"Without stronger evidence than we have, I doubt we'd get one," Gardner reminded him. "We have no possible motive in the Scott case, and except for his wife's affair, nothing against him in the Mitchell case."

"Anyone else with a motive in the Mitchell case?" Seymour asked.

"Possibly the son, Brian Mitchell. He is the chief beneficiary. But he's pretty much been ruled out as a suspect. There's no way he could have been in Connecticut when his old man was knocked off, not unless that BMW he drives is rocket-propelled. I also seriously doubt that Mitchell's former teaching assistant, Curt Daniels, had anything to do with the professor's murder despite their history." Gardner went on to describe the results of his trip to Vermont and Massachusetts.

"So unless there is someone we haven't yet considered, that leaves the Lawrences, as well as the former Mrs. Mitchell with the strongest possible motives, " Blaustein added, pouring some Pepsi into a paper cup.

"Alison Mitchell?" Seymour leaned back in his chair, his hands folded comfortably across his belly, "What if anything do you have on her?"

"Just a likely motive if she was aware of how much she stood to gain in his will," Blaustein explained. "Right now Alison Mitchell is practically broke and she likes the finer things in life. Likes them a lot. Which means the former Mrs. Mitchell needs or thinks she needs money real bad. Besides her extravagant tastes, the lady has a gambling habit. She's pissed away just about all she's got."

"How much did she have to start with?" Latima asked.

Blaustein took a sip of his soda. "She took almost everything Mitchell had when they got divorced and she has a sizable alimony. She also got half the couple's savings and investments and a beach house in North Carolina which she has since mortgaged to the hilt. In addition, she inherited a bundle from her father in tax free bonds and a house in Florida which she sold at a profit. But it's all pretty much gone now. Her only steady source of income is her alimony but that was tied to what Mitchell made as a Whitney professor ten years ago. And it's barely enough to keep the lady in chump change. Because of the wording in the divorce agreement, her alimony doesn't include any of Mitchell's royalties. But with his death everything changes. According to his will she and her son will each get fifty percent of his royalties. That's a substantial amount given the popularity of his books, and it's a fairly solid motive for a lady whose strapped, wouldn't you say?"

"How do you know she has a gambling habit?" Latima challenged.

"Because I followed her to the Mohegan Sun Casino and I've had a trooper keep an eye on her since. She's only been in the state since Mitchell's funeral but has made several trips there already. Always betting big. I also placed a call to the police in Sint Maarten where she usually spends the winter. They checked the island's casinos for me and reported back this morning. Seems she's a regular at the gaming tables and drops a bundle whenever she stays on the island."

"But I thought she was in Sint Maarten when Mitchell was killed," Latima reminded Blaustein with a gotcha smile.

"Maybe she was," Blaustein conceded. "At least we thought so at first because there were no visas in her passport to coincide with the time of the murder. But there are ways to avoid Immigration. Like chartering a private plane and landing on an unregulated airfield somewhere. So there's a long-shot possibility she could have come back to the States, knocked off her ex and then returned to the island with no one the wiser. Trouble is we can't prove it."

"I don't think we should consider Deirdre Lawrence a suspect," Gardner, who hitherto had been silent, chipped in.

"You're just sweet on her," Blaustein teased, balling up a paper napkin and tossing it at his partner.

"No I'm not!" Gardner blushed, his pleasant face lighting up like a schoolgirl's. "It just doesn't add up. You know it doesn't. She left a trail a mile wide in the kitchen and the bedroom. Why would she do that if she was careful to eliminate the fingerprints at the murder scene? And why would she want to kill him, anyway? What motive did she have?"

"Maybe he told her he was dumping her?" Seymour suggested.

"If he was planning on dumping her, he had a funny way of telling her. He took her up to his bedroom with only an hour to spare before catching a plane. Does that make sense to you?"

"Not much," Blaustein agreed, "and besides, it really doesn't look much like a crime of passion. It seems too planned. Too neat. Not exactly spontaneous. Which leaves us with just Lawrence and Alison Mitchell. The jealous husband or the greedy ex wife, take your pick."

"And then there's Augusta Scott. Where does she fit in?" Seymour reminded him.

"My guess is she found out something about the killer and he silenced her. Which brings us back to why she tried to call us. If only we knew that, we'd have the answer."

"If only," Gardner sighed.

17

FINALLY ALL THE PIECES WERE IN PLACE AND EDWARD MORRISON
left to assist in the search of Herman Archer's house. Assigned the role
of keeping an eye on the suspect, Dina had taken a seat in a carrel
along the far wall of the library. Occasionally turning the pages of
a book she was not actually reading, she had an unobstructed view
of the reserve desk. Archie, dressed in his customary jacket and tie,
hair combed neatly into place had a benign look on his face. He
was in his accustomed spot and apparently doing what librarians are
supposed to do. Dina saw no evidence of a transaction taking place.
That was not the object today, as long as Archer kept to his normal
routine, they could search his residence and all would be well. But
just before noon, when he usually took his lunch break, the head
librarian approached him and he went into the office to take a call.

Guessing that Archer might be on the move again and knowing
that the only way he could leave the library was through the front
entrance, Dina decided to preempt him. She gathered her books,
put on her coat and hat and went outside. A weak January sun was
filtering through leafless trees that usually shaded the quadrangle in

warmer weather. Despite a cold, unpleasant wind, cigarette-smoking students were huddled in a small group on the library steps. Joining them, not to smoke but to make herself inconspicuous, she completed the camouflage by putting on dark glasses. She did not have to wait long for Archie to emerge. In a matter of minutes, the reserve librarian appeared and scurried off across the quadrangle, his head bowed against the wind.

Immediately Dina dialed Edward's number. "He's on the move."

"Shit! I hope he isn't going home."

"I'm on his tail. When I know where he's headed, I'll call it in."

"I'll keep my line free."

With that, Dina was hurrying in pursuit. As before, Archie left the campus and headed toward the bus stop on the corner of Dixwell. Shielded from view behind a commercial van, Dina paused, hit the redial button and waited for Morrison to pick up.

"I think he's heading for the Dixwell Avenue bus stop."

"If he goes to the same place he did last time, we could be waiting for him and his contact. We'd catch them with the goods."

"My thought exactly," Dina agreed. "But just because Archer arrived first the last time doesn't mean his contact won't be there waiting for him. You don't want to spook the man."

"Good point. We'll arrange to go in several unmarked cars and arrive separately."

"I see the bus coming. Better go."

"Okay then. Stay with him and let us know if his rendezvous has changed."

Dina cut the connection, hurried across the street and boarded the bus just before the doors began to close. As she dug out her change and fed her fare into the coin slot, she looked up. Archie was looking in her direction. Was it her imagination, or had there been a flicker of recognition in his eyes? Hoping he had not made her, that he was merely looking at her as one might any fellow passenger, she kept her face blank as she made her way past him to a seat near the back of the bus. When he did not turn round to look at her, and made no attempt to call anyone on his cell phone, she began to feel reasonably certain that she was in the clear.

Just as before, Archie got out when the bus reached the strip mall. As soon as he did, Dina called Morrison.

"He just got off the bus. Same place."

"1 see him. We're in place. Three units."

"Any sign of his contact?"

"Not yet. No one has arrived here in the past fifteen minutes."

"I'll get off at the next stop and keep out of sight." There was no rush this time to keep an eye on the librarian. Her task was essentially done.

From behind the same ice cream kiosk as before, Dina scanned the parking lot. There was no sign of Archie, and if Edward had not told her that the unmarked cars were already in place, she would not have noticed them either. All was quiet. A woman emerged from the mini-market carrying two plastic bags of groceries. Dina held her breath as she watched the woman walk to her car and unlock the door. It would have really messed things up if Archie's supplier had chosen this moment to arrive. But he did not. The woman deposited her grocery bags on the back seat, got in and drove off.

After a five minute wait that seemed more like five hours, the black Lincoln drove into the lot. Simultaneously Archie appeared from the Laundromat and walked over to it. As on the previous occasion, he opened the passenger-side door and got in. The second that occurred, cars from three different corners of the lot converged on the Lincoln. One blocked it from the front, a second blocked it from behind and the third pulled up on the driver's side. As if choreographed, the doors of the police cars opened and six men in plain clothes got out, their guns drawn. Partially shielded behind the open doors of the three unmarked cars, Morrison and his five NHPD colleagues had the occupants of the Lincoln surrounded and their escape blocked. The two men in the Lincoln could not put up even token resistance. When ordered to, they got out of the car, their hands in the air. One was Carmen Mendoza, elegant in a double-breasted, camel- hair coat, a Burberry scarf and brown leather driving gloves. His dark hair was slicked back. And except for the dark eyes that looked daggers, he was the epitome of cool. On the other hand, Herman Archer looked like a rabbit cornered by a hunting dog, small and hunched over, an expression of sheer terror on his face.

As both men were being read their rights, cuffed and escorted into the rear seats of two separate police cars, the NHPD narcotics officers began to search the Lincoln. They did not have to look very hard. Inside the shoe box that was sitting on the front seat, they found a dozen glycine bags of white powder.

"Unless this is sugar, we've hit pay dirt!" Morrison cried.

"Let's check the trunk as well," Barrett had crossed the parking lot to participate in the collar.

One of the New Haven detectives hit the release button and the trunk flew open. "There's at least a kilo in here," a New Haven narc called out. "This would have fetched a quarter million on the street. Detective Barrett, you did good."

"It wasn't exactly a solo effort," Dina protested with an embarrassed smile.

Then her smile faded as she noticed a pair of resentful eyes staring at her from the rear seat of the police car. Archie definitely recognized her now. But it no longer mattered that her cover was blown. His arrest made it irrelevant. Or so she thought.

While Barrett and Morrison were arresting the drug dealers, Blaustein, Gardner and a team from the Major Crime Squad were taking advantage of a brief January thaw. With the daytime temperature above freezing for a change, they were combing Godfrey Mitchell's yard in the hope of finding clues previously buried beneath a blanket of snow. Neither Blaustein nor Gardner was optimistic about their chances of finding any material evidence after all this time. And the slight hope that they would find tire tracks evaporated when the driveway turned out to be paved. It yielded nothing, not even the odd cigarette butt. The brick walkways leading to the front door and around the house to the rear, were similarly sterile. So Blaustein, Gardner and their team of techs were concentrating on the flower beds that framed the house. Even though there had been no obvious sign of forced entry, they combed the ground beneath the windows. They could not overlook the possibility that the killer may have entered the house through an unlocked window, latched the window once inside and then left the house through the self-locking front door. What Blaustein hoped to find in the soil beneath the windows was a footprint with a clear and distinctive tread. But he was far from optimistic. It was much more likely that the killer had been admitted through the front door and that the killer was someone who knew Mitchell and knew him well. Someone who had a personal grudge to settle. Someone like Sidney Lawrence, for instance. For all the lack of physical evidence, Blaustein's money was still on the aggrieved husband.

But scouring the grounds proved to be an exercise in futility. They found nothing. And when it became clear that their search was fruitless, Blaustein sent the rest of the crew back to headquarters and he and Gardner drove over to Winslow Street to pick up the answering machine tape Kelly Richmond had promised them.

"I'll stay outside for a smoke, if you don't mind," Gardner said, when they got to the Winslow Street address.

Blaustein went up the sagging steps to the front door and rang the buzzer with Kelly Richmond's name taped under it. When she didn't answer, he opened the door and went inside. The downstairs hall was gloomy, wallpaper peeling off the walls, the smell of bacon grease pervasive. Feeling hungry and regretting that he had skipped breakfast, he climbed the stairs to the third floor. Kelly's bicycle was there, chained to the newel-post. He knocked on the door and waited. When there was no answer, he checked the landing for the message tape she had promised to leave for him if she went out. The landing was empty. Returning to the front foyer, he was greeted by an older woman with her hair done up in pink rollers. Her door was ajar and the bacon smell was even stronger than before. "Are you the Detective?" she asked.

"Yes, I am," he said, showing her his identification.

"Kelly said you'd be by. She left something for you. I'll go get it," she turned and disappeared, closing the door behind her.

After a brief pause the woman reappeared and handed him an envelope with his name on it. He thanked her and tore it open. It contained a small message tape and a note written on lined yellow note paper.

"Dear Detective Blaustein," it read. "I'm sorry I couldn't wait. I have a class at ten. Here's the tape. I hope your lab people can do something with it, Kelly."

"I hope so too," he thought, replacing the note and the tape in the envelope and pocketing it.

Outside, Gardner was leaning against the car. He flicked away his cigarette as Blaustein approached and opened the door., "I called headquarters," Gardner said getting in. "There was a message for you from Dina."

"What was the message?"

"She and Morrison have a collar in the Whitney drug case. They will be wrapping up the details next week. If she isn't reassigned, she hopes she'll be able to join us full time."

"Remind me to speak to Gordon about it," Jackson put the key in the ignition. "I have the message tape. Richmond wasn't in but she left it with a neighbor. After we've dropped it off at the lab, I'd like to grab a late breakfast. You agreeable?" he asked, knowing what Gardner's answer would be.

"Always," Gardner said predictably and folding the newspaper to the daily crossword, they headed back to the highway.

"There's only a slim chance the message tape can tell us much more than we already know. That Scott called to cancel her appointment with Richmond."

"Hopefully it will tell us why," Gardener replied, checking out the crossword as he spoke.

Blaustein hoped his partner was correct and not just putting a rosy construction on things as usual. But that was one of the good things about Huey Gardner, he always looked on the bright side.

Apparently untarnished by years in a job that bred cynicism, he remained upbeat no matter what the circumstances. It was why he had lasted so long. That and the ability to accept whatever life dealt him. Besides losing a son in the Iraq War and his wife after a long battle with cancer, tragedies that would have embittered the most sanguine, he remained a cheerful soul. Huey Gardner simply rolled with the punches, just like Greta, Blaustein thought. Greta had the same resilience.

"You have to come over for dinner one night soon," Blaustein said, voicing an unspoken thought. "You've never met Greta, have you?"

"No I haven't and I'd like to very much," Gardner looked up from his crossword puzzle and smiled. "If it isn't too much trouble."

"On the contrary, Greta loves it when I bring colleagues home for dinner. In New York City, when we were first married, I did it frequently. Even last minute. She enjoys having company. But now, except for inviting Dina over occasionally, I haven't been very sociable."

"I would be honored to meet Greta. She sounds like a special lady," Gardner favored his partner with a warm smile before retreating to his puzzle again.

They drove on in silence till they reached Meriden, parked in the headquarters lot, headed straight for the lab and went inside.

"This is the message tape I told you about," Blaustein said, dropping the envelope on a technician's desk. "The message has been erased. Please try to restore it if it's at all possible."

The technician took the tape out of the envelope and looked at it. "I'll do what I can. Should be able to tell in about an hour. That okay?"

"That's fine. We'll come in after breakfast."

"Breakfast? It's almost lunchtime," the technician looked at his watch.

"I know, but I have a hankering for bacon and eggs. I hope the diner down the road is still serving breakfast."

18

THE NEXT MORNING WAS SATURDAY AND DINA HAD THE DAY OFF. From the window in Freddie's kitchen, she watched as a couple of audacious squirrels raided the bird-feeder. Even on the bleakest day, life always seemed to be a lark for the spunky little creatures. Today they were frolicking in sunshine that had brought a welcome January thaw. A winter-faded lawn was emerging from its blanket of snow and in the warmer spots, precocious crocus leaves had surfaced prematurely. But the sun gave only the illusion of warmth.

Turning from the window, cell phone in hand, Dina dialed Elizabeth Randolph, chair of the Rutgers History Department. It was the last of the phone numbers on the list of calls Scott made before she was killed. Huey had already crossed Randolph's name off the list with the notation that Scott's call was to confirm her participation in the spring colloquium. But Dina was still not satisfied. There could have been more to the conversation. If Scott were thinking of taking on Kelly Richmond, a recent Rutgers graduate, wouldn't it have been perfectly natural to ask Randolph about her? And if she had, was it more than coincidence that Scott's very next call was to cancel her meeting with Kelly Richmond? Ignoring the risk of annoying Randolph with another call from the Connecticut Major Crime Squad, Dina decided to follow up on what was nothing more than a hunch. "I've already spoken to one of your detectives," came the clipped response when Dina identified herself as a detective on the Connecticut Major Crime Squad.

"Yes, I'm aware of that, Professor Randolph and I regret the inconvenience," Dina replied, apologetic but not obsequious. "But if you don't mind, there are a couple of things that still need clarification. You told Detective Blaustein that the intent of Professor Scott's call was to invite you to a spring symposium at Whitney?" Dina said.

"Yes, I agreed to present a paper," the response came with patient resignation.

"I know that's what you told my colleague when he called yesterday," Dina confirmed.,"but I have a couple of additional questions if you don't mind?"

"If it won't take too long," Randolph replied with the impatience of someone glancing at her watch.

"Thank you," Dina continued politely. "Did you know Professor Scott personally?"

"Only slightly. We've met professionally a few times, and I respected her work. I can't say that I knew her personally."

"Was the symposium the only topic you discussed when she called you?" Dina probed cautiously. She did not want to put words into the woman's mouth.

"Well," Randolph hesitated, "it was the main purpose of her call. But just before she rang off, she asked me about a former student here."

"Do you happen to remember the student's name?" Despite a rush of expectation, Dina asked her question in a calm professional tone.

"Why yes, Kelly Richmond," Randolph was giving away nothing but the barest facts. Dina felt she was pulling teeth, "And what did she ask about the student?"

"Whether Richmond was a good student."

"And what did you tell her?" Still more teeth.

"I told her that Kelly was one of the best students to graduate from the Rutgers History program in the past ten years. But frankly, her question surprised me."

"Why did it surprise you? You must get frequent questions about former students."

"Of course, we're routinely asked about former students applying to graduate school or going on to teaching positions but that's not what I found odd. What was odd, Detective Barrett, was that the question was asked about this particular student. As I told Professor Scott, Kelly Richmond was killed in a traffic accident a week after graduation. The driver of a pick-up truck ran a red light and broadsided Kelly's car. He was killed almost instantly. A tragic waste and a promising career ended before it had begun."

He? To make sure she had heard correctly, Dina rephrased the professor's words. "Did I hear you say he was killed?"

"Yes."

"And that's exactly what you told Professor Scott?"

"It was."

"Did Professor Scott tell you why she was interested in this particular student."

"No. And I didn't ask," Randolph paused before continuing. "If I were to offer a possible explanation, I'd say that Augusta wanted to cite a senior research paper that Kelly published in his final year. Perhaps she was curious about the student who wrote it."

"Was anything further said?"

"Not that I can recall," Randolph said with a long-suffering sigh.

"Thank you Professor, you've been an enormous help."

Dina hung up feeling confused. She tapped a finger on the kitchen counter wondering what to do next. Kelly Richmond looked and acted like a typical student. But if Kelly Richmond wasn't Kelly Richmond then who was she? More to the point, was it possible that Augusta Scott had confronted Kelly when she found out about the deception? And if so, was Scott killed in order to keep her from dooming Kelly's academic career? If that were the case, then Mitchell may have uncovered the same information and been murdered for the same reason.

Though convinced she was onto something, Dina was still puzzled. How did a student who did not own a car get to Scott's place? Or to Mitchell's for that matter? Both were far from campus and neither place was on a bus route. Of course, Kelly could have rented a car,. If so, it would be easy enough to check out the rental places. With this thought in mind, and in any case eager to share what she had learned, Dina dialed Blaustein's number. But he was not at headquarters in Meriden, nor at the East Haven command center. And when she dialed his cell phone, the line was busy. Frustrated and impatient, she called headquarters again and left a message for him to call her. Then she called information to get the number of the New Brunswick Police Department. When she got through, she identified herself and asked the policeman on duty to check out a traffic accident that had taken the life of a Kelly Richmond some time between May and September of the previous year.

"Sure, it won't take a second," the officer replied and Dina could hear keys clicking as she waited for him to come back on line.

"Here it is," he said. "The accident occurred in June of last year. Richmond was in a two-car accident at a traffic light in downtown New Brunswick. The other driver ran the light and plowed into Richmond's car. The male driver of the other vehicle and a female passenger in Richmond's car walked away unharmed. Richmond wasn't so lucky. He was killed instantly."

"He?" Dina wanted to confirm what Professor Randolph told her.

"Yes, Ma'am. Male Caucasian. Twenty two. Six five. Two thirty. Anything else I can tell you?"

"Can you give me the name and a description of the female passenger in Richmond's car?"

The computer keys tapped again before the answer came. "Charlotte Chapman. No description. And there won't be hospital records. She was never admitted. Her address at the time of the accident was 730 Newbury Street, New Brunswick."

"That's a big help. Thank you, Officer," Dina said writing down the name and address.

After disconnecting, she dialed New Jersey information a second time. But this time she drew a blank. There was no current telephone listing for a Charlotte Chapman and she had a feeling she knew why. By now unable to contain her excitement, she tried calling Blaustein again. Again without success. So she left a second message for him to call her back and hung up.

Frustrated she paced. She simply could not wait around in Freddie's house doing nothing. With Blaustein unavailable, she decided to go ahead on her own. It was Saturday and she had no other commitments. Rutgers was only three hours away, so why not just go over there and poke around? Without a second thought, she grabbed her coat, locked the house and hopped in her car. Her mind was already chasing down the New Jersey Turnpike, knocking on the door of 730 Newbury Street, and wondering what lay behind it.

Like a bench of dignified judges, a flock of imperturbable sparrows perched on a sign cantilevered high above the New Jersey Turnpike. At the tollbooth ahead, an impatient motorist honked his horn. A trucker rolled down his window and swore. The driver in a beat-up Thunderbird turned up the volume of its multi-speaker system so high that the vehicle vibrated with the boom of the bass. Ignoring the racket, Dina dialed Jackson Blaustein once again. She knew that she risked a lecture when she told him she was chasing down a lead on her own. But he needed to know that Kelly Richmond was not really Kelly Richmond. That Augusta Scott discovered the fraud when she called Elizabeth Randolph at Rutgers on the day before her murder. And that Scott may have paid with her life when she confronted Kelly Richmond with her discovery. But Dina's call to Jackson was never connected. Halfway through dialing, the loud warning beep of her dying cell-phone battery interrupted her. Now incommunicado, she tossed the useless phone onto the seat beside her, coasted toward the toll booth and sorted through her purse for change. She paid the tollbooth attendant and took the exit to New Brunswick. At the first gas station she came to, she bought a cup of coffee and a local map.

On the three-hour drive from New Haven, Dina had tried to analyze her feelings toward the woman she had known as Kelly Richmond. She had instinctively liked the tall blonde in her out-of shape sweaters, sensible boots and granny glasses. She had sympathized with her evident predicament. Even trusted her. But that was then, when she assumed Kelly Richmond was a struggling graduate student. Now she did not know what to assume. Professor Randolph's revelation had knocked Dina for a loop. Confused and left with a sense of betrayal, she no longer knew what to think except that there was a distinct possibility that Kelly Richmond's charade was tied to at least one of the two murders on the Whitney campus. Dina was coming to terms with the possibility that the woman was a killer. Perhaps a multiple murderer.

Determined to find some answers, Dina drove to 730 Newbury Street, the last known address of Charlotte Chapman, the passenger who had walked away from the crash that killed the real Kelly Richmond. The house was a two-family structure with an aging roof, a sagging porch and peeling paint. Dina got out of the car and climbed the rickety steps to the front door. Beside the door was an intercom with two names on it, neither legible. Hesitating, she pushed the downstairs buzzer and waited. Moments later a curtain moved in a window overlooking the porch and after a brief delay, the intercom buzzed. The outer door yielded to her touch and she stepped into a gloomy hall lit by a bare bulb in a rusted wall-sconce. To her right was a stairway with worn rubber treads. The door to her left was ajar on a chain.

"Yes, what is it?" Came a querulous voice from behind the door.

"Connecticut State Police, Ma'am," Dina said, proffering identification. "May I have a word?"

There was fear in the eyes of the woman looking back at Dina but she scraped back the chain, and let Dina in. The woman may have been in her fifties, but looked older. Prematurely worn. Of medium height and very thin. She was probably pretty once. Now she looked sad-eyed. Her hair was a faded blond. Her skin was sallow and lined about the mouth. She was dressed in worn, brown corduroy pants and a button-up cardigan with pockets that sagged. Everything about her seemed tired. Without saying a word, she led the way into the sitting room but did not ask Dina to sit down. Which was just as well. Dina had no desire to do so. The smell of cat litter was overpowering, and the source of the odor was ensconced proprietorially in the center of the couch. She got straight to the point.

"Does a Charlotte Chapman live here?"

"No she doesn't."

"Do you know where I can contact her?"

"I'm sorry, I can't help you," the woman's eyelids flickered like the nictitating membrane of a reptile. Dina half expected her to hiss. Her mouth was set in an obstinate line. There was going to be as little cooperation here as possible.

"She lived here about a year ago, didn't she?" Dina had come too far to be put off so easily.

"Yes," the woman admitted after hesitating for a fraction of a second.

"In this apartment?" Dina insisted.

The woman nodded.

"With you, I assume?" From the accumulation of clutter it seemed clear that the woman had lived in the same place for much more than a year. "Are you Mrs. Chapman?"

The woman nodded again.

"How are you and Charlotte related?"

"She's my daughter, has something happened to her? Why are you asking about her?"

"I have a few questions about a friend of hers, Kelly Richmond."

"She was with Kelly when his car was hit by a drunk driver. She's already told the police all she knows about the accident. I don't know what else she can tell you." With the focus of Dina's questions shifting, the woman's relief was evident and Dina wondered why.

"You knew Kelly?"

"No I didn't," Mrs. Chapman pulled a crumpled tissue from the pocket of her sweater and blew her nose.

"Well, I'd like to ask Charlotte about him. Do you know where I can locate her?"

"I don't. She left here shortly after the accident and I haven't seen her since."

"And you haven't heard from your daughter since?" Dina was incredulous.

The woman shook her head and sighed. "Charlotte and I had a disagreement. I don't really expect to hear from her."

"Do you have any idea where she went?"

Again there was a moment's hesitation before the woman shook her head. And Dina knew she was lying.

"Sometimes mothers and daughters don't get along," Dina said speaking from experience. "Perhaps she'll come around. When she does, will you let her know that I'm trying to reach her. Please have her call me collect. Here's my card. I'll write my home phone number on the back of it."

With her cell phone temporarily disabled, and not knowing when she would recharge it, Dina wrote down Freddie's number and handed Mrs. Chapman the card. "Can you tell me what you two quarreled about?"

"It was personal," the woman's pale cheeks flushed and her chin came up indignantly.

"Yes, of course it was. I'm sorry I asked," Dina managed to sound contrite. "If you hear from her please ask her to call me. I really need to ask her about Kelly Richmond."

The woman merely nodded. She did not bother to show Dina out.

Dina's second stop was the Rutgers History Department. She knew that Elizabeth Randolph would not be happy to see her so soon after their telephone conversation, but having come this far and having learned nothing, she decided to go for it. She drove across town and parked her car near a grassy quadrangle at the center of the Rutgers College campus. A student gave her directions to the History Department and she found it without any difficulty. Steeling herself for a possible rejection, she entered the building only to learn that Professor Randolph was not in and had only limited office hours on a Saturday.

"Is there someone else who can help you?" The Departmental secretary asked.

"I hope so," Dina did not to ask about Kelly Richmond. Instead she asked the secretary if she knew a student named Charlotte Chapman.

The secretary shook her head.

"She may have graduated with a degree in history about a year ago?"

"I'll check for you," the woman opened the menu on her computer. When the list of the previous year's graduating class came up, she shook her head. "No student by that name graduated. At least not in the past year."

Dina frowned, plainly perplexed. "Was a student by that name enrolled here at all last year?"

Again the secretary scrolled through a list. This time she nodded. "Yes, she was a declared History major. Completed her third year. Decent grades. But she didn't come back this year."

"Do you know whether she transferred her credits to another university?""

"You'll have to ask the Dean of Students. His office isn't far from here. Someone should be on duty today."

At the Dean's office Dina drew another blank. Shy only twenty-two credits, Charlotte Chapman had dropped out. The Dean's secretary did not oblige Dina with a transcript. That information was privileged, but when pressed, she told Dina which courses Charlotte had taken the previous year. Only one of them was in British history: a course in British Imperialism.

"Could you tell me whether Kelly Richmond was enrolled in that course?"

"He was," the secretary responded without further comment.

So Charlotte Chapman may have met Kelly Richmond when both were enrolled in the course on British Imperialism. With this thought in mind, Dina went back to the History Department. This time she trolled the hall till she found the lecture room where the professor who taught British Imperialism was giving a make-up exam. When the session ended and the students came out, she went in. The professor, a man who looked to be about forty, was in the process of taking down a map with a lot of pink on it.

"The once mighty Raj," he said, looking up as she came in.

Dina introduced herself as a detective on the Connecticut Major Crime Squad, neglecting to mention that she had no jurisdiction in New Jersey. "I wonder if you have a moment, Professor?"

"Not much more than that," he looked at his watch. "I'm playing racquet-ball in a half hour. So shoot."

"Did you happen to have a student named Charlotte Chapman in your class last year?"

"Yes, I believe so. Not a bad student. Mostly Bs as I recall."

"How about Kelly Richmond?"

"A real tragedy there," he shook his head sadly. "Kelly was brilliant. The type of student you fantasize about. A challenging mind and a hell of a writer. He was accepted into the graduate program at Whitney but sad to say, he never got there. He was killed in a car crash just after graduation. Is that why you're asking?" He frowned. "I thought it was ruled an accident."

"As far as I know it was. But Charlotte Chapman was with him when the accident occurred and I'm trying to locate her."

"Charlotte in some sort of hot water then?"

"Not at all. We think she might be a witness in another case we're working on and we've been unable to locate her. Do you happen to remember what she looks like, professor?"

He pursed his lips and drew his eyebrows together in an effort to conjure up an image. "Tall. Blonde. Good facial bones."

"Did she wear glasses?"

He shook his head. "Don't believe so."

"Do you happen to know why she didn't come back this year?"

"Didn't know she wasn't back. I see a lot of students in the course of a year, Detective. It isn't possible to keep track of them all."

"Just the brilliant ones like Kelly Richmond?"

He nodded, "Kelly was one of a kind."

"Do you happen to know who any of his friends were?"

"He was a bit of a loner. If he hung out with anyone at all it was with Keith Martin."

"As far as you know, did Keith also graduate last year or is he still around?"

"He was a basketball red shirt his second year. Stayed on this year to do his Masters. If you want to catch him, he'll most likely be working out with the team. They have a game against Michigan tomorrow. You can't miss him. Six eleven with bright red hair. But I'd wait for practice to end before button-holing him." Again he looked at his watch. "And now I really must leave, if you don't mind."

"Of course not. You've been most helpful. Thank you."

She left him stuffing his lecture notes into the side pocket of a gym bag and then found her way to the gym where she hung around until the players came out of the locker room. It was easy to spot Keith Martin. Two or three inches taller than the other players, he ducked as he came through the door. He was dressed in jeans and an unzipped varsity jacket. His red hair was damp from the shower.

"Keith Martin?" She asked.

"Yes," He obligingly turned to face her. "You the press?"

"No, sorry," she handed him her card. "Dina Barrett, Detective Connecticut Major Crime Squad."

"Whatever it was I didn't do it," he laughed, raising both hands in a gesture of surrender.

"And if you did, I doubt they'd send me to haul you in," she said, craning to look up at him. "I just have a few questions about your friend Kelly Richmond, if you don't mind."

Instantly the smile left his eyes. He waved to the team-mates who had been hanging around waiting for him. "I'll catch up with you guys later."

When the basketball players had gone, he gestured to a nearby bench. "Why don't we sit down so you can avoid neck strain."

Seated on the bench, she had a better opportunity to look at him. Her instinctive reaction was to like him. Pale-skinned and freckled like most red-heads, he had a friendly, open face. His hands and feet were enormous. The former likewise covered with freckles. The latter encased in the largest sneakers she had ever seen. Even seated, he towered over her.

"When Kelly was killed," she began, "a fellow student named Charlotte Chapman was with him. She was lucky enough to walk away from the accident, but she did not return to school this year. Any idea how I can locate her?"

"None," He shook his head.

"Did you know Charlotte?"

"Not really, I noticed her in class though. There aren't too many decent-looking tall women around, so I noticed her right off," he grinned.

"Was she a close friend of Kelly's?"

"Not as far as I know. At least he wasn't dating her or anything like that. He had a steady girlfriend but they broke up a few months before the accident."

"Yet Charlotte was in the car with him when the accident occurred, right?"

"Maybe he was giving her a ride home."

"Do you know who any of Charlotte's friends are? Anyone who would know where I can find her?"

"Sorry I don't. All I know is that she lived off-campus somewhere. The Registrar might have her address," he suggested helpfully. "Maybe she had a room-mate?"

But Dina knew that was not the case. In fact, if her hunch was correct, then she might be the only one who really knew where Charlotte Chapman was and what she was doing there. But why? Why had she used Kelly Richmond's college record to get into the Whitney Graduate School? Why take a chance like that with only one year left to graduate. She could have completed her degree and

210

then gone on to graduate school almost anywhere. Perhaps not to Whitney or Yale but certainly to a pretty decent History Department somewhere else. What was her hurry? Why take the risk? History was not a cut-throat business. It was not like trying to get into law or medical school. Her deception made no sense at all.

"Tell me about Kelly," she asked, trying a different approach.

"I sat next to him the first day of class our freshman year," Keith smiled sadly. "I guess I sort of gravitated to him. He was big like me, maybe six five, and I thought that maybe he was also a basketball recruit. But I was way off. Kelly was totally uncoordinated. A big klutz. Actually a big, shy, very gentle klutz. But a brilliant one, a true scholar. He was never happier than when he was buried in a book, or more excited than when he was writing a research paper. He actually enjoyed doing research," he shook his head in wonderment. "His father was a high school history teacher. I guess he passed his passion on to his son. It even rubbed off on me a bit after getting to know Kelly. But I became a history major because I didn't know what else to major in. For Kelly, history was a calling.

"Sounds like you were very fond of him."

"He was the best friend I ever had. When I had to red-shirt my sophomore year because of a knee injury, I was really down. It frustrated the Hell out of me. But Kelly stood by me. He encouraged me to rehab. Encouraged me to study. Man, he was really there for me. That's one of the reasons it's so hard to come to grips with the fact that he's no longer around. I feel I still owe him and I can't deliver."

Feeling there was no response she could make to that sentiment, Dina stood up. "Thanks for your help Keith. If you happen to be in contact with Charlotte, please let me know. I'll write my home phone number on the back of my card." Which she did as she spoke. "Call me collect."

"No sweat." The genial giant unfolded from the bench and gave her his huge paw to shake.

"Good luck against Michigan."

"Yeah. Let's hope we kick butt."

19

WHILE DINA BARRETT WAS CHASING PHANTOMS IN NEW JERSEY,
Blaustein and Gardner were engaged in surveillance, a duty Blaustein
considered the most horrendously dull aspect of police work. They
were parked down the street from Lawrence's house, sustenance
in the form of donuts and coffee on the seat between them. It was
below freezing but they could not run the engine without attracting
attention. To prevent fogging, the windows were cracked a little
and that made it seem even colder. As usual Gardner was doing the
Courant crossword. Blaustein was on the phone to the crime lab for
an update on Kelly Richmond's message tape. Before giving him the
bottom line, the technician favored him with a lengthy treatise on his
methodology. It proved to be an ominous beginning. Every known
technique had failed and despite their best efforts, the lab had been
unable to restore the message tape. Blaustein felt cheated, as if the
last slender thread that connected him with Augusta Scott had been
snapped. It did not much matter that the message on the tape was
likely nothing more than a postponement of the professor's meeting
with her potential graduate student. It was not knowing for certain

that left him frustrated. He thanked the technician, and asked to be transferred to Lennie Hoffman's line.

"Looks like a bust here, Detective," Lennie said when he recognized Blaustein's voice. "Professor Scott's home computer was wiped clean by someone who knew what he was doing and we can't restore it. We've also been all through Professor Scott's office computer and there's nothing much there. At least of a personal nature. Zip. Even her letters were work-related. You and Detective Gardner can look through the files for yourselves, but unless the killer had something against British history, I doubt you'll find anything useful," Lennie giggled. "Myself, I hated history in school. Even so, I wouldn't have gone so far as to kill my history teacher."

"We'll take a look when we get back to headquarters, but I'm inclined to take your word for it. Thanks a lot Lennie," Blaustein turned to his partner after disconnecting, "Well that's that then. There's nothing helpful on either of Scott's computers, and the messages on Kelly Richmond's answering tape can't be restored."

"Maybe Dina turned up something useful from that telephone list," Gardner was ever the optimist. "Perhaps that's why she left you a message. I'll try her number again."

He dialed. Waited and shook his head. "Still not answering."

"Try her at Mrs. Hathaway's number."

Which Huey did. Waited, and shook his head again. "No response there either."

Just then Lawrence emerged from his front door. He was wearing a navy sweatsuit with a Whitney logo on it, a wool cap pulled low over his forehead and over-sized mittens. Without preliminaries of any kind, he set off in their direction with long, practiced strides.

"Shit. Do you think he'll make us?" Gardner muttered, opening the newspaper so that it blocked the window.

Already ahead of his colleague, Blaustein had started the car and had pulled away from the curb before the professor came abreast of them. But there was no need, staring straight ahead, his breath preceding him in a frosty cloud, Lawrence seemed oblivious.

"What now?" Gardner asked when it was safe to come out from behind his newspaper.

"Well obviously we can't come back and set up shop in the same place. That'd be much too obvious. So where to?" Blaustein grumbled as Lawrence turned a corner and disappeared from the rear-view mirror.

"There's an elementary school down the block. He'll have to pass by there on his way back to the house."

"Good thought. The school lot will be filled with teachers' cars so we won't stand out."

"Also we'll be able to run the engine without drawing attention. So at least we'll be able to keep warm," Gardner said, blowing on his frozen fingers.

After identifying themselves but giving no explanation to the school security guard, Blaustein found a spot with a good view of the road and they prepared for another wait. About forty-five minutes later, Lawrence passed the school on his way home. He was still running effortlessly.

"The man's an athlete as well as a scholar," Gardner said wistfully.

"And perhaps also a murderer," Blaustein responded uncharitably.

They drank some more coffee, munched their glazed donuts and waited as another deadly dull half hour passed. Gardner had finished the puzzle and was working on the bridge problem when Deidre Lawrence drove by in her red Contour. She was alone.

"No point following her," Blaustein said for something to say.

"Uh huh," Gardner gave up on the bridge problem, folded the newspaper and shoved it into the pocket of his coat.

"There he is."

A moment later, Lawrence drove past the school in a maroon Chevy Blazer. Blaustein waited until he had turned the corner, before pulling out of the lot. He hung way back as the Blazer maneuvered the suburban streets and made for the highway. Tailing the Blazer would be easy, that was one of the things Blaustein liked about SUVs. They made highly visible targets. Once they got to the highway, he was able to keep several cars behind Lawrence and still keep him in sight. After a few miles the Blazer took the exit for downtown New Haven.

"Damn!" Showing more animation than usual, Gardner pounded his fist on the dashboard. "Lawrence's probably just going to Whitney. All that waiting for nothing."

"We not only waited for nothing, we got up at the crack of dawn on a Saturday morning to wait for nothing," Blaustein grumbled.

But Lawrence did not go to the Whitney campus. Instead he drove in the direction of downtown New Haven. Once there, he circled the downtown area slowly, as if he was looking for a parking space. Not finding one, he continued down Elm Street and turned into a public parking lot a few blocks from the Green. Blaustein, followed at a distance and pulled into an illegal space just beyond the parking lot entrance. With eyes glued to the rear-view mirror, he waited and watched as Lawrence parked his car. After the professor, no longer in running clothes, left on foot, both men got out. Blaustein affixed a police card to the sun-visor and they prepared to follow.

"Keep tailing him, I'll cross the street and shadow him from there," Blaustein said. "I doubt he'll be able to shake both of us."

But Lawrence, his head slightly bowed as he walked into a wind that had turned brisk and cold, did not act like a man intent on shaking a tail. He walked with a purpose and did not look over his shoulder once. When he reached the Green, he stopped to chat with a student wheeling a bicycle. Gardner immediately took a seat on a park bench and kept watch huddled behind his ubiquitous newspaper. Across the road Blaustein hesitated. He was out in the open, unable to simply stop and stare without being spotted. Seeing the New Haven Public Library to his right, he climbed the steps and, with a quick over-the-shoulder glance to make sure Lawrence was still engaged in conversation, dodged inside. From behind a glass door panel, he had a clear view of the Green. He could see that Lawrence was still in animated discussion with the student. And he could see Gardner, struggling to keep his newspaper from flapping in the breeze.

A city bus, stopping to drop off a passenger in front of the library, momentarily blocked Blaustein's view. And by the time the bus lumbered off again, Lawrence was no longer talking to the student. In fact Lawrence was talking to Gardner. Or more likely, judging by his body language, haranguing him. And Gardner, looking chagrinned, was merely shrugging in response to the tirade. The professor's fists were balled and his shoulders hunched. Even at a distance, Blaustein could tell he was irate. Obviously he had seen past the newspaper subterfuge. Which would not have been difficult. Reading a newspaper in a howling gale was a way to draw attention, rather than avoid it. When Lawrence finally stormed off, Gardner got up off the bench and slowly strolled in the opposite direction. If his partner knew Blaustein was watching, he gave no indication of it.

Lawrence, looking over his shoulder a couple of times to make sure Gardner's retreating figure was really retreating, took off across the Green toward Chapel Street. When he considered it safe, Blaustein left his sanctuary and followed, chuckling to himself. He was dying to know what had passed between Lawrence and his partner, but right now his priority was finding out where the professor was headed. Skirting the Green, rather than crossing it behind his quarry, Blaustein followed doggedly. With his hat pulled down over his eyes, his coat collar turned up and his scarf wound around the lower half of his face, he kept Lawrence in sight as the latter traversed the Green. At the corner of Chapel and Temple, Lawrence crossed to the commercial side of Chapel Street and walked purposefully west. Following several yards back and on the opposite side of the street, Blaustein had Yale to his right and nothing but a row of parked cars to his left. If Lawrence had turned to look in his direction, he would have seen him at once. But Lawrence looked like a man on a mission as he strode purposefully forward.

After a few blocks, Lawrence's pace slowed. He was referring to a folded piece of paper which he had taken from his coat pocket and he may have been checking street numbers. When he reached the place he was looking for, he squared his shoulders and went inside. After a couple of minutes, feeling it was reasonably safe, Blaustein crossed the road. The building Lawrence entered had once been a private residence, built in the nineteen twenties when families were large and the affluent still lived in downtown New Haven. In its present incarnation, it was a professional office building. A discreet brass name plate on the front door announced that within were the law offices of Marsh, Appleby and Hume. Blaustein knew the firm, and not only by reputation, their specialty was criminal defense. They had represented more than one of his collars. And the Chairman of the Whitney History Department was seeking their services? Interesting, but not necessarily incriminating. Just because the professor was consulting a criminal defense attorney did not make the man guilty. Merely cautious. Lawrence was far too smart not to realize that he might be considered a suspect. And to top it, he had spotted Gardner tailing him. Too bad. Now the man would be extra careful. Turning on his heel, Blaustein made his way back up Chapel Street. Across the Green. And back to where Gardner was waiting beside the car. His partner was holding two containers of coffee and handed one to Blaustein.

"So where did he go?"

"He's paying a visit to Marsh, Allenby and Hume as we speak," Blaustein said, unlocking the car to let his partner in.

"We scared him I guess. But that doesn't make him guilty."

"Right. He's just playing it safe," Blaustein peeled the lid off the coffee and savored the aroma. "If we don't want his lawyers crying police harassment, we'll have to be careful from now on."

"Yeah. Sorry about that. The damn wind blew my cover. Literally."

"Can't be helped," Blaustein sipped his coffee gratefully.

"So where do we go from here? We've got nothing in the Mitchell case and less than nothing in the Scott case. The only evidence we have linking Lawrence to the Mitchell murder is his wife's affair with the victim, but his alibi is solid for the day of the homicide. And though he doesn't have an alibi for the time Augusta Scott was killed, what possible reason would he have had for killing her?"

"None that I can see," Gardner sighed. "Which reminds me. I called the East Haven P.D. while I was waiting for you. They found a witness who swears that no vehicles drove up to the Scott house before Dina's SUV drove up."

"A pretty reliable witness?"

"One of Augusta Scott's neighbors. She was at home recovering from back surgery and was waiting for her physical therapist to show up. At the approximate time the homicide went down she was looking out of her bedroom window. She's prepared to swear on a stack of Bibles that she didn't see any other vehicles parked at or near the Scott house around the time the professor was killed."

"How come the East Haven cops didn't turn up this witness before?"

"She hadn't returned from the hospital when they stopped by her house the first time."

"Have the EHPD completed their canvass of the neighborhood?"

"They've covered everything within a six block area. And, except for the woman with the bad back and the woman walking her dog on the beach, they've come up empty."

Blaustein set his cup in the cup holder and started the car. "If the perp walked several blocks to the Scott house and then made a get-away through an icy surf, I think it lets out the elegant Mrs. Mitchell. I just don't see her doing that."

"But it would be a walk in the park for an athlete like Sidney Lawrence."

"It also implies premeditation," Blaustein reflected. "Yet unlike the Mitchell homicide, it doesn't look like a premeditated act. There is something very spur-of-the-moment about it."

"If only we knew what it was Augusta Scott wanted to tell us when she called that day."

20

WHEN DINA GOT BACK TO NEW HAVEN, THE ILLUMINATED CLOCK ON the dash read eleven fifteen. On automatic light-timers that switched off at eleven, Freddie's house was shrouded in darkness. To Dina, the gloomy old Victorian behind its barricade of bare-branched trees looked forbidding. Telling herself that Detectives in the Major Crime Squad ought not to be melodramatic, she locked her car and made her way to the front porch. But as she unlocked the door and let herself into the hall, she could not shake a sense of apprehension. Groping the wall, she felt for and flipped on the light switch. But nothing happened. Instead of flooding the foyer with light, the house remained ominously dark.

Outside, a streetlight cloaked in fog assured her that there was no general power outage. She guessed that the bulb in the the hall light had burnt out. So, waiting for her eyes to adjust to the gloom, she edged toward the parlor, felt along the wall for the light switch and flipped it. But again without result. Sighing, she resigned herself to a trip to the basement to check the circuit-breakers. There was no alternative. Though she was bone tired, she could not simply climb into bed, pull the covers over her head and wait until morning. No power meant no heat and the potential for frozen pipes. She owed it to Freddie to go down to the basement and investigate. Remembering that Freddie kept a flashlight in the drawer beside the kitchen sink, she groped her way through the dining room and pantry to the kitchen. Cautiously placing one foot in front of the other, like a drunk driver taking a sobriety test, she inched her way to the kitchen sink and opened the cabinet drawer. But where the flashlight should have been, her hand encountered only an empty space.

"Looking for this?" Came a strangely familiar voice from behind the suddenly blinding glare of the flashlight.

Her instincts instantly on high alert, Dina reached in her shoulder bag for her Sig Sauer. But before she could get it out, the purse was wrested from her hand.

"Considerate of you to provide a gun. Now put your hands above your head. I won't hesitate to use this thing," came the voice from behind the flashlight, the voice of the woman who called herself Kelly Richmond.

"What kind of game are you playing?" Dina willed herself to remain calm.

"You're the one who's been playing games. Snooping around. Playing Nancy Drew. Meddling where you have no business to meddle. And calling yourself Diana Bassett."

"Oh! And it's all right for you to call yourself Kelly Richmond?" Dina said with more bravado than she felt.

"Too bad for you that you found out about it," the other woman's meaning was clear. There was no attempt to veil the threat.

Regretting that she had not told Blaustein where she was going and why, feeling defenseless and exposed in the glare of the flashlight, Dina knew that her only hope was to surprise the woman hidden behind that light. To do that, she had to make the first move. And make it fast. Using a karate kick, she aimed at the flashlight. Dislodged it from the woman's hand, and as it fell to the floor, pounced on it.

"Touch it and I'll blow our head off."

Hearing the confirming sound of the magazine's release, Dina hesitated. And her momentary hesitation cost her. Instead of completing her grab for the flashlight, she watched helplessly as the other woman reached for it and turned its beam back on her.

"Who are you any way?" Dina decided that it was time for bravado. "And why are you calling yourself Kelly Richmond."

"It was quite clever of you to figure that out. But then you're a professional snoop, Dina Barrett, girl detective. My mother told me all about your little visit." The voice continued without inflection. "What I don't know is why you've been hanging out in a college library impersonating a student. Or why you latched onto me and weaseled your way into my confidence."

As Dina chose not to answer, the woman kept on speaking. "Does your friend Detective Blaustein know where you went today? Or why?"

"Of course he does," Dina lied, her words calmly assertive. "Make a move against me and you won't get away with it."

"Funny, but I don't really believe you. So why don't we just find out for sure?" Still caught in the beam of the flashlight, Dina waited as the other woman backed toward the wall phone.

"Move over to the phone and dial Blaustein's number."

Her jaw set in obstinate refusal, Dina did not budge. "It's almost midnight. I won't call him at this hour."

"Dial, damn you. Dial or I'll have no option but to shoot you."

Dina sensed rather than saw the gun barrel trained on her, but still she stood her ground, willing the woman to approach her. Perhaps if she came close enough, she'd have a chance to wrest the gun from her hand. But the woman stayed where she was, the flashlight steady in one hand. The gun cocked and ready in the other. Seeing she really had no choice, Dina went to the phone and lifted the receiver.

"When you get through dialing, hand me the phone immediately. Step back. And shut up. If you make so much as a sound, I'll shoot you."

Dina dialed the number hoping against hope that Jackson had Caller ID. If he did, he would know where the call was coming from and maybe figure out she was in trouble. The other woman shifted the flashlight to the pocket of her parka and took the handset from Dina's reluctant fingers as soon as the last digit was punched. With the flashlight no longer aimed directly at her, Dina could make out the gun and the gloved hand that held it. Clearly, Kelly or Charlotte, or whoever she was, had no intention of leaving fingerprints behind. She probably wasn't planning on leaving any witnesses either. For the moment all Dina could do was step back as ordered.

"Detective Blaustein, I'm sorry to bother you at this hour." The woman spoke in a soft, breathless voice. "No, this isn't Freddie, this is Dina's mother."

So, Jackson did have Caller ID! Heartened for a moment, Dina's rush of optimism was soon deflated.

Charlotte did not miss a beat. "I'm calling from Mrs. Hathaway's house. I came here when I couldn't reach Dina on the phone. You see, her father is gravely ill. I have been trying to reach her all day. Do you have any idea where she is?"

There was a pause as the woman listened, her eyes on Dina, the gun never wavering. "Or any idea where she can be?"

Another pause followed. "Well if you hear from her, will you tell her to come to Hartford Hospital. That's where her father is. Thank you."

Hearing the click as the connection with Blaustein was broken, Dina felt as though her lifeline had been snapped.

"He had no idea where you were today. You lied to me," she screamed. And with the gun in her right hand still trained on Dina, she grabbed the flashlight from her pocket with her left and sent a backhand crashing into Dina's temple. The blow took Dina by surprise. Stunned, she stumbled to her knees.

"Don't lie to me again! If you do, then the next time I'll use the nice gun you've so thoughtfully provided on *you*."

Yes, Dina thought, the victim's weapon just like before. It seemed to be the pattern. How convenient! If she once had any lingering doubts about the woman's guilt, she did not now. But what to do about it? None of her police training had prepared her for a surprise ambush in her own home. The intruder held all the cards. Dina's sole hope now was to gamble on another grab for the flashlight. Darkness would be her ally. In the dark the odds were in her favor. It is difficult enough to shoot accurately when you can see your target but virtually impossible in the dark.

Exaggerating the effect of the blow to her temple, Dina staggered to her feet. But before standing upright, she tensed her body and lunged like a cat on its prey. Catching the other woman off guard, she managed to hurl the flashlight from her hand and send it crashing to the floor with the satisfying sound of splintering glass. The instant the place was plunged into darkness, Dina turned and ran from the kitchen. Now the ball was in her court. She knew the house intimately, the other woman did not. Keeping low, she dashed through the pantry as a shot rang out. She heard the bullet whistle over her head and heard it crash into a glass-fronted china cabinet, shattering it with the tinkle of broken glass. Without breaking stride, she pushed open the swinging door that led from the pantry to the dining room. With the door still swinging behind her, she fled through the dining room overturning chairs as she raced past the dining room table. She made a beeline for the foyer and had the satisfaction of hearing her pursuer curse as she tripped over an upended chair.

"Stop bitch or I'll shoot!" But the woman did not shoot. She probably knew the odds of hitting a barely visible quarry were minimal.

Having reached the front door, Dina fumbled with the lock in nightmarish slow-motion, cursing her leaden fingers. She had seconds to open the door but knew with sickening certainty that when she did so, she would be silhouetted against the light from the street. A clear target. As the sound of footsteps came closer, the lock clicked open. Flinging the door wide, Dina leaped out and ducked to her left. But not in time. In the split second she appeared in the open doorway, her pursuer fired. A lucky shot perhaps, but it found a mark. Dina felt a sharp, searing pain in her shoulder. Trying to ignore the pain, she turned and stumbled toward her car. With numb fingers she groped in her coat pocket for her car keys. Pulled them out and clicked open the lock. But her long-legged enemy reached for the car door before she could wrench it open.

"Back off," the other woman hissed through clenched teeth. "And this time do exactly as I say."

Dina backed away, dizzy with pain, her resistance seeping away like the blood that oozed from her shoulder.

"Give me your keys."

Meekly, fatalistically, Dina handed them over.

"Hands together."

Just as in the Scott case, the woman had come prepared. She pulled a roll of duct tape from her pocket and as Dina stood unprotesting, her hands were bound together. Helplessly she watched as the woman opened the hatch of the SUV and folded down the rear seat.

"Get in," she was motioned inside. But Dina could not climb in. Not only were her legs like rubber, but she was determined to summon up a last attempt at resistance.

"Move it, damn you!"

This time, a vicious shove from behind, propelled Dina into the cargo area where she lay unmoving, wrapped in a cocoon of pain and anguish. She was having trouble breathing and just when she needed all her resources, her old wound was acting up too. Sinking in and out of consciousness, she smelled the duct tape before she felt it cover her mouth. Felt it around her ankles, bound so tightly that it hurt. Then a bicycle was dumped into the cargo area beside her, a pedal digging into her side, a wheel rotating perilously close to her eyes. She heard the hatch close and the car-door slam. Then the engine started up. She could see the misty glow of the street lights and the tops of trees as they pulled away from the curb. But trussed hand and foot, all she could do was lie still and hope that a neighbor had heard the shot. That someone had called 911. She strained for the sound of a siren. Yearned to see the blue and red flash of emergency lights. But except for the pounding of her heart and the hum of the car's engine, all was still. If anyone had heard the shot, they had not reported it. So with a sinking heart and fading hope, she faced the reality that no one would come to her rescue. She was utterly alone.

21

"WHO WAS THAT?" GRETA, STILL HALF-ASLEEP SWITCHED ON THE bedside light.

"Nothing. Go back to sleep," Blaustein put the telephone back in its cradle.

"Didn't sound like nothing. Something's wrong isn't it, Jackson? You look worried."

"Nothing we can do much about, I'm afraid. Dina's father is very ill. That was her mother. When she couldn't reach Dina on the phone, she drove all the way to New Haven to get her. The poor woman must be frantic."

"And Dina's not at home? It's past midnight?" Greta was wide awake now. "Do you think Dina could be in some sort of trouble?"

"I doubt it. Saturday nights young people stay out later than old farts like us," he threw the bedclothes aside and got up. "I might as well go to the can. Anything I can get you? A glass of water maybe?"

"Nothing, thank you. But I think I'll read for a while if you don't mind leaving the light on for a bit," Greta pushed herself into a sitting position and took a book from her bedside table. But when

Blaustein got back from the bathroom, she had neither opened the book nor put on her reading glasses, "Jackson, don't you think that you're being a bit too dismissive? I'm really worried about Dina."

"If anything were wrong, Freddie Hathaway would have called," her husband replied, climbing back into bed.

"And Freddie didn't know where Dina was when Dina's mother arrived at her house?"

"Mrs. Barrett didn't say. All she said was that Dina wasn't at home and she hadn't been able to reach her all day. But if it makes you feel better, I'll check things out on my way to work in the morning," he said as he turned onto his side so that his back was to the light and pulled the covers over his head. "Now if you don't mind, I'm going back to sleep."

Next morning at breakfast Greta reminded her husband of his promise.

"You probably lay awake all night worrying, didn't you?" Blaustein accused.

"Guilty as charged," she smiled as she buttered an English muffin. "I guess I'm just a typical Jewish mother. You can blame it on my roots."

"Well if it'll make you feel any better, I'll call Dina right away," he put down his coffee mug and got up. "Though I doubt she'll appreciate a call this early on Sunday morning if she was out on the town last night."

"Thank you, dear," Greta said, with a grateful smile, as her husband punched the number on the kitchen phone.

Blaustein waited a while and then disconnected, "No one's answering. Now I'm also concerned." He punched a few more numbers and waited. "She's not answering her cell phone either."

"Can you call Mrs. Barrett? Maybe she was able to reach her."

Blaustein nodded as he dialed 411. "Operator, I need the number for a Jeremy Barrett. Storrs or Mansfield. . . . Yes, please connect me." He waited till a woman answered at the other end.

"Mrs. Barrett?" he said. "I'm sorry to disturb you. This is Jackson Blaustein."

"Who?" Dina's mother sounded confused.

"I'm Dina's colleague at the State Police. You were trying to reach her when you called me last night," he explained, puzzled by the woman's confusion.

"You must be thinking of someone else, Detective. I didn't call you. Maybe my husband called you. Do you want to speak to him?"

"Your husband is alright?" Now it was Blaustein's turn to be confused.

"He's fine. And right here." There was a rustle of newspaper as the phone was handed over and a new voice came on the line.

"Jeremy Barrett here. Is something wrong, Detective?"

"I hope not," he didn't want to panic Dina's parents. "A woman called me last night at about midnight. She claimed to be Mrs. Barrett, Dina's mother. She said she had been trying to reach Dina all day because her father, you, were in the hospital. She contacted me because she thought I'd know where Dina was."

"She said she was Dina's mother?"

"She did."

"And she mentioned Dina by name?"

"She did."

"Do you think it could have been a prank, Detective?"

"It's always a possibility, Professor," Blaustein tried to sound reassuring.

"But you don't think so, do you?"

"I'm really not sure," Blaustein hesitated before deciding to level with Dina's father. "When I tried calling Dina at home earlier this morning no one answered. She's not responding to her cell phone either. That's why I called you." There was an intake of breath at the other end. "Please don't be unduly alarmed. If she was out late last night, she might have turned off the ringer. Or possibly she was in the shower and didn't hear the phone when I tried to reach her this morning. There's probably a simple explanation."

"It doesn't explain the call you had last night, Detective," the professor wasn't buying an easy explanation.

"True, and I'll do my best to find out what the problem is," Blaustein sounded more confident than he felt.

"Thank you, Detective. And please have Dina give us a call as soon as you locate her. We'll plan to be at home today."

Blaustein's expression was grim when he replaced the receiver. "I should have known to trust your instincts, Greta."

"You think something's seriously wrong, don't you?" Greta's expression matched his. They were both fond of Dina.

"I hope I'm over-reacting."

"Do you think the woman who called here's involved in a case Dina's working on?"

"Unlikely," he swallowed the last of his by now tepid coffee, took his cup to the sink and rinsed it. "Dina left a message on Friday to say they'd had just wrapped up their assignment. That the suspects had been taken into custody and she was looking forward to working full-time on the Mitchell case. But so far Dina hasn't had much involvement in the Mitchell case. And no one outside of law enforcement knows that she discovered Scott's body. We've managed to keep it out of the papers," he frowned, remembering the list of phone calls Dina was following up on. "On the other hand, if she's been chasing down leads, it's possible she may have rubbed someone up the wrong way."

"I hope she didn't get into a situation she can't handle," Greta's worried expression mirrored the one on her husband's face.

He leaned down and kissed her on the cheek, "Okay if I go over to Mrs. Hathaway's?"

"Of course," she patted his hand. "Let's hope you'll find Dina and there's a simple explanation for all this."

"Love, do me a favor. Call Huey and ask him to meet me at Freddie's house. Tell him why."

"I will, Dear."

"If by any chance Dina happens to call, tell her to call my cell phone ASAP." And with a wave he was gone.

An agitated Freddie Hathaway met Blaustein at the door. "Oh, I thought you were the plumber," she said, ushering him inside.

"Not one of my skills, I'm afraid. What's wrong?"

"I'm a bit miffed at your colleague Dina, that's what. I can't think what she's been up to," Freddie ran a distracted hand through her short gray curls. "I arrived home from the airport just a short while ago, and what did I find? No electricity. No heat. The pipes frozen. Chairs turned over in the dining room. My china cabinet shattered. And the front door not just unlocked but ajar. What could have come over her to leave the house in such a state!"

"It certainly isn't like Dina," Blaustein agreed diplomatically. But he knew now that something was very wrong indeed. Taking Freddie firmly by the elbow, he led her to the sofa in the front parlor. "Freddie, please sit down, and don't be alarmed by what I'm about to say. I think something may have happened to Dina."

"Oh my! I hope to God you're wrong!" Freddie's face blanched.

"Tell me, have you had a chance to check the fuse box yet?"

"No, I've only been back from the airport for a few minutes," she shook her head and as if to underscore the point, indicated the suitcase and golf clubs piled up in the front hall. "The place was like an icebox when I walked in. In this kind of weather, my first concern was for frozen pipes. And sure enough, when I tried to run water in the downstairs bathroom I got nothing. That's why I was expecting the plumber when you showed up." Hunched in her coat, she looked very small and unexpectedly frail.

"I want you to stay here and I don't want you to touch anything," Blaustein said, slipping on a pair of surgical gloves. "If the plumber arrives, tell him not to touch anything either and to wait right here with you till I get back. Where's your fuse-box?

"Do you think something bad could have happened to Dina?" Freddie looked up at him, fear reflected in her eyes. "Now I feel guilty for being cross with her."

"A perfectly natural reaction when you came home to a mess," he patted her shoulder reassuringly. "So let's hope my assumptions were wrong and your first reaction was the right one. Then you can give her a well-deserved scolding. Now tell me, where do I find your fuse box?"

"In the basement. Far corner on the north side of the house. The door to the basement is in the kitchen. You'll find a flashlight in the drawer by the sink."

But the drawer by the sink was empty. The flashlight lay on the floor, its glass shattered. Nothing else in the kitchen seemed out of place except that the back door had clearly been jimmied. Grim-faced, Blaustein took a plastic bag from his pocket and transferred the flashlight and glass fragments to it. Then taking a pen-light from his coat pocket and his service revolver from his holster, he opened the basement door and edged his way cautiously down the stairs. Not knowing what he would find and keeping his back to the wall, he flashed the pen-light left and right as he made his way to the north side of the house. But he saw nothing untoward, just the decades-long accumulation of family treasures and the discarded belongings one expects to find in the cellar of an old house. The furnace and the water heater were idle. Both cold and silent. On the rear wall, exactly where Freddie said it would be, he located an old-fashioned fuse box and opened it. All the fuses had been removed. They lay scattered on an adjacent table. As soon as he had replaced them, the ancient heating system creaked and rattled as it came to life. Simultaneously, the basement light came on and the place no longer looked as sinister as it had moments before.

Once back upstairs, he used his cell phone to dial headquarters. "Detective Barrett is missing from her home. I have reason to believe she's been abducted because there are signs that a struggle took place. Send a tech team over here ASAP," he gave the directions to Freddie's house. "Put out an APB for her SUV. Also, I want to find out where Detective Barrett was yesterday and who she contacted. Check her cell phone records and any calls that were made from the Hathaway house in the past forty-eight hours," he rattled off Freddie's address and phone number. He knew, because he had Caller ID, that his midnight call had come from Freddie's house. But if the woman who called him had made other calls from the same phone, he might be able to find out who she was and why Dina was missing. He could not shake the sense that something really bad had gone down here.

Freddie was sitting in the parlor, huddled in a multi-colored Afghan. The plumber had not yet arrived.

"The heat's back on and the house should warm up soon," Blaustein assured her. "I don't know how long it'll take the pipes to thaw."

"If there's water in the kettle I could make you some instant coffee or a cup of tea?"

"Actually, I'd rather you didn't go into the kitchen just yet."

"Why?" Her eyes grew round as saucers.

"Just a precaution. I've asked for a team of technicians to come down here. I want them to dust for prints and the kitchen is the most likely place to start," he patted her shoulder reassuringly though he was far from reassured himself. "But I think we could both use a cup of something hot. So I'll ask Detective Gardner to stop at Dunkin' Donuts on his way down." He dialed Huey's number. Gave him a thumbnail account and asked him to stop for coffee on his way into New Haven. Then he handed his cell phone to Freddie. "Do you mind calling the plumber and asking him to hold off for a while? I've turned all the faucets on and the furnace is chugging away. If we turn the thermostat up, I suspect the pipes will thaw on their own. Also, look around and tell me whether you think anything is missing, but don't touch anything."

"You think burglars?"

"There's always that possibility." His midnight phone call convinced him otherwise but he had to be sure.

Soon the place buzzed with activity. The technical crew showed up just as Huey arrived bearing sustenance and a worried expression. His expression turned even graver when the technical experts found a bullet inside the shattered china cabinet and traces of blood on the front steps.

"Dina was in surgery at Hartford Hospital after the casino shooting. They'll have her blood type. Get the sample down to the lab at once. Also, have ballistics check out the bullet," Blaustein ordered.

"Bullet's .40 caliber. Could be from Detective Barrett's Sig Sauer. But there's no sign of the weapon or of Barrett's purse," one of the techs said, holding up a plastic bag containing the bullet.

"A .40? I don't know whether that's a good sign or a bad one," Blaustein shook his head. "And when the hell is someone going to call in the phone records I requested."

The words were no sooner out of his mouth than his cell phone rang.

"Blaustein," he acknowledged.

"I have a list of yesterday's calls made from the Hathaway house. Do you want me to fax them to you?"

"Just read them to me. You can copy me later. Start with the last call."

"That was made to your home at 12:08 a.m. The previous calls were made more than twenty-four hours ago. Do you want them too."

"Those you can fax to my office. What about the calls made from Barrett's cell phone, do you have those yet?"

"I'll have to get back to you with that."

"Well, hurry it up. Barrett's life may depend on it."

"I know, I know. We're doing the best we can."

"Sorry, I know you are. Didn't mean to be short with you," he ended his call and turned to the tech. "Have you had a chance to dust the telephone in the kitchen yet?"

"It was wiped clean."

"Any other phones in the house?"

"There's one in the hall. A mess of superimposed prints, nothing distinctive. Ditto the two upstairs."

Blaustein had no leads and no way to identify the woman who had called last night. He searched his memory, trying to remember his caller's voice. It had been soft, unaccented. Nothing distinctive about it. If he had a tape of it, maybe a voice expert would be able to identify the caller. Maybe. Or then again, maybe not. There was no point in speculating. But even though he had been roused from a deep sleep, he remembered exactly what the caller said.

"This is Dina's mother .... I'm calling from Mrs. Hathaway house. I came here when I couldn't reach Dina on the phone." At first he had identified the woman as Freddie Hathaway because of the Caller ID. But when she figured that out, instead of being flustered, the caller did not miss a beat. She compensated for it. "You see, her father is gravely ill," she had said, "I have been trying to reach Dina all day. Do you have any idea where she is?"

He had answered in the negative. Was this what the woman wanted to hear? Did she call to find out if he knew where Dina was and where she had been in order to find Dina. Or had it been to find out what he knew about Dina's whereabouts? And why him? If the call was connected to the Whitney drug case, there'd be no reason to call him. He had not worked on the Whitney drug case. The only cases that he and Dina were working on together were the Mitchell- Scott homicides. Was this episode related to the Whitney murders? And if so, did that mean his caller was the killer? No other explanation came to mind and it sent a chill through him. Without an obvious suspect in the case, where could they begin a search? At least he knew now that they were looking for a woman. A woman who was either an accomplice, or the killer herself.

Time was not on their side. Although Blaustein wanted to believe that Dina was safe somewhere, and was reluctant to believe otherwise, he knew there was no palatable explanation for what had transpired in Freddie Hathaway's house the night before. The overturned chairs and the broken china cabinet convinced him that there had been a struggle. And if the blood on the front steps turned out to be Dina's, his worst fears would be confirmed. Returning to the problem of the midnight call, Blaustein decided to interpret the call as an attempt to find out what if anything he knew about Dina's whereabouts. Perhaps for some reason, the caller had been checking up on what he knew. Had he given the wrong answer? Had he reassured the caller by saying that he knew nothing of Dina's whereabouts? Had his response endangered Dina's life? Turning the possibilities over in his mind again, he held onto the faint hope that Dina was being held captive somewhere. That this was a second-worst case scenario. That she still had a chance. He did not want to think about the worst-case scenario. He knew only that he had to find Dina before it was too late. But where to look? He couldn't even hazard a guess as to where she had been yesterday. And not knowing made it next to impossible to figure out who had taken her or where they had gone. Being a Saturday and Dina's day off, there had been no need for her to file any reports or call headquarters. All he knew, and knew with gut-wrenching certainty, was that his midnight caller was most likely the Mitchell-Scott killer and that Dina, if still alive, was in the hands of a ruthless adversary, a brutal killer who had already murdered twice and would not hesitate to kill again. Though loath to admit it, he knew that Dina's prospects were extremely grim.

Forcing himself to remain calm, he tried to reconstruct the previous night's scenario. Piece by piece he examined the evidence, picturing himself in Dina's place. The fact that the power had been turned off had all the hallmarks of an ambush. Dina must have arrived home at about midnight -- judging by the time of the call to him -- to find the house in darkness. There, waiting for her like a spider ready to pounce on its unsuspecting prey, was her assailant. A woman, judging by the voice on the telephone. But despite evidence of blood at the front door, Blaustein did not think Dina was shot when she first opened the front door. There had not been a lot of blood in the front hall and if it had been only a superficial wound, Dina would have high-tailed it out of there. She had not. There was too much evidence to the contrary: the overturned chairs in the dining room, the broken flashlight in the kitchen, and the bullet fired into the china cabinet in the pantry. The trail seemed to lead from the kitchen and Blaustein suspected that was where Dina's assailant had lain in wait. With both Freddie and Dina out of the house, there had been time for her assailant to search the place. Time to turn off the power. And time to wait silently like an alligator in a swamp.

The woman probably figured out that when Dina arrived to find a house without lights, she would go to the basement to check the fuse box. And where better to surprise her quarry than in the kitchen beside the basement door? That was also where the phone was. And that was where the call to him must have been placed. Thinking back to his responses, he could only hope that nothing he told the caller would have reassured her. The caller could not be certain that Dina was working alone. And that uncertainty was Dina's ally. Maybe that was why Dina had not been killed on sight. Now, if she could only stall her abductor long enough, it might keep her alive. But for how long? And how badly injured was she? Again he puzzled over the woman's need to call him. He was certain now that the call had been made to find out if he knew whatever it was that Dina knew and whether he knew where she had been. But to find this out, the woman had taken a huge risk. She could not have known for certain that he would not follow up on the call immediately. That he would not send the local cops to make sure Dina was alright. If only he had!

"Phone's ringing, Jackson. Do you want to take it?" Huey interrupted his train of thought.

"Tell Mrs. Hathaway to pick it up in the hall after the next ring and to keep the caller talking. Try to get a trace going. I'll be listening in on the kitchen extension."

"Hello," Blaustein heard Freddie say as he picked up the receiver in the kitchen.

"May I speak to Dina, please," a male voice. Perhaps there were two of them after all, a male and a female?

"This is Freddie Hathaway," Freddie's voice sounded strained. "Who is this please?"

"Mrs. Hathaway, my name is Clive Atkinson. I'm a friend of Dina's."

Dina's ex-fiancé, Blaustein recognized the name. "Clive," he said speaking on the other extension. "My name is Jackson Blaustein, Connecticut Major Crime Squad. I'm a colleague of Dina's. I don't mean to alarm you unduly, but Dina seems to be missing. You wouldn't happen to know where she's been the last couple of days?"

"Missing? But I just saw her."

"When was that?" Blaustein pounced with a faint ray of hope.

"Night before last. We shared a pizza," Clive hesitated. "But I left kind of abruptly which is why I'm calling. To apologize."

Blaustein remembered that the relationship between the two had been somewhat rocky, "Did she say anything to you about her plans for yesterday?"

"Not that I can recall."

"Please try. Anything you remember would be helpful," Blaustein nodded as Gardner handed him a piece of note paper. Scrawled on it was the caller's phone number and the fact that the call came from Raleigh, N.C., "Uh, where are you calling from, Clive?"

"I'm in Raleigh, North Carolina. I left Connecticut yesterday morning."

"Flight number?"

"Look, if I'd kidnaped Dina, I wouldn't be calling," Clive bristled.

"Perhaps, but I need to follow up anyway."

"Sure, sure," Clive read the flight number from his boarding pass. "Look, I have to be in court in a few minutes. If I think of anything helpful, I'll get back to you. Give me your phone number." After writing down Blaustein's cell phone number, he added, "Please find her."

"What about Dina's other boyfriend? The current one?" Huey asked as Blaustein replaced the receiver.

"Philip, you mean? Good thought! Maybe Dina told him where she was going yesterday."

"It's worth trying. Any port in a storm," Blaustein frowned. "Do you happen to remember his last name?"

"No I don't. Perhaps Mrs. Hathaway knows."

Freddie was sipping coffee in the parlor. A half-eaten donut lay on a paper napkin beside her. She looked up expectantly when the two detectives entered.

"Any word?"

Blaustein shook his head, "Mrs. Hathaway, do you happen to know the last name of Dina's friend, Philip?"

"Porter, I think," she answered uncertainly. "No, Potter. Definitely, Potter."

"Huey, could you get Mr. Potter on the phone?"

While Gardner was doing that, Blaustein turned again to Freddie

Hathaway. She looked very small and miserable on the large Victorian sofa in the parlor.

"Have you been able to tell yet if anything valuable was missing?"

"Nothing seems to be," she replied, adding wistfully, "You are going to find her aren't you?"

"God willing," he sat down beside her and took her cold, little hand in his.

Just then, Gardner came in with a cell phone in one hand and a notepad in the other. "I have Philip Potter on the line," he said handing the phone to Blaustein.

Excusing himself, Blaustein relinquished Freddie's hand, stood up and walked into the hall, "Mr. Potter, did Detective Gardner tell you why we're calling you?"

"Actually, no. he didn't. I hope it isn't to do with Dina? Is she okay?"

"We don't know. That's why we called you. Did Dina, by any chance tell you where she was planning to go yesterday? Or what she planned to do?"

"I wish I could help you Detective, but Dina and I are no longer seeing each other and I didn't speak to Dina yesterday. Please tell me, that Dina's okay."

Blaustein did not answer Philip's question. He let it hang a moment because it occurred to him that if Dina and Philip Potter had had a falling-out, it could have been responsible for what had happened in the Hathaway house last night? But only partly. The voice on the phone had definitely been a woman's. Still he had to make sure. And though he would much rather have questioned the man in person in order to gauge his reaction, time was of the essence. So instead of answering Philip's question, he asked one of his own.

"Could you tell me what you were doing around midnight last night?"

"I was attending a farewell party. Mine. My company is sending me to Atlanta."

"Permanently?"

"Yes, permanently."

"Did Dina know about it?"

"She did. In fact, I asked Dina to come with me. She declined."

"You had a quarrel?"

"No, we parted friends. And, Detective Blaustein, just because I'm leaving the state without her, does not mean that I've stopped caring. I still love her," Philip said with conviction.

"Okay, Mr. Potter," Philip Potter's involvement in Dina's abduction had been a long shot anyway.

"You still haven't told me why you phoned. Has Dina been hurt?"

"We're concerned for her safety and are trying to locate her. We were hoping you'd have information that could help us find her."

"I'm sorry, Detective, I haven't a clue. I wish I could help. I'd like to help."

"Thank you, Mr. Potter. If you think of anything relevant, please call me, that would be a help," he gave Philip his number and hung up with a sigh. It was time to shift the search into high gear.

22

"THE BLOOD TYPE WE FOUND ON FREDDIE'S DOORSTEP MATCHES Dina's," Blaustein said somberly as he replaced the receiver. He and Gardner had returned to their office at headquarters. "It's not conclusive without a DNA test of course, but we can assume it's hers."

"And the bullet recovered from the china cabinet?" Asking a practical question, Gardner stifled his unspoken thoughts.

"It was a .40 caliber. Same as the ammo Barrett uses in her Sig Sauer."

"What about the APB?"

"No word yet on Dina's vehicle."

"I know you think Dina's abduction is related to the Mitchell-Scott case. But I think there's a chance it isn't."

"How do you figure that?" Blaustein looked at his partner, a glimmer of hope in his eyes.

"Well, we can rule out that the intruder was a burglar because Mrs. Hathaway confirmed that nothing appears to be missing. But I think there's always a chance that Dina's disappearance could be related to the drug investigation she's been working on. Her cover was clearly blown when she was involved in the arrests. It could simply be a case of retribution. I know it sounds far-fetched, but isn't it possible?"

"I suppose it's is," Blaustein sounded as dubious as he felt..

"The drug dealers might want a quid pro quo? This could become a hostage situation?"

"If it were, wouldn't we have demands by now?"

"Probably," Gardner admitted.

"I'm not dismissing the idea, but I think it's a long shot. And right now I don't want to take the time to go through Barrett's case files to find out who she and Edward Morrison were dealing with. Why don't you get hold of Morrison? Ask him to follow up."

Gardner nodded in agreement. "I hope I'm right. At least then we'll know with whom we're dealing. And she'll be safer than with you know. ..." Which was as close as either of them came to uttering their unspoken fears.

"If only she hadn't just filed things in her head. Told us what she was up to yesterday. What she suspected. Or who."

"Maybe that's why she tried to call you yesterday."

"Well, she didn't try hard enough. If I wasn't so worried, I'd be mad at her."

"At least we know now that we are looking for a female," Gardner reminded him, returning to the problem at hand.

"So if Dina's disappearance is connected to the Mitchell case then it lets Lawrence off the hook," Blaustein knew he was clutching at straws. "I seriously doubt he and his wife were working as a team. My gut tells me we're looking for a lone wolf here. A she-wolf."

"Mrs. Lawrence has a southern accent. Did the woman who called you last night have a Southern accent'?"

"No, not a trace," Blaustein admitted. "Still, I guess one can fake an accent." On the yellow legal pad in front of him, Blaustein made a note to check out the happy couple anyway.

"We're a bit short on female suspects."

"Well, number one on the list has to be the former Mrs. Mitchell.

She had an obvious motive to kill her ex. So we need to find out where she was at midnight last night," Blaustein jotted down another note.

"Mrs. Mitchell's a tall woman and strong enough to overpower Augusta Scott especially if she had surprise on her side."

"That doesn't automatically eliminate little Mrs. Lawrence."

"No, not necessarily. A little person can always overpower a big person with a gun in her hand."

"Or if she isn't working alone."

"What about Heather Leopold?"

"We're her alibi for the Scott homicide. But if the Mitchell and Scott homicides are unrelated – which is unlikely - then we have to consider the possibility that there are two killers. In which case Leopold isn't off the hook yet. But I don't like her for it. Let's find out if she has an alibi for last night to make sure." Blaustein added her to his list.

"Kelly Richmond?"

"Unlikely don't you think? What would be her motive. She barely knew Scott and Scott was about to offer her an assistantship. Still, we ought to have a word with her if only because there's a chance Dina bumped into her on campus yesterday. Dina might have mentioned where she was headed."

"That's a pretty short list with a lot of ifs. Something tells me we ought to be looking for some woman we know nothing about," Gardner threw down his ballpoint pen in frustration. It was a rare show of emotion from the usually stolid detective.

"For now the short list is all we have. So let's get on with it. Either way, we're going to need help." Blaustein picked up the phone and dialed Lieutenant Gordon.

After a short wait a woman answered. A youthful voice. Maybe a maid or a babysitter. Gordon had two fairly young children.

"May I speak with Lieutenant Gordon, please."

"I'm sorry, Lieutenant and Mrs. Gordon have gone to church. Would you like to leave a message."

"Ask him to call Blaustein as soon as he gets in. Please tell him it's an emergency."

Reluctant to call the lieutenant's pager while he was in church, Blaustein started looking for help on his own. He began by calling Edward Morrison. First he called him at home. When there was no answer, he left a message and then tried Morrison's cell phone.

"Morrison," came the answer after a couple of rings.

"Jackson Blaustein, Edward. We have a potentially dangerous situation here. Dina Barrett was apparently abducted from her home around midnight last night. There are signs that a struggle took place and that shots were fired."

"Christ!" Morrison listened in stunned silence as Blaustein gave a thumb-nail sketch of what he thought had happened the night before.

"We're inclined to believe that Barrett's disappearance may be linked to one of the cases she's been working on. I know it's your day off and I can't authorize over-time, but can you come to headquarters for a briefing? I'm getting a voluntary task force together."

"The wife and I were on our way to my in-laws for brunch. I'll have to drop her off first but then I'll come right over."

Next Blaustein telephoned detectives Harry Green and his partner Leon Anderson, both members of the Mitchell homicide team.

"Green? Blaustein here. Look I'm sorry to be calling you on a Sunday, but we have a crisis on our hands."

"Isn't there always," came a sleepy voice in response.

When Blaustein explained the reason for his call all reluctance vanished.

"I'll be there as soon as I throw some clothes on."

Blaustein called Anderson next. He was in his garage changing the oil in his car. "I'll take the wife's car," he said without hesitation. "Be there in a flash."

23

FIRST OF THE DETECTIVES TO ARRIVE WAS LEON ANDERSON, A handsome, dark-skinned, giant of a man. Somehow, he had managed to find the time to scrub the grease from his hands and to change into decent clothes. He wore his service weapon in a leather holster and carried a camel-hair overcoat over one arm.

By contrast, Green, a stocky balding man in his fifties and far from a fashion-plate, was unkempt. In his rush to get to headquarters, he had not taken the time to shave and his clothes looked as if he had slept in them.

Morrison was the last one to show up. Dressed for brunch with his in-laws, he had shed his under-cover student-look if not his fresh-scrubbed appearance. He was neatly attired in a blazer and tie, his shoes had been polished, and his hair was carefully combed. His normally pleasant face looked grim.

As they had not yet heard from Lieutenant Gordon, Blaustein had taken it upon himself to brief the detectives and hand out assignments. Though Gardner, who had partnered Blaustein when they questioned the arrogant Alison Mitchell, was the obvious choice to interrogate her, Blaustein decided to send the urbane Anderson instead. Gardner's assignment was to interview Heather Leopold. He already knew the way to Heather Leopold's shoreline residence, and would not have to waste time finding it.

"Harry," Blaustein turned to Green next. "I'd like you to find out if Richmond has spoken to Barrett recently. Dina may have mentioned her weekend plans to her in passing."

"But don't call her Dina Barrett," Morrison interjected. "Her under-cover name is Diana Bassett."

"Good," Blaustein accepted the correction with a nod. "I'll go to Woodbridge to find out what the Lawrences were doing last night. And that brings us to you Edward. What is the status of the suspects you arrested in the Whitney case?"

"Yesterday I would have said that both were safely housed in a New Haven lock-up. And Carmen Mendoza still is. He's considered a flight risk. Herman Archer on the other hand is a bit player with no previous record. He was released on bail sometime yesterday. Own recognizance."

"You think the charges will stick?"

"We have them dead to rights. They were caught in Mendoza's car with a shoe-box filled with goodies and a kilo in the truck. In addition, we used an existing warrant to search Archer's apartment and found a stash in his bedroom."

"Do you think Archer connected Dina with the bust?"

"Most probably. Dina thought he recognized her when she tailed him on Friday. And I saw the look he gave her after we made the collar. I'd say her cover was well and truly blown."

"Do you think either of them's likely to retaliate against her'?"

"Perhaps, but I was the one who read him his rights. If they wanted to go after someone, why not me?" Blaustein gave him a look which the big man answered with a sheepish grin. "Okay, okay. I guess the answer to that is obvious. But it still strikes me as out of character for a wimp like Archer to get physical. And it's highly unlikely Mendoza could have organized a kidnaping from behind bars. At least not so soon after his arrest. Anyway, what would be the point?""

"It's iffy, I know, but we have to cover all the bases. Is the library open on a Sunday?"

"Even if it were, we won't find Archer anywhere near the library. He's been suspended by the University," Morrison explained. "I'll try his house. After that I don't know. He has no known hang-outs."

"Well, do your best to find him. We need to know where he was around midnight last night," Blaustein looked at his watch and then at the circle of anxious faces surrounding him. "If anyone gets a lead, call me on my cell phone and I'll keep the rest of you posted. Let's plan to rendezvous back here in two hours."

"That's not a lot of time," Anderson said, slipping on his topcoat.

"It's more time than we have," Blaustein reminded him.

24

"I THOUGHT YOU WERE ROOM SERVICE," ALISON MITCHELL WAS wearing brown tweed slacks and a matching cashmere sweater. Not a hair was out of place but beneath the immaculate grooming and carefully applied make-up, her face looked drawn.

"Detective Leon Anderson, Major Crime Squad," Anderson showed her his identification. "May I come in Mrs. Mitchell?"

"Do I have a choice in the matter?" She said opening the door to her hotel room and stepping aside to let him in. Her eyes were flat and cold.

"I would just like to ask you a few questions, Mrs. Mitchell," Anderson said, hauling a notepad and pen from his coat pocket.

She shrugged elaborately and made her way to the couch, "Sit down why don't you."

When they were both seated, Alison Mitchell on the couch and Anderson in the armchair facing her, he began his questioning. "Do you mind telling me where you were last night?"

"That's rather personal," the snake eyes flashed.

"Alright, I'll put it another way. Is there anyone who can vouch for your whereabouts last night?"

"If I'm being accused of something, Detective, then don't I have the right to an attorney?"

"That is your right, Ma'am. But you're not being accused of any crime. I just want to know where you were last night," Anderson was all business. He didn't have time for the run-around.

"And if I refuse to answer?"

"Then I'll be forced to read you your rights and haul you down to the State Police headquarters. You can call your attorney from there," the usually soft-spoken Anderson was as close as he ever came to losing his patience.

She sighed before answering, as if weighing her options, "Well I wasn't doing anything illegal, so I might as well tell you, but I resent being questioned about something I consider a purely personal matter. I showered and changed at seven."

Anderson was regretting he had not asked her to begin her narration at midnight but he allowed her to continue without interruption.

"Around eight o'clock, I had dinner alone in the hotel restaurant, the Maitre 'D will vouch for that. Do you want to know what I ordered?"

"No, Ma'am," he did not want to play games. He just wanted answers. "Just get on with it."

"Alright," she pulled a cigarette from the purse that lay beside her on the couch and lit it slowly, deliberately, taking her time. She did not offer Anderson one. "Let's see. After dinner I went to the bar where a gentleman bought me a drink. More than one actually. We ended up in his bedroom. I didn't get back to my own room until midnight."

"The gentleman's name?"

"Robert something or other. We never got as far as last names," she shrugged her elegant shoulders dismissively.

"Try and remember. It may be important for you to prove where you were last night."

"Then I am being accused of something," she hissed.

"Do you remember the number of his hotel room?" Anderson persisted, choosing to ignore her question.

She thought for a moment before answering, "Fourth floor. Directly above this one. It could be Number 412, I guess."

Anderson wrote the number down and stood up, "Thank you, let's hope this checks out."

"It will," she did not get up to let him out.

In the hall, Anderson almost collided with a waiter pushing a room-service cart. "Is this for Room 312?" He asked.

"Yes Sir," the waiter was tall and skinny with the lilt of the West Indies in his accent. When Anderson hauled out his badge, fear flickered in his eyes.

"It's okay, I just need to ask if the room directly above this one is Room 412?" Anderson said, hastening to put the man at ease.

"Yes, Sir," the waiter frowned, not knowing where the detective was going with his questions.

"Could you tell me the name of the gentleman in 412?"

"They can tell you that at the front desk, Sir," the waiter replied, looking relieved. "But if you want to speak to him, you'd better hurry, man. He's checking out this morning."

"Thanks for your help," Anderson handed the waiter a couple of dollars and made for the stairs to the next floor.

When he got to room 412, the door was ajar. He pushed it open and saw that the bed was unmade and the drapes still closed. The closet door stood open, its hangers empty. The remnants of breakfast were on a room-service cart. It had the abandoned look of a hotel room that had been recently vacated. He went inside and used the phone on the bedside table to call the front desk.

"This is Detective Leon Anderson, State Police," he gave the clerk his badge number. "Could you tell me whether the guest in Room 412 has checked out yet?" He drummed his fingers on the nightstand while he waited.

"The gentleman checked out about half an hour ago, Detective."

Anderson felt like swearing, but instead, he said, "I'll need his name, his forwarding address and phone number. I'll be right down to get it."

When he got to the front desk, the clerk handed him a slip of paper with the information he had requested. His name was Robert Vorhees, he had a Columbus, Ohio phone number and business address.

"Do you happen to know if Mr. Vorhees is returning to Ohio today'?"

"As a matter of fact, he is. He said something about going home as he checked out."

"Did Mr. Vorhees take a limo to the airport?"

The clerk checked the computer. "I think he drove himself, Detective. When he registered, he listed a car with a Connecticut license plate. A rental."

"You've been most helpful, thank you."

If he had known which car rental company Vorhees had used, Anderson would have called them at the airport and stalled the man. But he did not know. And there was no time to find out. From a phone in the lobby Anderson called Bradley International Airport to discover that American Airlines had the next flight scheduled to fly to Columbus. It was due to leave on time in just over an hour. His next call, was to the airline which confirmed that Mr. Vorhees had a reservation on the flight. As Anderson had no authority to hold the plane or to have Vorhees detained, his only hope was to make it to the airport before the flight took off. Wasting no time and showing some of the agility he had displayed as a guard in college basketball, Anderson sprinted for his car. He was a good half hour behind Vorhees, but unlike Vorhees, he did not have to drop off a rental car or check-in, so with luck he could still make it before the flight took off. Driving well over the posted speed limit, siren blaring and lights flashing, he sped north on Interstate 91. Fortunately it was Sunday and the traffic was light. Cars pulled over to leave the fast lane free when they heard him coming.

He arrived at the terminal with only minutes to spare. Not wanting to be delayed by x-ray machines, he tossed his service weapon into the glove box, left his car at the curb, lights still flashing, and ran inside the terminal building.

"Look, the flight to Columbus is about to leave and I have to speak to someone before they board. It's urgent," he showed the baggage inspector his badge.

"Go right ahead," the inspector said waving him through.

After a quick check of the overhead monitors, he dashed to the gate. The Columbus flight had already been called and travelers were lining up with boarding passes in their hands. With a sense of relief that was palpable, Anderson went to the head of the line and spoke to the official about to process the first class passengers.

"I need to speak to a passenger on this flight, Mr. Robert Vorhees, could you page him for me," he said, showing his badge once again.

"I'm Robert Vorhees," the man who was second in line spoke up. "Is something wrong?"

He was fiftyish, tall, iron-haired and elegant in a well-tailored suit. A Burberry overcoat was slung over one arm. His only carry-on luggage was a bulging leather briefcase.

"Nothing's wrong, Sir. I just need a minute of your time," Anderson led the way to a bank of empty seats. Neither man sat down.

"I hope this won't make me miss my flight." It was not a question. Vorhees spoke like a man who was used to giving orders not taking them.

"I want you to tell me whether you know a Mrs. Alison Mitchell."

"Not really. Although more intimately than I did day before yesterday," he grinned shamefacedly. "I met her last night in the bar of my hotel."

Thus far, at least, Alison Mitchell's story was holding. "About what time was that, Sir?"

"I'd say around nine," as if to emphasize that he had a plane to catch, Vorhees pushed back his cuff and pointedly looked at his Rolex,.

"And you were with her till when?" Anderson went on doggedly.

"Look, if this is some kind of divorce case, I don't want any part of it."

"It isn't a divorce case. We are just trying to establish the whereabouts of Mrs. Mitchell at approximately midnight."

"Look, I'm a married man. I don't think I want to answer that question," he gave another glance at his Rolex.

"Sir, there's absolutely no reason your wife need know where you were last night."

"Well, alright then," Vorhees conceded reluctantly and this time with a glance at the diminishing line of boarding passengers. "I met Alison in the bar, as I said. We had a few drinks. We chatted. After that she accompanied me to my room. I hope I don't have to go into details."

"No, Sir. Just tell me what time she left your room."

"Not too late. I had a plane to catch this morning and I needed a little shut-eye. So I kicked her out a little after midnight. Not very gentlemanly."

"Had you known her prior to last evening."

"No," Vorhees responded shortly. "It was your classic one-night stand."

"Anyone see you both go upstairs?"

"Only the elevator operator."

And that was that. Vorhees's story supported Alison Mitchell's. The man had no reason to lie but just in case, Anderson intended to check with the hotel elevator operator.

25

BEFORE LEAVING TO CHECK ON SIDNEY AND DEIDRE LAWRENCE, Jackson called again for Dina's cell phone records.

"Still working on it, Detective. We're short-handed on the weekends," he was informed.

After replacing the receiver, Blaustein dialed his home number. He had almost forgotten his promise to let Greta know about Dina's whereabouts.

"Darling," he said, when she answered, "I wish I had better news. We have no idea where Dina is, but we're going all out to try and find her. I have several men working on it." He chose not to go into details.

But Greta was not about to be put off with platitudes or evasions. "Do you think she's in danger?"

"We just don't know yet but I promise to keep you posted," he answered. At this stage telling Greta that he feared the worst would be premature. "Keep your fingers crossed."

His last call before grabbing his coat was his third to Lieutenant

Gordon. The same young woman answered and gave him the same response.

"Look, please try to get hold of him. It's an emergency."

"I'm sorry, Detective, I'm not supposed to call him while he's in church. In fact I couldn't get hold of him if I tried. He turns his pager off." And that was that.

Blaustein shrugged into his coat and was on the point of leaving when a gray-haired, distinguished-looking man knocked on his office door. He was wearing a wool overcoat with the collar turned up, leather driving gloves and a blue and white University of Connecticut scarf. There was a worried expression on his face.

"Detective Blaustein?"

"Yes?" He did not have time for diversions. Not now when every second counted.

"Jeremy Barrett," the man took off his right-hand glove and shook Blaustein's hand. " I'm Dina's father. Any word of her whereabouts yet? Her mother and I are most concerned. Have been ever since your call this morning."

"Not yet, Professor Barrett, I'm sorry. We're chasing down every possible lead."

"You don't suspect foul play, do you?" The question was posed tentatively as if he did not want to hear the answer.

"We don't know what to think at this point."

Jackson did not want to unduly alarm Dina's father, but the other man was quick on the uptake and saw through his evasion. "The truth, please."

"It's a possibility, yes, but we don't really know yet. Wish I could give you a more positive answer."

Jeremy Barrett was silent before speaking again. "We haven't been close the past few years. Mostly my fault. I just hope it isn't too late to make it up to her."

"We'll try to make sure that you have the chance to do just that," Blaustein said, sounding a lot more confident than he felt as he took the older man by the elbow and steered him toward the door. "There are four other detectives trying to find her as we speak, and I was about to check on a possible lead myself."

"Well then, I certainly don't want to hold you up. But could you tell me why you think there's a possibility she may be in danger?"

Blaustein hesitated. "There are indications that a confrontation took place at the Hathaway residence."

"You're hedging, Detective. Please, I need to know the facts."

"Overturned chairs. The door left unlocked. No sign of Dina or her vehicle," Blaustein chose not to mention the blood on the doorjamb or the bullet that had smashed the china cabinet. "And she has not responded to calls on her cell phone."

"I know that. Her mother and I have tried to reach her on her cell phone ever since you called this morning. We're hoping it's because she turned it off."

"That's what I'm hoping too. And that she'll turn up any second and wonder what all the fuss is about. But be assured, finding Dina is our top priority. I'll call you the minute I find out anything. In the mean time, if you hear from her, please call me at once."

After seeing Dina's father to his car and reassuring him, once again, that they were doing everything possible to find his daughter, Blaustein went to the lab to check on the flashlight he had found in Freddie's kitchen. Assembled on the lab counter beside the the flashlight case were the carefully retrieved shards of glass.

"Any fingerprints?"

"The only ones on the flashlight were Barrett's."

Another dead end.

Sighing, his level of anxiety rising with each passing minute, Jackson drove over to the Lawrence home. There his welcome was less than cordial.

"I have nothing to say to you," Lawrence said when he answered the door.

"Actually I'm here to speak to your wife."

"She has nothing to say to you either," Lawrence made as if to close the door in Blaustein's face.

"I can speak for myself, Sidney. Besides, we have nothing to hide.

Please let the detective in," Deirdre Lawrence was standing right behind her husband, the front page section of the Sunday Register in one hand. She was dressed for church in a navy suit with a pleated skirt, a white silk blouse and low-heeled pumps. Her face looked pale and some of the sparkle seemed to have gone out of her.

Grudgingly Lawrence stepped aside to let Blaustein in. But he did not follow his wife and the detective into the living room. Instead he stood framed in the doorway glowering at them, his arms folded across his chest, his back leaning against the jamb. Pointedly ignoring him, Deirdre waved Blaustein to the sofa. When he was seated, she sat down next to him with a little flounce.

"What can I do for you Detective?" she asked politely.

"Do you mind telling me where you were last night, Mrs. Lawrence?"

"Don't tell him anything," growled Lawrence from the doorway.

"I went to Hartford. To the Bushnell to see *La Boheme*," she answered, paying her husband no heed.

"Just the two of you?"

"We went with neighbors of ours, John and Beryl Jacobs."

"Now she's getting the Jacobs involved," Lawrence muttered audibly.

"What time did the opera end?" Blaustein chose to ignore Lawrence's remark.

"Eleven something. We didn't get back home till after midnight. Isn't that right Sidney?" she said sweetly.

Her husband did not respond. He simply stood there working the muscles in his cheek.

"The other couple rode with you?"

"Actually we rode with them. It was their turn to drive. The four of us have season tickets to the Bushnell. We take turns driving."

If the Jacobs could collaborate Deidre Lawrence's story it would be easy enough to track them down without ruffling Lawrence's feathers any more than he already had. Blaustein got to his feet. "Thank you Mrs. Lawrence. Mr. Lawrence. I'll let you get on with your morning."

Somewhat mollified but still less than gracious, Lawrence ushered Blaustein to the front door and shut it behind him.

As soon as the detective got into his car, he called for a location on the Jacobs' house. Then he drove two blocks north, parked, rang the doorbell and waited. After a second ring, the door was answered by an anorexic-looking woman in a leotard, her face glowing with a fine sheen of perspiration, her faded blonde hair tied back with a flowered scarf.

"Sorry," she apologized. "I don't always hear the doorbell when I'm working out. I hope you haven't waited long."

"Not long at all, Ma'am," Blaustein introduced himself and showed her his badge.

"What can I do for you Detective?" She frowned.

"We're running down a complaint," he lied. "Apparently some kids were drag racing in this neighborhood between eleven thirty and twelve o'clock last night. Did you hear or see anything?"

"Last night? No. We weren't home by then. We went to Hartford last night with some friends."

"Were your friends from this neighborhood too?"

"Yes they were."

"Would you mind giving me their names," he pulled out his notebook. "That way I won't have to trouble them with the same question."

"Not all. We were with Deirdre and Sidney Lawrence."

Blaustein made a show of writing down the names before snapping the notebook closed and pocketing it. "Thank you very much Ma'am. You've been most helpful."

And that was that. Hoping the other detectives were having better luck, he dialed Anderson's cell phone.

"How's it going Leon?"

"Alison Mitchell was, shall we say, otherwise engaged last night. She couldn't have called you from Dina's. Her alibi's tight. How about the Lawrences?"

"Likewise. Both of them. So we're left with a couple of real long shots. I hope Gardner and Green are doing better than we did.

As he rang Heather Leopold's front door bell, Huey Gardner was overwhelmed by a feeling of deja vu. He and Jackson Blaustein had been here the morning Augusta Scott tried to call them. They had been here, when someone tied the professor to a rocking chair; choked the life out of her and left her slumping like a broken rag doll. Now it seemed highly likely that the person who had strangled Scott may have spirited Dina away. Gardner tried unsuccessfully to shut out the images that came to mind. But even old case-hardened professionals like Gardner had a soft inner core, especially when it came to one of their own. Putting his personal feelings aside was getting harder and harder for him, but he squared his shoulders and rang again. The drapes covering the front window were closed and a plastic wrapped Sunday newspaper lay on the doormat. If Leopold wasn't answering the doorbell, was that an ominous sign? He did not have a warrant to search the premises but he was quite prepared to break in if it meant saving Dina's life. Just as he started weighing his options, he heard the sound of a chain being pulled back and the door opened.

Heather Leopold stood there wearing a maroon quilted robe and a pair of pink, fluffy slippers. Her pale hair was uncombed and she seemed not quite awake. He saw honest surprise in her eyes, but neither wariness nor fear, when she recognized her visitor.

"Hope you haven't been waiting long," she mumbled, standing aside to let him in. "I was asleep," she said, stating the obvious.

"No problem. I'm sorry to disturb you on a Sunday. Won't keep you long."

"Please, come in and sit down," she replied pulling aside the drapes to let light into the living room. "Coffee? I'm going to need a cup myself. I always need a kick-start in the morning."

"That would be great, thank you," Gardner took a seat on the couch. In front of him, the coffee table was covered with blue books. Neat stacks of them.

"Freshman quizzes," Heather explained as she dashed off to the kitchen.

When she returned a few minutes later with a steaming mug

of coffee in each hand, she had combed her hair and changed into jeans and a sweatshirt. "I forgot to ask if you wanted cream or sugar. Obviously I'm not fully functional yet."

"Black will be fine," Gardner took the mug from her and waited for her to sit down in the chair facing him, "Ms. Leopold, can you tell me where you were last night?"

Balancing the coffee mug on the arm of her chair, her legs crossed in front of her, she turned to him. There was alarm in the green eyes under their light-colored brows. "I hope you're not going to tell me there's been another Whitney murder."

"No, there hasn't been. But I still need an answer to my question, Ms. Leopold, " he said firmly, hoping she wasn't going to be difficult.

"I was right here. Grading papers and listening to Mozart," the green eyes did not waver, but he could tell from the hunch of her shoulders that she was extremely tense.

"Here alone?" he was inclined to believe her but he needed to probe further.

"Quite alone."

"Did you make or receive any calls during the evening?"

"I did actually. Let's see. I had a call from a colleague who wanted me to take over her class on Monday. A family funeral, I couldn't refuse. Then there was a call from a bank who wanted to sell me a Visa card. I told them I already have quite enough plastic," she shook her head, "I really need to get on a 'no-call' list."

"What time were these calls?" Gardner took a tentative sip of coffee. It was still too hot.

"Around dinner-time. I'm not sure exactly."

"What about later in the evening?" he prodded.

"I called my sister in California. It was before nine on the West Coast. So I guess I called at about a quarter to twelve our time."

"Did you use a land-line or your cell?"

"My home phone."

"What's your long distance company, Ms. Leopold?" If the call from her land-line checked out, then Heather Leopold was in the clear. No way could she have been in New Haven if she made a call from home around midnight. Not unless she rode a broom.

"Cox," she seemed to sense that her answers satisfied him and the tension went out of her shoulders.

Gardner took a long, last drink of coffee, found a spot for the mug among the blue books on the coffee table, and stood up. "You've been very helpful, Ms. Leopold. And thank you for the coffee. It hit the spot."

"You're not going to tell me what this was all about are you?" She stood and escorted him to the door.

"I'm sorry Ms. Leopold, I can't go into that right now," he apologized.

No one answered the door at Kelly Richmond's apartment and unwilling to simply assume she was not there, Harry Green pulled out his cell phone and dialed Kelly's number. He could hear the phone ring unanswered in the empty apartment, so he left a message for her to call him back and went to check with the downstairs tenants. They yielded very little information about the graduate student or her whereabouts. The elderly woman on the first floor did not remember seeing Kelly at all the day before. The second-floor tenant, a garrulous retired mailman, was curious about the police presence and wanted to be helpful.

"A nice young lady," the former mailman said in answer to Green's question. "Very quiet. In the past when they rented the top floor to students it's been noisy. You know, loud music and late night parties. Not this one, thank God."

"Have you seen her today?"

"Not today, no," came the hesitant admission.

"How about yesterday?"

"Yes, as a matter of fact. A couple of times when she was taking stuff to the dumpster. And then later when she went off on her bicycle."

"Where does she keep her bicycle?"

"On the landing outside her door."

Feeling frustrated, Green turned to go. There had been no bicycle on the landing outside Richmond's door. Kelly Richmond could be wherever her bicycle took her. Green shivered involuntarily, Richmond had to be pretty tough to be out riding a bicycle in this weather. But where to? Where would a graduate student who didn't have a car go on a Sunday? Probably not to friends. The retired mailman had indicated that she was something of a loner. So if she had few friends then perhaps she had gone to the Graduate School or the library. With the university in mind, Green got into his car and drove first to the Graduate School and then to the library. Both were closed until noon, their Sunday hours prominently posted.

Unwilling to return to headquarters empty handed, Green placed a call to Jackson Blaustein.

"No sign of Richmond. Should I hang around for the Whitney library to open?"

"When's that?" Blaustein had barely arrived back at headquarters when Green's call came in.

"Noon. I'll grab a cup of coffee and come back."

"Well don't hang around too long if she doesn't show. There's only an outside chance that she knows where Dina went yesterday."

Their search was turning up empty and Blaustein felt more than disheartened. It had been almost twelve hours since his mysterious midnight phone call. Convinced that his colleague was in imminent danger, he was beginning to think it might be prudent to bring in the FBI. It was not something he was authorized to do, even in the case of a kidnaping. So, fighting to control a rising sense of desperation, he tried Lieutenant Gordon's home number again.

"Yes, Detective," Gordon answered himself this time and he sounded none too pleased at being disturbed on a Sunday. "I got your message and was about to call. What's the urgency?"

"Loo, it's serious, I'm afraid. It's about Dina Barrett. There's clear evidence she's been abducted."

"You're shitting me."

"Wish I were."

Blaustein provided a quick run-down of events beginning with the late night call from the woman claiming to be Dina's mother, and ending with the names of those who had come in to help out.

"You realize that you've gone over my head to make these assignments? I'm the one who has to authorize overtime, not you." As usual Gordon was thinking of the bottom line.

"We're each doing this on our own time, Loo. No one is going to put in for overtime."

"All right then," the Lieutenant sounded somewhat mollified. "What else have you done?".

"We have an all states APB out on Barrett's SUV and we're hoping to get lucky there. Otherwise we seem to be drawing blanks."

"No one saw her yesterday?"

"No one. Yesterday was Dina's day off, so we haven't a clue what she was doing."

"What have you heard from the others?"

"Detective Gardner questioned Heather Leopold. She's in the clear. Her phone records confirm that she called California from her residence around midnight last night."

"You still consider her a suspect in the Mitchell case?"

"Not if the same perp was responsible for both the Mitchell and Scott homicides. Detective Gardner and I were with Leopold when Augusta Scott was murdered. She's not off the hook for Mitchell's murder. But we have no evidence against her."

"Who else has been checked out today?"

"Sidney and Deidre Lawrence. Their alibi for last night is solid. And Detective Anderson has confirmed Alison Mitchell's alibi. I'm still waiting for word from Harry Green. He's looking for Mitchell's graduate student, Kelly Richmond. We're hoping Dina may have said something to her about her weekend plans."

"You're sure Barrett's disappearance is connected to the Mitchell-Scott homicides?"

"Sure? No. But it appears to be likely."

"If you've checked out all the suspects in the case and they're in the clear, then it means you haven't a clue who the Mitchell-Scott perpetrator is," Gordon gave a barely suppressed groan. "The Chief's going to be on my case tomorrow."

At that moment, Blaustein couldn't care less about Gordon's fate, so he chose not to go there. "On the off chance that Detective Barrett's disappearance is not related to the Mitchell- Scott homicides, Edward Morrison is checking on the men they arrested in the Whitney drug case. One is in custody. The other one is out on bail. I haven't heard back from Morrison yet."

"Keep on it," suddenly Lieutenant Gordon was all business. "I'll see you at headquarters in a few minutes. If nothing has turned up by then, we'll have to go on the assumption that this is an abduction and I'll put in a call to the FBI."

While the other detectives were checking on the Mitchell-Scott suspects, Edward Morrison was on what he suspected was a wild goose chase. First he went to Herman Archer's second floor apartment in the two-family house on the bus route from New Haven. No wonder the man didn't need a car. And without a car, Edward reasoned, Archer could not have gone too far.

Morrison did not bother to ring the front door bell. Taking two steps at a time, he ran up to the second floor and rapped loudly on Archer's door. There was no response and no sign of life, not even the sound of a television or radio emanating from the other side of the closed door.

"Police, if you're in there, open up."

Morrison did not know whether the subpoena they had used on Friday was still valid but he did not stop to think about it. He took a step back, tensed his muscles and was preparing to ram the door when he heard a noise on the first floor landing. Looking over the balustrade, he saw an elderly man dressed in a hat and coat come out of the downstairs apartment and walk toward the front door.

"Hold on a minute, Sir," Morrison called as he ran downstairs.

"Who are you?" The elderly man looked up suspiciously as Morrison approached him.

"Detective Edward Morrison, Connecticut Major Crime Squad," he held out his badge.

The old man squinted at it through his bi-focals,"Why are you people back again?"

"I'm looking for Herman Archer. Have you seen him?"

"What's he been up to this time?"

Instead of answering, Morrison repeated the question.

"No need to be snippy."

"Sorry."

"And so you should be," the old man scolded, but this time he answered Morrison's question. "I guess he went to church this morning. Like he does every Sunday."

Morrison was tempted to say that he hoped Archer was praying for his sins but instead he asked another question. "When was that?"

"Two, two-and-a-half hours ago."

"Do you know if he walked?"

"Saw him standing at the bus-stop when I went outside to pick up my paper."

"Do you know where Herman worships, Sir?"

"One of the churches on the Green. Not sure which one."

"Do you happen to know if he's had any visitors today? Or perhaps late last night?"

"Don't think so, I would have heard them. I'm a light sleeper."

Thanking the old man, Morrison went outside and hopped in his car. By now, he was convinced that this was in fact a wild goose chase. For one thing, he reasoned, it had been a female who called Blaustein last night. Herman Archer was a loner. Nothing in Archer's background check had revealed any female connections. For another thing, Archer had no wheels. He would have needed Dina's vehicle to pull off an abduction. If so, where was her missing SUV? Archer could not have taken it far, not if his downstairs neighbor had seen him on foot. Although the logical thing for Archer to have done if he had Dina's car was to park it within walking distance of his apartment. But state and local law enforcement authorities had been on the look out for the vehicle ever since the APB was issued and a systematic search of the New Haven area had come up empty.

Though he felt he was spinning his wheels, Morrison still needed to track Archer down. If the librarian had gone to church two hours earlier, chances were he was on his way back by now. Possibly on or waiting for a bus. So that is what Morrison did. He waited in his car for the bus. When it stopped on the far corner, Archie got off. And, before crossing the road, like any law–abiding citizen,which Morrison knew he was not, Archer waited at the corner for the 'don't walk' sign to change. Morrison did not wait. He raced his vehicle up to the corner and blocked the crosswalk. Then, in one fluid movement he hit the brakes, shoved the gear into park and with the engine still running, got out.

He grabbed the startled Archie by the arm and pulled him to the sidewalk. "I have some questions for you. We can either talk here, or you can come with me to the station. Which will it be?"

"Here," Archie stammered looking more than ever like a frightened rabbit. "I'll talk to you here."

"Alright, get in."

Still clutching Archer's arm, Morrison shepherded the terrified man to the car and propelled him inside. Then Morrison got in himself, piloted the vehicle across the intersection and pulled up at the curb. The man seated beside him was virtually in tears, but Morrison was unmoved. He had little sympathy for the drug dealer. He saw the man as a predator who exploited the weaknesses of others.

"Where were you last night around midnight?" He demanded without preamble.

"Home."

"Alone?"

"Yes, alone," Archer countered, he had regained some of his composure and was sounding more in control.

"So you have no alibi?"

"Why would I need an alibi?"

"I'm the one asking the questions. You are the one giving the answers. So, I repeat, do you have someone who can corroborate your whereabouts at midnight on Saturday?"

"I could ask to see my lawyer before answering your question," Archer smirked. "But as it happens, I have an air-tight alibi. One you cops can't question. As it happens, I called the New Haven Police Department just before midnight last night."

"Why was that?"

"Some sort of party in the duplex next door. They were making a racket and I couldn't sleep."

Morrison made no reply. Instead he took out his cell phone and dialed NHPD dispatch. "Is there a record of a disturbance call from a Herman Archer, on Fairhaven Avenue last night around midnight," he asked after providing the appropriate identification.

It took a few minutes for the operator to check the previous night's incoming calls before coming back on line, "Yup, a call came in at 11:56 p.m. Happens most every Saturday night. This guy Archer calls to complain all the time."

So that was that.

26

"ARCHER'S IN THE CLEAR," MORRISON TOLD BLAUSTEIN. "ANYTHING else I can do to help?"

"Thanks. I'll let you know if there is. In the mean time, why don't you go have brunch with your wife and in-laws."

It was at this point that the fax machine in Blaustein's office beeped and began spitting out paper. Blaustein grabbed the fax as it came off the machine. At last, the list of calls made from Dina's cell phone! Hoping that this was the break they had been waiting for, that Dina's phone calls could provide the lead they needed, he ran a finger down the list. She had made two out-of-state calls on Saturday morning. Both to New Jersey. He pulled the Augusta Scott telephone records from the file and was about to cross-check the phone numbers when Gardner came in.

"As I told you when I called, Heather Leopold's clean," Gardner said, taking off his coat and unwinding a scarf from his neck. "Cox confirms a call she made from her house to her sister in California. It was nine something Pacific time. In Connecticut it was just before midnight. Cox is faxing written verification. Are we still drawing blanks everywhere? " Gardner plonked dejectedly into the chair behind his desk. "Have you been able to contact Lieutenant Gordon yet?"

"Finally reached him at home. He's agreed that the Feds can cast a wider net than we can. He's coming in to make the call. Meanwhile there's no word yet on Dina's vehicle."

"What have you got there? Anything useful?" Gardner indicated the fax in Blaustein's hand.

"Dina's long distance phone records. I was about to compare them with Scott's last telephone calls. Remember, it was Dina's job to check out the professor's calls?"

Gardner nodded. "If there's an overlap, it could be the break we're looking for."

"If there's an overlap, it also means her assailant is responsible for the Mitchell-Scott homicides and she could be in terrible danger. I should never have invited her on board."

"You can't blame yourself," Gardner said, shuffling the stack of telephone messages that had accumulated on his desk.

Blaustein merely shrugged. He did blame himself. But nursing a sense of guilt would not help to find his missing colleague. Abruptly he got back to business. He set the two telephone records, Scott's and Dina's, side by side on his desk and began comparing them. Looking from list to list, he crossed off numbers that were on one and not on the other. In the end only one of Scott's phone numbers coincided, with the calls on Dina's list. It was one of the two calls she had made to the same number in New Jersey: a call to Rutgers University.

"Bingo!"

"Got something?" Gardner, about to make a call stopped in mid-dial and cradled the receiver.

"Let's hope so. Unless Dina drew a blank with this one," Blaustein said, dialing the number.

"I hope the Professor works on Sundays."

"Which professor?"

"Professor Elizabeth Randolph at Rutgers. It's the only call Scott and Barrett both made."

But there was no response to his call. Grumbling, frustrated by the delay, Blaustein called information and asked for the professor's home number. When he had it, he dialed again.

"Elizabeth Randolph," the voice at the other end of the line was crisp.

Blaustein introduced himself and apologized for calling on a Sunday.

"What now?" Randolph gave an exasperated sigh. "I spoke to your Detective Gardner, and I also spoke to your Detective Barrett. Don't you people communicate with one another?"

"If you don't mind, there are a couple of things that still need clarification and if it wasn't urgent, I would not have bothered you on a Sunday. You told Detective Gardner, when he called, that Professor Scott called to invite you to a spring symposium at Whitney?'"

"Yes, for the third time," the answer was accompanied by another sigh.

"What besides that did you tell Detective Barrett when she called you yesterday? It's really terribly important. Your answer may help us prevent another tragedy."

"Well naturally I'll do all I can to help in that case. Let's see. I told your detective that I had met Augusta professionally a few times, and I respected her work. But that I didn't know her personally," she paused as if trying to remember the rest of the conversation. Blaustein did not interrupt. "Oh yes, I also told your detective that Augusta asked me about a former student here at Rutgers."

"Oh? The student's name?"

"Kelly Richmond."

"And what exactly did you tell her about Richmond?"

"I told her exactly what I told Augusta, that Kelly was one of the best students to graduate from the Rutgers History program in the past ten years. I also happened to mention that the question, or rather Augusta's interest in the student, surprised me because Kelly Richmond was killed in a traffic accident a week after graduation. The driver of a pick-up truck ran a red light and broad-sided Kelly's car. He was killed almost instantly. A terrible tragedy."

"Did you say 'he'?"

"Yes I did," she sounded puzzled but Blaustein did not explain. He merely thanked the professor for her help and hung up.

"I think we may be onto something here," Blaustein could barely keep the excitement from his voice. "Kelly Richmond's dead."

"Poor kid. When did that happen?" Gardner sounded solicitous.

"Don't get bent out of shape, it happened last June," Blaustein answered grimly. "Not only that, but the late Kelly Richmond was a 'he'. Obviously the person we know as Kelly Richmond is a fraud. An imposter. And possibly also a murderer and a kidnapper. If we find her, and let's hope to God we do so in time, my bet is we'll find Dina."

"So who the hell is Richmond? Or whoever is passing for Richmond. And where is she? Green already tried her apartment, right?"

"Right. But she wasn't there and he didn't go inside. Besides not having a search warrant, he had no reason to at the time."

"Then let's get a bloody warrant. At the very least the woman's defrauded Whitney. We'll have probable cause."

"Her apartment's the first place to look. If Dina isn't there and we can't find Richmond, or whoever she is, then I haven't a clue where to turn. Unless. . . ." Blaustein snatched up Dina's phone records. "After Dina's call to Professor Randolph, she made a second call to New Jersey. Let's hope it provides some answers," he said dialing the number.

"New Brunswick Police Department," came a male voice at the other end.

"I'd like to speak to anyone who took a call late yesterday from Detective Dina Barrett of the Connecticut Major Crime Squad," Blaustein said after he introduced himself.

"That would have been Officer Brooks. He had desk duty yesterday. But he's off today."

"Look, it's urgent that I speak to him. Detective Barrett has been abducted from her home. In order to locate her, it's imperative we find out what Brooks and Barrett discussed. Can you give me his home number?"

"The best I can do for you is call Brooks at home and give him your number. Regulations you know. I'll get him to call you right back."

Blaustein thanked the officer and hung up. "So we know Dina called the New Brunswick Police Department," he explained, "But just our luck, the officer who spoke to her is off duty today. We're going to have to wait for him to call back."

"What's this about the New Brunswick Police Department?" Lieutenant Joe Gordon stood in the doorway, well-groomed and smelling of after shave. Under his overcoat he wore a navy blazer, a freshly pressed shirt, a tie knotted with his usual military precision, gray flannel pants neatly creased and Florsheims buffed to a blinding shine. Blaustein decided that even if the Lieutenant had been to church, he was a sick man. No one dressed like that on a Sunday.

"One of the last calls Dina made on her cell phone was to the New Brunswick Police Department. I was following up."

"We have no jurisdiction in Jersey and you know it. Why don't you let the FBI handle it. I'll place a call to them."

"They don't have a personal stake in it, we do. Right Huey?"

Gardner vigorously nodded his agreement.

"This isn't a request Blaustein. It's an order. There's an APB out on Barrett's car and the FBI will soon be on the case. Butt out."

"Sir, I'd like to take personal time, beginning right now," Blaustein said without hesitation, his face flushed and his fists clenched as he tried to control the anger and frustration percolating through him.

"Request denied. You're working two unsolved murders. I need you here."

"There's a very high probability both murders are linked to Barrett's disappearance, Loo. If we find her abductor, we'll find the killer," Gardner spoke up, the sweet voice of reason.

Lieutenant Gordon hesitated, "All right. I'll give you twenty-four hours."

"Forty-eight?" Blaustein knew he was pushing it.

But surprisingly Gordon semi-capitulated. "Thirty-six hours and not a minute more," he conceded reluctantly. "And try not to step on anyone's toes. Just let the FBI and the Jersey police do their jobs," he turned smartly on his heel and went to his office.

"Ass hole." Blaustein muttered when Gordon was out of ear shot.

"You've got that right," Gardner agreed.

It seemed like an eternity, but it was only ten minutes later that the phone rang and Officer Brooks of the New Brunswick Police Department identified himself.

Blaustein hastened to tell the officer about Dina's disappearance.

"Gee, I'm sorry to hear that. I'll do anything I can to help," Brooks offered.

"We think that her call to you and her abduction are connected. So tell me what you two talked about."

"Let me check my notes." There was a pause and the sound of pages turning before the officer spoke again, She asked me about a fatal traffic accident that took place last summer, a two-car at an intersection in downtown New Brunswick. June it was. She was interested in the driver of one of the cars, a Kelly Richmond. The other driver ran the light and plowed into Richmond's car. Richmond was killed. Succumbed at the hospital. Massive brain trauma. The driver of the other vehicle and a passenger in Richmond's car walked away unharmed."

"You gave Barrett a description of Richmond?"

"Yes, a male Caucasian in his twenties. Six five. About two hundred pounds," he paused a moment. "She didn't ask any questions about the driver of the other car but wanted to know the name and last known address of the female passenger in Richmond's car."

"And you gave them to her?"

"I did. Her name was Charlotte Chapman."

"Description?"

"No physical description available. And there weren't any hospital records. She was never admitted."

"If the officer on the scene questioned Chapman, maybe he can provide a description?"

"Unfortunately, he left the force shortly afterwards. I think he's living in Florida somewhere. But I gave Detective Barrett Chapman's home address at the time of the accident. She may have followed up. I have the address here." Blaustein could hear the rustle of paper again as he waited, impatiently drumming a tattoo on his desk. "Here it is: Charlotte Chapman, 730 Newbury Street, New Brunswick. I did not have a current phone number for her."

Blaustein wrote down the name and address and thanked the officer. "If you think of anything else will you let me know?" Blaustein gave him his cell phone number.

"Sure thing." Brooks hung up.

"For what it's worth," Blaustein said, turning to Gardner, "a woman by the name of Charlotte Chapman was the passenger in Richmond's car the night he was killed. At the time of the accident, Chapman was living in New Brunswick, New Jersey. What we don't know is whether she's still living there. We don't have a current phone number for her. And we also don't know whether or not she has any idea who's been walking around in Kelly Richmond's shoes. But she may. At least it's a place to start."

When Blaustein called information and found there was no phone number for Charlotte Chapman, he turned to his partner and shook his head, "No phone number."

"You're going to Jersey, aren't you?" Gardner thought he knew the answer before he asked the question.

"As soon as I've called Greta. She's as worried about Dina as we are," Blaustein said, reaching for the phone, "Meanwhile.. .."

"Yes, I know. I'll prepare a warrant and take a team over to the Winslow Street apartment *tout suite*. The problem is getting someone to okay a warrant on a Sunday."

"Maybe Gordon can pull some strings. And do me a favor, call Green and give him an update," Blaustein looked at his watch, "He's waiting outside the Whitney Library to see if Richmond or whoever the woman is shows up. My guess is she won't and he might as well stand down."

27

AT FIRST IT WAS THE STABBING PAIN THAT PENETRATED HER consciousness. Then the numbing cold. Even before she was fully awake. Even before she opened her eyes. She felt the pain that seared her left shoulder and radiated down her arm, and the cold chilled her to the bone. She was no longer lying in the cargo area of her SUV but on a hard, cold surface in a place that was dank and dark. She had no idea whether it was night or day. Or how long she had been there. She remembered lying, trussed like an animal, a bicycle wheel spinning in her face, the overhead street lights flashing by as she fell in and out of consciousness, the feeling of helplessness as she faced the inevitability of death. She only half-remembered being roughly awakened and dragged from the car, her body screaming in pain. Then nothing but a jumble of bad dreams: of Augusta Scott, a broken doll of a woman, laughing a ghoulish laugh as she rocked back and forth in her rocking chair, of the ambush in Freddie's darkened house, of the dream that was not a dream but the waking realization that she was facing an implacable enemy alone.

She was lying on a cement floor. Her wrists and ankles were

bound with duct tape. There was duct tape across her mouth. And her feet had lost all circulation. At first she could not make out her surroundings. With the modicum of light that filtered into the place, she sensed rather than saw that she was in some place cavernous: a barn or warehouse, high ceilinged and without windows. Listening, she thought she could hear the lapping of water, and smell its mustiness. Then as her eyes adjusted to the dark, she began to discern the sleek silhouettes of rowing shells. And realized that she was in a boathouse, a sizable one. The Whitney boathouse perhaps? From an inner reservoir of strength she did not know she had, she summoned all her energy and tried to sit up. But the effort and the pain were so intense that she almost blacked out again. Feeling feverish despite the cold, hot behind the eyeballs, light-headed, she lay still and tried to regroup.

She was still alive and she would fight to stay that way. Gritting her teeth, she again willed herself to sit up. This time she made it without blacking out. After taking a moment to catch her breath, she explored the extent of her wound. Bending both arms so that her bound hands could reach her left shoulder, she gingerly touched it with the tips of her fingers. The fabric of her jacket was sticky with congealed blood. That was a good sign. It meant that the blood had coagulated and that the wound had stopped hemorrhaging. Even so, the chance of surviving would be lousy once Charlotte Chapman returned.

Though it was in the spring semester that college crews practiced, she could not bank on the hope that someone other than Charlotte would come to the boathouse first. She had to escape, or at least try to. Struggling slowly, painfully to her feet, she steadied herself and tried to get her bearings. At the far end of the boathouse, light was beginning to creep in around the edges of a large double door. With her ankles bound, she shuffled slowly, uncertainly toward it, stopping every couple of yards to catch her breath. It was a tedious, excruciating process. Once she stumbled to her knees and had to force herself to get back on her feet. But the door drew her like a magnet and she did not stop to rest or permit herself to waiver until she reached it. It was like getting to the finish line in a marathon. But there were no roaring crowds to greet her, only the pervasive silence of the cavernous boat-house. With her bound hands outstretched, she touched the door and tried the handle. Of course it was locked. She expected nothing else.

Leaning against the door, she fought off light-headedness, permitted herself a moment's respite, and then began feeling for a light-switch. With the tips of her fingers she explored the wall to the right of the door. Nothing. Shuffling to the other side of the door, she tried again. This time her fingers touched a bank of switches. She flipped them up one after the other, flooding the boathouse with light. Blinking at the unexpected brightness, she took in her surroundings. Rows of sleek, gleaming shells: eights, fours, pairs and sculls. And racks and racks of oars. Not green and gold. Not the Whitney colors. But red and black. This then was not the Whitney boat-house. So where was she? A small motorized launch provided the answer. Painted on its side in scarlet letters were the initials 'RU'. Rutgers University. Her heart sank. The woman who called herself Kelly Richmond had taken her back to New Jersey. Who would think of looking for her here? Or finding her alive if they did. She had told no one of her trip to New Jersey or about her probe into Kelly Richmond's undergraduate record at Rutgers. No one else knew that Kelly Richmond was not Kelly Richmond but Charlotte Chapman. She was on her own. And she couldn't blame her isolation on a dead cell-phone battery. Pay phones were not yet obsolete. She could have found one and called Jackson. But she had not. Wordlessly she cursed her own arrogance. Cursed herself for keeping her discovery about Kelly Richmond's identity to herself. Though not admitting it at the time, she had been secretly pleased when her cell phone failed her. It had given her a convenient excuse to solve the Mitchell-Scott murders all by herself. Clever, Dina, look where it got you! Her present predicament was of her own making. She had only herself to blame. And now she had only herself to rely on.

Now that she could see what she was doing, Dina tried the door handle again. Again to no avail. Had she really thought escape would be that easy? That Charlotte Chapman had driven her all this way only to let her walk out of here? In frustration, she tried to ram the door as hard as she could with her good shoulder. The door did not give a millimeter. It did not even rattle. All the effort accomplished was to send a shock of raw pain through her injured body. And the last thing she wanted to do was to pass out again. Disheartened, exhausted by her exertions, she sank to the floor and forced herself to think rationally. As she saw it, her only option was to outwit her captor. To escape before Charlotte came back, or if not, to be prepared for the woman's return. Dina had no idea how much time she had. Nor did she know how long it had been since the confrontation in Freddie's house. Shocked by the realization that she did not even know what time it was or even what day, she tried to check her watch. But the bitch had taken it. Her wrist was bare.

It was light outside, so surely there should be people about. People who would respond to noise. But how much noise was she capable of generating trussed and gagged? The gag had to come off. Using her fingernails, she scratched and pulled at one corner of the duct tape that covered her mouth. Slowly, patiently, she worked at the tape till she was able to grip a small piece of it and tear it off with a single, painful tug. Feeling unwonted exhilaration at this small accomplishment, she pulled herself to her feet. Then, positioning herself so that her mouth was aligned with the crack between the double doors, she shouted for help as loudly as she could. But weak as she was, her shout was no more than a hoarse whisper and not nearly loud enough to be heard above the steady hum of the passing cars outside. Her old wound and the new one were ganging up to deplete her strength and her frustration was building. She cast her eyes about her for a lifeline. Something, anything that would help. As if in answer to a prayer, she caught sight of a shelf of old coxswains' bullhorns. The very thing. She hobbled over to the shelf. But being able to reach up far enough with her hands tied together proved impossible. Her injured shoulder would not collaborate with her good one. Biting back pain, she tried to force her body to cooperate but it refused. Despite a Herculean effort, she was unable to lift both arms above the horizontal. She would need to liberate her good arm in order to reach the shelf. That meant cutting through the duct tape and freeing her hands. But how? All she had were her teeth. Disregarding the throbbing in her shoulder and the urge to sink back into oblivion, she began to gnaw at the edges of the duck tape that bound her wrists. She tugged and pulled at it with her incisors and tore at it with her canines. It was very slow going. Agonizing and tedious. And still light-headed, she had to stop every now and then to keep from fainting.

When the final shred of duct tape gave way and her hands were free, she started stripping the duct-tape from her ankles. At first, her ice cold fingers refused to obey her. But she kept at it one millimeter at a time till at last her persistence paid off. Exhilarated by this monumental achievement, she almost laughed. Wriggling her toes to get the circulation going in her feet, she stood up and stamped them. She felt free, sort of. But the reality was something else. She still needed to get out of the boathouse. Reaching for and grabbing one of the bull-horns, she returned to the door, placed the bull-horn over the crack between the two doors and shouted as loudly as her aching body would let her, "Help! Help me! Please Help!"

Except for the distant squawking of a crow and the drone of passing cars, her only answer was leaden silence. Utterly drained, she summoned all her strength and tried again. Several times. Each time there was no response. And the silence alarmed and depressed her. Her only hope now was that someone would come to the boathouse before her captor returned. Given the time of year and the level of light she could see through the crack in the door, she guessed it was morning and not too early for crews to be out on the river. The semester would have started by now, and didn't crews practice early in the morning? But unfortunately no one came. Thus far she remained utterly alone.

She had nothing to show for her efforts and did not have the luxury of time, but she knew she had to rest. She knew it was imperative that she regain some of her strength before the woman returned. She did not want to be cornered like a defenseless animal.

If she was destined to go down, she was determined to go down fighting.

Having resolved to put up what defense she could, she helped herself to an oar from one of the racks and returned to her post by the door. Then she switched off the lights and took up a semi- recumbent position with her back to the wall. Her only chance as she saw it, and an outside chance at best, was to take her captor by surprise, to ram her with the oar or trip her up with it as she came through the door. At most, the element of surprise might give her a split-second opportunity to bolt through the door to freedom. It did not seem like much of a plan, but it was all she could think of.

Green and Gardner, warrant in hand and accompanied by Kelly Richmond's elderly landlord and a pair of technicians, knocked on the door of the third floor apartment. When, as expected, there was no response, they repeated the process.

"She still isn't here. I've been keeping an eye out for her," came a voice from the landing below. "You guys must want to speak to her real bad."

"We do," Gardner acknowledged as the retired mailman who lived on the second floor lumbered up the stairs to join the group upstairs.

"You brought an army this time," the old man's curiosity had clearly been piqued by the appearance of an ambulance and the mobile crime lab. The Crime Squad detectives had come prepared for all contingencies.

Ignoring the old man, Gardner turned to the landlord, "Please use your pass key."

The landlord complied and the door swung open.

"Now I'll have to ask you all to wait outside," Gardner said addressing the civilians. "This could be a crime scene," he explained politely.

Though chagrined, the onlookers obliged as Gardner, Green and the two techs went inside and closed the door behind them.

Gardner's first sensation was one of immense relief. There was no body. But there was also not much of anything else. The place had been stripped of everything but its second hand furnishings. Nothing personal remained: no books, no papers, no clothing. Nor was there a thing on the shelves in either the bathroom or the kitchen cabinets. There were no garments on the empty hangers in the armoire. Even the refrigerator had been emptied.

"Clearly the bird has flown. But maybe, she left some prints. If they are on file somewhere we'll at least be able to identify her from those. Dust the surfaces and see what you get," Gardner told the techs, and leaving Green in charge of the operation, went downstairs.

The old mailman was waiting for Gardner when he reached the second floor. "Did you find what you were looking for?" He asked.

"Not yet. But perhaps you can tell me something. Did you notice whether the upstairs tenant made any trips to the dumpster in the last day or so?"

"Yes, yesterday. I told that to the other detective when he was here earlier. Actually, I saw her going to the dumpster more than once yesterday," the old man answered, pleased to be making a contribution. "I asked her if she was getting a head start on her spring cleaning."

"And what did she say to that?"

"She didn't bother to answer. Just continued down the stairs and out the door with her plastic trash bags. Rude I thought. Young people have no respect these days."

Just what Gardner was afraid of. The Mitchell-Scott killer had left nothing behind in either crime scene, not even a fingerprint and she appeared to have done the same in her apartment. If the Richmond woman was their killer, they wouldn't find anything incriminating there either. Chances were she had wiped all the surfaces in her apartment and got rid of everything else she had touched. Unless the trash was still in the dumpster.

"When is the trash in your dumpster collected?"

"Monday morning. Before dawn. The garbage trucks usually wake me up and I have a devil of a time getting back to sleep again."

If that was the case, then Richmond's trash would still be in the dumpster. There was still a chance that a clue to her identity had been left behind. A break at last.

"Did you happen to notice the color of the plastic bags she was carrying."

"Black maybe, a dark color anyhows. You want I should point them out to you?" The old man, eager to be helpful, was already looking forward to the story he would tell his poker buddies the next time they played.

"Did Ms. Richmond have any visitors that you noticed?" Gardner asked as the two men made their way outside.

"Not what I was aware of. A real quiet girl. Like I told that other Detective. She didn't have no wild parties like some of the tenants we've had on the third floor," he pointed to the overgrown driveway at the side of the house. "Dumpster's over there."

"Does Ms. Richmond own a car?" Gardner asked as they walked over to the dumpster.

"Nah. Mostly rides that bike of hers," the retired mailman said as he helpfully pushed back the lid of the dumpster.

Gardner noted with satisfaction that it had not yet been emptied. In fact it was filled to capacity. On top lay six dark green, large-capacity garbage bags, "Are those the bags you saw Ms. Richmond carrying?"

"Sure are."

Later, back at headquarters, with Gardner standing over them, the technicians sifted through the garbage bags one at a time. In one bag they found the half-used contents of the refrigerator: an empty milk carton, a jar of ketchup and assorted vegetables. In another there were unopened cans of soup, an almost full box of herbal teas, a partial bag of flour, a pot of honey, a jar of organic spaghetti sauce, and half a box of linguine. A third bag contained kitchen-ware: inexpensive cutlery, a frying pan, a dented aluminum pot, a kettle, four coffee mugs and an assortment of plates, none of which matched. The fourth bag was filled with clothes: jeans, a skirt, a couple of sweatshirts, a pair of sneakers and several under-garments. The other two bags contained papers and books. Some of the books bore the *ex libris* imprint of the Whitney library. What looked like the entire contents of the young woman's apartment had been stuffed into the six plastic garbage bags. Though all she owned did not add up to much especially when it was all laid out, it was enough to yield several clear sets of prints.

"Not much she could take with her if all she had was a bicycle," Gardner said to Green. "Now, let's see if the lab can find a record on those prints. My guess is they all belong to Richmond. It will be a real break if we can match them with a name. Meanwhile, let's take a look at the papers the woman left behind."

"Probably a waste of time, they look like a bunch of class notes."

They hauled the papers up to the office and dumped them on Green's desk for further review. Gardner meanwhile called Blaustein's cell phone. When he reached him, Blaustein was on the far side of the George Washington bridge, and he had some news of his own.

"Dina's truck's been located. Local police caught a couple of kids trying to steal it off a street in Menlo Park."

"Did the kids see who parked it there?"

"That was my first question too. But the answer's 'no', sorry to say. Apparently the car was parked there overnight. The kids figured the owner wasn't coming back any time soon, so they jimmied a window and hot-wired the car. Unfortunately for them and fortunately for us, they were caught in the act by a beat cop. The license was traced and that's pretty much the end of the story as far as the vehicle is concerned. But the fact that it was found in New Jersey ties in with Dina's phone calls to Rutgers so we're on the right track. At any rate, that's where I'm headed now. I just hope we're in time," Blaustein cleared his throat of the persistent lump in it. "Anything useful turn up in the Richmond woman's apartment?"

"The bird had flown by the time we got there. Probably sometime yesterday. She cleared everything out before she left but not before the garbage was collected. We retrieved it from the dumpster and were able to find some prints. They're being checked out as we speak. I just hope she has a record. Even if she doesn't, it sure looks like she's the one responsible for Dina's abduction." Left unspoken was his hope that an abduction was all it was.

"She could have taken off in Dina's SUV."

"Certainly looks that way. According to the old geezer who lives in her building, Richmond, or whoever she is, didn't own a car. A nosey neighbor comes in handy every now and then."

"A bicycle's Richmond's only form of transportation?"

"Seems to be. But I'll double-check with Motor Vehicles just to be sure."

"And check the rental places. If she's the Scott-Mitchell killer then she probably used a rental to get over to Chisholm and to Scott's place in East Haven?"

"I'll call DMV and area car rental companies as soon as I get off the phone."

Blaustein thought for a moment, "You may come up dry. She could have gone to both places on her bike."

"That's quite a distance."

"Not really. Not for someone who's fit. From her apartment it's only about ten miles to Chisholm and less than that to Scott's home in East Haven. In my younger days I routinely cycled twenty-five, thirty miles, without breaking a sweat."

"Well if she rode her bike it would account for the fact that we found no car-tracks at either scene."

"Yes it would. It might also mean that she's holding Dina somewhere in the vicinity of Menlo Park. Within a ten to fifteen mile radius of where she abandoned the SUV. I'll plan to make Menlo Park my first stop on the off chance there's useful evidence in Dina's vehicle."

"Don't hold your breath. This woman's not only clever but clearly not the careless type. She tries to leave no evidence behind."

"Certainly she was smart enough to have seen through Dina's cover and to have gone after her."

"Either that or someone tipped her off. And when she found out that Dina was onto her, she needed to know how much *you* knew. That's why she called you late last night pretending to be Dina's mother. Not killing Dina outright was an act of self-preservation rather than and act of kindness. Let's just hope that Dina can stall her long enough for us to find both of them."

"Amen to that. The woman's doubts may keep Dina alive."

Neither of them wanted to contemplate anything else.

28

"HERE IT IS," THE MENLO PARK DETECTIVE SAID, LIFTING THE HATCH of Dina's impounded vehicle. "We didn't find any prints, but there are blood stains on the carpet in the back and some grease marks. Both look recent."

"Do you think the grease marks could have come from a bicycle chain?"

"Possibly. We could test it to find out."

Blaustein leaned forward and examined the blood stains, "Has the blood been typed yet?" He tried to sound professional, but the sight of what was probably Dina's blood had left him shaken.

"Not yet. Being Sunday and all. And our lab's still working overtime on a busier than usual Saturday night caseload."

The Menlo Park policeman did not ask why a Connecticut cop was in New Jersey asking questions about an abandoned SUV and it was just as well, Blaustein didn't have time for explanations. The blood stains in Dina's vehicle had escalated his sense of urgency. His only link to the real Kelly Richmond was his female passenger at the time of his accident, Charlotte Chapman. He needed to locate and question Charlotte Chapman before it was too late. The New Brunswick police had given Dina the Chapman woman's address and, knowing his former partner, he was convinced that Dina would have come to the conclusion that Richmond's female passenger held the key to the identity of Kelly Richmond's impersonator. If so, Charlotte Chapman was not only the last person to see the real Kelly Richmond alive, but she may have been the last person to see or speak to Dina yesterday.

Blaustein pulled up in front of Charlotte Chapman's last known address, got out of the car and climbed the sagging steps to the front door. Unable to decipher the names on either intercom, he pushed both buzzers and waited. He sensed rather than saw someone observing him from behind the curtain in a window overlooking the porch, and he favored the watcher with his most benign expression. Seconds later the intercom buzzed and opening the outer door, he entered an ill lit hall. The interior door to his left was ajar on a chain. From behind it came a woman's voice.

"What is it?"

Blaustein took out his badge and held it so that she could see it through the space between the door and the jamb, "Detective Blaustein, Connecticut State Police, Ma'am. Does a Charlotte Chapman live here?"

"No she does not."

"How about upstairs?"

"She doesn't live upstairs either."

"Ma'am may I please come inside?"

"Why? I already told you Charlotte doesn't live here."

"Ma'am, this was her last known address. She lived here less than a year ago, were you living here at the time?"

"Yes," the woman admitted with a sigh.

At last he was getting somewhere, but it was like squeezing juice from a lemon rind, "Ma'am, have you seen her lately?"

The woman hesitated. "What's this about, officer? A woman from the Connecticut police was here yesterday with questions. Why are you bothering me again?"

So Dina had been there yesterday. Blaustein felt a flicker of hope, "I don't mean to bother you Ma'am. But I need to speak to Ms. Chapman urgently. I think she can help us," Blaustein smiled pleasantly, trying not to let his irritation show.

His pleasant, nonthreatening demeanor seemed to do the trick. The woman scraped back the security chain and let him in. She was close to Blaustein's age, but looked older. Sad-looking. With joyless eyes. She had fine features and was probably pretty once. Now her hair had faded to gray, her skin was sallow and lined about the eyes and mouth. She wore a longish brown, plaid skirt with buttons up the front and a shapeless, navy zippered cardigan. Her shoulders were rounded as if in defeat. She stood aside to let him in and wordlessly waved him into the sitting room.

"Sit down."

"Thank you Ma'am," Blaustein sat down at one end of the couch. The other end was occupied by a large tabby cat which made no effort to move. The overpowering cat-smell made Blaustein want to puke, "Tell me if you will," he repeated his question, "do you know where Ms. Chapman is now?"

The woman had remained standing, her arms folded protectively across her chest. She shook her head, her face expressionless.

"Tell me if she's been here in the last twenty-four hours," he asked patiently, though he felt anything but.

The woman hesitated for the barest moment before shaking her head again. The hesitation tipped Blaustein off. That and the fact that she refused to make eye contact. Years on the force had made him an expert at reading body language. The woman's denial was an implicit lie. That meant that Chapman had indeed been here despite the woman's denial.

He tried a new tack, "Are you related to Charlotte?"

"Charlotte's my daughter," the woman admitted reluctantly.

"Do you happen to have a photograph of her?"

Although she shook her head, the gesture was accompanied by a flickering glance over Blaustein's shoulder. The glance was so quick that Blaustein almost missed it. He turned in the direction of the glance. On a table behind the couch lay a photograph album. He rose and picked it up. The pictures had been arranged in chronological order beginning with baby pictures and ending with two photographs that held his attention. Both were of a pretty blonde girl. In the first photograph she had her arm linked with that of an older man, maybe her father. He was reed-thin, as if he had a wasting disease. His hair was thinning and faded. His skin was tautly drawn over prominent cheekbones. His eyes had the mournful look of a Basset hound. In the second photograph the girl, by now in her late teens or early twenties, stood alone on the bank of a river. She was dressed in Rutgers University rowing shorts and jersey and was gripping an oar upright like the farmer in the Grant Wood painting. Even though the young woman in the picture did not wear glasses, he recognized her instantly as the student who called herself Kelly Richmond.

Immediately Blaustein went into attack mode, "Ma'am, did you know that your daughter was using the name Kelly Richmond?" It was as much an accusation as a question.

The woman turned pale and clutched at the arm of the couch as if to steady herself, "She didn't tell me," her voice was querulous and her shock obvious. But her denial unequivocal. And he believed her.

"Now why would she do that do you think?"

"I don't know," her voice was barely audible.

"Do you know where your daughter's been since last summer?"

"She told me she was finishing her degree at Whitney. I had a fight with her about it."

"Why fight Mrs. Chapman? Whitney's a fine school."

"Personal reasons," she said shortly, her lips setting in an obstinate line.

Blaustein switched tacks again, "Mrs. Chapman, what did Detective Dina Barrett come to see you about yesterday?"

"She asked about the accident that killed Kelly Richmond," again the answer was preceded by a cautionary hesitation.

"Did you call your daughter to tell her about Detective Barrett's visit?"

"I thought she should know the police were looking into the

accident that killed Kelly. I told her she should get in touch with Detective Barrett. The detective left me her home phone number."

"And where was your daughter when you called her, Ms. Chapman?"

"In New Haven."

So Charlotte Chapman had made a point of finding Dina in New Haven, finding her and abducting her. Blaustein thought caustically. But he did not let either his rancor or his sense of urgency show. Instead, he spoke calmly, using his most placating tone, "Alright Mrs. Chapman. You're being very helpful. Now tell me please, have you seen your daughter in the last twenty-four hours?"

"She arrived here late last night. Early this morning actually," the woman acknowledged reluctantly. "I don't know when exactly. I was asleep. She must have let herself in and gone straight to her room. She left a note for me not to wake her."

"And at what time this morning did she leave?"

"Just before you arrived," the woman wrung her hands in obvious distress now.

"She saw me drive up?"

The woman nodded miserably, "She went out the back way. She said she didn't need to talk to you."

"Do you have any idea where she went?"

"She didn't tell me. She just took her bike and left."

"She doesn't have access to a vehicle?"

Mrs. Chapman shook her head, "She doesn't own a car. And my car is still parked outside. The blue Citation."

Blaustein went over to the window and looked out at the ancient Citation parked at the curb. It confirmed what the mother had said, and Blaustein heaved a sigh of relief. Wherever Charlotte Chapman was, it could not be far.

"What was your daughter wearing when she left?"

Again the hesitation, as if torn between loyalty and doubt, "Black sweat pants and a black parka."

"Did she wear a hat of any kind?"

"A red knit cap."

"Was she wearing her glasses?"

"She doesn't wear glasses."

So the glasses, like the name she had stolen, were fake, both part of Charlotte Chapman's false persona. All to get into Whitney Graduate School? Even conceding the fact that competition to get into the top universities was tough, it didn't make sense. Neither the stakes nor the pay-offs seemed high enough. Not for a degree in history. Law maybe. Or medicine perhaps. But history? And even supposing Mitchell had discovered the charade, why did Chapman have to kill him? She could have simply walked away and disappeared. In all probability, Mitchell did not even know her real name. Or had the motive for the Mitchell homicide been simpler than that. More basic. Carnal perhaps? Given Mitchell's reputation, it could have been a crime of passion, a well covered up crime till Scott became suspicious. Then one thing led to another until Chapman was in so deep she couldn't get out. Like a cornered animal. And, like any cornered animal, extremely dangerous. He shivered involuntarily. Whatever her reasons, it did not matter now. Blaustein was convinced that the woman had already committed two murders. He hoped desperately that it was not too late to prevent a third.

"Mrs. Chapman, I would like to borrow these photographs of Charlotte," he said, and without waiting for an answer took both recent photographs and put them in his pocket. "If your daughter comes back here, or if you hear from her, I want you to call me at once, " he handed her his card pointing out the cell phone number. "I won't hurt your daughter but I think there is still time to stop her from hurting herself or someone else."

"Hurting someone else? Are you implying that Charlotte has hurt someone? Charlotte wouldn't do that," her chin went up defiantly and for the first time there was light in her dead eyes.

"Look," he said, as gently as possible, "I realize it may be difficult for you to accept, but I have reason to believe that Charlotte may have murdered at least one of her college professors."

"Oh God," the woman grabbed the mantle for support with one hand and clutched her chest with the other. "This is about Godfrey Mitchell isn't it?"

Blaustein blinked. The Mitchell homicide had been in all the papers and was widely reported on television, but why would Mrs. Chapman jump to the conclusion that he was referring to Mitchell? He wanted to know the answer but the answer would have to wait. He had no time to probe deeper. Not now. Now was not the time to think about the Mitchell murder. Now his only priority was to find Charlotte Chapman before it was too late to stop her from killing again.

After leaving the Chapman house, Blaustein called the local police department from his car. Officer Brooks, now back on duty, listened to the Connecticut detective as he explained what he needed and why.

"I'll put out an APB," Brooks said. "Do you have a description of the car Richmond is driving?"

"The woman will probably be on a bicycle. When last seen she was wearing black sweatpants, a black parka and a red knit cap. She's tall and blonde. I have a fairly recent photograph and I'm on my way with it right now. I'll see you at the station."

Following the directions Brooks gave him, Blaustein located the New Brunswick Police Department without any trouble. Brooks met him at the front desk. He was a pleasant-faced, African-American man, fortyish, about six foot three with a shaved head and a beginning beer belly. When Blaustein handed him the photograph, Brooks immediately went into action, photocopying the picture and faxing it to all the area precincts.

"Isn't modem technology great?" Brooks said with a grin.

Blaustein nodded absently and pulled out his cell phone, "Excuse me a moment while I call my Loo?"

Though explaining to Lieutenant Gordon what was still only a hunch went against the grain, not to mention his better judgment, Blaustein had no option but to brief the lieutenant. If Dina was still alive, they would be needing a first-class hostage negotiating team. And Gordon was their link to the FBI.

"Loo," he said, clearing his throat. "I'm certain that Dina's being held somewhere in the New Brunswick area. When we pin-point the exact location, we'll need an expert hostage negotiator. The best there is. That means calling in the FBI."

"Agreed. I'll ask them to stand by."

"Actually it might be best if they could mobilize ASAP. We may not have much time." Blaustein tried not to let his impatience show.

"Be reasonable Blaustein. I can't call in the FBI until you've located Detective Barrett. You've got to give me more than your guesstimate."

"This is what we have so far, Loo," to keep his temper in check, Blaustein took a deep breath and explained the situation as patiently as he could, "Our suspect is one Charlotte Chapman a.k.a. Kelly Richmond. Chapman was using the identity of Kelly Richmond in order to get into Whitney Graduate School. It was probably when Mitchell and Scott found out about the switch that Chapman killed them. Barrett probably figured it out when she checked Scott's telephone records. But Chapman found out that Barrett was asking questions. That's when she surprised her. She's holding her somewhere in the Rutgers vicinity."

"How can you be sure that's where Barrett is being held?"

"Barrett's car was located in Menlo Park, within biking distance of New Brunswick. Which was Chapman's last known address before she moved to New Haven. Chapman doesn't have a car. Just a bicycle. So the way I see it, Chapman has Barrett stashed somewhere in or near New Brunswick. The woman used to live here and she knows the area."

"That only tells us that Chapman could be within biking distance of New Brunswick. It does nothing to confirm that Detective Barrett is there too. Chapman could have dropped her off anywhere before ditching the car in Menlo Park. Barrett could be in Connecticut for that matter."

"That's true except for one thing, Chapman could have killed Barrett when she ambushed her in the Hathaway house. Instead she abducted her. I think she wanted her alive in order to question her. Maybe to find out what was known about the Mitchell-Scott homicides and who knew it. It's the only explanation for the snatch. Which is why I think Barrett's been stashed in or near New Brunswick. Somewhere within biking range. Chapman needs access to her and she can't go very far on a bicycle," Blaustein did not give Gordon time to interrupt. Instead he continued to stress the urgency he felt, "Loo, I think it's important to move quickly. Apart from the fact that we know what this woman is capable of, there is evidence that Dina's been injured and we don't know how badly. In addition to the blood-stains we found in Mrs. Hathaway's home, there were bloodstains in the back of Dina's vehicle."

"The same blood type as Barrett's?"

"That hasn't been determined yet. But they're highly unlikely to be anyone else's."

"And you're positive that the Chapman woman is responsible for the Mitchell and Scott homicides, or is this just another of your hunches?"

"Largely circumstantial, I admit," Blaustein conceded grudgingly. "But I believe we've got both motive and opportunity for Mitchell and Scott: a cover-up gone bad. Chapman was admitted to Whitney under false pretenses and did not want to get caught. When Barrett found out about it, she put herself at risk too. We need to get to her before Barrett becomes Chapman's next victim."

"It doesn't make sense. Even if Chapman was masquerading as Richmond, why would she go to such extremes to conceal it?"

Again Blaustein fought down his impatience as he watched the minutes tick by on the squad room wall-clock. Although he did not have an answer for Gordon's question, every instinct told him he was right. "Look Loo, I've seen a photograph of Chapman. There can be no doubt that it is she who assumed Richmond's identity. At the very least she's guilty of fraud. Furthermore, Chapman was seen in New Haven yesterday and has definitely been in New Brunswick in the past twenty-four hours. Her mother admitted as much to me. The mother also admitted that she called her daughter yesterday and told her that Dina had been here asking questions about her," he spoke as calmly as he could, repeating his rationale, enunciating each word through clenched teeth. "Chapman used Dina's car to get to the area. She left Dina somewhere around here and after ditching the car, went to her mother's house on her bike. Apparently she arrived in the early hours of the morning and did not leave until she saw me coming up the walk. When she did, she skipped out the back way. That tells you something right there."

"I'm still not convinced I have enough information for the FBI. I wouldn't hesitate to call them if you could tell me where she is. Or at the very least, where the Chapman woman was headed."

If I knew that I would be heading there myself instead of stuck here talking to you, Blaustein felt like saying. Instead he mustered what little patience he had left and said simply. "When we find out where that is, we'll find Dina. I'm sure of it."

"Assuming Dina's still alive."

"We have to assume that."

"Granted, I suppose if this Chapman person had wanted to kill Barrett, it would have been simpler to do it in the Hathaway house," Lieutenant Gordon conceded. He paused a moment and Blaustein could hear the shuffling of papers. "Alright, I'll call the FBI and request a SWAT team and their top negotiator. Do you have a description of the car Chapman is driving?" Clearly Gordon had not been listening.

"Negative. She does not have access to a car. She's on a bicycle," he repeated.

"Well that does reduce the search radius somewhat. I'll brief the FBI as soon as we get off the phone. Make a note of the FBI number," he dictated it while Blaustein wrote it down. "I'll tell them you'll call them directly when you can pinpoint a location. And don't leave us in the dark up here. We'll all be praying for Barrett," he abruptly cut the connection.

Blaustein hung up the phone and shook his head. "My Loo's a royal pain the ass."

"Sure sounded that way," Brooks gave him a sympathetic grin. "Now how about some coffee and a donut? You look like you can use something."

"To go maybe," though Blaustein hadn't eaten anything

substantial since his interrupted breakfast with Greta, he didn't have the luxury of time.

"Why don't you ride with me in my squad car," Brooks said, pouring coffee into two Styrofoam cups and slapping lids on them. "You know what the woman looks like. You'll be sure to recognize her."

"I'd appreciate that, especially as I can't legally make a collar in this jurisdiction. Everything has to be strictly by the book. I don't want this perp to get off on a technicality," Blaustein said, relieving Brooks of one of the coffee cups and helping himself to a jelly donut. "But before we leave I'd like to look at a map of the area if that's okay."

"No problem," Brooks pulled a map from a drawer and laid it flat on his desk. "Are we looking for something in particular?"

"Assuming Chapman'll cycle to wherever she has taken Barrett, I reckon we should first concentrate on an area within ten miles or so of the Chapman house."

"That would be the Newbury Street address," Brooks said, simultaneously pointing it out on the map. "A ten-mile radius will cover a lot of ground and extend beyond the city limits."

"Well, to start with, let's concentrate on places that are within city limits. Places Chapman is most likely familiar with. Places to which she might have access. And places where she could stash Detective Barrett that are relatively secure. Any ideas?"

Brooks shook his head, "Sorry, not offhand. All we can do is drive around and hope we get lucky."

29

ACHING ALL OVER, DEHYDRATED, HER HEAD SWIMMING AND
alternately shivering with cold and burning up with fever, Dina
fought her body's urge to lapse into unconsciousness. She had been
sitting with her back against the wall, the oar and megaphone on the
floor beside her. As the eons-long minutes passed and the morning
grew later, she began to hear a gradually escalating hum as the
volume of passing traffic increased. Then, a short time later, came the
tolling of distant church bells and it dawned on her that it was only
just Sunday. What had seemed like an eternity since her ambush in
Freddie's darkened house, had been only a few hours.

Perhaps she still had time. She realized now that thinking she
could solve a double homicide on her own had been both arrogant and
stupid. She should have told Blaustein about her suspicions and left it
at that. But instead of acting like a team player, she had gone it alone.
And she got careless. Careless and cavalier. A deadly combination as it
turned out. She should have considered the possibility that Charlotte
was more than a witness. And that by giving Mrs. Chapman Freddie
Hathaway's home phone number, she had enabled Charlotte to track

her down instead of the other way around. The ambush should have been predictable. But for once her instincts had forsaken her. Even the fact the electric power was off when she got home should have tipped her off. But she had neither drawn her gun nor beaten a strategic retreat. Instead she had walked into the darkened house like an unwitting fly into a spider's web. Now her only hope was that the midnight phone call to Jackson had set off alarm bells. Maybe he would call or come to check on her. But what if he did? What would he find except that she was gone? How would he know where she had gone or who had taken her.

Hoping she had left behind some clue to her present predicament, she went over the sequence of events. They started with her call to Professor Randolph at Rutgers. That call was a small but vital clue. If Jackson found it, it could be like the end of a thread which, if pulled, would unravel the sequence of events. That call could be her lifeline. It would tally with the Augusta Scott call to the Rutgers History Department. But would Jackson think to check the phone records? And if he did, would they tell him anything? Or tell him anything in time to help her? Damn, damn, damn, if only she had told Jackson where she was going and why. But she had not because she knew he would have talked her out of it. And, she thought ruefully, he would have been right to do so.

Hindsight and feeling sorry for herself were not going to get her out of her pickle. Sighing, she labored slowly to her feet and tried using the megaphone again. But each time the effort took more of a toll on her fading strength. And each time silence was her only answer. Perhaps crews didn't practice on Sundays and maybe no one else was close enough to hear. That was why Charlotte had chosen to lock her in the boathouse. She had known that no one would come near it. No one except for Charlotte herself. But when would she return? Hopefully not in broad daylight. If so, Dina felt she had some time. Accepting this rationale gratefully, she sat down again, still beside the door, her back propped against the wall. Closing her eyes, she allowed herself to fall into a fitful, disturbed sleep.

It was out of that sleep that a noise roused her into instant awareness. All her senses were immediately on alert. She grabbed the oar with her good hand and, using it as a crutch, pulled herself to her feet. The oar was very heavy, a dead weight. Not exactly her weapon of choice. She longed for her Sig Sauer. But Charlotte Chapman had taken that. All Dina had in her favor was the element of surprise.

A key was scraping in the lock. The sound magnified by the silence. Hoping that it was someone else turning the key and not Charlotte Chapman, Dina waited. Every nerve tensed, she forced herself to forget about the pain and cold and the gnawing hunger in her belly. All her energy and concentration went into her only chance to escape. She was determined not to blow it. Holding the oar the only way she could, under-handed like a battering ram, she watched as the door swung open. She knew she had to make her move the moment a figure was silhouetted in the doorway. Before the lights were switched on. Before she had time to recognize whoever it was. She knew that she might be attacking a potential savior. But she could not worry about that. Apologies would have to come later.

As the door swung open, she lunged at the figure framed against an overcast sky. And caught by surprise, her adversary stumbled.

"What the hell?" It was Chapman's voice.

Not waiting for the woman to regain her balance, Dina dropped the cumbersome oar and using every ounce of the strength she had left, pushed past her. Willing her unwilling body to obey her, she fled on feet that were leaden and legs that were rubbery. Slow as sludge, as if in a bad dream, she scrambled out of the boathouse and up a slight incline. Ahead of her was the road and a steady stream of cars. In her rush to get away, she slipped on the icy surface and fell to her knees. Get up! Get up! she urged her unwilling body as she used her good hand to lever herself to her feet. By some miracle, her body obeyed. Her focus was on the road ahead. She did not look back. She ignored the sound of footsteps closing in from behind. She did not want to know how close her pursuer was or even consider the possibility that she might be shot a second time. This was her one chance to get away. Probably her only chance. And she was determined to make the most of it.

In the rear, the footsteps were gaining on her. She could hear them pounding behind her. Louder and louder. Coming nearer. Laboring now, her breath coming in painful gasps, she kept going. She was within yards of the road, within sight of the passing cars. But her pursuer was very close now, she could hear her breathing. Sense her proximity.

Almost within haling distance of the road, tantalizingly close, a vicious football tackle brought Dina down. The two women wrestled. Charlotte grappling. Dina thrashing and kicking. It was not a fair contest. Winded and weakened, Dina was no match for her attacker. Hoping someone would either see or hear her, she screamed. But it was a barely audible croak. And before she could try it again, a gloved hand clamped down hard on her mouth.

"Shut up," Charlotte muttered through gritted teeth. "Shut up and get up."

A rough hand grabbed her by her bloodied shoulder and pulled her to her feet. Dizzying pain shot through her. The world swam. The passing cars blurred. She came close to blacking out. But she fought it. She was not about to make it easy for the other woman. Digging her heels in like a reluctant mule, she reared back, balled her fist and threw a punch at Charlotte's gut. The blow caught her opponent off guard and gave Dina a second to wrench free. In that second she made one more bid for freedom. Half scrambling, half crawling on hands and knees, Dina fought to get away. Desperation gave her strength. But the other woman was stronger and quicker and whole. With a lunge, she grabbed Dina's coat and reeled her in like a harpooned fish.

"Stop resisting. I won't hesitate to shoot you."

A suffocating hand was placed over her face, and with her good arm twisted behind her back and her wounded arm dangling uselessly beside her, she was frog-marched back to the boat house. Once inside, Charlotte threw Dina to the ground, kicked the door closed behind her, latched it, and flipped on the light. With Dina's weapon in one hand, Charlotte stared down at her captive. She was dressed in black sweats with the scarlet Rutgers women's crew team logo embroidered on one breast. Her fair hair was pulled back under a red stocking cap. She was not wearing glasses, and the pale eyes that bore into Dina were cold and hard.

"Aren't you worried someone from the crew team will come in?" Dina challenged, knowing she was snatching at straws.

"Nice try," Charlotte smirked. "But this time of year the crew practices across the river in rowing tanks. You and I have the place all to ourselves. Now get up and go stand with your back to the wall. Put your hands where I can see them. No tricks."

Dina had no tricks left. The attempt to get away had sapped her strength entirely. With her resistance at its lowest ebb, she did as she was told. Rising painfully to her feet, she walked over to the wall and leaned up against it, grateful for its rugged support.

"Now tell me," Charlotte said, pointing the gun at Dina's chest. "Tell me what you and your crime fighting buddies know about me."

So this was it. This was what had kept Dina alive thus far. Charlotte needed to know who else was onto her. It was the reason she had called Blaustein in the middle of the night. And Charlotte still needed to find out what he was privy to. She needed the reassurance that Dina had been working alone. That Dina was a loose canon and not part of a team, and that the mask Charlotte wore was still in place. It was a reassurance that Dina was determined not to give her. Charlotte's doubts were Dina's one remaining trump card. As long as Chapman did not know whether or not Dina a had been acting alone or whether she was part of an organized probe, she had a chance. So maybe a bluff would work. Or if not a bluff then a stall.

"Enough. *We* know enough," Dina put an emphasis on the word 'we'.

"What the hell does that mean?" Chapman waved the gun at her. "Tell me exactly what it means, or I'll save myself a lot of trouble and shoot you right now."

"What we don't know is why it was it necessary to impersonate Kelly Richmond? You could have been accepted to Whitney on your own merits."

"What made you think that I impersonated Kelly Richmond?"

"Because we know that the real Kelly Richmond died in an automobile accident last May and that you, a passenger in his car, walked away without a scratch. We also know that Kelly had been accepted into the Whitney Graduate Program and that you took his place." She looked at Chapman quizzically, "Did you really think you could get away with it?"

"I have till now, haven't I?"

"Look, can I please sit down," she hated to show any sign of weakness but her shoulder throbbed and her legs felt wobbly.

"Remain exactly as you are," this time Chapman jiggled the gun at Dina. "You still haven't answered my question."

"Look, isn't it enough that we know you killed Mitchell when he found out that you were masquerading as Kelly Richmond," again she emphasized the word 'we' and hoped that it registered.

"Hah! You've got it all wrong."

"Are you're saying that you didn't shoot Mitchell?" As long as Dina could keep Chapman talking, she had a smidgeon of a chance.

"I didn't say that," Chapman smirked, "I was saying that I didn't shoot him because he found out I was a phony. I shot him because *he* was a phony."

"You've got me there," Dina was genuinely puzzled. "How was he a phony?"

"He was a phony and lived a goddamned lie," the woman snarled. "Someone had to teach him a lesson."

"Come again?" Anything to keep the woman talking and to cheat death if only for a few more minutes.

"Godfrey Mitchell was a mediocrity. A mediocrity and a fraud. When he couldn't make it on his own at Whitney, he stole someone else's genius." Getting worked up now, flushing with anger, Charlotte's eyes blazed. Despite the circumstances, she obviously wanted to get her story off her chest, "When I registered as Kelly Richmond, I was doing exactly what he had done, trading on someone else's genius."

"So, he used students to do his research and didn't give them any credit. It's not very ethical but it hardly deserves the death penalty?" Dina gave voice to her confusion. "And why did you, who had only been at Whitney a few months, barely enough time to build up resentment, appoint yourself his executioner? There must have been more to it than that. Could it be you had a lover's quarrel?"

"Not bloody likely!" Chapman was obviously offended by the suggestion. "I wouldn't let that filthy bastard within ten feet of me."

"Then why?" Even given her situation, Barrett was frankly curious, her investigative instincts still at work despite the circumstances.

"He had to pay for what he did to my father.".

"Your father?" Now Barrett was truly mystified.

Chapman shook her head impatiently. She did not want to explain but the urge to do so, the need to justify, outweighed the necessity to get answers. "Mitchell could not make it on his own at Whitney, so he stole a letter from the Grosvenor and framed my father for the theft. He made a criminal of an innocent man. A brilliant man. A man infinitely Mitchell's superior. Godfrey Mitchell wrecked his career and ruined his life."

"You father is Harvey Thomas?" Damn! They had not followed up on the Harvey Thomas link because it seemed too long ago to be anything but far-fetched.

"Was! Was! My father was Harvey Thomas. He died a broken man. But Mitchell destroyed him long before his death. Mitchell robbed him of his reputation, his livelihood and his dignity," Chapman spat out the words.

"And that was the reason you went to Whitney? For revenge?"

"The operative word is 'avenge' not 'revenge'," Charlotte Chapman corrected primly.

"You saw it as a duty?"

"I saw it as justified."

"How come your name's Chapman and not Thomas?" The woman obviously needed to unburden herself and Dina was determined to string her along.

"My father changed his name. He was running away from a ruined reputation. Why else? He was living with a prison record for something he didn't do. Always terrified of being found out," her voice caught.,"that's why he never published again. Not so much as a sentence. He had been drummed out of academia and denied his genius because of Mitchell. You can't imagine how unbearable it was for me to watch a kind, brilliant man, eaten up by frustration and bitterness," the words were coming easily now, tumbling over each other to get out.

"You must have been too young to grasp what was happening at the time."

"You don't understand at all, do you?" The other woman's voice broke. "The persecution never stopped. My father was hounded constantly. He was a fugitive for the rest of his life. Dismissed from one worse than mediocre college to the next. And no matter how hard he tried, or how much he slaved, as soon as the college found out who he was, they terminated him. He was never given a second chance. He served a life sentence for something he did not do," there were tears in her eyes. Her shoulders slumped, and the hand holding the gun dropped to her side.

"I can understand how you must feel," Dina took a quick step toward her. If she was going to disarm the woman now would be the perfect time.

But like an animal cornering its prey, Chapman pounced, "Get back." she snapped, training the gun on Dina once again.

"Don't you think I deserve a second chance too?" It went against the grain to beg, but Dina didn't want to die either.

"You're crazy if you think I'll let you go," the woman's eyes narrowed suspiciously. "And don't think I can't figure out what you've been trying to do, turning the conversation around, trying to distract me. But you're not going to trick me. Discussion's over. So let's not prolong this any longer. Tell me what I need to know."

"Which is?"

"You know very well, so don't be coy with me. I want you to tell me not only how you found out about me but also who else knows. Now speak dammit!"

"I've pretty much told you already. We found out that you were not Kelly Richmond probably the same way Augusta Scott did, by calling the Rutgers History Department and learning that Kelly

Richmond died in an automobile accident. It wasn't difficult to figure out that you killed Mitchell and Scott when they confronted you. But until just now I, for one, didn't know why," Dina replied weakly, she wasn't sure how much longer she could drag out the conversation. "Look, I'm willing to believe your father was innocent. And that Mitchell framed him. It makes perfect sense. From what we've learned, your father was a shoe-in for the only available tenured spot. The chairman of the History Department considered him brilliant. And Mitchell, from what I hear was about to lose out. So I'm prepared to believe that he planted the Grosvenor letter in order to land the tenure spot for himself. But what I don't understand is how the other letter -- the one offering the manuscript for sale -- came to be written on your father's home typewriter. It was that letter that clinched the case against him, right?"

"No great mystery there. Mitchell and Dad were friends before this whole thing went down. He came to the house often and could have typed the letter at any time. Dad was convinced of it. That was what hurt the most: that a friend would wantonly destroy him," Chapman came a step closer. "Now it's my turn. I get to ask the questions and you get to answer them. And if you don't, I'll take you outside, shoot you and dump your body in the Raritan River."

"I have to admit you've been very clever," Barrett said, ignoring the threat. She knew that criminals typically liked to boast about their exploits and she desperately needed to play for more time. "You managed to surprise Mitchell in his own study. You shot him with his own gun. And you did it during the Christmas break when he had a trip planned and his newspaper and mail were on hold. You planned it well."

"But it wasn't planned, you see. None of it. It was not my intention to kill him," Chapman's need to explain her actions had begun to take precedence over her need to drag information out of Dina. "From the beginning my plan was only to discredit Mitchell. To discredit him the way he had discredited my father. It's something I've wanted to do for a very long time but I didn't know how. Then Kelly was killed. And it seemed like a sign from God. Without any real plan in mind, I went to Whitney in Kelly's place. At first I couldn't decide what to do, so I played my part to the hilt and waited. In fact, it wasn't till I found out that Mitchell was due to receive a special award in Atlanta, that I decided the time had come to act. I couldn't bear the thought of the smug bastard being honored as some kind of genius. So I went to his house to force him into admitting the truth *in writing*. I did not go there to kill him."

"What changed things?"

"Well when I got to Mitchell's house, Deirdre Lawrence's car was parked outside and the front door was unlocked. So I let myself in. The two of them were humping upstairs and it gave me a chance to check out the downstairs. That's when I found the gun."

"So you really hadn't planned to shoot him?"

"No, all I wanted to do was take him down, ruin his reputation and exonerate my father. I wanted to force him to admit the truth. That's all I intended to do. When Mrs. Lawrence left, I confronted him in his study. The gun was a plus. It made him realize I was serious. In fact, seeing me there with a gun scared him to death. He trembled so badly, he looked like a jellyfish. I ordered him to sit down at his desk and write down exactly what he had done to my father. To admit that he had planted the Grosvenor letter in my father's office and that it was he who typed the phony letter offering the manuscript for sale. But he refused to do it. He laughed at me. So I put the gun to his head. Just to make the point. But the fool made a grab for my wrist and the gun went off."

"So you really didn't mean to kill him?" Dina was incredulous.

Charlotte shook her head. "It was an accident, but I knew I'd have trouble proving that. So I decided to make it look like suicide and leave a suicide note, a *mea culpa* admitting what he had done to my father. In fact I started writing one on his computer and then had second thoughts. I was afraid a confession might lead back to me and my mother."

"I, Godfrey.... It sounded like the beginning of a suicide note."

"That's why I left it there," Charlotte couldn't resist taking a figurative bow. "I wiped off all the surfaces I had touched, in the hall, in the study and, of course, on the gun. Then I put the gun in Mitchell's hand, aimed it at the opposite wall and pulled the trigger. I wanted the gun to have his fingerprints on it and I wanted his hand to be covered with gunpowder residue."

"Good thinking," Dina was intentionally drawing her out, flattering her without being condescending. In part it was to play for time, but it was also with a touch of genuine respect.

"I was also lucky. It was Christmas break and Mitchell was expected to be away, so I knew that the body wouldn't be found for a while. To make doubly sure that the time of death would be a question mark, I turned down the temperature in the house."

"Cold enough to slow deterioration of the body, but just warm enough to keep the pipes from bursting," Dina nodded. "If not for his airline ticket to Atlanta, the time of death would have been a complete mystery. Tell me, " Dina was frankly curious. "How did you get to Mitchell's House? By cab?"

"The way I went everywhere, on my bicycle."

"It's ten miles."

"I'm used to it," she stated it as a fact not a boast. "Besides, it gave me a cover. No one notices a bicycle. If I'd taken a cab or rented a car, there would have been a paper trail. I'd have been nailed for sure."

"So you thought you were in the clear till Augusta Scott confronted you with the Kelly Richmond impersonation?"

"Till then, I went totally under the radar," Charlotte nodded. "I was doing really great until Scott found out I wasn't Kelly Richmond. Like you, she jumped to the conclusion that I killed Mitchell because he found out I'd been accepted to Whitney under false pretenses. That I was afraid of being kicked out of the University or worse, sent to jail."

"If she thought you killed Mitchell, she was crazy to confront you."

"For some reason, she thought she could talk me into giving myself up. And she tried," Charlotte sighed. "I really didn't want to kill Professor Scott. She gave me no choice. Just like you. I'll have committed three murders without having had the least intention of committing any."

"That would be in your favor when it came to trial."

"Forget it. I won't be going to trial," Chapman snapped. "If Scott failed to convince me, you most certainly won't." She took two menacing steps forward and planted herself feet astride. With the Sig Sauer in both hands, her arms fully extended, the gun aimed at Dina's face. "Now, Detective Barrett, it's your turn to speak."

30

AFTER ALERTING AND COOPTING THE LOCAL AS WELL AS THE
Rutgers campus police, Blaustein and Brooks began a slow,
methodical sweep of the New Brunswick streets. Figuring that a
lone cyclist would be fairly noticeable on a day when the wind chill
was in the single digits, they stopped to question everyone they saw,
pedestrians as well as motorists. No one they spoke to remembered
seeing someone on a bicycle. Next, with guns drawn, they checked
out two boarded-up buildings. In one they scared off a half dozen
teenagers smoking pot. In the second, they found only a sleeping
derelict guarded by an ancient, mongrel dog. They stopped off at a
church and questioned the pastor. They checked out a garage and a
barn. Still there was no sign of either Chapman or Barrett. When they
saw a bicycle chained to a bike rack in front of a college hangout, they
went inside. But no one there knew or had seen Charlotte Chapman
and the bicycle belonged to someone else. It was as if the woman had
simply vanished into thin air. Brooks kept in constant radio contact
with the other police units while he and Blaustein expanded the
area of their search to the outskirts of the city. Thus far, none of the

patrols had spotted anyone matching the right description. And with daylight beginning to fade, Blaustein's hopes began to fade too. He wasn't sure whether the lump of lead at the pit of his stomach was the donut he had eaten earlier or a feeling of dread. By now words had become superfluous and a mutual silence had fallen between him and Brooks. The latter, working on his own time, remained at the wheel without complaint. Beside him, Blaustein patiently scoured their route for the elusive Charlotte Chapman. By now they were on the road leading out of town, a four-lane roadway that ran parallel to the Raritan River.

"There's a large building on the other side of the road. I can only make out the roof," Blaustein said, breaking the silence. "What is it?"

"That's the Rutgers boathouse."

"Can you turn around? I'd like to take a closer look," Blaustein said, not even attempting to suppress a growing optimism. "Remember that photograph I gave you? In it Chapman was wearing a Rutgers crew uniform."

Brooks shot him a quick grin, "What better place to hide someone. The crew teams don't use the boathouse this time of year. They use rowing tanks on the other side of the river until it gets warmer."

"No lights and no siren."

Nodding in agreement, Brooks steered the car to the left lane and making an illegal u-turn at the first possible opportunity, swung into the west-bound lane. As they approached the boathouse, he slowed to a stop well short of the boathouse driveway. Ahead the boathouse had a deserted, closed-up look.

"Doesn't look promising but let's check any way," Blaustein said, getting out of the cruiser before it came to a full stop.

With Brooks a few steps behind him, they walked cautiously around to the front of the building. Then stopped dead in their tracks. There was a bicycle propped up beside the door. Instinctively Blaustein drew his weapon, took a step towards the building and halted. Sublimating his personal feelings, he willed the professional policeman in him to take over. If Dina was being held hostage in the boathouse then a frontal attack might well endanger her. He turned to face Brooks.

"One bicycle looks pretty much like another to me," he whispered, "but I'm almost positive this is Chapman's's bike." He said as he examined the bike's broken reflector. It was cracked in the same way as the one he had seen on the third floor landing outside the woman's Winslow Street apartment. "Go back to the car and radio for back-up. Tell them not to use sirens or lights," he handed a slip of paper to the other man. "And this number will get you the FBI's hostage negotiating team. I hope to God they're ready to move in. I'll wait here."

Hardly daring to breathe, Blaustein took up a position next to the door. He could hear voices. Voices too inaudible to be identified. Hoping against hope that Dina's was one of them, he waited while Brooks called from his cruiser. When the New Brunswick policeman returned to his side, the news was not good.

"The FBI SWAT team was not told to mobilize. Only to stand by for a possible hostage situation in New Brunswick. It could be hours before they get here."

"Damn that asshole Gordon," Blaustein muttered under his breath. "Okay, let's go to plan B."

"We have a plan B?"

"We do now," Blaustein said, speaking fast. "Do you have a local hostage negotiator?"

"We do," Brooks nodded.

"Okay, get the negotiator and as many men as possible. How long do you think that will take?"

"I honestly don't know, but I'll get things rolling right away."

"Tell them we want a silent approach. And when you've done that, send someone to fetch Mrs. Chapman. Tell her to dress warmly. There's no telling how long we'll be out here."

"The mother?"

"I've been involved with a few hostage situations in my time. Sometimes there's a better chance they'll end peacefully when a close relative is thrown into the mix. Brief Mrs. Chapman. Tell her that there's sufficient evidence to believe her daughter is holding Dina Barrett at gunpoint."

"I'll go get Mrs. Chapman myself."

In what seemed like hours but was in fact a relatively short time, Brooks arrived with Mrs. Chapman in tow. Moments later the local SWAT team showed up and took up stations around the perimeter of the boathouse. At the sight of so many armed men Mrs. Chapman was clearly terrified. Her pale, drawn face was etched with fear, "Are all these guns necessary?" She pleaded. "She's just a girl."

"We don't want anyone to get hurt, Mrs. Chapman. But we can't take chances. Your daughter is armed and dangerous."

"She doesn't own a gun. How could she be armed? Where would she get a gun?"

Blaustein ignored the woman's protestations. "Ma'am, as Officer Brooks told you, we think your daughter is holding Dina Barrett hostage in there. We want to prevent a tragedy."

"Let me talk to Charlotte," Mrs. Chapman pleaded standing up a little straighter. "I'm sure this can all be worked out. We don't need guns."

"No, I can't allow you to do that. It could be dangerous. For the time being I want you to wait here for the hostage negotiator to show up in case you're needed."

"Just wait?"

"Yes, wait."

"Well I won't," she squared her shoulders, her dignity restored. "Let me go in and talk to her. There'll be no need for guns if I can just talk to her. She'll listen to me, you'll see."

"We can't let you put yourself in that kind of danger. The only way we can let you talk to your daughter would be if you use a bull-horn."

"It won't be the same thing as face to face," insistent but calm, she stood her ground. "We may have had our differences but she won't hurt me. And you're not going to stop me. I insist on talking to Charlotte. I have a mother's right to do so. So you had just better get used to the idea." Transformed into the picture of mulish obstinacy, she planted her feet firmly astride, folded her arms across her chest and thrust out her chin.

Helpless before this maternal onslaught and against his better judgment, Blaustein caved, "Alright. But we'll do it my way."

After discussing the procedure with the local cops, Blaustein and Mrs. Chapman approached the boathouse door. "I want you to say.. . ."

"I know what to say Detective," she interrupted him.

"Very well," he gave her shoulder an encouraging squeeze.

Acknowledging the gesture with a nod, she went up to the door and in a loud clear voice announced her presence, "Charlotte, this is your mother. I'm coming in."

She tried the handle but the door had been bolted from the inside.

"Charlotte," she said again. "Let me in."

"Mother, go away, this has nothing to do with you," came the muffled response from the other side of the door.

"That's where you're wrong. I'm your mother, that makes it my business."

"Just leave, Mother."

"What you've done is just tearing me apart. For my sake, please open the door."

"Don't lay a guilt trip on me. It won't work. I am not opening the door."

"No one wants to hurt you," her mother pleaded. "Make it easy on yourself and surrender peacefully. The police have this place surrounded. You won't get away."

This information was followed by a heavy silence.

"Please Charlotte," her mother pleaded again.

"How do I know the cops won't come busting in the second I open the door?" Clearly Charlotte was hesitating now.

"They won't, I have their word," her mother replied after a reassuring nod from Blaustein.

After a brief pause, came a scraping sound as a bolt was drawn back. Then the door opened just enough to admit Mrs. Chapman before closing again and the bolt was slipped back into place.

Mrs. Chapman entered, smiling tentatively as she stepped into the boathouse. She reached out both arms as she approached her daughter. And only then did she become aware of the gun in her daughter's hand and of Dina slumped against the wall, her jacket blood-stained, her face unnaturally pale. The older woman's' smile became a frozen rictus. Her arms dropped to her sides. She stood stunned and immobile as if unwilling to let herself believe what she was seeing.

After a moment's hesitation she spoke, sounding more like a mother scolding a child for not doing her homework than a woman pleading for the life of a hostage, "Charlotte what have you done to this poor woman?"

"Mother, what do you want?" Charlotte half-turned to face her mother, the gun and the corner of her eye still trained on Barrett.

"What I want is for you to drop the gun and let this woman go. She's obviously in need of medical attention."

"Fat chance."

"Charlotte, please," her mother sighed. "They're saying you killed Godfrey Mitchell. Are they right?"

"You can't tell me that monster didn't have it coming to him? Besides, he was lucky. He died quickly. He made Father die a slow death."

"That all happened a long time ago and had nothing to do with you."

"What Mitchell did to my father had nothing to do with me?"

Mrs. Chapman stared at her daughter, her eyes bright with unshed tears, "Sweetheart, I want you to understand something. Something that I should have told you a long time ago." In a voice that was barely audible, Mrs. Chapman looked her daughter in the eye, "The man you thought was your father, was not your father. Godfrey Mitchell was your father. When you killed him, you killed your real father."

As the shock of what she had heard registered, Charlotte had grown very pale. She was momentarily silent before speaking again, "And Daddy? What about Daddy? Did he know he wasn't my real father?"

Mrs. Chapman bit her lower lip and shook her head, "I never had the heart to tell him."

"And Mitchell? What about him? Did he know he had fathered your bastard?" Charlotte spat out the words.

"I never told him either," refusing to meet her daughter's angry eyes, Mrs. Chapman worried a loose thread on one of her woolen gloves. "But don't think I haven't blamed myself over the years."

"Blamed yourself! And that's supposed to absolve you?"

"I'll never be absolved," her mother admitted with a heart-wrenching sigh.

"Right! You should burn in Hell for it."

"I've been burning in Hell for more than twenty years."

"And I'm supposed to feel sorry for you?" The knuckles of the hand that gripped the gun were white. Watching her, Dina was afraid the woman would lose control and kill them both.

"I don't deserve your pity," abjectly, her eyes lowered, Mrs. Chapman looked at her daughter, the picture of misery.

But Charlotte dismissed her mother's admission with a dangerous wave of her gun hand, "You probably let Mitchell hump you in your own house. In your marital bed. . . ." She stopped in mid-sentence and gasped as a sudden thought occurred to her. "That letter, the letter that sent Daddy to prison, that's when Mitchell wrote it, wasn't it? He wrote it using Daddy's typewriter when he was with you, didn't he?"

"I don't know," her mother's voice was barely above a whisper.

"That scum bag had as much access to Daddy's typewriter as he had to his wife. He did, didn't he?" Her mother lowered her eyes but said nothing.

"Didn't it cross your pitiful little mind that Mitchell was the one who typed that letter?" Charlotte demanded, her voice rising.

"I suspected it," by now tears were flowing unrestrained down her mother's cheeks.

"If you suspected it, why the hell didn't you speak up? How could you keep quiet? God woman, you let an innocent man go to jail and you never said a word! You stood by and let him lose everything!"

Charlotte flew at her mother and hit her across the face with the balled up fist of her free hand. "You adulterous bloody bitch! You let that poor, sweet man suffer for the rest of his life because you didn't have the guts to own up to a seamy love affair. I should kill you too."

Mrs. Chapman cringed as her daughter raised her hand to repeat the blow. Charlotte's right hand, the one holding the gun was at her side now, the barrel facing down. Her eyes were on her mother. Her hostage momentarily ignored.

Taking advantage of the distraction, Barrett pounced. She grabbed Chapman's gun hand and tried to wrest the weapon from it. But Chapman merely spun around and threw a left to Barrett's chin. Ducking, Barrett avoided the full force of the blow and fortified by the knowledge that help was just outside the door, she summoned the last of her ebbing strength, and came down hard on the other woman's instep with the heel of her boot. It was not enough. Barrett had come to the end of her resources. And Mrs Chapman, sensing a fatal end to the struggle, placed a restraining hand on her daughter's shoulder.

"Charlotte, please give it up. The place is surrounded. You're not going to win."

Her words broke the impasse and her daughter was finally forced to concede the fight. Her body sagged. She sank to her knees with a sob, and as the gun rolled from her fingers, Dina swooped and grabbed it. Training the weapon on the dejected form at her feet, she took a step back and spoke in a voice that was surprisingly calm and controlled.

"Mrs. Chapman, please open the door and tell the police to come in. This party's over."

Her distress mirrored in the stoop of her shoulders and the dejection in each reluctant step, Mrs. Chapman shuffled to the door. Dina watched as she drew back the bolt, opened the door and stepped aside to admit a phalanx of armed police officers. They were led by Jackson Blaustein. When he saw Dina, the tension in his face evaporated and his eyes glistened with unshed tears. He holstered his weapon and left it to Officer Brooks to read Charlotte Chapman her rights and escort her to a waiting patrol car.

"EMT stat!" Blaustein shouted in a voice cracking with emotion as he hurried over to his wounded colleague. He lifted her gently in his arms, and raced toward a waiting ambulance. Questions and explanations would have to wait.

Printed in the United States
By Bookmasters